Arcadia Falls

BOOKS AND BEWITCHMENT

ISLA JEWELL

TITAN BOOKS

Books and Bewitchment
Trade paperback edition ISBN: 9781835416334
Australian paperback edition ISBN: 9781835418093
E-book edition ISBN: 9781835416389

Published by Titan Books
A division of Titan Publishing Group Ltd
144 Southwark Street, London SE1 0UP
www.titanbooks.com

First edition: February 2026
10 9 8 7 6 5 4 3 2 1

This is a work of fiction. All of the characters, organizations, and events portrayed in this novel are either products of the author's imagination or are used fictitiously. Any resemblance to actual persons, living or dead (except for satirical purposes), is entirely coincidental.

© D.S. Dawson 2026.

D.S. Dawson asserts the moral right to be
identified as the author of this work.

No part of this publication may be reproduced, stored in a retrieval system, or transmitted, in any form or by any means without the prior written permission of the publisher, nor be otherwise circulated in any form of binding or cover other than that in which it is published and without a similar condition being imposed on the subsequent purchaser.

A CIP catalogue record for this title is
available from the British Library.

EU RP (for authorities only)
eucomply OÜ, Pärnu mnt. 139b-14, 11317 Tallinn, Estonia
hello@eucompliancepartner.com, +3375690241

Designed and typeset in Baskerville by Richard Mason.

Printed and bound by CPI (UK) Ltd, Croydon CR0 4YY

"Deliciously delightful! I adored this adorable book! You'll laugh, you'll swoon, and you'll want to stay in Arcadia Falls!"

SARAH BETH DURST, *New York Times*-bestselling author of *The Spellshop*

"Cozy and fun - break out the popcorn and a mug of your favourite warm beverage!"

CAITLIN ROZAKIS, *New York Times*-bestselling author of *Dreadful* and *Startup Hell*

"A sticky, southern-fried comfort dish combining nostalgia, magical romance, and the struggle of the capable sibling… The spells will delight you. The kisses will make your knees go weak. The ghost will make you want to open your own haunted small business."

MOLLY HARPER, *USA Today*-bestselling author of *Hex Around and Find Out*

"Brimming with charming characters, magic, a guy who might just be the world's sexiest handyman, and so much heart. Isla Jewell cast a spell on me that I never wanted to end!"

JENNA LEVINE, *USA Today*-bestselling author of *My Roommate is a Vampire*

"An utterly charming story for booklovers and anyone who has ever dreamed of a fresh start… Sharply funny and wonderfully kind."

LISH MCBRIDE, award-winning author of *A Little Too Familiar*

"A warm hug of a love story that perfectly balances magic, romance, and family secrets… A book you will want to curl up with and finish in one sitting!"

FALON BALLARD, *USA Today*-bestselling author of *Change of Heart*

"Absolutely cosy and full of whimsy, this romance enchants."

KATIE HOLT, author of *Not in My Book*

For my heroes, the matchmakers,
the keepers of magic: the booksellers.

And especially for the staff of Malaprop's
Bookstore/Café in Asheville, North Carolina,
who were so generous with their time and expertise when
I begged to visit them and ask a thousand questions.

And for the readers, too.
Because of you, I get to have the best job in the world.

1

No matter how bad my day is, someone in a book has it worse and will still get a happily-ever-after eventually. Maybe that's why I read so much. It gives me hope and an escape. If my life were a book, right now I would probably give it two stars. "The main character, Rhea Wolfe, has no agency," the review would read. "What does she actually want? No one's life is that boring. And her pet cockatoo, Doris, sings too many show tunes. Did not finish."

At least that's how it feels to me.

Almost like I'm always waiting for the story to start.

Like I'm longing for something I haven't found yet.

Then again, I've lived in the same place my entire life, and for the last four years, most of it was spent sitting at the front desk of Buckley Insurance.

"Mail for you, hon," my boss says, dropping a slender envelope on my desk. "Probably shouldn't be having your mail sent here to the office, but I'll let it go this one time. And about your raise request . . ."

I perk up.

"We'll talk later. After lunch." He winks and waddles into his office.

The screech that follows does not startle me. "No, Horace! Lordy! That boy's a mess!"

I look up at the pink-and-gray rose-breasted cockatoo bobbing her head from her perch atop an elaborate cage across the office lobby and say, "Hush, Doris. You know he hates that."

Doris chuckles and mutters, "Oh, poor Horace," in the voice of my boss's dead mother, her original owner. Horace—Mr. Buckley—hates this bird as much as he loved his mother, and that's why caring for her takes up more of my time than keeping his books and answering his phones. Honestly, I don't mind. She's better company than him, any day, and somehow she causes me fewer headaches. After several disastrous holidays and one destroyed taxidermy bear at his hunting lodge, Mr. Buckley asked me to keep her on the weekends, and then the weekdays, and now she's just with me all the time.

Once his door is closed, I set aside the envelope, cheeks burning. I've been working for Buckley Insurance since college, and though Mr. Buckley—I'm not allowed to call him Horace, even if the bird can—sounds cheerful and kind, he's going to turn down my request for a simple ten percent raise, I can just feel it. The man delights in finding fault with me, but the benefits are good, and my paychecks are always on time—in part because I write them. That's one of the few perks of being his only employee. I also have plenty of time to read when he's out golfing and the phone isn't ringing. This morning, he's watching me like a watery-eyed hawk, so I can't open the envelope or I'll get dinged again.

Books and Bewitchment

When I'm running out to get Mr. Buckley's daily burger and fries, I see a little lump in the middle of the road and slow to a stop, putting on my hazard lights and hitting pause on my audiobook. Hoping I'm not attempting to save a child's kneepad yet again, I hop out of the car and pick up a box turtle, who's heaving himself across the asphalt and doesn't stop waving his legs even when he's clearly off the ground. I know turtles only want to go one way, so I carry him to the other side of the street and carefully place him in the scrubby grass, nestled among cigarette butts and soda bottles. He doesn't even pause, just keeps waddling bravely on. You've got to admire that.

I'm dusting my hands off, feeling pretty happy about my good deed, when I hear a siren and turn to find a black SUV aiming for me, lights flashing. And since I live in my hometown, I know this is not a coincidence and that I'm not about to receive a medal of honor on behalf of reptiles everywhere.

"Oh, lordy," I mutter.

I go sit in my car, knowing this won't be good. The officer pulls in behind me but doesn't exit his vehicle. My window is already down, my license and registration ready. But this, sadly, is no meet-cute. More like an avoid-ugly—because I'd like to avoid it, and it's about to get ugly.

I wish we could just get it over with, but after five minutes, he hasn't even opened his car door. Still, I know better than to drive away. I'm not surprised when a tow truck pulls in behind the black SUV—but I am disappointed.

Billy Wayne gets out of his tow truck, blond hair billowing in the sun, and gives the officer a high five as he walks over to my window. "You bein' a bad girl again, Rhea?" He pulls down his sunglasses to wink at me with the prettiest baby blues in Cumberville, Alabama.

"Billy, c'mon. You know damn well I was saving a turtle. Will you please tell your brother to back off?"

He looks back over his shoulder at the SUV and jerks his chin. His brother Jimmy—Officer Jimmy of the Cumberville PD—who hates me, by the way, gets out holding his phone up. Recording us.

Oh no—

Billy gets down on one knee outside my car door.

"Rhea Wolfe, we've been dating on and off since middle school, but I think it's time we stopped with the 'off' part. Will you marry me?" He holds out a little white box with a ring in it.

A ring that is not my style and that is also several sizes too small.

"Come on, Billy." I lean in close so maybe Jimmy and his phone won't hear this part. "You don't want to marry me. You just want to sleep with me."

He wiggles the box back and forth. "Can't it be both?"

I don't even consider it. Not for a second. After our last breakup two weeks ago, I promised my sisters I wouldn't sleep with him ever again, and I can't imagine the hell they would give me if I ended up in Billy's bed, much less wearing his ring. Cait says that after a month of dating him, I always end up acting like his mama, and I'd be fine with never washing his tighty-whiteys again.

Because here's the thing.

We're *terrible* together.

I want to wake up at dawn for coffee on the porch while Doris sings bits of old musicals and eats her fruit salad; he wants to sleep in and get donuts at noon with his dog, Zeke, who can't decide if Doris is an intruder or a squeaky toy and won't shut up about it. I want to spend weekends tidying up the house and watching rom-coms about secret princes;

he wants to go out on his cousin's Jet Ski and drink a case of beer. I want to take a boiling-hot bath with a book and go to bed early; he wants to stay up until midnight lifting weights and fall into bed covered in sweat and smelling like greasy metal. And you can guess who ends up having to fold the sheets, recycle the beer cans, and vacuum the muddy pawprints out of the carpet.

We've tried everything—living together, casually dating, being friends with benefits. But it always ends up with him raising his voice, Doris screaming, and me crying, swearing that all the roses and chocolates in the world aren't worth finding his whiskery shaving scum in my sink and realizing, as he and his friends watch football in my den with their work boots on my coffee table, that we're just not compatible.

"I think that's a bad idea, Billy," I say with the sort of smile that says I'm sorry about it.

He pushes his sunglasses on top of his beautiful hair and stands up; he never has taken rejection well, not since I first dumped him in tenth grade. "Oh, come on, Rhea. You got to settle down. You're only twenty-six, and you're starting to look like a librarian. I'm right here, and the clock's ticking, girl." He snaps the white box shut and jiggles it in his hand.

"I love librarians." I sigh and put my hand on his just to stop the jiggling. "Billy, come on. It's the same old cycle. We get together, we have fun, we break up. Do we really need to go through that again? Aren't you sick of finding the same cardboard box full of stuff on your doorstep?"

"I don't want to break up anymore. I want to settle down, Rhea. I want the kids and the baseball games and the fence and a golden retriever—"

"Zeke would kill it."

"Fine! No yellow dog! But don't you want all that other stuff, too?"

God, it doesn't even feel like a proposal. It's just a last-ditch effort. His heart's not even in it. He just wants to be taken care of.

Before I can come up with the right answer that's sweet but still assertive, he snorts. "You don't even know what you want, do you? You just know it isn't me." Shaking his head, ring box in his fist, he turns his back and stomps over to his brother, pushing the phone down and whispering fiercely. Whatever he says to Jimmy, it's not good. After giving me the finger, my ex-boyfriend hops back in his tow truck and peels out at a speed that would have any other cop salivating. Instead, Jimmy puts his phone away and saunters over to my window, his sunglasses hiding his eyes but not his frown.

"License and registration."

"I'm literally holding them out to you, Jimmy."

"That's 'Officer' to you. Ma'am, did you know you are impeding the flow of traffic? That's a serious violation."

When I see the cost of the ticket he tosses at me—$190—I know it's over with Billy for good.

Billy knows just how little money I have, and he still asked his brother to punish me because he wanted me to hurt like he was hurting. My roof is leaking, and the septic system is bubbling threateningly in the side yard, and I'm pretty certain I'm about to be told a raise is out of the question.

But it's even worse than that. When I get back to the office with his lunch, Mr. Buckley gives me the bad news.

I no longer have a job.

His favorite niece, Sylvie, is about to finish her degree, and he promised her my position.

"You understand, sugar," he says, unclipping his tie and tucking a napkin into his collar. "Family is important."

I do not remind him that I am also supporting my family. It wouldn't matter. If a Buckley needs a job at Buckley Insurance, who needs a Wolfe?

He tells me to close his door and write up a list of all the "little jobs" I do to make things easier for Sylvie, but instead I pick up the letter I received this morning.

The envelope is nice, but its return address is very, very suspect.

I slit the envelope with my Buckley Insurance letter opener. The paper is thick and creamy, the message typed on an actual typewriter.

```
Dear Ms. Wolfe,

I am writing on behalf of my client,
your grandmother, Mrs. Margaret Lowell
Kirkwood. I regret to inform you that
she passed on recently as the result of
an automobile accident. As her closest
living relative, you are set to inherit
a nice piece of property, a business,
and all of her assets. Please contact
me at your earliest convenience. My
condolences for your loss.

             Sincerely,
             Colonel Roy Gooch, Esq.
             Attorney at Law
             Arcadia Falls, Georgia
```

It sounds good, right? *Inheritance* is a juicy word, especially when you're in dire straits. But here's the thing: I'm not supposed to accept it. Mama made us all promise to never,

ever return to Arcadia Falls and especially to never talk to our grandmother.

She never spoke of her own mama without cursing. My sister Jemma used to ask about our grandmother all the time, because Jemma's the youngest and is softer than a dandelion puff and Daddy's folks died young, but Mama would always pin her lips like an angry horse and shake her head.

"That woman is dead to me," she'd say.

"Whatever Grandma did, I never want to do it," our middle sister, Cait, said back when we were little. "Mama's scary when she's angry."

And she was. Even nature knew it. The sky always seemed to darken and thunder when Mama got mad, and it would rain when she cried. It was an unspoken rule among my siblings that we would avoid upsetting Mama on special days because nobody wanted their birthday party or graduation ruined by foul weather. I know it sounds crazy saying so, but we really believed it when we were little. Then we all grew up, and Mama and Daddy died, and now we never know what the weather will be like.

So it's not that simple. I promised Mama that I would never go back to Arcadia Falls, but . . .

Do promises count, when one person up and dies? Does it really matter if Grandma Kirkwood is dead now, too? Surely Mama's grudge died with the both of them, and as the eldest, I feel like this is one of those responsibilities that I need to shoulder. I'm desperate, and my sisters . . .

Well, let's just say I'm the smart, dependable one who does the difficult things no one else wants to. It's eldest daughter syndrome, big-time. Cait is the sharp, sarcastic one whose mind goes a mile a minute; she won't get tested for ADHD, but coffee actually calms her down. Jemma is the sweet, romantic, loyal one for whom setting foot in Arcadia

Falls would be tantamount to lying to Mama's grave. If one of us has to go back and sort through the detritus of our estranged grandmother's life, it has to be me.

I am intimately familiar with my own money issues, and I know my sisters—who live half an hour away in Birmingham—aren't doing any better. Cait lost her nest egg in a bad investment last year, and Jemma tries to live a posh lifestyle on an entry-level salary. They may not be included in the will, but whatever Grandma Kirkwood left me, I won't be stingy. We all need it.

I look down at my desk, dominated by the paper blotter Mr. Buckley insists I use to keep his calendar because he thinks cellphones are a fad. Mr. Buckley doesn't—*didn't*—pay me what I'm worth, but I check the job boards every week and I've never seen anything better within a reasonable driving distance. My life here for the past four years has been dependable but monotonous, boring, and uninspiring. The days all run together. Nothing new or interesting ever happens. There's never enough money. I don't have anything to look forward to. There's no dating scene, outside of Billy. The best things in my life are my sisters, the library books I bring home every week, and Doris.

I've never given much thought to Arcadia Falls before, not as a real place. It was more some imaginary nightmare land, dark and forbidding, like the ogre-filled forest in a fairy tale that all good children knew to avoid. I do a search on my phone and find a cheerful website with an idyllic downtown square filled with cute restaurants, a general store, a place for kids to pretend like they're panning for gold. There are no obvious ogres, although there is an old-fashioned town hall where you can take a photo in a crusty jail cell to post on social media.

It's . . . surprising.

Isla Jewell

What's so terrible about this place? I wonder. What did Arcadia Falls do to Mama that made her run away and never look back? When Jemma asked one day, Daddy said he'd never been there and had never met Grandma Kirkwood; he told us he'd learned very quickly never to ask his beloved wife about anything that happened before they met in college unless he wanted to ruin a good car wash.

I can see how my life in Cumberville would play out. I know that it will go on like this for the rest of my days, unchanging. The same breakups and makeups with the cute boy I've been dating since puberty. The same girls from high school at the Piggly Wiggly trying to get me to sell diet shakes with their MLMs. The same dead-end jobs with no raises or room for promotion—if I can even find one. The same worry each time I slide my bank card, unsure if I can keep up my folks' place and still have enough money to eat. The same "doing the best I can and it's never enough" feeling.

After work, I open my library book, desperate for an escape, and something falls out. A Georgia lottery ticket. When I scratch off all the little piles of money, I realize that I've won five hundred dollars.

I've never won anything before in my life besides a spelling bee.

The only thing is . . . I need to go to Georgia to claim that money.

It feels like a sign from the universe.

I have to go to Arcadia Falls.

2

The decision made, I get down to business. I rent my folks' house out to Leah and Tommy Billings so they can have their baby somewhere besides Tommy's mom's moldy basement. I convince Mr. Buckley to let me legally adopt Doris, as she hates him with a fiery passion and once bit a chunk out of his job-stealing niece's arm at Easter brunch. He seems relieved and immediately draws up a contract, promising to continue to reimburse me for her care using the trust his mother left in her name. I pack up my things and Doris's cage, tie everything down in my old Ford Explorer, and hit the road, praying that I won't run into a certain towheaded tow-truck driver or his conniving cop brother on my way out of town.

The road trip is easy and fast, thanks to an engrossing audiobook. Doris loves the car—Mr. Buckley's mother was very eccentric and took her everywhere—so she's happy enough on her perch in the back seat. On the other side of

Atlanta traffic, we stop so I can gas up cheap, get my five hundred dollars, and send my sisters a selfie with a giant water tower that says CUMMING, and then we're driving up into the mountains.

The moment I see the WELCOME TO ARCADIA FALLS sign, it's like something lights up inside me. I've spent all my life in that cramped little house in the boonies outside Birmingham, but apparently my body recognizes the fresh mountain air that once lived in Mama's blood. Maybe it's the elevation, maybe it's the collected oxygen of all these trees, maybe it's two Diet Cokes and a large bag of Skittles, but it feels like I'm breathing more deeply than I have in my entire life.

Colonel Gooch's law office sits on the outskirts of downtown proper, a quaint white house with green shutters surrounded by blue hydrangea bushes in full bloom and a massive fig tree that smells like boozy rot and sounds like happy bees. As I stand outside and stretch, the front door opens and a round little man with an eye patch, a shock of white hair, a mustache, and a dapper three-piece plaid suit steps onto the porch looking like the dandy piratical twin brother of the KFC mascot.

"Mr. Gooch?" I ask, hurrying to catch him before he can leave.

He looks up, startled, but his blue eye is dancing.

"Why, you must be Miss Kirkwood," he says. "I'm sorry. I mean—Wolfe. The spitting image of your grandmother in her day. Well, our day. She was just two years ahead of me in school. Pretty as a picture. And please, call me Colonel."

"Okay, Colonel." I reach out to shake his hand, one sturdy pump, like we're making a deal. "Were you in the armed forces?"

His visible eyebrow draws down like this is a sore and

constant subject. "No. My mother, God rest her soul, had delusions of grandeur. I got off light. My brothers are named King and Duke." He shakes his head and takes a cleansing breath. "I was just headed into town for lunch, if you'd care to join me?"

"Don't we need to . . . sign the papers?" I'm not hungry, but I am financially desperate. I still don't know if I've—we've—inherited an outhouse or a mansion, and the suspense is killing me. Every time I asked on the phone, he'd said, "You just have to see it."

He flutters a hand in the air. "A formality. We'll eat, and I'll show you the property, and then we can get down to brass tacks. I don't operate well on an empty stomach, do you?"

Without waiting for an answer, he takes off up the sidewalk at a sprightly pace, his leather shoes squeaking. I've already got Doris zipped into her hot-pink bird backpack, so I grab the handle and jog to keep up. She flaps her wings and mutters, "Lordy. Oh, lordy," which is really the only part of her vocabulary she's gotten from her time with me.

"You haven't been to town before, I presume?" Colonel asks when I catch up.

"Never."

"Well, welcome to Arcadia Falls. Your family used to all but run this town, and then, with the storm . . ." He sighs. "Doesn't really matter, does it? You've got a place here. Not much blood these days, but plenty of bones left in these cemeteries." He gestures to a small, fenced-in graveyard by an old gray church, all the tombstones leaning drunkenly and carved away by the elements. "See it there? Always plenty of Kirkwoods. Used to be, at least."

He's right. I count three Kirkwood stones nestled in the verdant clover. I'm surprised to see a stone-built church with spires and stained glass—most Southern churches are plain brick things like squatting toads, but this building looks like it was transplanted straight out of Ireland.

The sidewalk cants up toward a cluster of buildings, and Colonel isn't even huffing and puffing, although I am. Everything was a lot flatter back home.

"So this is downtown," he says as the sidewalk spits us out on the square I saw online.

It's even prettier in person. Birds sing in the trees and peck on the sidewalks, butterflies and bees buzz amid blooming bushes, and the canopy overhead glows a uniform shade of brilliant green. All four sides of the square are lined with colorful buildings, some regular brick, some whitewashed, some wood, some mostly windows. There are flower baskets planted with late-summer marigolds and those tufty magenta plants that look like something out of a Dr. Seuss book. Some buildings have balconies, and people laugh as they sit at bistro tables or sip wine at open bars. In the center of the cobblestone square stands the Platonic ideal of a town hall, crisp white with tall columns. There's a matching gazebo beside a sculpture of an old miner with a pickax and a pot of gold. I feel like I've just walked into the welcome brochure.

"Which do you prefer, country cookin' or rabbit food?"

"Rabbit food?" I ask, confused.

"Country cookin' sticks to your ribs. Fried trout, chicken 'n' dumplings, macaroni and cheese with that nice crumbly stuff on top." He puts a hand to his stomach and points to a brick storefront painted dark burgundy with gingham curtains in the window. "That's Marla's Home Cookin'. Whereas if you prefer rabbit food, Lindy's has little fiddly sandwiches and soups and salads, although you can't always trust the salads, just between us." He looks vaguely disgusted as he points across the square to a light blue building with a striped awning. "What's your poison?"

Realizing that there is no way to get out of lunch, I say, "Sandwiches sound good."

He deflates. "Yes, my wife and my cardiologist would both agree with you. Sandwiches it is."

When we reach the door, he holds it open for me, and I pause. "This is a weird question, but do you think anybody would mind if I brought in a cockatoo?"

He looks at me like I just barked at him, so I turn my backpack around to show the rose-breasted cockatoo sitting inside. She's about the size of a football, with a Pepto-Bismol-pink head and chest, and soft gray wings and tail.

"This is Doris."

"Oh, lordy," Doris says, raising her feathered crest curiously. "Shipoopi!"

Colonel's jaw drops.

"It's from a musical—*The Music Man*," I say, blushing just as pink as her crest. "The old lady who owned her kept musicals on all day long. She doesn't actually curse, I promise."

"Well, I'll be. I guess we'll see what we can get away with. If Chuck Hickman can bring in that rashy old dog of his, I don't see how anyone could complain about a well-cultured cockatoo. Just don't let her escape. Lindy'll have a fit. She's more of a cat person."

I step into the restaurant, and it's hopping. There's a bakery counter and at least a dozen wobbling wooden tables filled with all sorts of folks, from moms with little kids fresh out of school to a man who's got to be older than God sitting alone with a half-bald mini poodle that's got to be older than God's oldest dog. Colonel leads me to the counter, and I'm reading the chalkboard menu when a loud voice drawls, "Oh my golden gravy, Miranda Kirkwood, is that you?"

Isla Jewell

I turn around to see who asked the question, and the woman's face falls, and I instantly know why. She's about Mama's age, and she's just realized that I'm not her.

"Close," I say, because I feel bad for her. She looks shaken, like she's seen a ghost. "I'm her daughter."

"Where's your mama at?"

The look on my face tells her everything she needs to know. She puts a hand to her prow of a chest and shakes her permed hair, blond running to gray. "She said she'd never come back come hell or high water, so I should've known. I'm so sorry for that. Can I ask—"

"Cancer."

She blinks rapidly as her eyes go wet. "She didn't deserve that. She was a good friend. Still, it's nice to see a Kirkwood around these parts, now that your grandma is—" She stops, eyes flying wide. "Oh, Lord. I did it again. Always putting my foot in my big ol' mouth. No wonder my pedicures don't last long."

Colonel steps in gallantly so she'll stop panicking. "Tina McGowan, this is Rhea Wolfe. She's come to take care of her grandmother's estate."

I can't quite decode the face Tina makes. There's some pity and disappointment there, but also . . . amusement?

"Well, good luck with that, honey. Does that mean you'll be sticking around?"

"Maybe," I begin.

"Has he shown you the—"

"The girl just got here, Tina. Don't scare her off with your stories," Colonel chides, a little sharp.

Tina pulls me into a big, warm hug, like she really means it, and rubs my back. "You're gonna do fine," she says softly. "You just remember you're a Kirkwood and don't take shoo-shoo off nobody, you hear?"

"Yes, ma'am," I say reflexively, because what else is there to say?

She releases me and bustles out the door, and now it's my turn to order, even though I haven't really had time to peruse the menu. I almost get a salad, but then I remember what Colonel said about the salads and think about what the plumbing must be like in the back of this ancient building. I order a grilled cheese and a side of fruit because it's almost impossible to make a bad grilled cheese, and Colonel insists on paying for us both. He guides me to a table for two up front by the window that looks out on the square.

My chair is spindly wood with a rounded back, and there's no room for Doris's backpack. As I turn in place in the cramped space, trying to find somewhere to put her, a toddler charges past, screaming about cookies. I back up, and my butt hits a chair, which knocks into the next table. I whirl around to apologize, forgetting I'm holding a neon-pink bag full of cockatoo. Doris is already screaming as her backpack knocks over someone's sweet tea—

Spilling it all over the table and a tablet, and into the lap of the best-looking man I've ever seen.

3

"I'm so sorry!" I blurt.

The poor man is using his napkin to try to contain the spill, but his tablet has gone dark and his chips are now soaked. He's around my age, with tanned skin, longish palomino hair pulled back at his nape, and tattoos peeking out of his rolled-up flannel.

He looks up, annoyed. His eyes are an arresting hazel gray, his eyebrows dark. "Do you have any napkins?"

"All I have is an angry cockatoo and abject mortification."

He does a double take as if actually seeing me—and Doris—for the first time.

"You know that chicken salad's a little underdone?"

"She's not lunch—she's my emotional support cockatoo."

"She's doing a real bad job of it. Are you okay?"

I must look like a complete idiot, standing in the middle of this crowded restaurant holding a pink bag and having a panic attack.

"Oh, Captain!" Doris shrieks. "Shipoopi!"

Colonel, who's been watching all this play out, collects napkins from the surrounding tables, and all three of us mop up the spilled tea. It's as awkward as it sounds, and Doris isn't helping. Any moment, I'm afraid I'm going to get kicked out of the sandwich shop, which is the only way I could be more embarrassed.

"I'm okay. But I really am sorry. Looks like I killed your tablet."

He picks it up and messes with the buttons. Brown liquid drips out of every tablet orifice. "My sister gave it to me for Christmas, and she's going to be furious with me until she finds out a bird did it." And then—a devastating smile. "A bird, and a pretty girl. That should mollify her."

I'm not sure which is more swoony, his smile or the fact that he can correctly use the word *mollify* in a sentence.

"I'll pay for it," I say, knowing full well I can't afford to. "Or—is there a bookstore downtown? I'll buy you a copy of whatever you were reading."

A wry shake of the head. "I wish we had a bookstore, but no. Closest we've got is a spinner rack of cookbooks at the—"

"Abraham?" Colonel barks, drawing my attention.

The second-oldest man in town sits down at the table beside ours. The last customer's trash is still there, and the man picks through the abandoned basket, crunching on someone else's pickle. With his long gray beard, shiny pink head, and sleepy brown eyes, I wouldn't be surprised if this guy was Abraham from the actual Bible.

"Yessir?" Abraham says, blinking in surprise as if he has no idea where he is.

"Who's watching the store?"

Abraham looks around in alarm. "Which store?"

"The one you're supposed to be watching."

Abraham scratches his beard and inspects whatever he found there. "I reckon it's watching itself. Hasn't got into trouble, so far."

"We'll see about that," Colonel says disapprovingly. "Ah, lunch!"

He turns away from Abraham and wiggles with joy as Lindy, a harried-looking woman in her forties wearing a cat sweatshirt and leggings, places our food on our table. "Enjoy!" she calls before galloping back into the kitchen.

But I can't sit down to eat—I'm still holding a parrot backpack and a wad of tea-soaked napkins.

"Are you using your extra seat?" I ask the handsome man with the destroyed tablet. "I need someplace to put this miscreant bird before she ruins someone else's lunch."

"I'm meeting a friend, but I think I have something that might work." He fumbles with his keychain, pulling out a weird little device that looks like brass knuckles and a coat hanger had an awkward child. "It's a purse hanger," he tells me, showing me how to hook it on the edge of the table. "If your emotional support cockatoo likes swings."

When he holds it out, I take it, and soon Doris is indeed dangling happily from the table. I pull a baggie of her favorite nut mix out of my tote bag and give her enough to keep her busy. The guy is still watching us like we're the best show on TV.

"So why do you have a purse hanger?" I ask, because honestly, he's the first attractive man I've seen in years who wasn't also in my kindergarten Christmas pageant, and I want to keep riding this high.

"Oh, it's for all my purses," he says. "I've got at least a dozen. One for every day of the week and an extra big one for Sunday, with a matching hat."

Just then, his friend shows up—a sharply handsome Latino guy in his early twenties. He gives me a mischievous smile, holds up his phone, and says, "Could you please say that again while I'm recording? The thing about all your purses?"

The first guy bursts out laughing again. "Nothing wrong with a good purse. But to answer your question, my grandmother is terrified of the flu and gave me that thing so I could open doors without touching them. I put it on my keychain so she won't ask me why I'm not using it. But you can keep it. For your parrot."

"And what will your grandmother say when she finds out it's gone?"

He grins, making me feel a little giddy. "I'll tell her I gave it to a beautiful woman, and she'll stop trying to set me up with that nice girl from her yoga class."

I'm about to say something else vaguely flirty, but with the new guy there, we have an audience. Instead, I thank my knight with shining purse hanger and sit, my back to him.

My grilled cheese is delicious, and my attention is captured by the black-and-white photos on the wall, showing the downtown square in times past. Soon Colonel is dabbing at his chin with his napkin, having eaten his sandwich in basically one big gulp like a snake. I'm not done eating, but I'm anxious about having uprooted my entire life to come here, and I'm still a little flustered by talking to the cute guy, so I put the rest of my sandwich in the basket and help bus the table. On the way out, I glance back, but the two men are having an intense discussion, scribbling on a napkin as they eat. I pocket the purse hanger. The cute guy said I could have it, and anyway, if I stick around, maybe I can try to return it some other day.

"So, you certainly had an effect on Hunter Blakely,"

Colonel begins once we're outside, as if he were reading my mind.

"I had to help clean up his tea," I say innocently, tucking that name away for later.

Colonel raises his eyebrow. "As my granddaughters say, there was definitely tea involved." He clears his throat. "Well, anyway. If you're ready to get down to business?"

I can't wait a moment more to ask all the questions bubbling up about this place, my grandmother's will, and my future here, but Colonel seems to live on his own schedule.

"Ready as the day I was born."

He leads me to the corner and across the street, then stops in the middle of the row of storefronts, most of which are closed or abandoned.

"What do you think?" he asks.

The building before us hasn't been painted recently. It's not cute like Lindy's or homey like Marla's Home Cookin'. The brick is patched and stained, and the big plate-glass window is dirty and mostly blocked by old cardboard cutouts from the movies of my parents' childhood, sun-bleached and sad. There's Arnold as the Terminator, Howard the Duck, Morticia Addams, and Darth Vader, all gazing out from within like they're trapped in a time capsule. When I look up, the second-story windows are all similarly unwashed and covered by ivory-yellow blinds, crooked and bent like someone's been playing basketball inside. Across the big front window, barely visible unless you're standing in just the right spot without too much glare, someone has painted, badly, the words ARCADIA FALLS VIDEO EMPORIUM, and even more badly, underneath that, & BOILED P-NUT PALACE.

"I think this is the last video store on earth, if it's still open," I say. "Does this town not have a library? Or decent Wi-Fi? Does the peanut part of the business bring in more customers?"

"The peanut part does do pretty well," he admits. "But the library is closed for renovation, and plenty of folks around town still rent videos. Time moves slower up here in the mountains. Shall we go inside?"

"Why? Are you hungry for peanuts?"

Colonel grasps my hand as if offering condolences. "No, darlin'. This is what your grandmother left you. This place is all yours. Upstairs and down. And the next three buildings in the row, besides, although I'll admit they're in worse condition."

I gently pull my hand away and take a step back to get a better look. Sensing my disquiet, Doris flaps her wings and squawks, "Oh, lordy."

There are five storefronts on this side of the square, and I'm standing in front of one of the only two that are open; the other is a candy store with a psychedelic gnome theme on the other corner. Honestly, I kind of wish I'd inherited that instead.

Except, well, when I look more closely, this place is . . . not *that* bad. The brick is grimy, but that can be cleaned. Or better yet, painted. A nice, crisp white, maybe, with the framing stark black. It needs a real sign, at least. The coterie of dingy cardboard heroes has to go. The windows upstairs look gross, but blinds are easy to take down and cheap to replace. It has good bones, and if I understand correctly . . .

"So we would own it all outright—me and my sisters? It would be ours free and clear, with no mortgage or liens or anything? The whole thing?"

Colonel nods and gestures grandly, as if he were offering me the world. "Upstairs and down, free and clear, all yours," he agrees. "Although your sisters aren't on the paperwork. You can split things with them however you like if everything goes according to plan."

"So we would own all four . . ." I trail off, considering it.

"The video store, then the next three storefronts." He points off to the left, to a closed hardware store, then a closed antiques market, then what looks like an ancient movie theater, big enough for just one screen. "Your grandmother owns—*owned*—most of the block. Everything except the candy store. This is the only business she could keep up, toward the end."

"So all I have to do is sign some paperwork?"

And then there's a pause. A very meaty pause.

"Yes, but . . . there's just one condition."

"What's the condition?" I ask, because that's the obvious question.

Colonel's lips purse. "Let's go back to my office and discuss it."

Now that I know it could be mine—*ours*—the homey brick building is vastly more interesting. Cardboard Arnold calls to me from behind his sunglasses. "I thought you said we could go inside?"

There's a sigh as Colonel fusses with his bow tie. "We can, but we'll need to hurry. I have a three o'clock, and I'd rather not pick up any . . . odors."

I'm not sure why odors would be a problem, but when I open the glass door, I'm immediately slapped in the face with the scent of salty brine. There's a ruckus in the backpack as Doris smells junk food that she's absolutely not allowed to have. Right beside the door stands an old mini air hockey table with two big Crock-Pots on top, their glass tops steaming. REGULAR $2, reads one in Comic Sans. CAJUN $3, reads the other. There are two ladles sitting on mismatched flowered saucers, as well as stacks of Styrofoam cups, tops, brown paper sacks, and a fishbowl stuffed with coins and crumpled bills. I see Colonel's problem; the smell of boiled peanuts is aggressive, and I move farther inside to avoid the cloud of nut steam.

The rest of the video emporium comes into focus, and I'm having flashbacks to Eighties Night at the Cumberville Skate-a-Rama, but that's partially due to the neon geometric-patterned carpet. No two shelves are alike—some white, some black, and some plain wood—and the DVDs are face-out, their cases dingy and dinged. Much to my absolute surprise, there's a whole bookcase filled with old VHS cassettes, including all the Disney movies in their ivory plastic boxes, somehow freed from the darkness of the Disney Vault. The shelves have hand-lettered signs pointing out their genres: HORROR, COMEDY, DRAMA, 4 KIDS, ROMANCE (with little hearts all around it). The movies aren't even in alphabetical order, and most of them are at least five years old, if not ten. Or twenty. Lots of these movies are older than me. I begin to see why the boiled-peanut half of the business gets more play.

By the front counter, there's a spinner rack full of self-published books. I see *The Official Arcadia Falls Cookbook*, *The Arcadia Falls REAL Official Cookbook*, *The 100% Genuine Real Honest-to-God OFFICIAL Arcadia Falls Cookbook*, *Ghosts of Arcadia Falls*, and *The Mountain Whispers My Name: The Life and Times of Darla Gooch*, among others. If these are the only books available for purchase in town, no wonder Hunter Blakely was annoyed at the loss of his reading tablet. With no library and no bookstore, I'm already annoyed myself. This selection is not going to bring in the crowds.

Books and Bewitchment

And that's when I realize there's not a single person in the store, besides us. No customers. No workers.

"So is it on an honor basis?" I ask.

Colonel looks out the plate-glass window, his hands in his pockets. "You saw Abraham in the sandwich shop? Maggie hired him to run this place when she wasn't around. He's doing a real bad job of it."

I think back to the man I saw at lunch, so old that I can't imagine him being able to stay vertical long enough to scoop out a cup of peanuts. He seems like he might keel over while counting out change.

"Can I fire him?"

A heavy sigh as Colonel squinches his eye shut. "Okay, so I suppose there are actually two conditions. Unfortunately, he comes with the shop. You're welcome to reduce his hours, as long as he makes enough money to live on."

I gesture at the haphazard shelves. "Can anyone make enough money to live on here?" I pick up the nearest DVD. It's *Starship Troopers 2*. "Do you even know how bad this movie is?"

He draws himself up tall. "I've rented that movie twice. When I tell you things move slower up here, I mean it. The first one is much better—the part about the ferret always makes me laugh." He clears his throat. "Thing is, Maggie was very specific about Abraham. He stays, and he earns minimum wage. Now, if you'll follow me to my office, I can answer all your questions without being bombarded with the scent of peanuts, to which I am sadly allergic."

"But we can't just leave the store . . . without . . ." I trail off as he gives me a look that suggests I'm not very bright.

"It's kept well enough like this for the last thirty years. I'm sure one more day of horrible mismanagement won't burn the building down." Colonel laboriously bends over to check the outlet into which the Crock-Pots are plugged. "Hopefully."

He opens the door, and I walk outside, vastly preferring the scent of late summer to thirty-year-old videos and overheated peanut hulls with too much paprika. Colonel is just as fast returning to work as he was heading to lunch, and soon I'm settled in a leather chair as he hunts through his massive desk. He opens a manila folder and jabs his finger at the paper-clipped sheaf of documents within. Doris's backpack is on the floor, and she's softly whistling "Bali Ha'i" from *South Pacific*, which is one of her happy songs. I have to wonder if she feels at home in the office, after all her time spent at Buckley Insurance. They both feature a lot of plaid.

"Your grandmother's trust is very peculiar," Colonel begins, and a little trill of worry skitters up my neck.

Peculiar isn't the sort of word that generally signifies something a person wants. Nobody ever says, "I won the lottery, but it's peculiar."

"It's straightforward, at least," he continues. "You are set to inherit buildings B through D at 375 Main Street, including the Video Emporium and Boiled P-Nut Palace. The second story of that storefront in particular is a furnished apartment. Probably needs some upgrades, but Maggie lived up there for the past twenty years or so. You also get two parking spots in the alley, which might be worth more than the building."

"I feel like you're just telling me the good parts," I say.

He chuckles. "Well, there's no bad part—just a few bizarre parts. In order to accept your inheritance, you have to take your grandmother's ashes to Arcadia Falls and, well, scatter them in the waterfall."

"Okay. That doesn't sound too bad. Is it a really rough

waterfall or something? Do I have to wear a bathing suit? Are there bears?"

He shakes his head. "The falls are decently calm—you can probably just roll up your jeans. And bears aren't typically a problem around here except on trash day, and even then they're little ol' black bears. So we just need to make the trip today. Since you're not from around here, it falls to me—ha, falls!—to take you up there and show you the right place." He's entirely focused on the papers, straightening them again and again.

"And that's it?"

I want to reach for the papers, but he's keeping them close.

"Can I read the will?"

He snatches up the folder. "Once you've distributed the ashes, then you'll sign the papers and have your copy—of the trust."

"What about my sisters? Do they need to come up and sign anything? I plan on giving each of them a building, even if they want to sell it. Is that allowed? Selling?"

He holds up the folder. "Nobody gets anything until those ashes are put to rest, and you can't sell the properties, although you can rent them out. That's what's so peculiar about the trust, you see. Maggie wanted things done her way, that's for sure."

Since I'm not going to wrestle the paperwork away from him, I don't have much of a choice. My sisters are counting on me. Money is scarce, so unless somebody suddenly marries rich, we're all doomed. We need this inheritance. If nothing else, we can rent out all these buildings and finance our lives back in Alabama, I guess. All I have to do, apparently, is spread some ashes by a waterfall. People have done a lot worse for a lot less. Hence reality television.

"Okay," I tell him. "Let's do it."

He cheers back up once I agree, his cheeks pink as he locks his office door again and confirms that Doris doesn't get carsick. He isn't comforted when I explain that birds vomit on purpose all the time, often out of love.

His car is expensive, the seats black leather and the suspension so smooth that I don't even feel the bumps and potholes in the winding mountain roads. As he drives, Colonel points out local spots of interest, from the Biscuit Barn to the animal shelter where his granddaughters read to cats every Wednesday afternoon. The falls aren't too far from downtown, but there are no sidewalks on either side of the road, the asphalt dropping off to what seems like an endless, dizzy tumble through the trees to the deep valleys below. I can already imagine what it's going to look like when the leaves start changing color in a few weeks, a glorious crazy quilt of yellow, red, and orange. Finally, he pulls into a gravel parking lot, tires crunching. There are no other cars here, and the ARCADIA FALLS PARK sign is small and brown, nearly blending in with the environment. It would be easy to drive right past the turnoff—no wonder he brought me himself.

As I get out of the car and let Doris look around from her bag, Colonel shuffles to his trunk, where he changes into a pair of lime-green sneakers before holding up a silver urn that looks a lot like a cocktail shaker.

"Is this all of her?" I ask. "It seems small."

He offers it to me and, when I take it, dusts off his hands, although it doesn't feel dusty at all. "This is how she wanted things done. As I've previously mentioned, she was very specific. Her best friend, Diana McGowan—you met her daughter, Tina, at lunch—was supposed to do all this, but Diana left us in the same car accident, rest their souls."

I realize that in all the talk, no one has told me any details about how my grandmother died. "How did she—"

"Ashes, first," he says, keeping me on task.

The urn feels warm in my hands, and I resist the urge to pop off the top and see what human cremains look like. I'll find out soon enough. Better to do it by the waterfall than to test it out here and lose some of my grandmother to a wayward breeze.

Colonel leads me up a trail, pumping his arms and walking with cheerful determination. I follow with my grandmother in one hand and Doris's backpack on my back, glad I'm just wearing old Chucks and not something more formal. The carpet of brown pine needles gives way to wood stairs during the especially vertical parts.

"Getting my cardio today," Colonel puffs. "That's for sure. Should've had the fried chicken. As fortification."

My heart rate is up, both from the steps and from a weird sense of anticipation. I'm not sure why. I'm just going to dump some ashes, which is completely normal when people die and don't want to be buried in an expensive coffin. I didn't even know my grandmother, so it's not like it's going to be a deep, emotional moment where I say goodbye to a loved one. These ashes might as well be sand for all the connection I feel to them. I don't know a single thing about my grandmother, other than that my mama hated her, that her will is weirdly persnickety, and that she didn't know how to run a video store.

I hear the falls before I see them, a busy rush like a cantankerous white-noise machine. I've never been near a waterfall before, but the air is charged and filled with mist, and I eagerly breathe it in. It's exhilarating and exciting, the temperature cool and the forest alive all around us. Our path runs along something halfway between a creek and a river, the churned-up waters that need somewhere to go after pouring down the mountain.

We come around a bend, and there it is.

Arcadia Falls.

It's strange, when a plural noun is also a singular.

The mountainside rises up hundreds of feet, craggy and mottled gray, and the water trickles from high overhead and then plummets, sheeting down heavily for the last twenty feet or so in a wide wall of water. I'm in awe of this wonder of nature, of the way the cascade has chosen exactly this place to reach the ground and has worn down its path over millennia. I wonder what the water tastes like, if it has the sharp tang of minerals or is gritty with dirt.

Colonel stops, one foot up on a rock, breathing heavily. "You go on now. You've got to get her *behind* the falls—she was very particular about that."

"Is there a cavern back there or something? Like, a secret cave?"

He looks at me like I'm a child asking how many carrots the Easter bunny ate to get so big. "I don't know what's back there, but I guess you'll find out. Always preferred the swimming hole farther down the creek, myself." He glances back toward the trail. "I'll let you know if anyone's coming. Do watch out, though—the rocks are slippery."

None of this information is helpful, but it's not like it matters. I'm here, and I have to go through with this next, strange step. This inheritance is the only way I can hope to offer any possibility of stability to my sisters—and myself. I hold out my backpack.

"Will you hold Doris, please? She's happier off the ground."

He raises a white eyebrow at my cockatoo. "Does she bite?"

"Not unless you start singing anything from *Cats*. She hates *Cats*."

He takes the backpack and holds it at arm's length. "Never was an animal sort of person, but she seems like a polite creature."

"Oh, Captain!" she says happily, and I begin to think she's a little in love with him.

Now armed with only the urn, I consider my approach.

The falls tumble down into a wide pool before emptying away into a creek littered with slime-coated stones. It's only knee-deep, maybe, and if I'd known the setup, I would've changed out of my jeans and into shorts; I've got most of my wardrobe packed in the many tubs shoved in the back of my old Explorer parked at the law office. As it is, I set down the urn and scrunch up the legs of my jeans, forcing them up over my knees. I take off my shoes and socks, leaving them on a flat rock.

The first step into the water is startlingly frigid, my feet going numb. I pick my way toward the falls, stepping on the biggest, flattest rocks. It's loud, up close, and I'm guessing that even if Colonel started squawking about visitors now, I wouldn't hear him. I glance back, and he's not watching the trail—he's watching me. Intently, seriously, with his one good eye. Which is all the funnier when you consider his three-piece suit, lime-green sneakers, and pink backpack full of worried cockatoo.

"Oh, lordy. Oh, lordy. Shipoopi!" she squawks, flapping her wings in frustration at my distance. I give her a little wave of reassurance, and Colonel waves back and gestures for me to get on with it.

I turn back around. Eyes on the prize. I'm close enough now to feel the spray of the falls hitting the rocks. The water is deeper than I thought, wetting my jeans up to my thighs.

Mist fills the air, rainbows shimmering as the sunlight hits the sparkling droplets. I unscrew the cap of the—

No, wait. If I have to get behind the falls, I should probably keep the cap on the urn, or else the falling water will just turn my grandmother's cremains into gray soup. But once I'm on the other side, my hands might be too wet. . . .

I unscrew it most of the way, to where it just needs one tiny little twist to come off. I read about three books a week, and I hate it when the main character doesn't think of these little details.

Looking up at the waterfall, I accept that I'm about to get soaked. I wonder if Colonel considered this part of the process, what he's going to say when my sopping-wet jeans squelch onto his fine leather seats.

Oh, well.

Not my leather seats, not my problem.

I take a deep breath and hold out my right hand as I enter the falls, expecting to bumble through the sheet of water into some sort of open area.

Instead, my hand hits solid stone, and the pounding water slams into my head, into my eyes, into my mouth, into my nose. I stumble back, gasping and gargling for air, and the urn goes flying. My bare heel catches on a slippery stone, and I fall on my butt in the pool, surrounded by floating human cremains. Colonel panics, dropping my bag, and Doris bursts out from the door she has yet again half unzipped because she's as smart as a toddler and just as reckless. Screeching, she flutters toward me and tries to land on my head. I throw up my hands, and her claws scratch bird calligraphy down my forearms. I finally get her settled on my wrist, and she shouts, "No, Horace, bad boy!" and bites my finger, holding on for dear life.

I flail and screech—I can't help it; that bite *hurts!*—

and she flaps away and lands in the water, squawking and splashing as gritty gray rivulets soak my hair and run down my face, the world's grossest baptism. I reach for her, the cool water thankfully chilling my bleeding finger.

It doesn't hurt anymore.

It feels . . .

I feel . . .

Weirdly amazing.

"What the hell?" someone shrieks—and it's not Colonel Gooch.

And then everything changes.

5

I swipe away the hair matting over my eyes and struggle to stand, my senses overwhelmed by being wet and hurt and covered with moistened grandma cremains.

"Diana? Diana!" the shrieking voice continues.

Once I can see more clearly . . .

Well, it doesn't help at all.

It's just me, Doris, and Colonel, who is decidedly not a shrieking woman.

Doris is struggling in the water, flapping her wings, her puffy feathers waterlogged.

"Come here, fool," I tell her, scooping her up and holding her to my chest.

"I don't know what the hell happened," the strange voice continues, sounding panicked and annoyed, "but you'd better put me down." It sounds like an elderly woman, but there are no women in the area, and Colonel isn't reacting to the voice at all.

"I say, Miss Wolfe, are you all right?" he calls from his perch at the edge of the pool. "That looked like quite a tumble."

"Well, for future reference, there's no cavern behind the falls," I tell him, sloshing toward land. "Just solid rock. Was my grandmother a practical joker?"

"I would not say that she was. Maybe you need to try a different part of the falls?"

I look back at the pounding water doubtfully.

"Tell him the ashes hit the falls, so it counts," the voice says.

I reckon I might be losing my mind—maybe the waterfall gave me a concussion, or I inhaled too many cremains—but the voice is making as much sense as anything else right now.

"The ashes got behind the falls. That's what the will said, right? That they had to go behind the falls?"

Doris tries to fluff herself, but I'm holding her tight as a football as I watch Colonel's nose scrunch up.

"Well, now, that is true. I suppose there are definitely ashes behind the falls." He looks down at the murky, gray-coated water with immense distaste. "The ashes are everywhere. I certainly do hope the sheriff doesn't show up. I wasn't expecting such a mess."

"Me neither," I say.

Satisfied that I've done my duty, I carefully step up on the shore. My jeans and shirt are soaked—every bit of me is soaked—and I'm quickly learning that wet cremains would never work as a beauty treatment. Maybe I should be more grossed out, but honestly, what's the point? Running wild in the neighborhood with my sisters, I learned long ago that dirt and blood both wash off. This is just a temporary state, and at least I've already booked a room at the Magnolia Inn, a local B&B with great reviews. Although . . .

"Now that we're done here, can I sign the papers and take possession of that apartment?" I ask. "And does it have a washer and dryer?"

Colonel's nostrils flare as he takes a step away from me. "You certainly can, and I would hope it does." He points back at the pool. "You'll want to collect that urn, though. Definitely not biodegradable."

The urn is bobbing around not too far away, so I place Doris back in the backpack and zip it up, knowing full well she'll make a mess. Then again, that's one of the only absolute truths about cockatoos—all pet birds, really.

Once she's secure, I wade back into the pool and toward the waterfall, dodging the floaty bits of gray. Now that I know what to expect, I use the flowing water to rinse off the cremains as well as I can. I'm aware that I look like a goth shampoo commercial as I dip my head backward in the falls and shake out my hair. Soaked but no longer a walking biohazard, I scoop up the urn and its top. "Take nothing but pictures, leave nothing but a big goddamn mess," I murmur. Doris chuckles and shakes her wet feathers. The tuft on her head is all spiky with water, like a tiny pink mohawk.

"I do still have a three o'clock, so we should hurry," Colonel reminds me. "There's a yoga mat in the back of the car, if you wouldn't mind sitting on that?"

Soon we're zooming back toward town, Colonel's bright blue yoga mat uncomfortably squeaky under my wet jeans. Doris is quiet in her backpack, which is unusual but not unwelcome. I pull down my mirror and grimace. Despite my attempt to clean up and wind my hair in a tidy bun, I look like a swamp monster.

"This is not how things usually go when people pass," Colonel says, possibly more to himself than to me. "Spread my ashes in the ocean, they say. Put me on the mantel. But of course ol' Maggie would want to be deposited behind a waterfall."

"I thought you said she wasn't a jokester."

He shakes his head. "She wasn't. But she wanted things done her way. A very stubborn woman. That's why—"

He breaks off and gives a huffy little sigh, and Doris flaps her wings in her bag and screeches, "Bullshit!"

"I thought you said she didn't curse," Colonel says, primly.

I look down into her brightly blinking red eyes. "She never has before. But that was probably a little traumatizing, what happened back there. I may need to get her into cockatoo therapy or something." I silently try to find a pun based on *psittacosis* and *psychiatry* and fail.

Back at Colonel's office, once I'm sitting on a towel, I'm allowed to read through the trust. It's strange but straightforward. Everything was supposed to go to her best friend, Diana McGowan, who was a few years younger and in excellent health, then the next of kin, with no mention of my mother or me or my sisters. Although the paperwork I sign is very official, the original trust is handwritten and witnessed by Colonel himself. With both Maggie and Diana dead in the same car accident, everything is left to me. Abraham will have a job and be paid minimum wage for thirty hours per week until he's dead. And most annoyingly, I can't use the reasonable-but-not-life-changing money in my grandmother's trust for anything other than paying him or improving the properties on the downtown square. Colonel is the executor and I'm the trustee, which means I can't just withdraw all the cash and run.

"Aren't wills supposed to just—give you stuff?" I ask. My folks' will was easy, even if probate was a pain; they just downloaded it off the internet and filled in the blank spaces.

Colonel hands me a weighty silver pen. "*Supposed to.* Those words don't mean much, do they? Maggie chose a trust instead of a will because it was imperative to her that her legacy remained in Arcadia Falls. She has paid me to enforce her requirements whether I believe them wise or not."

I sign on the line because there's no reason not to. When you've got nothing, pretty much anything is an improvement. I return Colonel's pen, and he bustles around, muttering about his assistant being out for the day as he makes a copy for me and then places the signed paper in the file as if it's precious.

"I'll file everything for you, go through all the proper motions, but as far as I'm concerned, you are now the sole beneficiary of all your grandmother's holdings. Should you wish to divide them up with your sisters, I can handle that for you legally, and if you'd rather rent out the spaces, I can help with that, too. Any money you spend improving the properties, whether to occupy them yourself or rent them, must be reported to me with receipts, but I'm here most business days from nine until five."

"And that's it? That's all there is?"

"Everything in her apartment is yours now. You would've had her old truck, but I'm afraid there was nothing left but scrap. Drunk drivers on these roads, I swear." He shakes his head sadly. "I understand Maggie has an account at the bank up the street, so they can help you sort that out. In any case, welcome to Arcadia Falls." His smile is genuine, his eye twinkling. "I do hope you'll enjoy it here. Your family has always been part of this place, and I pray it will continue that way."

He slides a battered leather key ring across the desk, and there must be at least two dozen keys of all shapes and sizes on it.

"Do all of these keys go to something?"

He stands, struggling into his blazer. "Not a clue, darlin'. The stairs up to the apartment are out back in the alley. The parking spaces are marked. Beyond that, I'm afraid I don't know much. A very private woman, your grandmother. I've never even been upstairs, so I have no idea what condition it's in." He holds open the door and seems to relax a little once I'm dripping on his porch instead of his rug. "Just one more thing."

Colonel locks his office door and looks suspiciously from side to side like he's expecting someone to pop out from behind the shady fig tree. "Your grandmother was tough and feisty," he whispers. "I'm not sure what happened, but the town seemed to turn on her a while back—some families, at least. No one would tell me why. You might encounter some unfriendliness when the locals find out who you are. Not that I would know, as I'm not a gossip, but just . . ." He smooths back his white hair. "Just watch out, is all I'm saying."

With that, he gives me a jaunty nod, gets in his car, and drives away before I can drip on anything else of value, leaving me alone in his parking lot with a moist bird and a soggy butt.

"Well, that was strange," I mutter to myself as I head for my car.

"It certainly was," someone says—that same female voice from the waterfall.

I look around, and there isn't another human being anywhere near us.

This is . . . too much.

I slam into my car seat, shut and lock the door, and put Doris's backpack on the passenger side.

"Who keeps talking to me?" I say to my empty car.

"Come on, girl. You've got to be smarter than this."

I look over and Doris is staring at me through the mesh panel of the backpack, her red eyes blinking expectantly like she knows I have popcorn and is hoping for a handful.

"My cockatoo is not talking to me," I say, and I'm thankfully staring straight at Doris, so I know her mouth—beak!—isn't moving when the next words are spoken.

"Well, yes and no," the voice says tiredly. "Your cockatoo is now your grandmother, and it seems you can hear me. So I guess that's our introduction. This was not supposed to happen." Doris ruffles up her feathers and flares out her tail like she always does when she's annoyed.

"Not what was supposed to happen?"

"I wasn't supposed to die this early, and you're not supposed to be here at all," she snaps. "The trust only goes to next of kin in case of catastrophe. Which is what's happened. It's all gone wrong. I worked too hard to see everything go to waste."

That raises my dander. "Your granddaughter inheriting your estate is a waste?"

"Yes!"

"Well, I'm so sorry to disappoint. Since it seems like you don't want me around, shall I open the window so you can go do your own thing? Maybe find a flock of pigeons to infiltrate?"

The voice in my head huffs a sigh.

"Look, honey, I'm mad, but I'm not mad at you. I was supposed to come back as my cat and help Diana—" The voice cuts off. "But Diana is gone." She makes a few weird *gerk-gluck* noises before saying, with some surprise, "Huh. Birds can't cry. This body is going to take a lot of getting used to."

I can't currently trust this bird, so I buckle the backpack

into the passenger seat instead of letting Doris—or whoever she is now—sit on her car seat perch.

"Nope," I say, putting the car in reverse and backing out of the space. "Nope, my dead grandmother is not a talking cockatoo. I will get to a safe place and shower and put on dry clothes and drink a glass of water, and then I'll figure out why I'm hallucinating."

I'm on the road now, headed up toward the main street. Doris flaps her wings, and I hear the thump of her landing in the bottom of the backpack.

"Oh, lordy!" the voice says. "This is harder than it looks."

My cockatoo ward, who should definitely not be talking with the voice of a seventy-year-old Southern woman, makes a ruckus as I drive. I think she's struggling to get back up on the rope perch.

"Balance is all off," the voice mutters. "What are these creepy chicken feet? Ridiculous things. Couldn't you have a pet with a little grace? It's like wearing flip-flops with thumbs."

"I'm not hearing that," I say, leaning forward as I hunt for the alley that contains my promised parking spaces. I find a turn-in behind the row of buildings, a road wide enough for a delivery truck with parallel parking spaces running alongside, and one sad dumpster. All the parking spots are taken except one, which has a sign that reads MAGGIE KIRKWOOD. DON'T EVEN THINK ABOUT IT.

I think about it. I pull in.

Or, I try to.

I'm not good at parallel parking. Getting the car passably close to the curb takes me five nervous minutes, which are not made any easier by the running commentary of a disembodied voice fussing in my head.

"This is easier when they respect the second space, but I

reckon the moment I keeled over, Marla decided she could park there. You're gonna have to put up another sign. Oh! Maybe a bit less sharp braking. Hard to hold on for dear life when you don't have hands."

I try to ignore the voice and fail, but at least I don't argue with it.

Because that would be giving in to lunacy.

Once I'm mostly in the space, I hop out and snag the backpack. Surely it is a coincidence that the voice says, "Whoop! Well, that's a fine how-do-you-do!"

The alley is silent and shadowy, and smells vaguely of chocolate. I pull out the new key ring and head up a set of sturdy wooden stairs to a second-story balcony above the video store. There's a worn welcome mat and a concrete statue of a cat, and the door is painted purple.

"Which key?" I mutter to myself, because, honestly, when you're losing your mind, sometimes you're the only person worth talking to.

"The round silver one with purple nail polish," the voice says, and I ignore the fact that Doris is pressed up against the mesh of the backpack, watching me closely.

I can be stubborn and work through the keys my way, or I can do what the mysterious voice says and possibly be showering off human cremains and stepping into a dry pair of pants five minutes faster, so I try the round silver key with a swash of purple and am almost disappointed that it works. The door creaks open on a kitchen/living room combo, but I barely register that as I hurry back out to the car, grab the roller bag I packed with my most immediate needs, and drag my suitcase up the steps with the bird backpack in my other hand.

"What's it called, that thing where a bird's body moves but its head doesn't?" the disembodied voice asks.

"Insanity," I growl.

"No, that's not it. There's a specific sciencey term."

At the top of the stairs, I nudge open the door and get my first glimpse of who my grandmother must've been.

And to tell you the truth, it's a total shock.

6

I expected florals and quilts and pastels and maybe more cardboard movie stand-ups.

I would not have been surprised by faded country chic and mothballs and, I don't know, ceramic roosters everywhere.

And yet here I stand in a full-on hippie retreat.

There are crystals on every windowsill, macramé plant hangers in every corner, shawls over every lamp, dried flowers on every surface, posters of Stevie Nicks and Picasso's peace dove and Woodstock. The dominating odors are incense and patchouli.

"Home sweet home," the annoying voice says, relieved.

Now that I'm in a private place, I close the door behind me, put down my bags, unzip the backpack, and gently take Doris in both hands, holding her up to face me.

"Are you talking?" I ask, inspecting her for a hidden speaker.

"Not with my mouth," she admits. "It's telepathy. Pretty neato, right?"

There's nothing new or unusual about the cockatoo that's been my ward for the past three years, aside from the dried human cremains dusting her pink feathers. When she struggles in my hands, I place her on the floor. She waddles back and forth, looks at her foot, spreads her wings, raises her crest.

"This body didn't come with an instruction manual. Gonna take some getting used to. But I always wanted to fly—"

"One of your wings is clipped, so don't get too excited."

She looks up at me, her eyes dilating in annoyance. "I thought you young people believed in personal freedoms."

"You do not currently have the personal freedom to fly into a school bus. I actually don't approve of wing clipping, but until recently, my boss, Mr. Horace Buckley, was your legal owner, and you did attempt to attack a couple of his clients—" I drag my hands down my face. "Oh my God, I'm trying to reason with a cockatoo."

I scoop Doris up and walk over to a long, low bookshelf filled with paperbacks by Danielle Steel and Nora Roberts, plus several photographs, a crystal ball, and a big vase of dried flowers. The bird struggles in my grasp, so I help her perch on my wrist. The image that's caught my attention is a beautiful young woman with long auburn hair wearing a slip dress and swinging a chubby baby around near the very waterfall I'm currently soaked in. The woman looks like me—and she looks like Mama.

"I sure was pretty, wasn't I?" the voice asks, sounding wistful. "Then again, I guess it's easy to be pretty when you're young."

I look from the bird to the photograph. I don't want to

ask the question I need to ask, because I know it's absurd, but . . . I have to ask.

"Am I talking to my grandmother, and are you, um, *possessing* my pet cockatoo?"

Doris—is it Doris, still?—clucks a laugh.

"That's one way to put it. I had everything planned out with Diana. I was supposed to come back as my cat and become her second familiar."

"A familiar? Like, the pet of a witch? And if you're in there, where did Doris go?"

The cockatoo nearly falls off my wrist, so I gently place her on the floor. She fluffs her feathers and hesitantly walks around, her head bobbing. "Every witch needs a familiar. And if Doris is what you called your bird, then yes, I'm talking about her. As for where she went, I don't know. I don't think cockatoos have souls."

"But they have feelings," I argue, annoyed by this assumption. "She had a personality. She liked musicals."

"Feelings and a love of musical theater are not a soul, honey. I'm sorry if you're going to miss her, but hopefully you'll be comforted by the fact that your grandmother performed a very complicated spell that— Well, it went totally wrong. But now that you're here and you fumbled your way into the waterfall, at least I'm still around to teach you how to be a witch."

The whole world goes silent in that moment.

I can hear a clock ticking, somewhere deeper in the apartment.

"I need a minute," I say.

Leaving the cockatoo—*the cockatoo that is apparently my estranged dead grandmother*—to peck at her own rug, I run out the door and down the stairs to the alley, grumbling to myself.

"This can't be happening. Weird-ass will, and no cavern behind the waterfall, and I'm wet and covered in dead grandma, and my pet bird is talking, but she's actually speaking in sentences instead of Rodgers and Hammerstein lyrics. Maybe I have a brain-eating amoeba from the water and I'm hearing a disembodied voice—"

I have tunnel vision and am extremely preoccupied, which means I run smack into someone, but they're sturdy enough that we don't go tumbling to the concrete. Instead, firm hands grasp my shoulders, and I flick my damp hair out of my eyes as I prepare to give somebody the what-for.

Oh.

It's him. The guy who gave me the purse hanger. Hunter. And he looks amused.

"Well, I'm not disembodied, if it makes you feel any better. Can't be disembodied if you have a body," he reasons.

And he does. Have a body. I have definitely noticed it. I was just momentarily pressed up against it. I'm very close to it right now. I'd like to—

Nope. Not now. I have bigger problems.

Leaving home for the first time, driving from Alabama to Georgia, being soaked to the bone, suddenly having a talking bird, inheriting a store that has no business existing, paying a salary to an absentee centenarian employee with money I don't possess. What else could go wrong?

"Sorry. I'm having . . . a day."

He looks me up and down with concern in his stormy gray eyes and apparently decides I'm not going to fall over, as he releases my shoulders. I immediately miss the way he made me feel all tingly and grounded. In that moment I realize that I'm farther away from everyone I love than I've ever been, and since I turned down Billy Wayne's crappy proposal weeks ago, no one has touched me, beyond Colonel's meaty handshake and Tina's awkward hug this morning. I feel both disconnected and yet also right where

I'm supposed to be, and these two sensations are playing tug-of-war with my heart.

The good-looking man standing before me knows none of this.

He doesn't know about the tingles.

He just sees a strange woman talking to herself, looking like she recently crawled out of a well.

He sticks his hands in his pockets as if trying to appear nonchalant. "Seems like it's not just a day, but a bad one. Are you okay? Did you get in a fight with a fire hydrant? And where's your emotional support cockatoo?"

A mad laugh breaks out of me at that thought.

The cockatoo in question is currently the cause of most of my problems.

"Let's just say she's currently in Cockatoo Jail for committing a crime of passion. I'm Rhea Wolfe, by the way."

He sticks out his hand, and I feel a jolt of electricity when we touch.

Not in the "oh, it's like it was meant to be" sort of way.

A literal shock, like touching a doorknob on the coldest day of winter.

He pulls his hand back and winces. "Oh, sorry. That happens all the time. Dry hands, thick shoes. I'm Hunter. So you're new in town, huh?"

I nod and force myself to look up. "Brand new." The longer I look at his muscular, tattooed forearms, the harder it's going to be for me to avoid doing anything but that.

"Well, normally I'd warn you about parking in Maggie Kirkwood's space. She's got a mean fastball with an egg from that balcony. Or she did. Sometimes she would try to snipe me just for tossing work trash in the dumpster. She was mean as hell, if you'll pardon my saying so, but she died a few weeks ago, so I guess you're probably safe."

I tuck away that bit about being mean. Didn't Colonel say she wasn't well-liked around town?

"So much for free eggs."

There's a frantic slapping noise, and we both look up to see a pink-and-gray blur caught in the ivory blinds and flapping madly.

"Oh, lordy," I mutter.

"Looks like your parrot is currently the one who needs the emotional support. She's not going to hurt herself up there, is she?" Hunter asks.

Doris—

No. *Grandma Maggie.*

Grandma Maggie pecks wildly at the glass as her wings strike the window again and again and her gray toenails scratch and scrabble furiously. She looks like she's about to have a cockatoo stroke.

"She'll be fine," I say, waving at her. "At zoos, they call this enrichment."

"Wait." He looks at me more closely. "Why is your bird in Maggie's apartment?" He glances at my Explorer, which is stuffed with most of my belongings. "Are you renting it?"

I'm not sure how much to tell him. I barely know what's happening myself.

"I'm staying here awhile. Well, maybe. Probably. It's complicated."

Hunter peers into the back of the Explorer, where Doris's enormous cage sits folded up on top of everything I own. He gazes up the wooden stairs to the apartment. "Do you have someone to help you move in?"

That thought did not occur to me until this very second, and suddenly the world feels desperately heavy. "Nope. Just me and Doris, and she had to give up powerlifting."

With a winning smile, he walks over and opens the

cargo area. "Think we can get the cage up there together, or should I get my friend Cisco to stop by after work?"

I'd honestly hoped I'd be on the ground floor somewhere. I never thought I'd be moving to a walk-up above the last video store in the world. Once unfolded, the cage is on wheels and is extremely sturdy, but I'm strong, and I know Hunter is strong, and he's right here. . . .

"If you have time and don't mind, I'd appreciate it," I tell him. "I think I can get everything else on my own, but the cage is a beast."

He inspects the metal bars. "Okay, so you weren't lying. Was this thing built to hold the Hulk?"

"Parrots can be a handful. Imagine an emotionally volatile toddler who has a knife for a nose and wolverine claws, and who's probably going to outlive you."

He chuckles, a pleasant rumble. "I think I'll stick with dogs. All of the innocent sweetness, none of the knifework." He maneuvers the cage into position and looks back at me as if measuring my grip strength.

I head over and heft the other side. "I helped load it, so I can help unload it. It weighs around a buck-fifty, but it's unwieldy."

"If you don't mind walking backward, that'll have me carrying the brunt of it."

It's a good plan. I nod and lift with my legs, not my back, and then the banter stops and the grunting begins. We cross the alley, and I begin the laborious work of walking backward up unfamiliar stairs while carrying something that weighs as much as I do in sopping-wet clothes and squelching sneakers while staring down at the taut forearms of the best-looking man I've seen in ages. I somehow manage not to trip or drop the cage on him, and soon we have it sitting on the balcony.

"You're strong," he says. "Are you a powerlifter, too?"

"I'm an office manager," I tell him. "But it's very heavy stuff."

He raises his eyebrows and reaches for the cage.

I hold up a hand. "Let me get Little Miss Knife Face into her backpack, just in case."

Hunter nods, and I squeeze through the door.

As soon as it's shut, I hurry to the next room, where Maggie is tangled up in the blinds. I gently extract her and whisper, "What on earth are you doing? You were better behaved when your brain was the size of a walnut."

"Life's a lot easier with hands," she says as I smooth down her feathers. "It's like I'm wearing oven mitts and stiletto heels, and my eyes go in opposite directions."

"Then why'd you decide to get in a fight with the blinds? Apparently, you can still think like a person, even if you're not great with this body." I snort. "God, that sounds completely unhinged."

"I was trying to tell you to get away from the Blakely boy, but I guess my telepathy can only go so far. Didn't you hear me shouting?"

"We both heard you screeching. And smacking your beak on the glass like a damn fool."

"That's cockatoo for 'Get away from the grandson of my mortal enemy Joyce Blakely.'"

"Mortal enemy?" I ask her.

She shakes herself. "Well, let's cross that bridge when we come to it. Not that it matters. When that boy finds out you're a Kirkwood, he won't want anything to do with you."

7

"And what's wrong with being a Kirkwood?" I ask.

For the first time in our life together, the bird goes absolutely silent.

"Maggie?"

She turns her head away, but at least she's not struggling against me, so I pop her into the backpack and firmly zip it up.

"Fine. Enjoy your silence in the Hot-Pink Backpack of Shame."

"You okay in there?" Hunter calls from outside.

"Just the usual Bird Problems," I shout back. "You know, like tax fraud."

I hurry to the photos of young Maggie I saw earlier and hide them all in a drawer. If she's right, I don't want him to put two and two together and figure out I'm her granddaughter. Not yet. I need to know more about this "Joyce Blakely is my mortal enemy" business, and I want to know more about him. After I do a quick scan to make sure there's no other damning evidence of my relationship to the egg-throwing menace, I hurry back to the door.

"Did you turn her in to the feds?" Hunter asks.

"Oh, yeah. She's already in prison. Ten-to-life for a pyramid scheme."

He grins and rolls in the cage—which he has already set up on his own! Swoon!

"Where do you want it?"

Those words . . . could mean something very different, in another context.

But in regard to the actual bird cage, I have not given this topic a moment's thought. "Over here against the wall would be great," I say.

He gets it in place and even checks that it's centered. "Anything else heavy I can bring up for you?"

As much as I would love to watch him carry ten boxes of my junk through the door, I want a shower even more than that. Plus, I'm Southern. If someone is going to do manual labor for me, I feel obligated to feed them, and I am in no position to feed him anything other than organic parrot pellets. I don't even know if the water is still on or what's in the fridge, although if Maggie died a few weeks ago, I'm not sure I want to find out.

"No, you've already helped so much. I really owe you one." I smile at him hopefully, praying he sees the appreciation and interest more than the wet rat.

He looks down at me—

And his face falls.

"Wait. You're bleeding. Did you cut yourself moving the cage?" He reaches for my hand, which is absolutely covered in blood, and I feel sparks again.

For a moment, I don't actually know. *Did* I cut myself?

But then I remember Doris—*Maggie*—bit me at the waterfall. The water seemed to staunch the blood at the time, but the wound must have opened up again.

"Self-inflicted friendly fire. By which I mean a parrot mistake. You know how they say a falling knife has no handle? A scared bird has no friends. It's not a big deal. Happens all the time."

We both look down at the excessive blood dripping to the ground.

"Please tell me this doesn't actually happen all the time. . . ." He trails off, worried. "Or at least that you're on good terms with the Red Cross."

"You're right," I say. "It doesn't happen much. She hasn't nipped me like that since our first week together. She was just startled, and I forgot about it."

Hunter turns on the faucet, and I'm grateful to see that it works. "Run your hand under the water, and I'll look around for a first-aid kit."

"There's not one," Maggie says in my head. "Unlike some people, I wasn't clumsy."

"You were pretty clumsy when you bit me," I mutter.

"What?" Hunter looks up from a junk drawer.

"I don't think you're going to find anything," I tell him, louder. "Maybe just hand me some paper towels? I'm sure it'll stop bleeding if I settle down." My heart has been doing jumping jacks since he got here, probably pumping out all sorts of extra blood, which I definitely do not mention.

There's half a roll of paper towels on the counter, and he brings over several and gently wraps them around my finger. "Compression will help," he says. "Trust me, I know. I work with a lot of power tools. I have a first-aid kit in the truck—"

"It's fine," I say.

He's still holding my hand, and I want him to stay there.

"I mean, it's not deep. I'll wash it with soap, make sure it's dry, keep an eye on it. I've had my tetanus shot." He still looks concerned, so I add, "Hopefully I won't get rabies. Or turn into a were-parrot. *Caw, caw,* I want to suck your blood."

He grins. "Wouldn't that be a vam-parrot?"

"Oh, please, no. The last thing we need is a parrot with fangs that will live forever instead of just a century."

He laughs, and it emboldens me.

"See, here I was just thanking you for helping with the cage, and now I owe you twice, this time for saving my life."

His answering smile makes my middle go all warm and swimmy. "Maybe you could buy me a drink sometime, if I'm not being too forward? Coffee or wine, as you like."

It's like a tiny orchestra begins to swell in my chest. I haven't felt this way since the first time Billy asked me out in eighth grade, as if the world is a new book just cracking open, full of delicious possibilities and adventure.

"Sure. Yes. Wine would be great." I'm smiling so wide my cheeks hurt. "And I won't be covered in blood and feathers. Promise."

"There's a nice vineyard, maybe three miles from downtown. The sunset view is beautiful."

"I love a good vineyard sunset," I say. "I mean, I've never seen one, but I can't imagine complaining about it."

He pulls out his phone. "Would you be okay with giving me your number? I would give you mine, but your hand looks like a mummy's."

He's right—I'd be pretty bad at texting right now. My phone is in my back pocket, though. Thank goodness they're waterproof these days. "Sure, I trust you. And my lawyer already knows your name, so I'm guessing you're probably not an axe murderer." I pause and look up, realizing how ridiculous this sounds. "Unless he knows your name *because* you're an axe murderer?"

He just grins in a very un-axe-murderer sort of way. "It's a small town. Everybody knows everybody. If somebody disappeared, believe me: They'd notice."

I spell out my name and rattle off my number. My phone immediately vibrates in my back pocket, and I jump, making him grin with dimples.

"My last name is Blakely, by the way. I guess I just assumed you already knew. Again—small town."

I did know. It was seared into my mind like the lines on a Burger King hamburger.

"Got it," I say, so he doesn't learn about the searing. "I'll put that in my phone once the mummification process is complete."

His phone pings—not me—and he looks down and frowns. "I'd love to stay and chat, but my grandmother is getting antsy. I was just here to toss some wood scraps in the dumpster, but now I'm fifteen minutes late and she's pretty sure I'm dead. Grandmas, right?"

"Grandmas," I agree with newfound vigor.

Hunter looks over to the bird backpack, where Maggie is watching us like a pink hawk. "And if you need a vet, you'll want Mountain Veterinary. The other vet in town, Wag and Purr, overcharges outsiders."

"I don't know if I'm an outsider, if my family's from here—"

"Are they?" He looks at me with curiosity.

I blush at my stupidity. "Maybe. I think so. A long time ago."

He chuckles. "Then you're not *from here* from here, but I'm glad you're here now."

With a little wave, he heads outside, shutting the door

softly behind him. I go to the yellowed blinds that Maggie recently mangled and secretly watch through one of the many cracks. Hunter gets in a black truck parked a few spaces away from my Explorer and drives off. A black Lab watches me from the open back window, ears flapping in the wind.

I suddenly realize I'm in a bedroom—Maggie's bedroom. It's odd, being in a stranger's personal space, especially when it's a grandmother you've never known and even more especially when she's currently a cockatoo.

The blinds are as messy as they looked from the alley, and I can see now that a cat was involved in this process. There are even little tooth marks.

"Is your cat still here?" I look around, suddenly worried for soft, feathery Doris, even if she's no longer exactly *my* Doris.

"Not anymore," Maggie says sadly from the other room. "I had two cats. My familiar, Artemis, and a young tortie named Moon. My trust left everything to my best friend, Diana McGowan, including the cats. And she was supposed to bring Moon to the waterfall, and then I'd be a cat and I'd be laughing about this with Diana right now. But I'm guessing that after I passed someone else took the kitties in."

That stops me. "Wait. Why'd you want to be a cat?"

"Well, I didn't want to die. No one does, I reckon. But I figured that your mama was using magic to hide from me and that when I died maybe Diana and I could find her—and any kids she might've had. Diana still had a decade in her at least, and we would've found a way to set up my trust—well, honestly, about like it is now. Keep the legacy in place. So it all worked out, in the end."

The bedroom is neat, with a very bohemian feel. More macramé, more flowers, more crystals. The walls are painted a soft rose, and the furniture is old-fashioned: a dresser, a blanket chest, and a vanity with a glass tray covered in perfume bottles. A big rag rug in shades of purple is placed right where bare feet would hit the wood floor every morning. Flowy velvet robes with fringe drip from hangers on the back of a closet door. Everything smells of incense and the uniquely crispy, herbal scent of dried greenery.

This room—I would've loved it as a child. It would've felt so magical, so mysteriously feminine, like Stevie Nicks's dressing room.

"So you were all in on the witchy-woman thing, huh?" I ask, getting used to the situation.

Because I'm starting to realize that if I can just accept that my grandmother's spirit has been transferred into the body of my pet cockatoo, I suddenly have a lot more answers to all of my many questions.

"I *was* a witch," she says, proud and sniffy, if cockatoos can sniff. "Obviously. You think I just randomly ended up inhabiting this bird? You think it's easy to refuse to die? Oh no, honey. Your mama might've tried to outrun it, and she might've gone to great trouble to hide you from me, but we come from a long line of witches. And you're a witch, too."

This is the craziest thing she's said yet. I stand in front of the vanity mirror, which is bedecked with crystal mala beads and skinny scarves glittering with metallic thread. I have never felt so alien and out of place.

"Me? I'm not a witch. I'm the most normal person in the world." I cock my head. I look horrible. I do not belong in this room, with its prism rainbows and rose petals. "Right?"

There's a pause. "Come get me out of this goddamn box, and let's talk."

I head back into the kitchen and unzip the backpack. Doris—*Maggie*—jumps out and struts into the bedroom as if she knows I was just in front of the mirror. She stands there, turning from side to side, raising her crest, her eyes dilating wildly as she regards herself.

"At least I'm not a chicken," she mutters. "The pink is nice." She looks up at me. "What the heck am I? The corgi version of a flamingo?"

"You're a galah, or rose-breasted cockatoo," I tell her. "The only member of the genus *Eolophus*, originally from Australia. You're eleven years old, with a possible lifespan of seventy-two. You were purchased from a breeder in Tennessee by an eccentric woman named Hilda, and after she died, you were inherited by her son, my old boss. And you hate him and were constantly trying to peck his eyes out, so I became responsible for you, and now I'm basically your owner, according to a hastily signed piece of notebook paper."

Her red eye pins me. "You don't own me."

"Fine. I'm your babysitter."

"I don't need a babysitter!"

"You have no hands, no money, no common sense, no ability to fly more than ten feet, and hundreds of natural predators. Also, you can't open doors. So unless you want to go peck for scraps at Lindy's and die early of fatty liver disease, you might as well get back to telling me about the witch thing."

She blinks at me and shakes her head. "Yeah, you're definitely a Kirkwood."

"I'm a Wolfe."

"Half of you, the important half, is still a Kirkwood." She bobs her head. "The witchy half."

I look around the room. "So this isn't all just wishful thinking? This is real witch shit?"

She sighs tiredly in my head, then launches herself at me. I have to either catch her or deal with her scrabbling against my chest. I naturally tuck her up in the crook of my arm, and she nestles down like this is perfectly normal.

"This is real witch shit," she says. "Which is how we're having this conversation."

"Just one problem, GamGam," I say. "I'm not a witch. There is literally nothing magical about me. I can barely keep my own life going, much less anyone else's. People with magic in their blood don't have leaky roofs."

I walk over to a front window and peek out through a crack in the blinds, watching the flow of life around the square. It's somewhere between sleepy and busy, aged and idyllic. The dinner crowd is trundling around, families and couples stopping to look at menus taped in windows as children turn cartwheels on the grass. It's nice to think I could be something more here, but my talking cockatoo is clucking nonsense.

"Didn't you feel it?" she says, fidgeting against me.

"Feel what?"

She breaks free of my grasp and flutters to the ground, where she paces back and forth. "The magic! The moment the water of the falls hit you. I still remember when it happened to me. It was like a big ol' party cracker full of golden glitter breaking over my heart. You're a Kirkwood, Rhea. I know you felt it, too."

And I had.

Even flailing in the ashy water, half drowned, coughing, sputtering, *I felt it*.

Like everything changed and good things were coming, like a swoop in my belly.

"I did," I say grudgingly.

"The falls—they're a catalyst."

"That's an awfully big word for a cockatoo," I say, because everything else is so ludicrous that I'm grasping at straws.

"Just because I'm from the mountains doesn't mean I'm an uneducated fool," she says coldly.

"But just because I fell in some water and started hallucinating doesn't mean I'm a witch. It just means my hair's frizzy and I'm covered in cremains—your cremains! It's crazy. Doesn't that seem weird to you?"

She flaps her wings and laughs. "They're all over me, too, but you don't hear me complaining. Look, honey, I can tell you're not particularly comfortable right now. The bathroom's right there, if you want to shower. I always bought the nice shampoo."

I follow her to the bathroom, with its old-fashioned seafoam-green tile. Her tiny talons *click-click-click*, and she fluffs herself like she's back on familiar ground. I'm enraptured by the clawfoot tub and glad to see the tiny separate shower stall. I note the folded lavender towels, the bottles of salon shampoo and conditioner. I can imagine how good it would feel, to be completely squeaky clean and putting on dry clothes, but something is still bothering me.

"If I'm a witch, what can I do?" I ask. "Are there magic words? Do I need a wand?"

"Wands are just silly claptrap," she declares. "But crystals give you a little boost. Hence"—she flaps her wings—"everything around here, pretty much."

The crystals and polished rocks and candles lined up on every windowsill begin to make sense, but it's still a lot to take in.

"I don't know why it's easier to believe my grandmother was reincarnated into a cockatoo than to accept that I could do magic," I admit.

"Then let's try something, because I can tell you're not a believer. I was, because I started early and grew up with it. I helped my mother and grandmother in the kitchen, and saw firsthand what they could do. But then your mama . . ."

My jaw drops. "Hold up. My mom was a witch, too?"

She flaps her wings in annoyance. "Doesn't matter. Focus on you." She jumps up onto the carpeted toilet seat. "Now, look, magic requires four things: ingredients, water from your source, a spell"—she bobs her head—"and blood."

8

I stare at her. "Blood? Gross."

"Not a lot of blood," she allows. "Just a few drops for most spells. We're not talking gallons. A drop of blood, a little water, some ingredients, and the right incantation, and you can do all sorts of things." Her crest raises. "Wanna see?"

"Now? You want me to do magic now?" I hold out my arms to show the absolute wreck that is my current situation. I am totally unprepared to do magic; I don't even have a pointy hat. It almost feels like one of those dreams where you realize you're back in school and have to take a test you haven't studied for, except I'm fully clothed and talking to a parrot.

"It's not hard. You already did half a spell today."

At first, I'm puzzled, but then I think about what happened at the waterfall. She—Doris—bit me, I bled in the water, and then it was like I was upside down on a roller coaster for a moment and suddenly my grandmother was talking in my head. "My blood, the waterfall . . ."

She bobs her head excitedly. "Plus the spell I'd already done, just waiting to happen. It was supposed to be Diana and Moon, but—" She must see my face harden. "Okay, okay, I've got to stop putting it like that. I wasn't expecting . . . you. I didn't know you existed. I didn't even know your name until I heard you give it to the Blakely boy. Your mother must've used the last of her magic to shield you from me. Rhea, honey, I know we got off on the wrong foot, but I've always wanted a granddaughter."

"You have two more."

I hear the gasp in my head as the cockatoo flaps her wings and raises her crest in excitement. "Three! Three granddaughters! Well, how do you like that? I swear, your mama—"

"Do not say one bad word about her or I'll feed you worms for dinner."

"Honestly, I don't think I'd mind. I guess I'm getting used to this body. Anyway, I want you to look under the sink. There's a milk jug full of water. But don't you spill a drop. That's not *normal* water."

It looks normal, and it's definitely not 1% milk, as the sticker suggests, which is good, because it would be totally curdled.

"See the little seashell dish by the sink? Pour out maybe a teaspoon of water into that dish."

I do. It's honestly pretty difficult, because the jug is very, very full, and there's a frantic cockatoo dancing on the toilet, urging me to be careful.

"Now, there are two ways to do this spell. You can use an eyelash or a marigold petal."

"I vote marigold," I say, not wanting to pluck myself bare.

"Tough. Today it's eyelash. Just run your finger over your eye and half the time, one will fall out. I'd give you one of mine since I'm too old to be that vain, but it appears I don't have them anymore."

I lean close to the sink and am fortunate to find an eyelash already on my cheek. I hold it out on my finger to show her. This all feels very silly, but literally everything today has felt silly, starting with the water tower labeled CUMMING, which, I mean—*what's in there?*

"Now just drop the eyelash in the water, add a drop of blood, and say—"

The word she says sounds like a drunk person saying, "Bear slick."

"Slow down, GamGam. I don't currently have an open wound."

"Yes you do, and I'll give you another one if you call me GamGam again. Just pinch your bit finger, for Pete's sake."

I unwrap the paper towel, and, yeah, it's not hard to get a drop of blood. It plunks into the tiny puddle and disperses as the single dark eyelash floats on top, coated in waterproof mascara.

"Bear slick?" I ask.

She repeats the word in my head, and I do my best to mimic it. In answer, the dish of water catches on fire.

I immediately shriek and swat it into the sink, breaking the dish. Maggie squawks and flaps into the bathtub, screeching in parrot. I turn on the sink faucet, but the fire is already out.

"What are you doing, you goose?" she asks in my head, still clattering around in the bathtub. "It wasn't real fire!"

I stare down at her. "How would I know? You didn't tell me what it was! I was not expecting literal flames!"

She flaps up and struggles to sit on the edge of the tub. "I thought you'd be smart enough to know!"

"My intelligence is not the issue here!"

There's an annoyed pause in which, in perfect time, we both mutter, "Lordy!"

And then, against my will, I laugh along with her.

"Got that from your mama, didn't you?" she asks softly.

I nod.

"And she got it from me, and I got it from my mama. It's as close as she would come to cussing. Nice to know it's still in the family. Same auburn hair, too." A sigh. "Lordy, I missed out on so much. Look at you! You're fully grown already. We never even got to make cookies."

I smile and help her out of the bathtub. "But we can apparently make magic, and that's even better. What else can I do? What are the rules? Is there a book? Do I get sorted into a house? Where do I buy my pointy hat?"

Maggie settles on my arm. "No hats. No schools. Let's say it's like cooking. There are all sorts of recipe books but no Bible, you know?"

"There's *Joy of Cooking*," I start.

"And how many editions does that thing have? Lordy, you'd argue with a post." She clucks. "There is no formal study. Everything is inherited. The rest of the world has no idea."

"So I don't get to go to witch college?"

"This isn't some ridiculous story, Rhea."

It's weird, hearing such an annoyed, human tone coming from the comical pink parrot who usually just sings show tunes.

"It's real, but magic . . . well, it's imperfect. It keeps itself a secret. You'll see."

"But you're telling me there are witches all over the place?"

Maggie flutter-jumps up onto the windowsill, nearly falling over before finding her feet. This window has no ivory blinds; it looks out on the alley, showing only a wall of kudzu peppered with tiny purple flowers.

"Witches cluster together along magical bodies of water. You can't cast a spell at all without the right water. And if you get too far from the wellspring of your magic, it fades. Our wellspring is the falls."

I consider the dish in the sink. "So that's one spell. What else can we do?"

She sighs, and even in my head, her voice sounds very old. "I can't teach you much. Not without my grimoire."

At that word, I perk up. "A grimoire? Like a magic diary? You have my full attention. Where is it?"

"Lost." She fidgets on the windowsill, weaving her head. "Like so many other things. I remember a few everyday spells, but without a grimoire, you might as well have infinite monkeys trying to write Shakespeare. And if they write it incorrectly, things get . . . explosive."

I can't believe I'm disappointed about magic, but here we are. "So I can do magic, but you can't teach me much. There is no cool book of spells. I don't get to live the witchy life and make potions and, I don't know, dance around under a full moon and curse people?"

Maggie flutters to the ground and walks past me into the hall. "I'm afraid not. Magic isn't what it once was. Most of the young folks moved away, after it began to dry up. You might have a knack—just something you can naturally do—but you won't know until it decides to reveal itself."

"You mean like levitating?"

She sneezes like this is ridiculous. "No. Nobody levitates. What's the point? Ladders exist. More like being able to figure out what's wrong with a car or having horses love you or never getting lost."

"Those sound kind of boring, honestly. I was hoping we could fly. Or make money."

Maggie hunches over and raises her tail in annoyance.

"Oh, well, I'm so sorry the magic doesn't impress you! Your generation, I swear."

If I had a tail, I'd raise it, too; I'm just as annoyed as she is. "I don't understand. If the magic is mostly gone, why'd you show me a spell at all? You could've just convinced me I was hallucinating. Or just stayed quiet. You don't have to constantly talk in my head. We could go back to communicating by singing duets." It feels like she showed me something wonderful, shining on the horizon, and then let the curtain fall, shutting off my beautiful view, and I begin to see why perhaps my mama didn't like her so much.

Maggie stops pacing and stares in at me, her beady red eyes as sharp as lasers. "I guess I shouldn't have shown you anything. Maybe I just wanted to see if you could do it. Maybe I was hoping you would stop questioning everything. But what's done is done. None of this is going the way it was supposed to. I guess it's not going how you expected, either. We'll just have to find a way to live with each other."

She sounds exhausted, deflated. And I'm feeling a little bit emotional myself. It has been one hell of a day, and I'm at the end of my rope.

"Maybe you're right," I say. "But if I don't shower soon, we're going to have a bigger problem, and the problem is me sitting on the floor and screaming."

"That's totally fair, honey, but I've got needs, too. First of all, food. Birds are built to eat all day, you know?"

I'm about to cry from the stress of it all—I don't like conflict—but it's so absurd that, as always, I go for bad puns. "So you're feeling *peckish*, huh?"

She shakes her feathery crest. "Just throw some crackers at me and get in the shower or I'll start screaming, too."

"Absolutely not. Crackers are junk food. But I'll get you some nice pellets."

I head out to the car to fetch the feeder and waterer that once belonged to a cockatoo named Doris. It feels strange, watching Maggie consider the little pellets with a critical eye, like I'm trying to poison her, and then figure out how to eat with a beak. I miss the old Doris, the brainless one that I snuggled like a football while reading books in my dad's old recliner. Still, I get to have a relationship with the grandmother I've never met, even if she's annoying, and . . .

"Why did my mama hate you so much?" I ask.

She looks up from her bowl. "That's a very long story, and you're a mess, and I'm starving, so maybe it can wait?"

I point at her. "Okay, but you have to tell me. I deserve to know. I promised her I would never come back here, and you made me break that promise."

"Your mom broke promises, too," she grumbles between bites. "And I didn't make you come here. Like I said, I didn't even know you existed before today. But yes, fine, I'll tell you. Later."

"I'll be in the shower. Don't die."

She looks up, pellet chunks clinging to her beak. "Once is enough, sugar."

I grab a pair of comfy pajamas and fuzzy socks from my overnight bag and head into the bathroom. The water takes a while to get hot, and the pipes sing and thump, but soon my hair is full of Maggie's expensive shampoo and I no longer smell like pond scum. It's been possibly the longest and strangest day of my life, and I can't wait to tell my sisters all about it.

Once I'm dressed with my hair twisted up in a towel, I find my grandmother in the main room, chasing a ladybug up the window glass.

"You ever been compelled by something you don't really care to do?" she asks, beak scraping the glass in vain.

"Yeah, that's pretty much the story of my life."

She gives me a sharp look and goes back to the ladybug without comment. I pick out the comfiest-looking place in the room, the squishy couch, and sink down into the cushions with my book and my phone. I tell myself that after this call, I'm going to find the greasiest takeout food in this town and stuff myself, because half a grilled cheese is not enough to keep me going.

"Do we have Wi-Fi here?" I ask.

"What's that?" is all the answer I need.

My phone has signal, at least, so I FaceTime my sisters, hoping they'll both be available.

"Where have you been?" Jemma all but screams, right as Cait shouts, "You haven't answered a single text since you sent the Cumming picture!"

Jemma gasps. "Uh, phrasing?"

"Things got away from me," I say weakly.

Which is very, very true.

"So what is Arcadia Falls like?" Cait asks.

"And what did we inherit?" Jemma chimes in, which is really what Cait means, because they are both in dire financial straits.

"Arcadia Falls is nice. It feels like home in a weird way." It's the farthest I've ever been from Cumberville, Alabama, and I'm actually pretty surprised by how much I like it, but I'm not sure how to tell my sisters that.

"How was the lawyer?" Jemma asks.

Maggie flutters up onto the couch, hops on the arm, and then lands on my shoulder, staring at the phone as she cocks her head back and forth, just like Doris used to. "So these are my other granddaughters," she says. "Pretty as a picture. Which one is which?"

I touch Jemma's face, and her name appears at the top of the screen.

"Ooh, that's clever. I'm glad I can still read."

"Well?" Cait presses.

"The lawyer is a character, and he was very helpful. Even bought me lunch. He has an eye patch. You'd want to put him in your pocket."

"Love an eye patch!" Jemma giggles. "I'd also love to hear that we've inherited a mansion with a pool."

"So the will was pretty strange," I admit. "I had to deposit Maggie's—our grandmother's—ashes in a very specific way, and once that was done, I signed some paperwork, and now I—*we* are the owners of four pieces of property on the downtown square."

"Ooh, like Monopoly?" Jemma asks, cheeks pink with excitement.

"If Monopoly was a broken-down video store that also sells boiled peanuts, an ancient movie theater, a hardware store, and the most haunted parts of an antiques market. With apartments on the second story. Right?"

Both of my sisters look at me quizzically. I've momentarily forgotten that I'm speaking to, well, a ghost they can't hear.

"Right, but the other apartments aren't as nice as this one. They're not livable as is. No one's set foot inside 'em in a couple of years. Things got away from me," Maggie says.

"Right," I answer myself for the sake of my sisters. "The apartments are probably going to need a ton of work, but the buildings are supposedly pretty solid."

"How much can we sell them for?" Jemma asks.

I grimace, and her face falls.

"C'mon, Rhea. We can't sell them? How does that even work?"

"It's a legal thing. We own them, and we can rent them out, but we can't sell them. Sorry." It's annoying that I feel guilty for something Maggie put in her trust, but I can see how upset my sisters are. They thought this was our big windfall, but . . . well, it's more complicated than that, isn't it?

God, there's so much I haven't had time to figure out.

I may be here to finally explore my own options, but my sisters are still depending on me.

How am I going to get a job in a tiny mountain town that probably has no jobs? If there's no actual money, what can I do to get by? I barely have any savings at all. I've been living paycheck to paycheck my whole life. The five hundred dollars from the lottery ticket isn't going to go far. And if Maggie's right, it's not like magic is going to be any help.

"Rental property is cool," Jemma says, trying to be cheerful. "Passive income."

"Well," Cait says, "but then Rhea has to get them cleaned up and ready to rent, turn on utilities, find renters, call the lawyer with the eye patch. . . ."

She trails off, and I'm annoyingly aware that she didn't say *we*. She said *Rhea*.

"I haven't even been here a full day, you guys," I remind them. "Don't put all your eggs in this basket."

"Um."

I know that *Um*. We all do.

It's the one where Jemma is in trouble.

"What's wrong, Jem?" I ask softly.

"I may have kind of rage quit my job today?"

I clench my teeth so hard I wonder if there are any good dentists in the area.

"A piece of work, this one," Maggie mutters.

"Jemma . . ." I start.

"It's just, you said there was an inheritance, and I pretty much hated it there, and my boss was so mean. I figured at least there would be some money, and you could float me until something better comes along."

The look I give her is the same one Mama used to give her—loving but beyond exasperated. "I can only use the money in the trust to improve the properties. Colonel—the lawyer—said there might be something additional in the bank, but who knows? I'll go tomorrow and see." And then I remember who's currently sitting on my shoulder. "Sure would be helpful to know if there's anything in that bank account," I add.

"Nothing," Maggie says quickly. "No need to go to the bank."

Which, as far as I'm concerned, is Cagey Grandma Speak for "Definitely go to the bank, because I am hiding something else."

"You got any savings?" I ask Jemma.

She turns even redder. "Maybe four hundred? If I only pay the minimum on my credit card. I'm sorry, Rhea. I should be more responsible, I know."

"Kids these days, I swear," Maggie grumbles.

"You're only twenty-one," I say to Jemma and for Maggie's benefit. "And you have a good degree. I'm sure you'll have a new job in a week or two. I can send you a little to get you by, but this inheritance isn't going to be a lottery ticket. You're going to have to keep working."

Jemma raises her chin. "Of course! I'm a good employee, it's just . . . the market is really hard right now. I'll double down on my influencing."

"We might need somebody in the front office," Cait says. "I can ask, if you like."

Jemma squeals and shakes her raised hands. "Would you? God, Cait, you're the best. I wish you were both here so I could hug you!"

I think about how much I already miss them, and my heart twists like a wet rag. If I were back home, I'd be in my car on my way to Jemma's apartment, stopping off for ice cream on the way. We'd watch nineties teen movies and eat sundaes, and I'd tell her everything is going to be all right. Halfway through, Cait would show up late with store-bought cupcakes, and we'd get Jemma laughing and everything would be okay again.

But I'm four hours away. A familiar guilt engulfs me. I'm supposed to be there for my sisters. I'm supposed to take care of them. With our parents gone, this is my responsibility.

But I left my sisters, and I don't even have the decency to throw gobs of cash at them.

We all say our usual goodbyes, and Jemma pops off the screen, but Cait stays.

"So . . . ," she starts.

"How much do you need?"

Her head hangs. She tries, but her mind vibrates on a different level, and she's known for accidentally overdrawing her account. "It's not my fault! I have a root canal next week. I ground my teeth so hard in a meeting that I cracked an old filling."

It's taking everything I have to resist opening my banking app and checking to make sure it hasn't sprung a leak.

Not that it matters—I know exactly what's in there, and it's not enough to fix everything that's wrong. I'm in a new town, I have no job, both of my sisters are in debt, and the inheritance isn't an immediate infusion of much-needed cash.

Maybe I should've just stayed home.

9

I turn my head to address Maggie. "Can—"

I want to ask her if magic can help with any of this crap, but the words won't come out. My throat is constricted, like right before you're about to cry.

But I'm not about to cry.

If anything, now I'm more mad than sad.

"Guck," is all I can say.

"Oh, and the magic will not be spoken," Maggie mutters. "In front of outsiders, I mean. Might as well stop trying."

I clear my throat and manage to swallow. "This is a lot for me to take in," I tell Cait. "I'll call you tomorrow. Love you a bushel and a peck."

"More like half a tablespoon right now, I'm guessing," she says dryly. "But I love you a bushel and a peck, too."

The call ends, and I fall back into the cushions, disrupting the cockatoo on my shoulder, who squawks and flaps to the sofa, sending feathers into the air.

"Those girls are completely irresponsible," Maggie says.

"Jemma is young and Cait tries hard," I shoot back.

Maggie blinks at me.

"And they're both used to me solving their problems," I admit.

"Beautiful girls, though. Wish I could've seen you-all when you were little. Always wanted grandbabies, and now you're taller than I am. Was. Definitely bigger than me now."

Which is nice and all, but I have questions. "So there's no mortgage to pay?" I ask.

Maggie struts. "Own everything outright."

"No internet or cable?"

"Don't need any of that junk. When there's a movie store downstairs, you just pop something in the VCR and settle in."

"What are the bills like?"

Maggie flutters up to the table. "Just got here and you're already in money mode?"

"I quit my job and rented out my folks' old house to move up here. I need to know where I stand. This is . . ." I look around the kitchen/living room, notice how the afternoon sun slants prettily through the broken blinds. "This is my life now, apparently."

For a moment, Maggie just stares at me, head bobbing. "You make bad decisions, too, huh? Miranda really did a number on you girls."

I snatch her off the table and hold her up to my face. "Don't you say one word against my mama! She put herself through college, married a good man, was a good mother, and taught us to be responsible members of society."

"Then why'd you quit your job and move up here on a whim?"

"Your lawyer said it was a significant inheritance!" I

have to look away. "And it just so happened that my boss fired me so he could hire his niece, and my ex and his cop brother were making my life hell. Truth is, I felt trapped. I needed a do-over. And if you hadn't made your will so bizarre, we would all be fine. Why'd you do that anyway? We're your next of kin; you were dead. Why can't we just sell and move on?"

Her wings flap like crazy, but I hold her in place.

"Because this is my legacy—"

"I'm your legacy! Those two irresponsible ninnies are your legacy. Why can't you trust us?"

"I didn't even know you! Your damn mama—"

I squeeze her a little too hard, and she pecks me, so I almost drop her.

"My damn mama loved me, and she told me I had to take care of my sisters when she was gone. I have had a job since the day I turned twelve," I say with gritted teeth. "I drive an old car. I use coupons. I eat store-brand cereal. The only way I could live cheaper is by being an only child. I didn't ask for any of this."

"Then just run away from your responsibilities like your mother did!"

My jaw drops.

I can't believe—

I place my grandmother—the cockatoo—on the kitchen table. "I can't listen to this anymore. I need some space to think. You've got food and water, and if you can't control your own cloaca, that's your problem. I'm going to go check into my B&B and come to grips with"—I gesture madly around me—"all this. You."

"None of this is my fault," she snaps. "All I did was die!"

"Die and leave me buildings I can't sell in a town where there are clearly no jobs that young people can live on?"

I stomp into the next room and change into a new pair of jeans and a T-shirt as I continue to shout at her. "Die and take over the body of a bird that was honestly my best friend, and now she's just—just banished to the ether so my uppity grandmother can insult my entire family? And I can't even tell you to drop dead, because you already did."

Maggie runs into the room and flaps into my face. I bat her away carefully, but she doesn't stop hollering in my head. "You should be grateful! You have a free home and a thriving business, with an extra bonus grandmother! And again, everything would be a hell of a lot easier if you had the good sense to have a cat instead of a stupid pink bird!"

"I didn't know I was going to become a witch today, so thanks for making me dump your ashes in the stupid magical waterfall. Really enjoyed having human remains in my hair. I guess now I know why Mama hated you. You're an asshole!" I shove my pajamas in my bag, zip it closed, and slide on my boots before stomping over to the door. "I'll see you tomorrow once I've cooled off a little. Then you're going to tell me how to rent out all this shitty property so I can move back home with my sisters. I'll drop you off with your real owner, and you can screech at him all you want, because he actually deserves it."

The door slams behind me, and I'm barreling down the stairs and out into the alley. The nerve of that woman! I had always pictured my missing grandmother as sweet and kind with curly white hair and an oven filled with cookies and cornbread. Fluffy pink sweaters and house slippers and rosy cheeks. Never once did I imagine she might be an infuriating, self-righteous cockatoo.

I feel guilty for just a moment—I have essentially locked a conscious adult in a room with no way to escape—but she'll be fine. There's enough food and water to last a week, now that she's a bird, and she's in her own apartment, and whatever she does next is her own business.

After I get my car unwedged from its spot in the alley, I head for the nearest drive-thru, get some food, and come back into town. The Magnolia Inn is just around the other side of the square, so it feels a little ridiculous parking close enough that I can see the video store from there, but I didn't really want to be seen dragging a suitcase around the sidewalk and crying. It is a small town, after all. As I stuff fries and chicken nuggets in my mouth in the inn's passive-aggressively marked parking lot, I wonder if I should go close up the video store, but what's the point? Honestly, if somebody broke in and stole all the movies and both slow cookers, I don't think I would mind. It was a terrible business idea even ten years ago, and there's no chance it could support me into retirement. Thriving business, my ass.

The faster I rent it all out, the better.

I'm so desperate to escape this whole situation that I call Colonel. His voicemail warmly informs me that the law office closes promptly at five. Damn it.

Once I've eaten an adequate amount of my feelings, I grab my chocolate milkshake and drag my suitcase toward the front door. This place seemed pretty expensive to me, but I felt like it was okay to splurge a little, considering the situation. I've only stayed in three hotels in my entire life, and I wanted to try one without a number in the name. Now I'm mad at myself for not sticking with the Motel 6 just outside of town, which would've cost half as much and not required me to stare across the square into the dingy windows of the last video store in the world.

When I walk in, there's no one at the front desk, and I let out an explosive sigh because honestly, it would be nice if one single thing was easy today.

"Rough travels?" someone asks, and it's then that I notice the figure sitting in a wingback chair by the fireplace, reading a book. He's a blue-eyed, prematurely gray silver fox, probably mid-thirties, but definitely not outside the realm of possibility. There's a bookshelf beside him filled with a wide range of titles, not just the usual 1980s used books people buy to take up aesthetic space, and I grudgingly tell myself I picked the right place. A dog sleeps peacefully on the rug, stretched out as if warming itself by a fire that doesn't exist. It doesn't so much as blink an eye at me, but I suppose a B&B dog would get used to constant customers.

"The travels were fine, but the destination is proving to be a challenge," I tell him, wishing my eyes weren't so wet and runny.

He stands and walks behind the counter. "Rhea Wolfe?"

"That's me."

His smile is sympathetic as he checks me in. When he takes my ID, I notice the wedding ring, and I'm honestly kind of disappointed. It would've been nice to know there were two hot, available men in town, especially considering the first one is apparently related to my grandmother's sworn enemy, not that she'll give me details on anything pertinent to that fact.

"So I'm Nick, one of the owners, and you can let me know if you need anything. My husband, Nathan, will have the included breakfast on the table from eight to ten. Do you have any dietary restrictions?"

"Nope. Give me all the bread and nuts. And there will be coffee?"

He puts a hand to his chest and closes his eyes. "If not, what's the point? We bring in beans from Atlanta, and we got a really nice espresso maker for our last anniversary."

"Sounds like I have no choice but to wake up, then."

"Please do. We supposedly have enough ghosts as it is." Nick hands me an old-fashioned key on a metal ring. "Not in your room, though. You have the Dogwood Room, on the second floor. Hope you don't hate pink."

"How much pink are we talking?"

"A . . . tasteful amount."

I have to laugh. "I'm sure it will be fine. It'll be dark soon." I glance back at the bookshelf, and he waits for me with professional patience. "So this place. Is it . . ." I trail off, unsure how to continue.

"We have excellent reviews and no bedbugs," he hurriedly assures me. "I wash the sheets myself, and I'm very fussy. Almost annoyingly so."

"No. It's not that." I glance at a black-and-white photo on the wall behind him of the inn in a different time, with a horse tied to the fence out front. "My family is from this town, and my mom left and made me promise I would never visit, and then my grandmother died, and now I just got here to take care of her will and everything is going wrong. So I guess I'm asking if it's as terrible as I think it is. Small-minded and boring and utterly lacking in Wi-Fi."

He purses his lips. "It's a little small-minded, but folks will generally accept you once you don't feel like a stranger. I'm from here, and people were leery of Nathan at first, but once everyone tried his biscuits, they were all in. The Wi-Fi actually isn't that bad—the code is posted in your room. It's getting more cultured all the time, with live music and the farmers' market. I left for college, but I missed it. These days, we're very happy here. Does that help at all?"

I smile with a little sniffle. "Good news about the Wi-Fi."

"And we have a system for dealing with the turkeys."

That's got my attention. "The turkeys?"

He grimaces. "Oh yes. There's a whole flock—more like

a gang, honestly—and when they come through downtown, we all take cover."

"I thought I'd have to worry about bears."

"Bears?" He waves a hand. "They're lovable little scamps by comparison. It's the turkeys you will learn to fear. Seriously, though, any questions, just let me know. We have lists of restaurants, maps, all that sort of thing. Are you thinking about staying a little longer?"

"Oh, I won't be staying," I say. "Saw the lawyer, signed the papers, tossed my grandmother's ashes. Tomorrow I talk to the bank, and then I think I'm out of here."

Another grimace, which does not bode well. "Then you must be Maggie's granddaughter. It's a small town, and her death surprised us all—hers and Diana's. Maggie always seemed so much younger than she was, you know? A real free spirit. I'm sorry for your loss."

I feel the tiniest stab of jealousy that all these strangers knew my grandmother when she was still around. I never got that chance. Maybe she was nicer before she was a small, angry bird. Colonel had said that she wasn't necessarily well-liked, but that doesn't seem to be the case for Nick.

"I never knew her," I tell him. "Were y'all friends?"

"She was on the Chamber of Commerce. Fiercely loved Arcadia Falls. And she took good care of poor ol' Abraham. He never got married, never had kids, outlived his whole family, but she made sure he had what he needed. Maggie was a bit much for some people, but she was always nice to Nathan and me."

I refuse to feel guilty for locking my grandmother in her own apartment. I'm sure Nick has fond feelings for Maggie, but he doesn't know the whole story. People often put on a mask in public that they quickly drop around family. My mom had good reason to hate my grandmother, and I should've given that more thought before I dumped my entire life and came here.

I can't move back home, not without breaking the Billingses' lease and crushing their dreams. Maybe I can move to a beach bungalow for a year or rent a little trailer and visit all the national parks.

Except—I'd have to bring a judgmental, know-it-all parrot with me, wouldn't I?

I'm now morally obligated to drag my grandmother with me wherever I go until she's lived a full life as a rose-breasted cockatoo, which could be . . .

Sigh.

Sixty more years.

Nick is smiling the benign and practiced smile of a service worker who has other things to do, so I thank him and wish him a good night before heading up to my room.

The amount of pink in the Dogwood Room is not what I would call tasteful, but at least it's more blushing rose than Pepto-Bismol or electric flamingo. Maggie could actually use this room as camouflage, but I'm glad for a little quiet.

I wolf down the rest of my fast food hunched over the elegant desk while watching a competitive cooking show on my laptop, glad that the Wi-Fi, at least, is indeed functional. Then I draw a bath in the big tub, grab my book, and sink into the rose-perfumed water, courtesy of a sachet of Epsom salts left thoughtfully for my use.

The tub in my house back home is one of those small 1970s things, and I can't squeeze in there without at least half my body outside of the water. This tub—like the one in Maggie's apartment—is deep and perfectly curved for lying back while reading, and I sigh as I settle into the heat and try to disappear into someone else's story. Usually, I use books as an escape because my life is so boring, so lacking in any kind of excitement or passion. Now I need something to take my mind off all the ways today has gone wrong and all the annoying work I'll have to do to make my life boring again.

All I inherited was a big ol' pain in the ass.

Tomorrow, I'm getting the hell out of Arcadia Falls.

10

I'll say this for Nick and Nathan—they sure know how to run a B&B. The bed is like a cloud, the linens are somehow crisp and soft at the same time, and the pillow is like the world's biggest marshmallow. I would say I sleep like the dead, but the only person I know who's currently dead is in the body of a cockatoo, so she's probably sleeping upright on one foot.

When I go down to breakfast at eight, I find a muscular Black man with immaculate facial hair placing a basket of biscuits on the sideboard.

"You must be Rhea," he says, looking up with a smile.

"And you must be my new favorite person, because this smells amazing. Nathan, right?"

He inclines his head. "The one and only. Now, what can I get you from the coffee bar?"

"Anything with caffeine is fine."

"Don't do that to me. Please. Demand something complicated and frothy."

"He needs a challenge," Nick says as he exits the kitchen holding an insulated tumbler.

"I hate to be a bother...."

They both groan in unison.

"Be a bother? He lives for this." Nick kisses Nathan on the cheek and heads back toward the lobby.

"Surprise me, then," I say. "I like sugar."

"Then you're going to love my French toast bread pudding." Nathan points to a steaming casserole that smells like fall. "Back in two shakes. Help yourself."

I pick up a plate and work through the spread, amazed at how much food there is. I didn't hear or see a single other guest last night, but I suppose that doesn't mean I'm the only one here. I pour a glass of orange juice from the carafe and sit down at the long table with a full plate. I've barely had a mouthful when a couple who look like newlyweds appear, fill up two plates, and leave, never taking their eyes off each other. Next is a businessman who stuffs a biscuit with bacon and scrambled eggs before tucking it into a napkin and running off. I'm surprised that the dog I saw last night isn't running around and begging with all the good smells in the air, but maybe they put him away during busy times.

Nathan approaches with a handmade mug and presents it to me with an eager grin. There's a little swan drawn in the foam.

"It's too pretty to drink!"

"Hush your mouth and get sugared up. That's a caramel latte, by the way."

He goes to straighten the matching dishes on the sideboard, and I ask him, "So are we expecting a full table?"

Nick pokes his head in through the door. "There are two rooms that haven't shown up for breakfast yet. And then there are the regulars."

"Regulars?"

He and Nathan share a knowing grin.

"Not a lot of breakfast choices downtown. Marla's place always has a wait, so we have plenty of folks who sort of cruise through," Nick says.

As if on cue, Colonel Gooch flaps into the room in another three-piece plaid suit. "Miss Wolfe," he says, giving me a warm smile and a nod. He drops a five in a fishbowl I hadn't noticed and flutters his fingers over the biscuits before plucking one up and stuffing it with bacon and eggs. "Best biscuits in town, but don't tell Marla I said so or she'll cut me off."

"Oh, Colonel, I meant to ask you—" I start.

With an apologetic wave of buttery fingers, he's back out the door.

"Why's he in a hurry at eight in the morning?" I ask.

"If his wife catches him eating biscuits, he'll be in the doghouse." Nathan rearranges the breakfast dishes. "Can't imagine being married to someone who scares me to death. And believe me: Geraldine Gooch scares me to death. You got a special someone, Rhea?"

I think back to Billy's feet on my coffee table. "My high school sweetheart asked me to marry him recently, and I told him no. So no." My shoulders sink a little. "And he owns the only tow truck in my hometown and likes to throw nails in my driveway when his feelings are hurt. Oh, and his brother is a cop, and he recently gave me a hundred-and-ninety-dollar ticket for pulling over to help a turtle cross the road. Said I was impeding traffic flow."

"What kind of monster . . . ," Nathan begins, affronted.

Nick glowers. "You did the right thing. I bet you could contest that in court, though."

"Billy would show up in his only suit just to propose again

with a bigger audience." I don't really like the pity in their eyes, and I've already accepted the fact that if I go home, I'll never see Hunter Blakely's vineyard sunset, so I change the subject. "How'd y'all meet?"

This topic lights them both up like Christmas trees.

"Right in this very building," Nick says. "Back when I was a blond and this was the Harrison House."

"We refused to run an inn named after a Confederate general," Nathan snaps.

"So we changed the name, first thing." Nick reaches over to give Nathan's hand a squeeze. "I was in town to visit my dad, who loves to hike."

"And I was here for a bachelor party. Extremely hungover. But I dragged my sorry carcass down to breakfast—"

"It was barely a continental!" Nick wails. "Prepackaged Danishes and soggy fruit salad."

"It's true. And the sweet little old lady who ran the inn was getting forgetful with her sell-by dates. Anyway, we met over this breakfast table. Even half dead, I was enraptured."

Nathan bats his eyes at Nick, and Nick goes for a cheek kiss, and then I have to look away and focus on my bread pudding because it feels like a terribly intimate moment.

"And here we are," Nick says breathlessly. "Ten years later."

I make a point of looking around the room. "Well, I'm not hungover or ready for a hike, but if my dream man would like to walk in, I'm ready."

As if on cue, the front door opens, out in the lobby, and Nick and Nathan look at each other like Sleeping Beauty's fairy godmothers waiting for their spell to come true.

And then they promptly burst out laughing.

"Morning, Abraham," Nick says as the thousand-year-old man shuffles into the room in his house slippers.

"Mornin', boys." Abraham drops a crumpled dollar in the fishbowl and loads up an extra-large margarine tub with as much breakfast as it can hold. "Ma'am." He gives me a nod but doesn't appear to have any idea that I am currently his boss. Without another word, he shuffles right back out the door.

"So we need to work on your foreshadowing skills," Nick starts, and they both try not to laugh.

I drag my hands down my face; I cannot cry again. "I can't believe I have to pay that man actual money to run a video rental store. For the rest of his life. He's probably going to outlive me."

Nick and Nathan share another look.

"You know that store is a money pit, right?" Nathan asks, but gently.

I sigh and put down my fork. "I know. My plan is to close it down, rent out all the storefronts and apartments, and send Abraham a check from Alabama because it's honestly the least depressing of my options. Y'all know any good real estate agents?"

Nathan grimaces. "Oh, honey . . ."

"What he means to say is that"—Nick rubs his beard—"if those properties were rentable, they'd be rented. Maggie used to bitch about it all the time, said she was too old to do that much work and didn't have any young people she could bully into doing it. The theater has water damage, the hardware store is full of old hardware and not fit to be anything else, the antiques market has vermin. One of the apartments got trashed by an angry renter she kicked out, and the other one was owned by a hoarder. They would take a significant amount of work to get in shape to rent."

Shit.

Shit shit *shit*.

Colonel didn't tell me how bad it truly was before I signed those papers.

Maggie definitely lied about it.

And now I'm stuck with it.

"Your best bet is probably to just sell it all to Joyce Blakely and call it a day."

I slurp the last of my amazingly delicious latte, knowing I'm going to need every bit of caffeine within to keep from sliding onto the floor like a defeated slug. "I can't sell it. The trust says it all has to stay in the family. And my grandmother hated Joyce Blakely, so even if that was an option, I'm pretty sure that would be the last thing in the world she wanted."

At that, Nick and Nathan exchange a grimace.

"Yes, there were several feuds. Bad blood," Nick says.

"Little old people in little old towns, I swear," Nathan adds. "Like they just need something to fuss about. And I never could get the actual story out of anyone. But here's someone we can ask. . . ." He smiles like butter wouldn't melt in his mouth. The front door opens and closes, and there's Hunter Blakely.

11

The moment I see Hunter, I know it was a mistake to come down to breakfast in my polka-dot pajamas with my hair still in a ratty bun. He's wearing a plaid flannel over a white T-shirt with well-fitting jeans and work boots, his hair still a little wet from the shower, and he looks absolutely delicious; and that's from someone already stuffed to the gills with bread pudding.

"Rhea!" His face lights up, which just about makes me do one of those dances bees do when they find honey. "You here for biscuits?"

"I'm here for everything," I say. "How about you?"

"Biscuits and coffee. Best way to start the day. I was just about to text you—"

"Hunter, your grandma hated Maggie Kirkwood, right?" Nathan calls from the other room, where the hiss of the steamer suggests he's making something to sweeten Hunter right up.

Hunter seems surprised by the question. "Yeah, I guess so. Why?"

"Because Rhea said—"

I cut Nathan off. "I just keep hearing that folks didn't like her, is all."

Hunter gives me a very peculiar look that I can't quite decipher. "Wait. Aren't you renting her apartment? Why are you at the inn?"

Because I locked my grandmother in there to punish her for dragging me out to the boonies and dumping me with a shitty inheritance, I want to say but can't.

"I'm moving in there, but I'd already reserved a room here for the first night. The bathtub and breakfast were worth it." I give Nick and Nathan my most grateful smile, hoping a bit of praise will mean we can stop with the gossip and neither of them will bring up the fact that Maggie was my grandmother. If Hunter's grandmother hates my grandmother, we might be forced into a Hatfield-and-McCoy situation, and I still want to see that vineyard.

Nathan enters the room and hands Hunter a to-go cup. "We were just telling Rhea that—"

I cut Nathan off again. "They were telling me that most of Maggie's properties are a wreck. That she couldn't rent 'em out if she tried."

"She had Cisco run some quotes for her to get them in shape once." Hunter chuckles. "When she saw the estimate, she just about had a stroke."

"Yeah, I hear she didn't have much money, outside of the properties," I press.

"I wouldn't know. She certainly . . ." A thoughtful pause. His phone pings. He looks down, frowns. "Kept her secrets."

"Do you know why she and your grandmother hated each other?"

Hunter gives me a probing stare. "Something that happened a long time ago. Maggie—" He abruptly stops speaking and shakes his head. "I'll text you later, okay?" With a warm nod, he heads out.

Nathan snatches up my empty coffee mug and heads back to his magical machine, but Nick pulls out a chair and sits at the table beside me.

"Hunter's going to text you, hmm?" Nathan sings from the other room.

I focus on my biscuit and mumble, "Maybe."

Nick taps the table. "But he doesn't know Maggie was your grandmother? You didn't tell him."

My cheeks are hot, my mouth dry with biscuit crumbs that I have to choke down before I can speak. "Okay, Dr. Phil. I didn't tell him because I want him to text me, and he might not, if his grandmother thinks I'm a bad seed or something."

"Rhea, lies are not a great way to start a relationship." He says it gently but knowingly.

"Tell me about it."

It's too bad we can't discuss Maggie's current situation.

Or maybe we can.

"Do you guys know about— *Grrrk!*"

"You are not choking on my biscuit, because my biscuits are not dry." Nathan puts another drink down in front of me. "And if you are choking on something else, you'd best stop it right now."

I take a hasty sip of the latte. Maggie said the magic would not be spoken, but I didn't know it was going to be so literal. Apparently, Nick and Nathan do not, in fact, know about magic.

"Look, I just got here yesterday," I tell them. "I have to find someone with great credit who wants to pay me money to rent out an apartment that looks like Stevie Nicks's dressing room while they run a video store that is older than Stevie Nicks. And the only thing giving me any hope at all is the thought that for one beautiful night, I might get to sit outside and watch the sunset with that pretty man while I drink some nice Moscato before driving back to my boring old life in Alabama with my annoying pet cockatoo." I snort. "A video store. Why'd it have to be a video store?"

"But, Rhea," Nick says, excited. "It doesn't have to be a video store. You can turn it into whatever you want. There are all sorts of needs that aren't being met downtown."

"Oh my God!" Nathan calls from the kitchen. "Think of all the possibilities. We haven't had anything new in ages. All the shops are a million years old, and nothing ever comes up for sale or lease—nothing in good condition, at least. Most of the business owners are at least sixty. The Chamber mixers are so depressing."

Nick scoots his chair closer, and I can see now that he's one of those people who absolutely loves a good dream—or maybe a good story.

"I'm being very serious. You have a functional storefront in an up-and-coming tourist area. We don't need another general store or tchotchke shop, but I swear, this square has excellent foot traffic and a dedicated Chamber of Commerce that would love a new venture to support. So let's see." He leans back, grinning. "A bar would make the most money, hands down. We have MacGillicuddy's and the pizza place, but no actual, dedicated bar."

"Something classy," Nathan calls. "A speakeasy! Bespoke cocktails! Small bites! Charcuterie! We have family restaurants but no fine dining until you get to the vineyards outside town—"

"Oh, wait." Nick shakes his head. "Not a restaurant or

a bar—remember when that couple from Portland tried? It would take a ton of money to get that space up to code. And you don't have any of the equipment. Right?"

"Right," I echo.

Nathan joins us at the table with his own drink. "Okay, no bar or restaurant, to my sadness. But the tourists love culture. You could do a funky little art gallery. Or painting parties or Pilates—"

"Or literally anything but video rentals." Nick shoots Nathan a wink. "Aaaaand we know someone who's done a lot of work on downtown buildings—"

"He rebuilt this place gorgeously!" Nathan cries. "He can build whatever you want!"

"But I'm not . . . I mean, y'all are so kind, trying to help me, but honestly I think I just want to give up." I feel like such a mood killer, saying it out loud. "I came up here thinking there would be a real inheritance for me and my sisters, but it's just a lot of work. They need me back home."

"Are they young?" Nathan asks.

"Twenty-one and twenty-four. They're grown and functional." I sigh and take a long, fortifying sip of my latte. "But not fiscally responsible. I'm still taking care of them, pretty much. I thought this was our lottery ticket."

"Well, maybe it still can be," Nick says. "For real, Rhea. When we reopened the B&B, we didn't know if we'd be bankrupt in a year, but we're constantly booked. Business is booming. Every person on the Chamber is seeing the best crowds in years. You own prime real estate. There is literally no reason you couldn't start a business that took care of your family. We have savings now. Do you know anybody our age with savings?"

Nathan comes up behind me and puts big, warm hands on my shoulders. "Let yourself dream. Close your eyes.

Picture it. If you could open any business in the whole world, what would it be?"

The answer seems to float up from my heart and plop right out of my mouth. "A bookstore."

"Yes!" Nick nearly shouts. "Yes, please! The closest bookstore is forty-five minutes up the highway, and the library has been closed for years with no end in sight. And you've already got shelves."

"And let's not forget that you own what's left of the hardware store, so you wouldn't even have to pay that much for materials," Nathan adds. He gives my shoulders a friendly squeeze and steps back around the table to hip-bump his husband. "And like I said, we know an excellent builder."

Nick leans forward, his eyes aglow. "Please tell me you'll consider it, Rhea. That old building deserves to shine. Arcadia Falls needs new blood. And I personally need a bookstore like a flower needs the sun."

"He does," Nathan agrees. "The only thing he loves more than books is me. And this place. Which, might I mention, looked about as crappy as the video store when we bought it."

They put their arms around each other and gaze at the historic home around us, glowing with pride.

I think about what it would feel like, owning a successful business. Being the master of my dreams, my own boss. Actually having savings. God, it would be so nice to never have to work for a Mr. Buckley again. I can almost see it in my head, the stained ivory VHS boxes replaced with rows and rows of books. Book clubs with chairs arranged in a circle, little kids on the rug for story time, a gift-wrapping station during the holidays. Maybe I could invite local artists to showcase their works, sell their prints and stickers and jewelry. All the bookstores I've visited lately have a whole section for little gifts. And—

Wait.

No.

What am I doing?

Yesterday, I swore I would leave this place.

Then again, yesterday I thought I could just rent out all the buildings and run right back home.

But what is there to run back to?

The same small town, the same low-paying jobs, the same tow-truck driver with a box of nails and a brother on the force who'd love nothing more than a reason to put me in handcuffs. The same boring story told again and again. My entire life back in Alabama would feel like treading water. Like waiting for something real to happen. I would never make enough money to support my sisters and have a life of my own choosing.

But maybe . . . maybe if I stay here, I could.

Maybe if I stay here, I can be part of a new story.

I feel like I'm standing on the edge of a cliff.

"Where's the bank?" I ask.

12

I'll be able to make a better decision about my future once I see what's actually in Maggie's bank account—and learn whether or not I can access it. After showering Nathan with compliments for the best breakfast of my life, I head back upstairs to wash off the meat sweats and get dressed in my nicest jeans.

I check out with Nick, drive my Explorer back to the alley, and park in Maggie's spot again. From there, it's a quick walk to the bank, and as I step inside, I don't know what to expect. Nick and Nathan told me everyone in town uses this same branch, as its proximity makes deposits and change runs easy as pie, but I don't even know the right words to ask for what I need.

"Can I help you?" asks a familiar voice at the counter. "Oh! Miranda's daughter. Honey, I'm so glad to see you."

It's Tina McGowan, the woman I met at Lindy's yesterday.

My mom's old friend and Diana's daughter.

Tina leaves the counter to pull me into another soft, sugar-scented embrace. She pulls away and looks me up and down. "You're just the spittin' image of Maggie and Miranda, I swear. Ever since I saw you yesterday, I kept hoping you were gonna stick around. This town needs a Kirkwood."

"Officially speaking, I'm a Wolfe, but that's kind of why I'm here. Colonel Gooch said y'all handled my grandmother's accounts?"

"Come into the office, and I'll show you what we're looking at." She pats my hand, leads me into one of the open offices, and closes the door. We sit across from each other, and she focuses on the desktop computer, lifting her glasses onto the tip of her nose and determinedly typing with two fingers. "Maggie's account—it's not a fortune, I'm afraid, but it's not nothin'."

I struggle to keep my smile up. It sure feels like nothin'.

She leans in close and looks around like someone might be listening in. "You're not officially on the account since probate takes a while, but if you can find her debit card or checkbook, well, I reckon they belong to you. If you were to access her account, this number might be of interest to you." Using a pencil, she writes $13,612.46 on a Post-it, shows it to me, then rolls it up in a ball and tosses it under her desk. "Now, with that *not* being officially said because you certainly didn't hear it from me, would you like to see what's in her safe-deposit box?"

I perk up at that. "She didn't mention . . . I mean, Colonel didn't mention—"

"Yes, well, us ladies don't always tell the menfolk about our secrets, do we? Now, do you have her big ol' key ring? And your ID?"

She gives me an exaggerated wink and heads back out to the counter, returning with a key. I hand over my license and sort through Maggie's keys until I find its twin. I've never even seen a safe-deposit box outside of movies, and I feel like I'm in an Agatha Christie book as we enter a vault and Tina shows me how to find box 103.

We each put in our keys and turn them, and a little door opens. I'm not sure what to do, but Tina says, "Just reach in and pull it out by the handle."

The box is long and narrow, made of mint-green metal. I place it on the pedestal table in the center of the vault and fumble with the catches, heart racing against my will as I think of the endless possibilities within. There could be nothing, or there could be a thousand diamonds. There could be stacks of cash or a single moth.

But what's actually there is a gallon Ziploc bag full of . . . stuff.

Papers, photos, jewelry, a big wallet.

Tina points at it. "Oh, would you look at that? Maggie's wallet. With her checkbook and bank card."

I look up at her, confused. "Wait, why is her wallet in here if she died in an accident?"

"Oh, well now. You're quick like your mama, too." Tina grimaces. "Colonel and I, we wanted to keep things safe. It was returned to me with my mama's belongings, so I made sure it got put in here with Maggie's old family stuff. She's probably got her PIN somewhere in there, but if not, you can withdraw cash as needed here at the bank. Colonel controls the trust, but this is yours free and clear." I haven't made a move to open the bag yet, so she adds, "Go on, honey. I'll give you some privacy, but I'll be right outside if you need anything. Dig around and see what you find."

She gives me an encouraging thumbs-up, and then I'm

alone in an old-fashioned bank vault with whatever my not-so-dead grandmother left for me. Well, not for *me*, exactly. For her friend Diana.

I check her wallet, which feels extremely intrusive, and find an old-fashioned checkbook, one debit card, an ID, and a huge wad of coupons, plus a lucky clover flattened between tape. She's even, helpfully and foolishly, written her PIN on a Post-it stuck to the card, and I'm horrified to see that it's 1234. Next up is a packet of photos held together with a rubber band, and my eyes prick with tears as I realize that these are images of my mother. I've never seen photos of her as a child before, her hair in pigtails as she stands barefoot by a big white farmhouse. There's one of her bareback on a palomino pony with a rope halter, one of her holding a rabbit, and one of her standing defiantly in the rain, arms crossed and glaring at the camera.

Wait—

When we were growing up, the weather always seemed to mimic my mother's bad moods. Was she like that as a kid, too?

Was that her . . .

Her magic?

For a moment, I'm upset that I'll never know the truth until I remember that dearly departed Grandma Maggie is back in her old apartment, waiting for me to return. I can ask her whatever I want. Whether or not she'll answer honestly is another story.

The objects in the Ziploc bag are peculiar. There's a big ring with a stone that even I can tell is fake, a fancy gold lipstick, an old L-shaped nail, a fountain pen, a silver teaspoon, a dog whistle, a piece of fool's gold, a thimble, a chess piece, a pair of readers, a gold dollar, junk upon junk upon junk, just a bunch of old-person detritus that doesn't make a ton of sense to me, hundreds of little doodads. The only thing I find interesting is a tiny, ancient dictionary, titled *The Little Webster*. It's bound in leather and has a snap closure. I open it and flip through it lovingly, marveling at the eighteen thousand words contained in such a small package. I slide it into my pocket, where it nestles down like a field mouse softly going to sleep in a flower.

All the other doodads can stay in the bag. I put everything but the wallet back in the box and slide it into place, but I'm unsure how to proceed from here. When I stick my head out of the vault, Tina rushes over and tidies everything up for me.

"Did you find what you needed?"

I sigh. "I don't know what I need, if I'm real honest."

"None of us do, really. You think you'll suddenly understand everything when you're an adult, and then one day you have bunions and just as many questions. Look, I've got to get back to work, but can I give you my number? I'll do anything I can to help with your grandmother's affairs." She leans in close. "Or if you just want to know more about her. Or your poor mama. I've got so many stories."

I can't tell Tina that my grandmother is still around to personally get on my last nerve, so I just take the business card she gives me and thank her. She hugs me again, and I hug her back, because it occurs to me that this is as close as I'll get to hugging a matriarch who cares about me and actually has arms instead of wings. That's when I realize that we have something else in common.

"Tina, I'm so sorry about your mother," I say.

She just holds me closer. "And I'm sorry about yours. I'm here whenever you need a hug."

I don't dare tell her there's only a fifty-fifty chance she'll ever see me again. Thirteen thousand dollars could give my sisters and me the breathing room we need to get by, even if it won't solve all our problems forever.

It's a beautiful morning, so I figure I'll walk around town and see everything it has to offer. I'm sitting on this enormous decision, and I've really only seen a couple of places here. Giant elms or oaks—I don't know which, but they're really big—stretch over the streets and make the sidewalks buckle dangerously around their roots. I pass a toy store, a pizzeria, a bakery, a seafood place, a yoga studio and juice bar, a potter, a couple of clothing and jewelry boutiques, a soap and candle store, a crystal store where my grandmother must've been a platinum card holder, a store that looks like it's nothing but dog stuff, the Chamber of Commerce and Visitors' Center. There's MacGillicuddy's, a big, sprawling restaurant off the main square that kind of looks like a treehouse, and a brewery and meadery that still has horse ties out front. Again, I'm struck by how much foot traffic there is, and by how many cars are clearly cruising for a parking space along the packed main drag.

Just across the square are Maggie's properties—my properties, I guess—and I squint and stare at the video store, trying to imagine the possibilities. A coat of paint, a good cleaning, some flowers outside. Just getting rid of the movie cutouts and washing the windows would be transformative. I walk toward it, imagining what it would be like to see it as a destination, a haven, a home, instead of a rock tied around my neck while I'm stuck in the middle of a river.

What if this were my town?

What if I made a life here, a life that didn't involve constantly avoiding a persistent tow-truck driver and his angry cop brother, where I could become whoever I wanted to be? What if I closed the old book and started a new story?

On the other hand, what if it's an utter failure? Maybe

a car will drive into the plate-glass window, and a raccoon will scamper in through the hole, and then it'll bite me and I'll have to get those awful rabies shots in my stomach?

I can picture a thousand ways things could go wrong. I'm good at telling those stories.

The simplest is this: I put my heart and my soul into this place, and it fails, and my sisters and I lose everything.

I'm directly in front of the video store now. Inside, the boiled peanuts gently steam as Abraham sleeps in a lawn chair off to the side. An older couple inspects the movies, picking up boxes and reading the backs before putting them down again. The fishbowl is full of coins and crumpled bills. What is it with this town and fishbowls full of cash, anyway? If nothing else, that dusty glass bowl contains enough to pay Abraham each day, so I guess that's considered breaking even.

My hand slips into my pocket, and my fingers trace over the old leather dictionary I found in my grandmother's safe-deposit box.

Maybe it seems silly, but several times in my life, I've found my answer in books. Words are my Magic 8 Ball. I unsnap the leather case, close my eyes, and flip to a random page, putting my fingertip down on the thin, crispy paper.

When I pick it up, I learn that the word I've blindly landed on is *destiny*.

13

Or *destitute*, maybe, which is just under it.

Could be either one, and I don't trust one-offs.

I flip through the dictionary nine more times.

Nine.

Nine.

The words I land on: *stay, tome, inherit, absolute, stores, future, dream, succeed,* and, oddly, *squirrel*.

"One more time," I say firmly.

As if laughing in my face, the dictionary gives me one more word: *magic*.

"This shit is rigged," I mutter.

Fate seems determined to keep me here, but I am a very logical woman, so I need to do more research. I start by walking into the video store and standing at the counter. The two customers are still browsing. Abraham is snoring gently, so I call his name, but that doesn't help.

"Just drop a few dollars in the fishbowl when you find

what you want," the lady customer says. She and the man are in their seventies and at the point where they're starting to resemble each other, outside of his mustache and her perm. "He's hard to wake up during naptime."

"So how does the store keep track of the videos?" I ask, because these folks seem local and friendly.

"There's a clipboard on the counter. You just write down whatever you take."

The office manager in me is horrified as I look over the clipboard. It's a copy of a copy of a copy, a form with spaces for date, time, name, and movie. A stump of pencil is taped to a string attached to the clipboard, and many of the entries are borderline unreadable. There is no computer, no cash register. Just a fishbowl full of green and silver and the goodwill of the town.

"So they don't take cards?"

The man laughs. "No, but checks are okay, if they know you. Which it sounds like they don't. You new or visiting?"

"Just visiting for now. Y'all come in here a lot?"

He holds up a copy of *Batman Returns*. "I probably ought to buy this one I watch it so much, but this place is pretty convenient. VHS is getting hard to find."

"We're in here a couple of times a week," the woman says. "Sure do wish they had some new stock, but I'd hate to see one of those newfangled robot boxes show up. We like the homey touches."

"Can't get boiled peanuts like that from a robot box!" the man agrees, going to grab a Styrofoam cup.

I don't have the heart to tell them that the robot box company went bankrupt.

As an unknown quantity, I don't really feel comfortable snooping around, even if this place legally belongs to me lock, stock, and barrel of peanuts. Luckily, I have an easy

BOOKS AND BEWITCHMENT

source of information locked in my apartment.

And that's another positive if I stay in Arcadia Falls: a comfortable, safe home that's paid for outright and doesn't seem to have any major problems. I don't even know what it's like to live in a place where you don't have to put down pots and bowls every time it rains. I can use the rent from the Billingses to pay the mortgage on my folks' place in Cumberville, which means my living expenses here would be almost nothing. Something in my shoulders relaxes when I think about that—not owing anybody anything.

I wave to the customers getting their peanuts and head out the door and around back to the alley, where I stomp upstairs loud enough that Maggie will know I'm coming. Even though she has everything a cockatoo could conceivably need, including food, water, and the enrichment of playing parkour on her own furniture, I still feel guilty for locking her up, but I am not the only one at fault here.

I take a deep breath and unlock the door. Something flies at my face, and I instinctively bat it away with my hands.

"You nasty little so-and-so!" Maggie screeches, landing on the floor and immediately launching herself at me again. "Locking me up! In my own home! When I've done nothing but help you!"

I gently push her away as she telepathically chews me a new one as only a little old Southern lady can. At least she seems to have forgotten that she has a very sharp beak, because if she wanted to, she could definitely draw blood. Again.

"Rude! I would tan your hide—"

"Nobody spanks their kids anymore, Grandma Cockatoo," I say, guiding her away. "Now, did you get it all out of your system?"

"The disrespect!" she screeches. "You're worse than your mama!"

That gets my attention. I set her down on the ground and prepare myself for another winged onslaught, but she just bustles back and forth angrily, her feathers ruffled.

"What did she do that made you so mad?" I ask. "And why'd she hate you so much?"

She stops and blinks at me. "Oh, so we're doing this now?"

"I need to know. I have some decisions to make."

I get a Diet Coke out of the fridge—it's the only thing in the fridge, which means the family Diet Coke addiction runs deep—and sit down on the couch. Maggie flutters up beside me. I can see now that she apparently took out a lot of her anger on one of the uglier throw pillows. I am very familiar with the decorating sense of a furious—or even bored—cockatoo.

"Oh, sure, just help yourself to my Diet Coke. Didn't even ask!" she grumbles.

"May I please have one of your Diet Cokes, seeing as how you can't drink them anymore and you can't actually stop me?"

She chirps irritably. "Fine. Help yourself. When I planned this spell, I didn't really think about what it would be like, being trapped in such a powerless body. It should've been Moon. A nice little cat, tidy and cozy. This is so . . . undignified."

She watches me as I sip my refreshing Diet Coke. I'm ready to give her the silent treatment. After all, I can walk right back out that door and leave her alone in here, and she knows it.

"Your mother was a hellcat," she finally says. "From the day she was born. High energy, rebellious, adventurous. Falling out of a tree or into a creek every day. Broke a bone every year. ADHD is what they call it now, but back then we just said, 'She's a mess.' And she'd argue with a stump."

"Well, none of that changed." I smile. "My sister Cait takes after her."

"Still can't believe there's two more granddaughters." Maggie fluffs her feathers and settles down, all tucked up. "When Miranda was born, I almost died. I couldn't have any more children. And I never married, so it was just me and her. I could tell she had the Kirkwood way about her early, so I tried to raise her the way my mama raised me—to be responsible and respect her legacy. I taught her the little spells to help the bread rise or keep the mice out, but she just saw it as work. She was like a horse that wouldn't take to the saddle. I'd ask her to do something—hell, I'd command her to do something—and she'd just run off."

"Sounds like a typical teenager."

"Teenager? I'm talking about when she was seven!" Maggie flaps her wings. "Headstrong from the start. She wanted to go far away for college, but I needed her back home to help with the store, and there's a perfectly good college nearby. She had a knack for weather, and even if Miranda and I were the only ones who ever knew the truth of it, her magic meant the world to the farmers in these parts. The vineyards, the greenhouses, the little old man with the tomato stand on the side of the road. Everywhere else in Georgia was in a drought, so dry the trees were bribing the dogs, and she could give us rain. And if a tornado came from somewhere else, she could make it veer off."

"I thought you said knacks were little things."

She clicks her beak in annoyance at that. "Some people are born with a little basic power, and some people are born with gifts, and some people are gosh darn Mozart. Your mama was that last type, and lordy, she hated it. She called me a nag, but this wasn't like asking a normal kid to do the dishes—one spell from her was the difference between a farming family having enough money for Christmas and going bankrupt."

But what she's saying does not describe the mama I knew.

"My mom was all about responsibility," I say sharply. "She was dedicated to her daughters. Never late on a payment for anything. Worked hard, and always took good care of us."

Maggie hops up onto the back of the couch. I guess even when they're run by people brains, parrot bodies can't sit still. "Well, people change sometimes. See, your mama and I had a big argument. We needed rain, and the moon was right for big magic, but she refused to do the spell. It was homecoming and she didn't want to lose blood or have a Band-Aid in her pictures or rain for her date. I remember her standing on the front porch with her hands in fists, shouting, 'I never promised to hurt myself for you, not for anybody. It's my life.' Like it was ever for *me*. Ha!"

She's quiet for a minute, and even though cockatoos don't have expressive faces, I can tell that this wound runs deep.

"And I'll admit—I was angry, too. I'd sacrificed things in my life to keep food on the table and be at every school play, and I always did my bit to help the community, even though I'd never had powers like hers. So I brought the basin full of water and ingredients and told her . . ." A cockatoo sneeze. "Lord, I'm ashamed of this, but I was mad, and she was seventeen. I told her she had a responsibility to the community that was more important than one selfish night of dry-humping a boy on the dance floor in a glittery dress."

I grimace. Arguing with Mama never went well for anyone at our house. I can't imagine having the gall to call her selfish—or the thunderstorm that would follow.

"She was madder than I'd ever seen her, and the sky went black as she pulled out her pocketknife and slit her wrist, and screamed, 'If you won't be happy till I'm bled dry, maybe this'll do it!' And then she did her spell to bring the rain, but . . . her anger plus all that blood pouring out meant the storm she summoned was stronger than anything she'd brought before, stronger than anything the region had ever seen. We had floods. Chunks of roads washed away. Hundred-year-old trees fell. Houses were blown to kindling. Whole herds of cows swept away by swollen rivers. The weatherman didn't know what to say. A freak summer tornado, he called it. Around here, it was catastrophic. Leveled my family's old farmhouse. We lost everything we had, except the properties downtown."

"And what did Mama do then?" I ask in a tiny voice.

"Well, first, she fainted from the blood loss. Scared the bejesus out of me. Thank heavens she missed all the big veins. I carried her to the neighbor's farm and patched her up, had to give her stitches myself because the road to the hospital was blocked. As soon as she was better and the roads were clear, she ran away, and I never saw her again. She never called, never sent a letter, nothing." I can hear strain in her voice. If she were human still, she'd be crying.

"And you didn't go looking for her?"

Maggie runs her beak over a few long wing feathers. "She always kept a little bottle of falls water in her purse, and I reckon she did a spell to hide from me, probably the last magic she ever did. She kept up with Tina McGowan for a while —they were best friends when they were young—and Tina has never been good with a secret, so she told her mother, Diana, and Diana told me. Your mama didn't even invite me to her wedding. Your daddy—was he a good man?"

"He was. His name was Ed. They were in love until the end—until his heart attack. And he was good to her. No worries on that part."

Maggie deflates a little in relief. "Thank goodness.

The local boys she dated were not up to snuff. It's a relief, honestly, to know that she had a good life. We needed her here, but I always assumed she was too ashamed to come back after that flood, and it was easier to blame it on me. Better to hate me than hate herself, I reckon. I loved that girl with all my heart, and I'm so sorry we never made up before she passed. If only I'd known. When did it happen?"

"Two years ago. It was so sudden. We'd barely found out before she was gone." Which brings up a new question about magic. "Do you have a gift? Could you have changed things? Is there magic that can cure diseases?"

A raspy chirp. "No, honey. Nobody can stop cancer. I have—I had—more influence than average. I could make folks do what I wanted. Except your mama, I guess. She was immune. You are, too, it seems." She flaps her wings. "Or maybe parrots just ain't magical."

I tuck my arm around my grandmother and give her a gentle squeeze. "I can't imagine anything more magical than a parrot who talks in complete sentences and always poops in her cage. It's just . . ."

When I woke up today, I did not expect to be running therapy for my grandma, a pink-feathered witch from an entirely different era.

"You and Mama were both stubborn, and you butted heads," I start. "I'm just as stubborn as y'all, but my generation does things differently. I'm angry at the situation, I guess. When you set up your trust, you had plans that didn't involve me and my sisters. It's not your fault you didn't know about us. I'm sure you would've done things differently if you had. Right?"

An annoyingly long pause. "The thing I need you to understand is that this building is part of our legacy. I had to protect it. These are not just empty stores. We've owned this land for generations, and I've lived in this apartment ever since that storm. I couldn't allow some horrible developer to sweep in and turn this place into—I don't know—Apple stores and cheap condos."

"It takes money to make a business profitable," I remind her. "And thirteen thousand dollars is not enough to do that and pay taxes and everything. Is there any way to change the trust? Maybe just sell one storefront so we can use that money to fix everything else? I could make a life here, but . . . the video store is dying. Even you have to see it."

"Nothing gets sold!" she barks. "You have a responsibility—"

"Woman, how well did that argument work with my mother? Do not push me."

She quiets.

"Thank you," I say. "Now, I am currently debating whether to go back to Alabama and drag you there with me or try to patch together a life here, and it's about fifty-fifty. So what can you tell me—without using words like *legacy* or *responsibility*—that might induce me to stay?"

Maggie flutters down to the floor. "Just so undignified," she mutters. "Trying to be serious in this body. But I think I'm getting the hang of it. Let's see." She looks up, mischief sparking in her shiny red eyes. "What did you choose from the Ziploc bag?"

14

"What Ziploc bag?" I ask.

"You know there's thirteen thousand dollars in my checking account, which means you went to the bank, which means Talky Tina probably gave you access to my entire life and you opened the safe-deposit box and poked through that bag full of goodies. So what called to you?"

My hand goes to the tiny leather dictionary in my pocket, and I pull it out and show it to her. "I wouldn't say it called to me, but I love words. And books."

"What do you think *called to* means, you ornery child?" Her eyes focus on the leather cover. "Lord, I want to bite that. This bird body is wired to destroy things." She ruffles her feathers and steps away. "Has anything interesting happened with that little book, since you stuck it in your pocket?"

I hate how knowing she sounds, and I hate that she's right. "I may have consulted it a few times when I was trying to make my decision."

She shakes herself excitedly. "Yes! Good. And how'd that go?"

I sigh. "The dictionary is biased. It probably accepts bribes."

"Ha!" she cackles. "Let me guess—every word you saw suggested you should stay here."

"You think you know everything," I grouse.

"Around here, maybe I do know everything. Ever think about that, smarty-pants?"

I hold up the dictionary and unsnap the cover. "Magic *Webster* in my palm, should I lock up Grammy and have some calm?"

I close my eyes, flip to a page, and put down my finger. And frown.

"What's the word?"

I don't want to say it.

"Well?"

"It says *listen*."

"I could've told you something like that was gonna happen," she gloats.

"So what does it mean—is this a magic book?"

"Only when *you* use it. Wouldn't do a thing for me." She struts around, full of energy now. "Okay, so I told you about knacks. Just like some normal folks are good at math and some are good with animals and some can sing like angels, most witches have a special skill. That's your knack. All the stuff in that bag—it was chosen for a reason. It can help identify your area of expertise. Been in the family pretty much forever."

I think back to how random it all was and begin to make connections. A dog whistle. A lipstick. A teaspoon. So someone who's good with animals, someone with charisma or acting ability or beauty skills, a baker or chef.

And I chose a book.

"So this dictionary is magic, or I have magic with all books?"

"Stop. Think back. Was there anything in your past life you couldn't explain?"

I roll my eyes. "Mawmaw, my life is not past. I'm still living it. I haven't decided if I'm going back or not."

"Your life in Alabama, before you knew about witchcraft. Was there anything that you were drawn to, something that just brought you comfort and joy?"

When it dawns on me, it feels annoyingly obvious.

"Yes, yes, I've always loved books. But that's not rare—"

"But when things were hard or you needed answers, you were drawn to books, right? And sometimes you found the answers you needed?"

I stand and stomp over to the nearest window, thinking about the five-hundred-dollar Georgia lottery scratcher in my library book. "You don't have to be smug just because you know more than I do." I pull on the cord to raise the blinds, but they don't budge, so I yank hard until they rip free and fall to the ground like a dying accordion. "I'm sick of everything here being pee-pee yellow."

"Does that mean you're staying? You can decorate however you like."

"I know I can do whatever I like, because a parrot can't stop me. And that doesn't mean I'm staying; it just means I'm tearing out all these ugly-ass blinds. Now, what makes you think my relationship with books is any different than your average bibliophile?"

I focus on the blinds, but I can hear her tiny little claws pattering around the room with the nervous energy expected of any excited bird.

"Because you don't just love books—it's like they love you," she says. "They want to help you. And when you're in Arcadia Falls, that feeling will be magnified. When you're far away, it grows weak. Without water from the falls, you can't do much. But there's a sort of . . . longing. A connection. It may fade, but it's always there. Pulling at you. Like being homesick."

"There's a word for that." I look out into the alley, down at my car's box-stuffed interior. "*Hiraeth*. It's Welsh. Means 'a longing for a place or time that's lost or inaccessible.' I used to feel it all the time, and I didn't know why. Books came closest to scratching that itch."

"And does it itch less, now that you're here?"

I give her another sour glance; she sure is annoyingly pleased with herself when she's right. "Well, it was pretty itchy when I got duped into bathing in a waterfall and ended up wearing your remains as setting powder." I yank down the next set of blinds, and sunlight pours into the room. It's satisfying as hell.

"After that, though. Since you activated the magic and found the book."

I stare at her, hands on my hips, as motes of dust dance in the light of the tall windows. The place already looks a thousand times better, just by letting in a little light that isn't the color of old piano keys.

"I guess so. Are you saying being here is like calamine lotion for an itchy soul?"

She flutters up to the window and looks out. "Some people go their whole lives never knowing their calling. They never develop a passion or find something they're really great at. They don't have a purpose. But for me—for most of the witches I've known—magic gives us that feeling. That satisfaction, bone deep. Especially using our knack. The magic wants to be used. It's been waiting for you. And it sounds like maybe you were waiting for it."

I yank down the third and last set of yellow blinds in the room and can finally appreciate what a nice apartment it really is. Twelve-foot ceilings with pressed tin, tall windows in front that look out on the idyllic square, wide wood floors the color of clover honey. Compared to the house I grew up in—with its fake wood paneling, ragged shag carpet, and wet spots on the popcorn ceiling—this place feels like a dream, like I'm the main character in a romance book where a beautiful girl moves to Manhattan and lucks into a rent-controlled apartment overlooking Central Park.

"So here's the real question," Maggie continues, cocking her head at me. "Why would you turn all that down? You got fate telling you that you're supposed to stay here. You got a dictionary giving you ten synonyms that all mean 'stick around.' You got me telling you, over and over. What else is it going to take? How many times does destiny have to knock before you answer the damn door?"

I stand in the middle of the room, trying to imagine a life here. I would move the furniture around for sure, get some new throw pillows and blankets, add some plants. I need less Stevie Nicks and more Dixie Chicks. And some candles to clear out all the incense. What exactly is holding me back?

My sisters, for one. I've never been this far away from them. They need me.

And I need a job, some way to bring in money. Maybe this place is almost free, but there would still be taxes to pay, utilities, food, upkeep on my car, tons of Epsom salts for all the bookish baths I'll need to take.

And . . .

Well, those are the main things. On the other hand, I don't have a job back home, either. Or a home, considering the lease I signed way too quickly. And I'm fairly certain Officer Jimmy Wayne wouldn't stop tailgating me until he found a reason to arrest me for breaking his brother's heart. I don't even want to think about all the nails Billy would toss in my carport.

"Well?" Maggie demands.

I still need confirmation.

I hold up a finger to shush her and pick up my phone. Mr. Buckley's office number is in my contacts because that man had a terrible habit of calling me every time I wasn't within shouting distance. It only rings once before someone picks up and a bright, bubbly voice says, "Buckley Insurance, this is Sylvie, can I help you?"

"Hi, Sylvie," I say, realizing I didn't think this through, either. "This is Rhea Wolfe. I used to work for Mr. Buckley."

"Oh, Rhea, hi!" She sounds like talking to me is the best thing that's ever happened to her. "You did such a nice job getting everything ready for me, I swear I haven't had to think a bit. Your filing system is just beautiful."

"Thanks?"

"Did you want to talk to Uncle Horace?"

I'm not sure how to answer that. I definitely don't, but it seems rude to say so. "Um—"

"Because he's in a meeting right now, but I can have him call you back. Is there a problem with Doris? You're not giving her back, are you?"

I splutter a little. Yes, there is definitely a problem with Doris, and no, I am not giving her back.

"Nope, she's doing great. Um, Sylvie, quick question. How are things going around there? You plan to stay awhile?"

"Definitely. I just graduated from Jefferson, and my folks live down the street and are letting me live in the suite over the garage, so this is perfect for me. I'm not going anywhere. My only worry about taking this job was dealing with Doris, and you took care of that. You took care of everything!"

She sounds so sincere and happy to be there that I can't really question her. Plus, I've heard Horace talk about his favorite niece before, and I know that short of her dying in a freak accident, there's no way I could get my job back while she's settled into that chair. I thank her again, and hang up.

"You convinced yet?" Maggie says, sounding pleased.

Instead of answering, I call Leah Billings at my folks' old place.

"What's wrong?" Leah asks right away.

"Nothing, just calling to see how y'all are doing."

She exhales. "Oh, thank God. I was afraid there was a problem." I can hear the sporadic buzz of a saw in the background. "I'm on bed rest now, so us renting your place was the best thing that could've ever happened. Can you imagine me stuck in bed in Tommy's mom's house? Lord, she'd be hollering at me day and night to stop being lazy and get up and dust her fans. This is like a vacation, Rhea. And Tommy loves working on things. He's happy as a pig. Got the roof patched up, and now he's fixing the soft spots in the ceilings. Did you know you can scrape the popcorn off? This place is a dream come true for us!"

Hearing that, I instantly know I can't ask Leah and Tommy to move out so I can go home. Tommy's mom is the devil, which I've known since she was my third-grade teacher and plucked *James and the Giant Peach* out of my hands to keep me from becoming a communist. I honestly don't think she knows what a communist is, but let's just say that I was careful to read my Marxist literature in private after that. Leah and I were in school together all twelve years, and she always gave me discounts at the grocery store, and I know how big and tired she is right now. The house I grew up in, my parents' house, my house—it has a new life, and that life does not involve me any further than a monthly rent check.

"I'm glad it's going so well," I tell her, meaning every word. "It's nice to know y'all are looking after things."

"Did you need something, Rhea? Did you forget something?"

The saw buzzes behind her, and I can imagine her in my big queen bed, cozied up in a nest of pillows while Tommy waits on her hand and foot and she doesn't have to dread every waking moment.

"Nope. Just wanted to check in."

"Well, the house is in great hands, and you're an angel for letting us have it for the year. If things keep going like this, maybe we can stay here even longer? It's a great place to raise a family, as I reckon you know."

I all but fall onto the couch, feeling defeated by reality itself.

"Of course. Take care of yourself and that baby, Leah. I'm so happy for you guys."

"You take care, too, Rhea. Hope you're as happy where you are!"

We hang up, and Maggie does a triumphant little cockatoo jig.

"See? The world is conspiring to keep you here. This is exactly where you're supposed to be, and as long as you're here, things are gonna go real well for you, I promise."

"What aren't you telling me—"

I'm startled by a loud knock.

"Someone's at the door," Maggie observes.

"Is that normal?"

I can't forget the weird warnings about folks with a grudge against my grandmother, and as far as I'm aware, only five people in town even know I'm here. Most of the buildings around me are empty, and I doubt Abraham down in the video store would hear me screaming bloody murder if I was bisected with a chainsaw right over his head.

I am not sure I want to answer the door.

Maggie shakes herself and stands. "It was normal when Diana was alive. Now? I don't know what's been going on, or even how long I've been dead. I almost felt like I was drifting around up here, all restless, but I reckon that's a problem for another day. Just answer the door."

I offer my wrist to Maggie, and she steps up and settles down. I almost ask her where she kept the knives as I approach the kitchen door, but honestly, a scared parrot is probably just as lethal. I don't even know what I'm worried about.

"Let me see out," she says.

"Manners," I whisper.

With a small snort, she mutters, "Please."

I hold her up to the peephole, and she angles her head to get her bright little eye right up against the glass.

"Well, that is unexpected."

15

I suddenly wish I'd brought my pepper spray along—the pink can Billy Wayne bought for my birthday after I was surprised by a skunk in my garage one night and just about had a panic attack.

"Unexpected good or unexpected bad?" I ask.

Maggie chuckles in amusement. "Unexpected good. It's just Shelby McGowan. Tina's daughter, Diana's granddaughter. Sweet girl, but she's never been here before, so that's the unexpected part. Come on in, Shelby."

"Yeah, she can't hear you because you're a cockatoo," I whisper before putting on my "totally normal girl who doesn't converse with cockatoos" smile and opening the door.

The woman standing there is about my age and looks just like her mom, short and curvy with wavy blond hair. She's wearing black leggings, brown UGG booties, and an oversized pink sweatshirt with a couple of chocolate stains.

"Hi! You must be Rhea. I'm Shelby. Our grandmas were

best friends. And our mamas, too. I hope this isn't weird. Is it weird? I'm so sorry."

The words tumble out of Shelby like a leaking pipe, and I smile and say, "It's not weird at all. It's real nice of you to stop by. Do you want to come in?"

"Yes, please! I always wanted to see inside this place, but your grandmother—God rest her soul, I am so sorry—kept it locked up tighter than a chicken's butt. Or a parrot's butt? I don't know what kind of bird you've got, but she's real cute. She'd match my bathroom perfectly. It's all flamingos."

I realize she's never going to stop talking, so I open the door wide for her, glad that things are pretty tidy, thanks to Maggie's ability to control her cloaca, unlike Doris, who when free to roam seemed to have a bull's-eye for family heirlooms and cute shoes. Shelby steps inside and sets a white bakery box down on the counter, looking around with wide eyes.

"Dang, girl. It's pretty in here! Get some new plants in those hangers, maybe a gold-framed mirror over there, some furry pillows, and it'll be a glow-up. You're so lucky! The apartment over my shop is so cramped. I'm a baker, by the way. Not sure what you like, so I brought a little bit of everything. Mom said you'd been to the bank, so I figured it would be safe to stop by. We never get new folks in town—well, except retirees, which is great for business, but not much fun, you know? Oh, and Nick said you were super sweet, and he's such a good judge of character."

"Does everyone in this town know each other?" I ask.

She nods solemnly. "Lord, yes. Everyone on the square, especially. All the businesses. Because so many of us live on the second floor over our shops, we're all neighbors."

"Did I mention she's a flibbertigibbet?" Maggie says.

I wish the telepathy worked both ways so I could let her know that it's actually comforting to have someone talk my ear off without a single word of admonishment. Honestly, Shelby reminds me of Cait and Jemma—as in, she talks as much as both of them combined. I hover over the white box. "Okay if I open it? I never could resist goodies."

She dimples and nods. "Please! The best part of baking is watching people eat. Not in a weird way. It's just satisfying."

"I always thought the best part of baking was eating what you'd baked while it was still hot enough to burn your fingers." I untie the light blue ribbon and open the box, and let me just say I'm very grateful our families are friends. There's an éclair, a donut, a vanilla cupcake, a plain croissant, a chocolate croissant, a bear claw, and one of those giant monster cookies that could feed a family for a week, studded with chocolate chips and M&M's. I select the bear claw and bite it, eyes rolling back in my head. The closest thing we had to this sort of glutenous goodness in Cumberville was the bakery at the Piggly Wiggly. "I think you're my new favorite person," I mumble through the crumbs.

"Aw! You're so sweet. I knew you'd be sweet. You know, our families have been besties for, like, centuries. I mean, our grandmas died together, like Thelma and Louise! Except on accident. Gawd, that sounded better in my head. I'm real sorry about Maggie."

I almost say, *Don't be,* until I remember that, for everyone else, Maggie is dead and gone and not just an annoying sidekick with a taste for mealworms. "I'm sorry about your grandmother, too. Your mom was really kind to me. I hope everyone's holding up okay."

Shelby waves a hand at me; her eyes are wet and pink now. "Nope. Not a chance. My granny was real young at heart and busy as a bee, and I keep thinking I hear her right behind me when I'm alone in the bakery, but then I remember, and . . ." She waves a hand as if dispelling an annoying cloud of smoke and sits on one of the kitchen stools and puts her elbows on the counter. "Well, dust to dust, right? I'm not gonna cry about it today. Again. What's done is done. She lived a good life, but we're here now. So you've got to tell me everything and take my mind off it. Where's your mama been all these years? What's your life like? And what's your knack?"

I just met her, and she's asking for not just a story but a whole book. Except—

"Did you just ask about my . . . ?" I trail off. I don't want to choke on this bear claw.

She gestures to the baked goods. "Your knack. Mine's baking. Obviously. My grandma had endless energy, and mom's real good with paperwork. And I'm assuming you have the magic, or we wouldn't be talking about it. I'd be all—" She grabs her throat and makes frantic choking noises.

"So melodramatic," my grandmother adds in my head. "Now how about some of that bear claw?"

I toss down one teeny-tiny crumb to shut her up and look to Shelby. "But you and I are allowed to talk about this stuff? I only found out about it yesterday, so I don't know all the rules yet."

"We both have magic, so it's physically possible. Talking about it is considered tacky among the old folks, but I've never understood why. 'Magic stays in the family' is how my granny put it." She rolls her eyes. "But I'm an only child and I don't know any other witches my age, and our families might as well be family, so as long as you're not offended, neither am I."

"I tried asking Nick and Nathan, and I totally choked."

"As talented as Nathan is in the kitchen, they are both sadly lacking magic. Anyway," Shelby goes on, "what can you do? Or do you know yet?" She leans forward, blue eyes alight, and I am overcome with the strangest mixture of shyness and pride.

"I'm just figuring it out," I admit. "But I think it's . . . books?"

Shelby cocks her head. "Your magic is books? Like, writing them? Or making them appear? That would be real helpful with the library closed."

I feel ridiculous talking about it. "So I have this little dictionary, and if I ask it a question, it kinda tells me the answer." I glance at Maggie, hoping she'll interrupt and give me a better way to explain it, because as it is, this does not sound properly magical.

"Is she your familiar?" Shelby asks, focusing on the cockatoo, who's too busy pecking around for more pastry that will not magically appear because bird obesity is actually very dangerous.

"Just say yes," Maggie breaks in, sounding cagey.

"Yep. My old boss back in Alabama inherited her when his mom died, but she hates him, so now she's mine."

Shelby reaches a hand toward the bird. "May I?"

I nod, biting back a grin, and Shelby scoops up my grandmother like she's a chicken. Maggie squawks and flaps a bit before Shelby firmly snuggles her under her arm. This is not a way I would ever deal with a parrot, but Maggie seems too stunned to fight it.

"She's a little sweetie, isn't she?" Shelby pets the soft gray feathers of Maggie's back. "What's she saying?"

Which tells me that regular familiars can talk, a fact that my grandmother neglected to pass along. I could've had Doris —my Doris!—but talking? And instead, I'm stuck with—

"You can't just go picking people up and swinging them around, even if they are birds!" Maggie splutters. "Shelby McGowan, you put me right back down!"

"She says that's nice and cozy," I say.

Shelby looks down, smiling. "Wow, sounds like she's a talker! My cat, Peekaboo, is pretty grouchy. I can barely get three words out of her, and most of them are *no*. But, you know"—she shrugs—"cats."

I am now entirely full of questions about familiars, and also full of bear claw, but I don't want to seem horribly ignorant, and I can just interrogate Maggie later anyway. When Shelby asks if I want to go to lunch, I agree, even though I'm nowhere near hungry. Honestly, it would just be nice to have a friend. My sisters and I were close, and when they moved out of my folks' house and into the city, I got lonely. It's hard to meet people when you're in your twenties if you don't go to church or work in an office with more than one person. Every time I took an art class hoping to meet quirky young women like me, I found mostly older ladies in established friend groups and couples trying to spice up their Thursday nights with glassblowing. And my one attempt at online dating resulted in a way-too-obvious catfishing attempt. Thus my best friend was pretty much Doris, and now even she is, to some degree, gone.

"Let's just get you in the cage," I say, reaching for Maggie, but she screeches and flaps out of Shelby's arms and away from me, landing on the floor and running behind the couch.

"No! Just take me with you. Put me in that ugly portable thing. I'll be quiet. But I just really, really don't want to be locked in and left alone. It's against the Geneva convention!"

I can understand that, I suppose—the part about being locked in, not the part about the Geneva convention, which I'm pretty sure doesn't apply to birds. "Oh, you want to come along? Let's just get you in the backpack." I put it on the floor with the door unzipped, and she eagerly runs over and jumps in, settling on the perch.

Shelby talks the whole time as we head down the stairs and out into the alley. "So we've got five choices for lunch down here—four if you don't like food poisoning. By which I mean you never want to go with the raw oyster bar. So that leaves us with Lindy's for sandwiches, Marla's for Southern food, or MacGillicuddy's for bar food. There's also My Pie for pizza, but the lunch crew is always hungover and super slow."

I'm too full for dumplings, and I'm not ready for the absolute chaos of Lindy's or the absolute annoyance of hungover staff, and I definitely don't want to barf oysters, so I say, "I haven't been to MacGillicuddy's before."

"Yay! They have the best fries."

As we walk along the sidewalk, Shelby fills me in on each storefront and the owners and workers within. It's kind of funny—I've lived in my own hometown all my life, in the exact same house, and I don't know anything about any of the businesses there. Cumberville doesn't have a cute downtown or a Chamber of Commerce, so while I may see the same cashiers at the store and run into folks I went to school with, there's just no real sense of community.

"Lindy comes to our weekly Craft Night," Shelby says as we pass by the sandwich shop, which is as mobbed as it was—just yesterday? It seems like it was eons ago. "So does Nathan from the inn and Edie from the soap shop and Keelie from MacGillicuddy's, and Riley—he's Mr. Gooch's assistant, not sure if you met him?"

"Nope. Just Mr. Gooch."

"He's such a character. That eye patch, right? And then some other folks come and go, but that's our core group." She eyes me hungrily. "Are you crafty?"

"Not as crafty as my sister Cait, but I know enough to make a really wonky scarf."

"Perfect! Excellent. We meet at MacGillicuddy's next

Saturday night. There's a room upstairs for private events, and if nobody's using it, it's ours as long as we all spend at least ten bucks each."

We're in front of the toy store now, which has one of those BACK IN 15 MINUTES signs up, and I pause to look in the front window. Even as an adult, I wish I could go inside. There's just something magical about toy stores.

"Mr. and Mrs. Cove," Shelby says disapprovingly. "Meanest people in town. They seem to hate children. Can't imagine why they opened a—"

She's interrupted by a ringing bell. Her eyes go wide, and her hand clamps down on my wrist.

"Oh, crap," she says. "We have to get off the street."

I look up and down the charming scene, trying to figure out what's going on. "Is there a tornado or something? The sky seems really blue."

She knocks on the door of the toy store, frantic, like we're in a horror movie.

"Come on, Mr. Cove," she murmurs. "I know you're just in back eating a sack lunch." She looks at me. "Nora would let us in, but they fired her. Their own daughter, can you believe that? Mr. Cove!"

When no one appears, she grabs my arm again and pulls me toward the corner, her eyes darting everywhere.

"Are we about to get murdered?" I ask.

She nods. "Maybe. We've got to get somewhere safe. Now."

"Shelby. Stop. What the hell is going on?"

She looks at me like I'm an idiot child. "The turkeys are coming."

16

"The... turkeys?" I ask.

But then I remember Nick saying something about them—

It's the turkeys you will learn to fear.

As if on cue, I hear the distinctive sound of a turkey gobble. The big birds round the corner with the confidence and lethality of a phalanx of mafia bosses. One huge tom turkey, two more husky gobblers that seriously look like his lieutenants, and at least twenty gurgling ladies.

I have only ever encountered turkeys wrapped in plastic and removed from the freezer to defrost in an aluminum pan. But let me tell you now that a male turkey is about four feet tall and four feet wide, and when his eyes lock on you and his face furiously engorges with blood and he runs right at you with his wings flapping madly, your brain will tell you you're living in the velociraptor scene of *Jurassic Park*.

"What do we do?" I shout, because it seems like a reasonable time to shout.

"Run!" Shelby shouts back, and then two grown women are hauling ass to escape a bunch of bloodthirsty gobbling brown dinosaurs.

I can hear them clucking and calling, hear the *clicking* of their awful talons, imagine the rasp of their beaks as they charge behind us.

"Faster!" Maggie shrieks from the backpack, which really gets me moving. A turkey might hurt me a little, but one could outright kill her. This could be the beginning of the world's most expensive and tragic turducken.

We're almost to the street corner when the passenger-side door of a parked truck flies open, blocking the sidewalk.

"Get in!" someone says, and Shelby doesn't hesitate. She pushes me up into the waiting truck, and I don't even think about who or what is inside it. I dive in and scoot over with the backpack in my lap, only to find myself on a bench seat, pressed up against . . .

Hunter Blakely.

Shelby slams the door, and something hot and wet slurps up the side of my face and into my ear. It's the black Lab I noticed when Hunter was driving away from the alley, and I can already hear his tail thumping.

"Hello to you, too," I say, reaching back to rub the dog's sleek black head.

"Bongo, c'mon," Hunter says. "Give the poor girl a break."

The dog immediately backs off, although I can hear his feet tapping excitedly on the black leather back seat.

I'm turning back to thank Hunter when something splats against the window—a turkey, trying to get inside. Then another and another, battering the door with their massive bodies.

"They're aggressive re-nesters—it's like a second mating season for the hormonally imbalanced," Hunter explains, as if this excuses it.

"Those dang Coves wouldn't let us in at the toy store," Shelby complains, fixing her hair in the mirror.

A turkey jumps up on the hood of the truck—one of the smaller females, thank goodness. Another one lands in the bed. Hunter turns and reaches past me to slide the back window shut, and my face is smashed nearly into his armpit. It's not nearly as horrible as it sounds. His deodorant smells like rain in a forest, and once the window is closed, he leaves his arm along the back of the seat, almost sort of around me. Our eyes meet for a brief, electric moment, and my heartbeat kicks up as I fight the urge to snuggle into him.

"Gotta be careful," he says, resettling—but not moving his arm. "Some of the smaller ones might actually make it inside, and I wouldn't want you to get pecked to death."

At the word *peck*, I can only think about his lips. They're so close—

"Get out of this truck right now!" Maggie screeches from the backpack in my lap. "You will not consort with Blakelys!"

"There are worse ways to go," I murmur, leaning into him.

"The turkey gang seems like it's bigger this summer," Shelby says. "You good, Rhea?"

Nearly crushed against Hunter?

Somehow I will find the tools to survive.

"She'll be fine when she's out of this ding-dang truck!" Since her grandma voice in my head isn't doing any good, Maggie screams incoherently in her parrot voice and bashes herself against the screen.

"I'm good, and you're only hurting yourself, Doris," I say.

Behind us, Bongo is on full alert and trying to climb over the bench seat but seems more curious than murderous.

"Sorry about her. Parrot brains are actually quite large compared to other animals, but they're still just about the size of a gumball, and sometimes she forgets she has one." I pat the backpack. "It's safer in here, honey. There's a dog in back. And we don't shout at the people who just saved our lives."

The turkeys aren't leaving, though—they're all over the truck now. There are three on the hood, several on the piles of wood in the bed, and judging by the scratchy thumps overhead, at least two making gobbling love on the roof.

"I need to get driving if I don't want to spend the rest of my day washing turkey shit off someone else's lumber. Is there somewhere I can drop y'all off?"

"We're headed to lunch at MacGillicuddy's," Shelby says, "if you want to join us."

But the weird thing is that she doesn't sound flirtatious at all. I wonder if maybe she's known him all her life, or they're related, or maybe she's not into dudes, because I'm just barely touching this man my grandmother doesn't want me to talk to and every atom in my body is at full salute.

Hunter nods and looks back to the bed of the truck. "I've got an appointment, but I'll drop y'all off. Buckle up. I'm gonna give these turkeys a ride."

I lift my hip so Shelby can buckle, then shuffle around looking for my seat belt. The middle seat of the bench is smaller, and I brush Hunter's shoulder as I buckle in. I'm almost sorry I don't have to dig under his butt to find my own seat-belt latch. His arm is no longer around me; he's all business now, hands at ten and two. As soon as my seat belt clicks, he commands Bongo to lie down and then hits the gas. The truck erupts out of its parking spot, sending turkeys literally flying. The air is full of angry brown feathers as Hunter hits the brakes and lays on the horn, scattering birds everywhere in a gobbling tornado. I notice he's careful not to hit any of the turkeys or run them over, but they have definitely moved from predator to prey, yelping at each other as they try to find someplace to roost that isn't moving and honking. I'm surprised that Bongo isn't barking up a storm, but he's lying behind us, calm and silent.

After a few staccato stops and starts as we escape the turkey flock, we're finally free and driving around the square. Shelby asks Hunter if he's coming to the Chamber meeting, and he says he's not sure, and she tells him he absolutely has to, and he asks what she's bringing. When she tells him she's bringing monster cookies, he reluctantly agrees to attend. And then he's pulling up in front of the restaurant, which looks like a treehouse. Shelby and I anxiously scan the area for any rogue turkeys, but it seems safe.

"Thanks for saving us," I say, and Shelby adds, "Sorry for being a bother."

Hunter smiles down at me. "No bother. It'd be more work cleaning your turkey-stripped carcasses off the square, if I'm honest."

"Aw, that's sweet," I say. "Because if you thought otherwise, I'd have a *bone* to pick."

His eyes light up. "Well, that *remains* to be seen."

"I could really only suggest that you *carrion*, then."

"Oh my God, please stop making death puns," Shelby wails. "I'm gonna lose my appetite."

"Someone's maintaining a *stiff* upper lip."

"The turkeys can have you—you turkeys!" Shelby says as she unbuckles and hops out.

Hunter and I grin at each other like idiots for a minute before Shelby sighs dramatically. I unbuckle, whisper "You'd better text me!" and slide down out of the truck.

Maggie is already berating me before Hunter is even out of the parking lot.

"I don't care what anybody tells you, that boy is not your friend! None of the Blakelys are!"

"So he's a Blakely," I say as Shelby and I head for the front steps. "They're magic, too, right?"

Shelby stops and looks around, making sure we're alone; I guess nobody likes the feeling of choking on their own magical spit. "They are. Or they were. Joyce used to be the most powerful witch of the older generation, and then there's our moms and their generation, but our generation is kind of a mess. Neither of the King girls seem to have powers at all, same with Nick and Nathan. Colonel's side of the Gooch family tree is a bust. To be honest, the witch thing is kinda dying off."

"Maggie said—" I start, then break off. I can't tell anyone what Maggie said, because they all think she's dead. "That is, I heard most of the young folks keep moving away?"

Shelby nods. "People are having fewer babies these days, there aren't that many jobs in the area, and kids want to go to better colleges." She leans closer. "And over the last couple of years, some folks just . . . lost most of their magic. Like the Blakelys. And the Malcolms. And the Halls."

"Lost their magic?"

She shrugs. "I don't know much about it, and I don't know why mine still works. Like I said, the older folks think it's tacky to talk about. But I heard . . ." She nibbles at her lip. "I heard your grandmother might have had something to do with it?"

"I did hear folks were mad at her," I start. "And I've been wondering why."

Maggie's voice in my head is flustered. "It's all lies. People just want someone to blame. I told you: Shelby is a flibbertigibbet."

"So what's the dating scene like around here?" I ask, changing tack. "Did you and Hunter ever—"

Shelby laughs as she walks toward the restaurant steps, her UGGs crunching in the gravel. "Nope. I think we're cousins twice removed or something, and I've known him all my life. I'm more into the big, burly outdoorsy type, you know? Give me a bushy beard and some camo and a freezer full of meat, and I'm good. Hunter is not a hunter. He was always kind of a nerd, to be honest."

I internally sigh in relief, and we step into Mac-Gillicuddy's and wait to be seated. On the way to the table, Shelby stops at the bar to talk to two dark-haired women who must be sisters. The bartender looks like she could crush a watermelon with her thighs while mixing a martini, and the younger one in the waitress apron looks like she's barely out of high school.

"Rhea Wolfe, this is Cash and Keelie King," Shelby says, pointing first to the bartender, then to the waitress.

"I'm so glad we've got somebody new for Craft Night!" Keelie practically squeals, and I realize that I absolutely have no choice but to be there now because making her sad would be the equivalent of kicking a kitten.

"Do you go to Craft Night, too?" I ask Cash.

She winces. "No, but my boyfriend does. The only thing I craft is cocktails. Shelby says you're from here originally?"

"My family is, but I've never been here before."

"How are you liking it?" Cash leans in. "Because I left for five years, and it's definitely different, being in such a small town again."

"*Definitely different* definitely covers it. The hardest part is being away from my sisters. They're still in Alabama, and we're very close."

Cash throws a fond glance at her sister. "I feel that. But, hey, you've managed to land in a special place. You'll find your feet quick."

The hairs on the back of my neck rise and my shoulders hunch up, and that's when I feel a dog's growl deep in my chest.

"Peach Pit, what's the matter with you?" Cash says firmly, looking directly behind me.

"She smells a stranger," a new voice says.

I turn stiffly and find a short woman with big bleached-blond hair and a penchant for rhinestones. Beside her a chestnut-colored pit bull stands, staring at my backpack with her hackles up.

"What's in the bag, new girl?" the woman asks, looking me up and down.

I want to sink into the floor as I slowly hold it up. "A cockatoo?"

"The sign by the door just says no raccoons," Shelby says helpfully. "So I figured a cockatoo wouldn't be a problem? Right, Farrah?"

"You brought a *cockatoo* into a *bar*," the woman begins, like she can't believe it. "And don't tell me it's an emotional support cockatoo, because I don't see a little red vest."

The tension is weirdly high, so I raise the backpack, and Maggie unhelpfully shouts, "Shipoopi!"

"Yep, you caught me. I'm Rhea, and this is my pet cockatoo, Doris, and she gets upset if she's left alone for too long in a new place and shreds everything I own and then plucks herself bald. But if her being here is a problem, then I'll apologize and get out of your hair."

"You're Maggie Kirkwood's granddaughter," the blond woman says. "Right?" But she's looking at Maggie when she asks it.

"You know damn well she is," Maggie mutters. "Stop giving the poor girl a heart attack."

The blond woman laughs, and it's then I know she can

hear Maggie, too. "I can't fault you, honey. The sign doesn't say anything about cockatoos. Peach, this is a friend. Settle on down."

The pit bull exhales, her hackles go down, and she gives a tentative wag.

"So we're okay?" I ask.

Peach Pit bustles over to me, her whole body wagging now. She looks like an entirely different dog when she's not about to attack. I tentatively reach one hand down to stroke her flat, silky head, holding my backpack out of reach with the other, just in case she changes her mind about Maggie.

"We're good. Always nice to see a new face in town." The woman glances at my bag and smirks. "And old friends are always welcome. I'm Farrah MacGillicuddy, owner of MacGillicuddy's."

I shake her hand, and it's like grabbing an iron girder covered in jangling bracelets and rings.

"You'll be at Chamber, right?" Farrah asks.

"Chamber of Commerce meeting," Shelby fills in for me. "Since you're the new owner of the Video Emporium, you kinda have to."

"Then I guess I'll be there."

Farrah finally releases my hand, and I want to rub my aching bones.

Shelby and I sit, Keelie brings us menus, and from then on, it's a perfectly normal lunch, outside of the pit bull that has decided to happily lie down on my feet. The food is surprisingly good, and Keelie is a great waitress, and Maggie mostly shuts up when I give her some fresh fruit to peck at.

As for the Chamber of Commerce and all that entails, that's a problem for future Rhea.

17

"Stop fussing," Maggie says from the floor. I'm in front of the bathroom mirror, trying to get my hair to behave. "It's just a Chamber meeting."

"Easy for you to say. You're a fancy pink parrot, whereas I actually have to impress these people."

"Which means you finally decided to stay?"

I huff a sigh. "Maybe. Probably. We'll see how it goes tonight. If it sucks, I still might hightail it back to Alabama, where I've never been chased by bloodthirsty turkeys before."

When I asked Shelby what to wear, she just shrugged and said, "Something cute," like that helps. I think Shelby might be one of those people who just looks cute in everything. Or maybe every woman thinks every other woman is that kind of woman. I ended up choosing dark jeans with a blazer and flats, trying to aim for professional but fun. If I'm going to open a bookstore, after all, that's the perfect persona.

Books and Bewitchment

Every time I think that word—*bookstore*—I can't help grinning.

The idea is so delicious that I'm scared of it.

Can I really just . . . open a business?

Choose exactly what to sell, where to put things, when to open and close?

I've spent so long working for someone else and taking care of other people that I've never considered what it might be like to do exactly what I want to do, exactly how I want to do it. Talking to Shelby at lunch really brought things to light. She told me how she started up her bakery, how she keeps her books, how she changes things like hours and prices to see what will work, and I realized that if someone as flighty as Shelby can bring in enough money to live comfortably, maybe I can, too. Especially when I factor in my newfound knack. Books are the perfect choice. Before, my future just felt like endless drudgery, but now I can visualize a life I truly want.

The only thing missing is my sisters.

As if by magic, my phone rings. It's only Cait calling on FaceTime, though, which is weird. I understand immediately what's going on when both of my sisters' worried faces appear, squished in together.

"You're alive! Thank heavens!" Jemma points a finger at the screen. "You are not answering texts like you're supposed to!"

"I've been busy. I had to fight a flock of turkeys today."

"You what?" Jemma shrieks.

Cait laughs, then her eyes narrow in accusatory suspicion. "Forget turkeys. You're wearing makeup. Lots of makeup. What's going on? Do you have a date?"

"A date?" I splutter. "I've only been here a couple of days! How fast do you think I move?"

"Well, I just can't think of another reason you'd be fully done up at six p.m. And Lord knows you've been in a dry spell since the last time Billy Wayne changed your oil."

I roll my eyes. "That's a terrible euphemism. And our entire hometown is a dry spell."

"So are there cute boys in the mountains? Mountain men? Burly men?" Jemma gasps. "Are there lumberjacks?"

"I'm going to the Chamber of Commerce meeting," I tell them, if only so they'll get off the topic of men and stop making me think about being squished up against Hunter Blakely's armpit in his truck. "As a local business owner, I need to meet everybody and figure out how to get the video store making money."

"Wait, you're serious? The Chamber of Commerce? What is this—the 1950s?" Jemma asks, giggling.

"They have a lot of influence around here. Every business downtown is involved. So I want to make a good impression."

Cait leans in, excited now. "So you're really doing it? You're really going to stay there and try to run a video store that also sells peanuts? Because I don't want to burst your bubble here, but that sounds deliciously bananapants."

I take a deep breath. I haven't told them yet, which feels like a betrayal. But a lot has happened in two days. I'm still getting used to it myself.

"Well, I—*we*—own the buildings. And the store doesn't have to do video rentals and peanut sales. It can be anything, you know? I've been told the other properties are too messed up to rent without a lot of work, but that it wouldn't be too hard to convert the open shop into . . ." I pause. Deep breath. "A bookstore?"

My sisters pause, too. Jemma's mouth falls open, but I can see the hamster wheel in Cait's brain spinning.

"Oh my God, that's perfect!" Jemma squeals.

"It kinda is," Cait admits. "But do you have the capital for that?"

"It won't take much money," I assure them. "Just a few new bookshelves, a coat of paint. I can start small and build up."

"And you have to order, like, a million books," Cait reminds me, but not in a negative way. She loves a project. "And you'll need a name and a logo, maybe some permits. Then there's marketing and bookkeeping. . . . This is a lot of work, Rhea. Are you ready for it?"

I look into the screen and break out into a grin. "Yeah, I really think I am," I say softly.

"That place must be amazing. Arcadia Falls." Cait tilts her head. "Mama always made it sound like the devil's butthole, but . . ."

"But it's not buttholey at all. It actually feels like home. You guys might like it."

Jemma leans in. "Is there room for us?"

"Kind of? Not in this apartment. I guess I need to explain how Maggie set things up—"

"Maggie? You mean"—Cait switches to Mama's accent—"that witch?"

It's how our mother often referred to her own mother, but Cait doesn't know how right she is.

"Sure. That witch. We're not dealing with a will. We're dealing with a trust. Which means we don't get a lump sum. I can't just wave my wand and make all your dreams come true. With a trust, the dead person gets to tell you what you can and can't do with the money. And the money in Maggie's trust can only be used in relation to the buildings in Arcadia Falls. There's not enough money to fix everything at once and give y'all shiny new apartments, but there's enough to get started."

Jemma blows her bangs out of her face. "Well, that's annoying."

"You're goddamn lucky!" my grandmother shrieks in my head as she perches on the carpeted toilet seat. "This is a gift!"

I point at her. "Shut it, you."

Cait and Jemma look at me like I'm hiding a cute boy under the table.

"Is there someone else there?" Jemma asks, eyes sparking mischievously.

"Just the usual troublesome cockatoo who won't stop making a ruckus and will soon be locked up in her cage if she doesn't settle down."

"Well, I never!" Maggie ruffles her feathers but goes quiet, at least.

I glance at the time. "I've got to go. I told y'all I wanted the chance to try something new, and I'm going to take it. Worst-case scenario, the business doesn't work, and I learn something and have a free apartment while I figure out how to fix up the properties to rent. Best-case scenario, I start a successful business and y'all move up here and do the same. But it's gonna take time, and it all starts with this Chamber of Commerce meeting, so please tell me I'm going to rock it."

"You're absolutely going to rock it," Jemma says with complete confidence.

When Cait doesn't immediately agree, Jemma nudges her.

"You're going to rock it," Cait echoes.

I hear her reluctance, but I know her well enough to understand that her anxiety is getting the best of her and she's worried about the future.

"I'll text y'all after and let you know how it went," I say.

"Or you'll do what you've been doing and forget to text

us entirely." Jemma sticks out her lower lip, her secret pouty weapon since she was a baby.

"If I'm not answering texts promptly, it's only because there's so much going on. And you know what? It's nice, having things going on. It's been a long time since I've had anything interesting in my life outside of makeups and breakups with Billy. So . . . sorry not sorry, I guess."

My sisters gape at me for a minute, and then Cait bursts out laughing.

"That might be the first time you've ever stood up for yourself in your entire life, Rhea."

I raise my chin. "Yeah, well, it won't be the last. Just remember, whatever good comes of this place, y'all will benefit. Now, I'm off. A bushel and a peck—"

"And a hug around the neck!" they call.

Once the screen goes dark, I check my lipstick one more time and look around for Maggie. She's fluffed up in the corner, glaring at me resentfully.

"I just want to see my granddaughters," she mutters.

"Then ask nicely. I'm always happy to show off a well-behaved cockatoo. I might even kiss your fluffy pink head. Now, what do I need to know about this meeting?"

I hold out the backpack, and Maggie flutters in and settles on the perch. If I knew she was going to behave, I might just carry her on my shoulder like a normal parrot, but it's almost like sometimes she forgets she's not human and that even if I can hear her talking, other people only hear squawks and see a pink-and-gray football flying right at them.

"Okay. The Chamber. Well, you've met Colonel and Shelby and both of the boys from the inn. There are the Coves—nobody likes them—and Edie. Farrah's usually there, plus Rocco from the pizzeria, Lindy and Marla from the lunch places, Tim from the oyster bar, Harry the potter

—don't bring up the books!—Alex from the brewery, Joelle from the crystal shop, Don from the general store, and Gabrielle from the dog store—which, a dog store? Honestly? Barb owns the boutique, and Irene manages the clothing shop where the young people go. Smokey, who owns the candy store, has been boycotting the Chamber for decades. We sometimes get the mayor or the head of the police when there's something of general importance. Considering we have someone new, you'll most likely see a big crowd."

It takes me a minute to realize that I am the someone new and that these locals might show up just to take my measure. I'm glad I'll have friends there—or allies, at least. When I think about what it would be like to be real, actual friends with Shelby and Nick and Nathan; to go to Craft Night and chat over the clicking of needles; or, I don't know, just go have coffee on a random Monday morning without a boss to stare at his wristwatch the moment I walk in the door, it's like my whole body relaxes a little. I never dreamed big—I don't need millions of dollars and boats and a house in the Hamptons, whatever a Hampton is—I just want a little breathing room from the daily anxieties that have hounded me since I was a kid. I want a lunch date with a girlfriend, enough money to give a nice birthday gift, the opportunity to pick out a couch that doesn't come with someone else's butt indentation.

Which only adds to the pressure of this meeting. I've committed to staying here, at least for a while, and I'm going to need all the help and goodwill I can get.

I pick up the bird backpack, plus another tote with the two big cups of boiled peanuts I've been ordered to bring along, and head down to the alley. It's well-lit back here, at least. I look up and down both ways, and Maggie chides, "It's safe, you goose."

"Tell that to the turkeys," I mutter, holding a key between

my knuckles like bootleg Wolverine.

I quick-walk toward the main street, and as I approach the dumpster, something bangs against the metal. I stumble back, reaching into my tote for the pepper spray that's somewhere under five pounds of salty nuts.

"Hey!" Maggie barks when I set down her backpack a little too roughly.

"There's something in the dumpster," I tell her. I grab the cool metal cylinder and pull it out, my thumb instinctively going to the lever, like Billy taught me.

"It's just raccoons."

"You don't know that."

"I absolutely do know that. Go on over and look in. There are usually two. Big John and Buttercup."

Holding my key in one hand and my pepper spray in the other, I approach the dumpster, which I was bound to pass anyway. I tell myself that a murderer wouldn't hide inside a dumpster or make an obvious thumping noise before they jumped out to hatchet-murder me, but my body tells me that Jason Voorhees is in there with a machete.

Another clank makes me jump, and I hear a noise that can only be described as a light skittering. A chubby raccoon appears on the dumpster's edge, staring at me like I'm interrupting something important.

"That's Big John. He's a rascal," Maggie informs me. When a second inquisitive head pops up, she adds, "And that's Buttercup. She's looking pretty chunky. We might get some babies this year."

"Kits."

She snorts in my head. "Those are clearly not cats."

"I know that, GamGam. Baby raccoons are called kits. I guess I need to buy some cat food for 'em, huh? If they're going to have babies back here."

"You're worried about baby raccoons in the dumpster? That's a new one."

I put the pepper spray back in the tote, shoulder my backpack, and continue walking as the raccoon-sparked adrenaline ebbs away.

"Listen. I've got to say something." Maggie's voice in my head is more measured and formal than usual. "I've only known you two days, but it's clear to anybody with eyes that you're a born martyr. Oldest daughter of a rebellious mom, you were always gonna be the little caretaker. Didn't have a choice about it. And I'm not judging. I can tell you love your sisters, and that's how it should be."

"But?" I press, uneasy with where this is going.

"But you're a Kirkwood, and Kirkwoods don't take shoo-shoo off anybody. You got to put your head up and claim what's yours. Fight for what you want. I can see the fire in you, but you've been smothering it your whole life, at least in relation to fighting for yourself. This is your chance, Rhea. Your chance to grab what you want."

"You just met me, and you're a parrot. How do you know what I want?"

"I know because I've been watching you. It's pretty boring being a bird, you know? Every time you're reading, you're smiling. I've seen your face when you talk about a bookstore. It glows. *You want this.* So whatever happens tonight, you got to remember to put yourself first for once in your life. You deserve a chance at your own happiness."

I want to say something smart, but . . . no one has ever said anything like that to me before.

Take care of your sisters. Nurse your mother. Cook for your boyfriend. Keep up the house. Make my coffee just right (or get a passive-aggressive Post-it). Can I have a hundred to float me until payday? Those are the things I've heard over and over again.

And I've done everything that's ever been asked of me.

But maybe Maggie is right.

Maybe it's time to put myself first.

Whatever that means.

"I'll think about it," I tell her, because I know that if I outright agree, she'll either get smug or start spouting more phrases stolen from Scholastic Book Fair posters with kittens hanging from tree branches.

The downtown square is even more charming at night than it is during the day, with fairy lights strung up in the trees and orange streetlights casting a warm glow along the sidewalks. The whole scene is just so homey. So welcoming. I already know my way to the inn, and Shelby is waiting for me on the sidewalk outside. She waves when she sees me, and my mouth waters when I see that she's holding a big bakery box. All I've had since lunch was another one of Maggie's Diet Cokes. I've got to find the nearest store and get something in that fridge that isn't carbonated.

"You ready?" Shelby asks as we head inside.

"Does it matter?"

She chuckles. "It's so funny—for me, this is about the same as Sunday dinner at my mom's, but I guess for you, it's a pretty big deal, huh?"

I nod. "Feels like a job interview, if I'm honest."

"Sure, a job interview with twenty nosy people excited to have something to talk about besides whether we need to put the stalls in a U-shape or three lines for the farmers' market. Don't worry—once they're full of sugar and peanuts, they'll be eating out of the palm of your hand."

"As the owner of a cockatoo, that's more dangerous than it sounds."

The front door of the inn is wide open, and there's movement and excited chatter wafting out. I follow Shelby in and through to the dining room where I had the best biscuits of my life and was inspired to turn a dumpy video store into the bookstore of my dreams. The long table seats twelve, but there are already more people than that, and white folding chairs are set up all around the walls.

Shelby opens her pastry box and sets it down in the middle of the table, where it reigns over cheese, crudités, cut fruit, and the supper version of Nathan's biscuits. "Just pop the top off the peanuts and put 'em down," she tells me. "They'll be gone soon enough."

"Where's the dog?" I ask her, because that wide-open door worries me.

Shelby looks genuinely confused. "What dog?"

"I saw it my first day here. Long and lanky, stretched out by the fireplace?"

Okay, now she's looking at me like I'm crazy. "There's no dog. Nick is allergic. That's why they only have one dog-friendly room and it's the farthest away from the lobby."

I don't have time to contemplate the nonexistent dog as the room is filling up. Nathan waves as he brings out bottles of wine, and I spot Colonel hurrying over to get first pick at the monster cookies. Lindy opens a bag of potato chips with a pop that startles Nick and makes him put a hand to his heart. Since I grew up without a big extended family past my sisters and parents, there's a warmth and energy here, a pleasant camaraderie that calls to me. When I see Hunter Blakely pause at the door, it takes everything I have not to stare at him, so I focus on filling my plate with a cookie, a couple of chocolate truffles, a scoop of boiled peanuts, and some mini quiches that Nathan has just brought out, piping hot, from the kitchen.

"And how are you settling in, Ms. Wolfe?" Colonel asks with cookie crumbs twinkling in his mustache.

"Pretty well," I have to admit. "Everyone's been so nice."

"Well, prepare yourself—"

He's interrupted by someone clinking silverware against a wineglass.

The room goes silent as everyone looks to the head of the long table, and I'm the only one who hears Maggie mutter, "Oh, shit."

18

"Of course Joyce Blakely is here," Maggie grumbles. "Don't make eye contact. Don't tell her you're a Kirkwood."

And the annoying thing about having a telepathic-dead-grandma cockatoo is that I can hear her, but I can't get clarification without looking like a lunatic who converses with birds. I also can't remind her that it's kind of hard to hide that I'm a Kirkwood when I'm the spitting image of my mother and grandmother.

The woman at the head of the table looks—well, exactly like how I thought my grandmother *would* look, and not just because she's currently human and decidedly not a pink parrot. Joyce is soft and round, sweet and harmless, with a smooth white bob and laugh lines and that exact shade of pink lipstick that appears on every seventy-year-old woman at church. She's wearing a barn coat and stretchy jeans, smiling warmly and benevolently as she looks around the table.

"Welcome, y'all," she says. "It looks like we have a new prospective member. Wanna introduce yourself, honey?"

Everyone smiles at me and claps, and Shelby elbows me in the side. I smile brightly and give a little wave.

"She's got something up her sleeve," Maggie hisses. "That snake!"

"Hi! I'm Rhea Wolfe. I'm hoping to start a new business downtown."

Joyce smiles, and her whole face crinkles up in a friendly way. "Can't wait to hear more about that. We're always happy for new blood. I hope you like what you hear tonight."

"Shut up, you lying bitch!" my grandmother yells, which feels so unnecessary. Joyce seems nice, and the way everyone else is smiling at her suggests that she *is* nice.

"So now that we've all got a plate of goodies, let's settle down to business. Lindy, you're taking notes? Thank you so much, sweetheart. I guess I'll turn it over to our president, Nick Harris."

Nick stands and calls the meeting to order, and everyone quietly eats as he runs through housekeeping items and the treasury reports, none of which mean much to me. Whenever he closes a topic, he snappily bangs a little gavel on a coaster, and he looks so pleased that I figure it's his favorite part of this duty. I spend my time looking around the room at the other members—and trying not to steal too many obvious glances at Hunter Blakely, who's posted up in a corner, standing with his arms crossed. A pretty blond girl around my age, maybe a little younger, sits in the chair closest to him. I haven't met her yet, but he's standing closer to her than he has to, which makes me want to bare my teeth even though I have no business doing so.

"And that brings us to new business," Nick says. "We have several members discussing a memorial for Maggie

Kirkwood and Diana McGowan. So far, a bench has been mentioned, as has a piece of artwork or a small garden. Does anyone have strong feelings?"

"Maybe a bench?" Shelby says.

"Absolutely not!" Maggie mutters. "We've got enough damn benches, and every time we build a garden, folks let their dogs pee in it. I don't want folks peeing all over my memorial. You tell her no. Say it should be art."

"But—" I murmur, hoping to keep a low profile.

"All for a bench?" Nick holds up his gavel.

"No!" Maggie barks.

"A piece of public art might be nice," I say, feeling awkward as hell. "Maybe a—"

Maggie flaps her wings. "Mural. Sculptures are too expensive. And heavy."

"A mural. On the side of the video store, since it's on the corner?"

An appreciative murmur goes up, and I'm glad that Maggie gets a say in her own memorial, even if she's not actually dead, in the usual way. Joyce is studying me, squinting like she's trying to get a better look, and I am very aware that I wasn't supposed to let on that I am Maggie's granddaughter. Not that I can help the way I look. Then again, I only spoke up because it seemed like Maggie wanted me to, and—

God, it's hard to keep up with the secret life of a reincarnated cockatoo-whispering witch.

"All in favor of commissioning an artist to paint a memorial mural for Maggie and Diana, say *aye*?"

Everyone in the room says, "Aye!" as Maggie preens a little in her backpack.

"Lindy, can you collect some possible artists and have some quotes for our next meeting? Yes? Thanks. Now, Rhea, if you join the Chamber, can we convince you to volunteer?

With our recent, uh, losses, we've got openings on several committees. If you're not interested, that's totally fine, but we need to know on behalf of the Chamber how you plan to move forward."

Nick's grin is so friendly and hopeful, and all around me, these people look like dogs desperate for a treat.

"Come on, girl," Shelby says quietly. "You got this!"

"You've got to commit to something," Maggie warns me.

And, sure, I decided that I was going to see this through, but it's a lot easier to decide that while holding a lucky dictionary and talking to a bossy cockatoo than it is to have twenty people waiting breathlessly to hear what you're going to do. I begin to wonder if it's silly, dreaming of a little bookstore, and a life here, and . . .

"You really should," Colonel says warmly. "We need you."

I meet Hunter's eyes, and I would swear there's a twinkle there, a yearning. He nods encouragingly.

And that's what pushes me over the edge.

"I guess I'm going to give it a try," I finally say.

The whole room erupts in applause. I haven't felt this universally liked since I won the county spelling bee in second grade with the word *ahoy*.

"That's great news, Rhea. We're all so glad." At Nick's raised voice, the room calms down a bit. "So will you keep running the video emporium or try something different?"

I take a deep breath.

Saying it out loud makes it real.

Once it's out there in public, not just an idea but a declaration, this decision will be heavy, demanding . . . something I *have* to do. Something that can actually fail.

But, then again, can I really fail worse than a video store?

"I'd like to keep the videos but shift the main business over to books with room for some gifts and artwork. A bookstore."

This statement is met with whispers and exclamations, all of which seem positive. Only Joyce and Hunter Blakely don't meet this news with joy. Joyce is still squinting at me, frowning, and Hunter's look is no longer flirty. I told him I'm renting Maggie's apartment, and now that he's made the connection between me and the video store, he knows something is fishy. I feel a brief press of guilt, but it's not like I've ever straight-up denied I was Maggie's kin. Nick gleefully bangs his gavel to bring everyone back to order, and I decide it's in my best interest to avoid looking at either Blakely just now.

"That's great," Nick assures me. "A bookstore would be a very valuable addition to our downtown. And I know our residents will be glad to still have the option to rent videos. And buy peanuts, I hope?"

"We need those peanuts!" cries a silver-haired lady in a caftan and tons of beaded necklaces. She sounds like I just threatened to abolish peanuts altogether, and I'm glad she won't be an enemy.

"A bookstore is just the thing," Colonel Gooch agrees. "More culture always brings folks downtown." He taps his chin. "And possibly some event space? I'd love to see a literary festival one day."

"Sure," I allow, although suddenly it sounds like a lot more work.

"And you're going to need a builder to help with all that," Nathan says with a smug little grin. "Due to the fragile and historical nature of our downtown architecture, you'll have to use our only approved contractor."

This is news to me. "Okay . . ."

"Do you have availability soon, Hunter?"

I feel like I've fallen directly into Nick and Nathan's dastardly meet-cute plan.

"Of course," Hunter says.

But he's wary, not warm at all, with a sort of professional detachment.

Like he knows we're all hiding something from him, and he knows he's not going to like it.

"Even though he's our only contractor, you can trust Hunter and his work," Nick assures me, as if he understands that Nathan's winking and grinning are not making me any more comfortable with the situation. "He's a genius and his prices are more than fair."

There are mumbles of "It's true" and "Yep" and "He saved us a thousand dollars."

Again, everyone looks at me expectantly. I begin to realize that along with the idea of being part of a community comes the part where you have to answer back.

"That sounds great," is basically my only choice.

"He'll stop by tomorrow to talk about what you need. Right?" Nathan prompts.

Hunter gives me a tight smile. "Of course. I'm available after lunch, if that works?"

"Sure. I'll be there."

"Then it's settled," Colonel says.

"And we'll still have the peanuts," the caftan lady adds like a prayer.

"Don't you dare let that boy on my property," the cockatoo in my backpack hisses in my head. "The Blakelys are a bunch of snakebelly, no good—"

I nudge the backpack with my foot to shut her up.

The Chamber moves on to old business and new business, and everyone has thoughts about how to deal with the turkeys, how many traffic cones we need to buy for the farmers' market, and whether or not the new visitors' center brochure should have the old gaol or the toy shop on the cover, as the candy store has already had a turn. It's pretty obvious that the toy shop is a better choice for bringing in visitors, but everyone hates the Coves, so they're putting up a fight. I can see why. The Coves oppose or question nearly every motion put forth and never seem to smile; these people would argue with a stump.

As the meeting drones on, I steal glances at Hunter. I get the weirdest vibe off him—curious but guarded, interested but puzzled. He knows there's something I'm not telling him, and I'm going to have to face the music soon. I wonder if it will be awkward when he stops by the shop tomorrow, and I realize, now that I'm committed, I have a lot of actual work to do.

Finally setting down his gavel, Nick asks if there's any further business, and I nervously raise my hand. "I've never run a business before," I admit. "Can anybody help me with—I don't know, permits and that sort of thing?"

Joyce Blakely smiles, friendly again. "You know, I'm a notary. I'd be happy to stop by the shop and help you."

"Over my dead body!" Maggie is so upset that she squawks, "Shipoopi!" and flaps around, nearly knocking over the backpack under the table. Across the room, I see Farrah struggling to contain her laughter.

Joyce's eyes narrow. "Did I just hear a bird?"

I hold up my backpack, revealing a pink cockatoo who is currently calling Joyce Blakely every name under the sun. "My pet cockatoo. Sorry if she's disturbing the peace."

Everyone has a good laugh, and Colonel Gooch raps his knuckles on the table. "As talented as you are, Joyce, I promised Rhea I'd be here for all her legal needs. It's on me to help her navigate the business side of things." He looks to me and winks—or blinks, hard to tell with the eye patch. "Rhea, whenever you're ready, give my office a call, and Riley will get you on the calendar so we can sort all that out."

"You're goddamn right you will, you old coot," Maggie mutters.

With no further business, Nick gets to happily bang his gavel one last time, dismissing the meeting. Everyone goes right back for the food, and I don't know why I'm surprised to see that all the peanuts I brought have been devoured, leaving wet brown shells on everyone's plates.

I am entirely unprepared for how many people want to shake my hand in welcome. No one, other than Colonel and Shelby, seems to connect me with Maggie, and it's honestly a relief that I don't have to accept condolences, especially considering Maggie is currently in my backpack, cursing like a sailor. I can see Joyce trying to edge her way around the table toward me, but everyone else wants to talk to her. I move as she does, keeping the table between us. It's not a disappointment when Hunter ends up leaning against the wall beside me.

"That was a little intense," Hunter says.

"Are Chamber meetings always like that?"

"Historically speaking? Never. It's usually a lot more droning and gavel banging. One time Barb and Irene almost got in a catfight because they both wanted to use Papyrus on their signs."

"Okay, so I definitely won't go with that for my new logo. Not that I was going to. I'm more of a Comic Sans girl."

Hunter grimaces.

"Joking," I hurry to add. "Love a good font joke. In fact, I'm a *font* of font jokes."

He tries to resist chuckling, but he can't quite get there. It turns out he has dimples, but maybe they only come out when he's trying not to laugh.

"Sounds like you really keep up with the *Times*," he says.

"Well, we are in *Georgia*."

He holds up his hands. "Uncle. I don't know any more fonts."

"Good. I didn't have anything that worked for Trebuchet, so I just threw that joke out."

For a long moment, we just smile at each other like idiots, and then he looks down, awkward again.

"I hope Nathan didn't make you uncomfortable," he finally says. "He can be a little aggressive in the nicest possible way. It's true that I'm the only person in Arcadia Falls certified to work on downtown buildings, but since you don't know me, I totally understand if you want a second opinion. Cisco and I work together—he was at lunch with me yesterday—but he can give you an independent quote, and I'll accept whatever number he gives you. You don't have to use me—I mean, you don't have to *trust* me, is what I'm trying to say. Badly."

"Don't trust him," my grandmother huffs from her backpack.

But why wouldn't I, when the whole town does?

It's not like anyone enjoys the process of contacting contractors and gathering estimates. Working with Hunter would make it easy. Hopefully also easy on the pocketbook, and definitely easy on the eyes.

"Even Nathan and his biscuits can't bully me into something I was going to do anyway," I say, keeping the tone light and playful. "I'll take all the help I can get."

"Are you still at the inn or staying at Maggie's place?"

Ah, yes. Here it comes. He's not going to let this go.

"At Maggie's," I say. "But—"

"Oh," someone else breaks in. "You're staying at Maggie's apartment?"

Finally, the moment I've been weirdly dreading arrives. Joyce Blakely has made her way around the table to stand before me.

Books and Bewitchment

Joyce may look like the Platonic ideal of a storybook grandmother, but the way she's glaring at me now suggests there is some truth to Maggie's dislike. Her eyes are sharp, her mouth turned down.

"That's so interesting. My Elizabeth was about the same age as Maggie's daughter Miranda, and you're just about Hunter's age and have auburn hair, just like Miranda. Just like Maggie. Living in her apartment. Taking over her store right after her death. Helping plan her memorial." She clears her throat and looks around the room as if waiting for attention before saying, loudly, "Why, you must be a Kirkwood!"

The room goes completely silent.

Worst of all, the look Hunter gives me? Pure disgust.

"Of course you are," he mutters, shaking his head sadly.

19

I'm immediately swarmed by Southern people who have smelled a tragedy and need to sink their teeth in. Hands grasp my shoulders and pat my arms. I'm told my grandmother was a spitfire, a saint, a beauty, a character. I'm told I look like her, the spitting image, how didn't they notice? I'm told that Arcadia Falls has been waiting for me. A few people, however, Joyce included, keep their distance, whisper behind their hands, and look me up and down like I might secretly be a reptile.

"Can't believe she never told us! And you weren't at the funeral!" the caftan lady mutters indignantly, like it's somehow my fault.

"They didn't know each other," Colonel shoots back. "I only found out a few weeks ago when Riley tracked down the prodigal granddaughter. Now let the poor girl breathe!"

It gets awkward after that, once all the condolences have been condoled and the monster cookies monstrously devoured. I swiftly make my exit, glancing around the room in hopes that I can avoid either of the Blakelys. Of course, in the crush of people navigating the furniture-strewn lobby of the inn, I manage to end up at the door at the same time as Hunter. The look he gives me is resentful, but I guess I deserve it.

He stands back. "Please. Go ahead."

And I'd argue, but I want out of here. So many new people, so much to keep up with, so many eyes on me. I'm not accustomed to being the center of attention, but I'm learning that being the new girl in a small town is like being a chicken nugget in a flock of pigeons, especially after Joyce's truth bomb about my ancestry.

I nod and murmur my thanks, aware of him waiting to follow me out. The night air has a welcome coolness, and I exhale a big breath and close my eyes for a moment, grateful for the space. The scent of late summer rides the breeze, heavy with jasmine and camellia, their glossy leaves rustling prettily behind the inn's white picket fence, and when I look up, it seems like the stars are closer than usual.

"You never mentioned you were a Kirkwood," Hunter says.

I take a deep breath. "That's because I'm not a Kirkwood. I'm a Wolfe. I never met my grandmother. My mother hated her and left this place to escape her. So whatever beef you have against her has nothing to do with me. I'm sorry she left y'all angry."

"You don't understand," Maggie starts, but I give the backpack a slight shake. This moment feels important, a make-or-break thing between Hunter and me.

He looks around, buying some time to think. "*Angry* doesn't quite cover it, but that doesn't mean it's your fault— or that it's safe for you to walk around at night by yourself. Can I see you home? That alley is dark, and you're the only person going back there tonight."

He's right. I own the next three properties, so they're all empty, and the candy store closes early. There's no reason for anyone else to be in that alley, which means that if they are, it's not good. And I'm pretty sure Big John and Buttercup would be of no use in case of an attack. Hell, they'd probably wring their little raccoon hands and bide their time to eat my corpse.

"Sure. Thanks." We start walking, and, not gonna lie, it's awkward. I slip out of my blazer, let the breeze hit my shoulders and flutter my silk shell. "Speaking of which—would it be really expensive to make an interior staircase that goes directly into the store? Or even just a ladder. Or a fireman's pole? I don't like the idea that if I heard something down there in the middle of the night, I'd have to go all the way around the alley first."

Something about him softens. He's relieved, I think, to have something to talk about besides our whole Romeo-and-Juliet vibe. "There actually is a stairwell already. Maggie had me wall off the door upstairs. She liked her privacy. So really, I'd just cut out the drywall and reframe the door in the apartment."

I try to imagine where a hidden door might be and, failing that, try to remember any spare doors in the actual store. A wave of guilt sweeps over me as I realize that I, the business owner, have only set foot in my store for a combined total of five minutes, maybe. I just assumed Abraham would be running it, or not running it, as usual. Since he didn't contact me at all and Maggie didn't suggest I talk to him, I kinda forgot all about it.

So far, I am not the ideal entrepreneur.

As we reach the square, I squint across the darkened street and note that the lights are still on at the Arcadia Falls Video Emporium & Boiled P-Nut Palace. Then again,

Books and Bewitchment

I guess people with a hankering to rent *Mannequin Two* on VHS don't want to wait until the morning. I haven't seen hours posted anywhere, but that fits in with everything I've seen so far of my grandmother's business. The best time to peruse twenty-year-old VHS tapes is clearly when an entire town of old folks is already asleep.

"Will you show me where that door is—in the store?" I add this last part hastily because I don't mean to imply that I'm inviting a good-looking single man up to my apartment two days after meeting him, even if I'm definitely thinking about it. We haven't spoken of the fact that he asked me out and then never texted, and I'm too embarrassed to bring it up. I have to find out what Maggie did to the Blakelys before I can truly untangle everyone's feelings, including my own.

Hunter nods and holds open the glass front door for me, and I step inside to the scent of possibly overboiled boiled peanuts. I don't see a single person—no one browsing the stacks and no Abraham sleeping in his usual chair. I have inherited the world's emptiest store, filled to the brim with the world's least viable product.

He points to the far door on the left. "That one goes into a shared storage room with the hardware store next door. Lot of good space in there, but it'll need some cleaning out if you want to use it. Bathroom door is marked, of course." He points to a door on the right. "And that one has the stairs." He nods at Abraham's lawn chair. "Huh. That's weird. He's usually asleep in that chair about this time."

A small but persistent alarm bell begins to ring in my head as a chill strokes up my spine. This doesn't feel right.

"Where does Abraham live?" I ask nervously. "I know he just abandons the store sometimes. . . ."

"No idea. He's a private guy."

I move the backpack around front and gently bounce it. "I

wish someone around here knew more about Abraham," I say.

Maggie shakes herself awake. "Abraham? He's my uncle. Never married. I was his only family, which is why you have to keep paying him."

"But where is he, I wonder," I continue.

She perks up and presses a beady red eye against the screened front of the bag. "He should be in that chair, sleeping. He usually wakes up and locks the door around ten."

"Does anybody know where he lives?" I ask again.

"Maggie might've. She knew him better than anyone," Hunter says, oblivious to my private, half-telepathic conversation with a sleepy parrot.

We're both still standing just inside the front door as if something is holding us back from venturing farther within.

"Abraham?" I call.

No answer.

"Sometimes he sleeps in the stairwell," Maggie admits.

Fine, then. This is my business, he's my employee, and I'm going to check the stairwell. I walk a circle of the entire store first, just to make sure he isn't curled up in a corner or using the restroom. He's not behind the counter, and the only places left to look are the two doors Hunter has just pointed out to me. Both possibilities seem equally creepy, so I head for the stairwell.

"Abraham?" I call again.

There's no answer, not even a rustle or snore from the other side. Hunter is right behind me, his hand out like he wants to be supportive but doesn't want to accidentally touch me. I grab the doorknob, and it's colder than it should be.

When I open the door, we find Abraham, right where Maggie said he would be.

But he's not asleep.

He's dead.

20

"Abraham!" I call, even though I can already tell there's no point.

I haven't seen a lot of dead people, but I've seen a lot of alive people, and they are never, ever that pale and still. Also, when they're asleep, their eyes aren't wide open and dry.

"Shipoopi!" Maggie screeches from the backpack.

It's apropos, at least. The stairwell has . . . that smell.

I'm about to ask what to do, but Hunter already has his phone out. I've never called 911 before, but it seems like he knows whoever answers. I'm yet again shocked by what a small town Arcadia Falls is.

"Hey, it's Hunter. I'm at the video store. Looks like Abraham died. Uh-huh. Thanks." He turns to me. "They're on their way. There's nothing we can do, but there are steps to follow."

The next hour is beyond surreal. Hunter and I leave Abraham where he is and go stand just outside the front door as if trying to put as much distance between us and death as we can. He lifts his arm like he might put it around me, but it wavers there in a stretch and then drops sadly to his side. I'm grateful for his presence but rendered mute by the shock of finding a dead body. Sirens start up and get closer and closer. There's an ambulance, a fire truck, and a police car, the placid night now full of blinking lights and cacophonous noise. The EMTs go in first and confirm that Abraham is gone. They roll in a gurney and place him on it, flat on his back under a white sheet. Hunter and I stay by the door, giving them space to do their work as they slide him into the back of the ambulance and drive away.

"You don't have to stick around," I say, suddenly self-conscious. "I'm sure you've got better things to do."

"I don't," he says simply. "I know you didn't know him, but this still can't be a fun thing to go through alone."

I feel like a burden on him, this kind stranger who also sorta half hates me, until a policeman walks toward us with a grim expression.

"Hunter."

"Officer Ferguson. This is Rhea Wolfe, Maggie Kirkwood's granddaughter."

He inclines his head to me. "Ms. Wolfe, I'm sorry you had to see this tonight. Is it okay if I ask you some questions?"

"Of course. I don't know much, but I'll tell you what I can."

He pulls out a notebook and pen, and I tell the story of how we discovered Abraham. I feel a little guilty that I can't tell the officer when Abraham got to work or how he looked or what he said. The closest I've come to an actual interaction with him was at Lindy's on my first day, when Colonel asked him who was watching the video store—and we didn't actually interact.

"Do you know how old Mr. Kirkwood was?" he asks me.

"Oh, gosh," Maggie mutters from my bag. "Let's see. My father was born in 1930, and Uncle Abe was three years younger, so—"

"Around ninety, I think," I say.

"Looks like he went peacefully. Was there anything unusual about the store that might indicate foul play?"

I look around, but honestly, I wouldn't know what constitutes *unusual* here.

"The door was unlocked and the lights were on," Hunter says. "Like always."

"And the fishbowl is full of cash, so it wasn't a robbery," I add.

"We'll ask around, but this seems pretty open-and-shut." Officer Ferguson puts away his notebook. "I'm sorry for your loss, ma'am." He winces. "Loss*es*. Grandmother, too. That's rough."

"He was probably waiting for me to go," Maggie says softly. "Always thought he could look after me, even when I was looking after him. Then you got here, and I guess he reckoned you could handle it yourself."

"Maybe he was waiting for Maggie to go," I say. "I know old folks do that sometimes."

Officer Ferguson nods. "Maybe so. Usually we'd alert the next of kin, but I think that's just you. Not that many Kirkwoods around these days. Again, I'm sorry for your loss. Y'all have a nice night and give us a call if you think of anything else we need to know."

It's after ten by the time he drives away, and the square is dark and still. I give a decisive sigh and head inside to unplug the boiled peanut slow cookers before something catches fire.

"I wonder if there's a manual for opening and closing,"

I say out loud, and I know I might sound like an absolute idiot, but Hunter isn't aware that someone in the know is secretly answering all my questions.

"No manual. It was only ever me and Uncle Abraham. I tried hiring teenagers a couple of times, but it was an absolute failure," Maggie says. "Just put the cash in the safe, turn out the lights, lock the doors, and head upstairs. Nothing you can do now." Maggie sounds sleepy and sad. I can't imagine how strange it must be, to die and return to life in the body of an animal, to be staring straight at your friends while they think you're dead, and then to lose someone you're close to and not even be able to cry. It is possibly the weirdest situation I can think of, and I read over a hundred books last year, one of which was about romancing Bigfoot.

Hunter is still at the door, giving me space to do whatever I need to do.

I grab the fishbowl, and Maggie mutters, "The safe is in the back corner under a tablecloth."

"There's got to be a safe around here, right? Because Maggie wasn't stuffing cash under the bed," I say for Hunter's benefit. Then, after a few minutes of poking around, I lift up the flowered tablecloth on what appears to be a small table with an ALF doll on it and find a safe that's got to be older than both Maggie and Abraham combined.

"No combination. It doesn't lock anymore. We called it the Unsafe Safe," Maggie tells me.

I open the door and my jaw drops.

This thing is *stuffed* with cash.

Almost a solid block of wadded bills.

"Holy shit," I mutter.

"Yeah, we're not great at bank runs," Maggie admits. "Weren't great. Whatever."

I try stuffing today's cash into the safe, but it just keeps falling out, so I stick the fishbowl in the stairwell where we found Abraham. It's cold in there, with a definite odor rising up from the pile of crusty blankets and graying pillows.

Hunter waits as I fumble with my key ring, and Maggie tells me which key to use to lock the door. The street is well lit but almost totally silent, aside from what sounds like a live guitarist somewhere mangling Ed Sheeran. We're quiet as Hunter walks me around the corner, past the dumpster, and up to Maggie's door.

My door.

"You gonna be okay tonight?" he asks me. "I'm sure Nick and Nathan have a room at the inn if you want company. And if not, there's another B&B a few miles away, deeper into the mountains."

I can't tell him how despite everything that's happened, this place already feels like home and safety. How Maggie's couch is more comfortable than mine ever was, and how I can't wait to be inside, finally able to shed this stupid blazer for good and soak in a hot bath in the clawfoot tub until the day floats away. Although I feel bad for him, I'm not horribly upset by Abraham's death; I can't be. I didn't even know him. I'm just exhausted from all that has happened in Arcadia Falls. It feels like I've been here a month.

"No, I'll be fine. Thanks for sticking around, though. I would not have known what to do if I'd been alone."

"Me neither, but that's what 911 is there for, I reckon."

I open the door and step into the kitchen, and he leans against the jamb.

"I'll be by after lunch tomorrow," he says, "if you still want to talk estimates. And I hope this doesn't seem presumptuous—"

Go ahead and try me, I think but don't say as I flip on the light, my heart full of hope despite the family drama.

"But you might want to order a doorbell cam or some kind of security system for this alley. Maggie's generation still thinks that nothing bad could possibly happen in a small town like this, but they're wrong."

My smile falls. That is not what the word *presumptuous* generally implies.

"Yeah, I'm definitely going to need some upgrades. Thanks again for everything. Today was just—" My voice hitches.

Our eyes meet with an electric thrill, and I think he might reach for me, but his hands go to fists at his sides. He's taut as a bowstring, and I'd like to be the kind of woman who could make the first move, but I can't. Whatever happened between our families is keeping him at a distance, and I'm not going to push him. He asked me out. I said yes. He never texted. He's mad about ancient history that has nothing to do with me, but I'm the only person left to blame. I can tell he's conflicted, but the ball is firmly in his court, no matter how much I truly need a hug right now.

"Today was just," he repeats, as if it means something.

I give a little wave, and he gently shuts the door. I can feel his presence outside. I already know he's the kind of man who isn't going to leave until the door is locked again and I'm safe.

"Don't you dare get all twitterpated over that boy, you hussy," Maggie says vehemently as I unzip the backpack to let her out.

"We don't use words like *hussy* anymore, Grandma Cockatoo," I remind her, wagging a finger. "Slut-shaming is not cool."

"I don't care what's cool! He's Joyce's grandson, and I'm sure she's poisoned him against me. He might be a spy."

"He doesn't seem like a spy."

"Spies never seem like spies! That's what makes them good spies!"

"What's he going to spy on—who's renting *FernGully* on VHS? He seems like a decent man. Didn't want me to walk home alone after dark, refused to leave me alone to deal with a corpse. So now it's your turn. I need you to tell me right now what beef you have with the Blakelys."

Instead of answering me, Maggie flutters into her cage to drink some water. I'm fuming, but I know I can't force her to do anything, so I head to the bedroom, put on my pajamas, and start doing some cleanup. I'm already making plans for this space, imagining what a little elbow grease and a trip to Walmart can do to make it my own. I hope Maggie won't take the changes too hard, but what's she going to do?

"Joyce Blakely is a snake," she says as she struts into the bedroom. "Hey, what are you doing?"

"I'm pulling all your scarves off the lamps so I can get some actual light and avoid starting any fires."

"They add ambiance! And they're not a fire hazard."

I hold up a silky scarf, showing a browned section that had been dangling perilously close to the light bulb. "Not anymore they're not, Firestarter."

I toss the scarves into a corner, and Maggie runs over and nestles down among them.

"I'm sorry, but it's time to redecorate," I tell her. "If I'm all in, I'm all in."

Even her chirps sound disappointed in me. "I'll have to come to terms with it, I know. Just promise me you'll donate my things. Don't just throw 'em out like garbage."

"I would never do that. I'm not that kind of person."

"Then I guess someone must've raised you right."

It's the closest she's come to any sort of compliment to me or my mom. I'm half proud and half insulted.

Isla Jewell

Finally it's time to try out Maggie's tub for the first time, and I put her to bed in the open cage and allow myself to sink down in absolute bliss. I've wanted a tub like this all my life, and the windowsill is right next to it, perfect for paperbacks. Maybe I should feel weird that someone died downstairs today, but it's not like I knew my great-uncle Abraham. I feel bad for him in the way that you feel bad for people you don't personally know, but it certainly seems like he lived a long life and died peacefully in a place where he was content.

I read until I'm pruny and the water is tepid, dry off, remove my makeup, and snuggle down in the cozy bed, already looking forward to seeing Hunter again tomorrow, even if it's going to be weird. It does not escape me that Maggie yet again dodged the question about why she was feuding with the Blakelys, but I'm going to find out eventually. We're pretty much stuck together unless she wants to go join the turkey gang.

I fall asleep, and my dreams are filmy, misty things, wisps of trees and waterfalls and something elusive, just out of reach. Some time later, when all is dark and still, I wake up straining to hear some odd sound, but whatever it was, it's gone. The room is freezing, colder than it should be in late summer, the moonlight shining in through the window to make a patch of icy white on the ground. I breathe out and my breath hangs in the air like a question.

"Bye, Uncle Abraham," I say, half dreaming.

I burrow deeper under the covers, and as I fall back asleep, it feels like someone pats my hair.

21

The next day dawns gray and rainy, and I spend ten minutes just lying in bed, luxuriating. The misty morning filters gently through the tall windows, making the rosy walls a pretty periwinkle and giving me the sensation of being wrapped up in a cocoon. The sheets are soft and worn, the quilt just heavy enough. I am not hurrying through breakfast or driving exactly the speed limit so I won't get pulled over on my way to work. I am not being yelled at by Mr. Buckley or scrubbing the black charcoal out of the coffee pot he insists on leaving on all day long. I'm not cleaning dirt off my coffee table after Billy and Jimmy monopolized my TV to watch football and refused to take off their work boots. I'm in my own soft, puffy bed, in my own apartment that I own without a mortgage, which is right over the business that I will soon make my dream store. This bed—

"GamGam?"

She bustles into the room and jumps up onto the bed. "You know you can call me Grandma, right? Or Grammy? I never got my chance to be a Grammy."

"GamGam, did you ever . . . get up to any funny business in this bed?" I ask her, looking down at the pastel quilt.

"I am not a GamGam!" She fussily shakes out her feathers. "And no, I did not"—she doesn't want to say it, either—"have relations in this bed."

"So you didn't date? No hookups? Hot parrots in your area? Were you on the lookout for a big cock—"

"Lordy!"

"—atoo boy?"

The look she gives me is one of avian disgust. "Are you normally this interested in the sex lives of your elders?"

"No, but I don't usually inherit their mattresses. So who was my grandfather?"

Maggie paces across the quilt. "I don't see how that's important."

"Then tell me why the Blakelys hate you."

"No!"

I grab her and stand, carrying her to the big cage. "I'm getting sick of you dodging my questions, so you can be in the Cockatoo Clink until you decide to get honest with me. You have nothing to lose. You have no dignity. You're a parrot who poops on a puppy pad. So just tell me the truth."

I close the door and snap on the carabiner that always kept Doris from breaking out.

"This is against the Geneva convention!" Maggie shouts.

"Yeah? You keep saying that, and I'm pretty sure it doesn't apply to birds. Legally, I can eat you and put your feathers in my pillow." I open a kitchen cabinet and find plates and bowls in neat stacks. "Do you have a coffee maker?"

"I was more of a tea person," Maggie says, which isn't helpful.

"Then you can stay in the Cage of Truth and Bad Choices to contemplate your sins."

Long-term, this lack of coffee supplies will not work for me, but short-term, I know where to get the best latte in town. I take a quick shower, slip into jeans and a tee, fluff my hair, add some eyeliner, and spritz on some perfume, because I now know that I can't leave this apartment without seeing a new acquaintance. Before I head out with my raggedy old umbrella, I figure out which keys open the apartment door and the store door, and separate them, sliding them onto my regular key ring.

"You can't leave me in here!" Maggie screams when she realizes I intend to walk out while she's still in the cage. "This is illegal! This is torture! You can't—"

"You're not as loud as Doris, so this is actually an upgrade. Let me know when you're ready for real talk."

The walk is pleasant enough despite the rain. All the flowers outside are soaking up the water, bursting with color. The trees are beginning to turn, pops of orange and yellow and red flashing among the lush green. As I pass by Marla's, I look through the window and see people I've met, laughing and eating as an older woman in an apron hurries around with cast-iron skillets full of steaming scrambles. I almost want to splash in a puddle, it's all so homey. The inn is bustling, thanks to a bachelorette party, and Nathan is happy to make me a mocha. My five dollars also gets me a biscuit, and I realize that this is a wonderful system.

Then I realize that I wasn't necessarily invited into this system.

"Is this okay?" I ask Nick. "Am I taking someone else's biscuit?"

"You're one of us now. We'll always have a biscuit for you, girl," Nathan assures me as he brings out my drink in a to-go cup. He winks at me. "Have fun talking to Hunter today."

For a minute, I'm shocked that he knows my business, but then I remember—Nathan himself made my business quite public last night when he set up the appointment.

"If I don't like his quote, is Cisco really just as good?"

"Honey, you're going to like his quote just fine. He truly is a gift. And not just visually."

I blush as I head back to my place—somehow, with Abraham gone, it really does feel like *my* place. I'm the only one left to run it. At least no one is standing at the door to the video store, waiting for me to open up. I probably need to make a sign to let folks know we're closed and under construction. And that makes me think of fonts, which makes me think of Hunter and flirting with him over fonts.

As soon as I'm back in the apartment, Maggie is screeching at me in true Doris style; I should not have dared her to be more annoying. I sit at the table, just a few feet away from her cage, glad we don't have any neighbors to hear her caterwauling. The moment I unwrap the biscuit, she stops.

"Nathan's?"

"Yup."

"Did you bring me one?"

"Human food is horrible for cockatoos. It'll make your liver explode. You have your pellets, and I'll give you fresh fruit and veg each day, plus some nice mealworms. Yummy yummy."

"But I can still taste biscuits, and Nathan's are the best."

"Then tell me about the Blakelys. And why Colonel said you had some enemies—enemies who gave me the stink eye last night."

I peel off a chunk of biscuit—not too much, because it

really is absolutely terrible for her health—and hold it up to the light.

She fluffs up her crest. "I always dreamed my granddaughter would be a sweet and respectful girl."

"And I was told from the start that you were a stubborn old witch, so here we are."

After a long pause, she sighs in defeat. "I made a decision. An important decision meant to keep Arcadia Falls safe. To protect this place. Needless to say, some people didn't agree with it."

I hold out the crumb of biscuit, and she gently pecks it from my fingers and gobbles it down. "Got any bacon on there?"

I tear off a piece of bacon and consider it. "Okay, next question. What was this altruistic decision of yours that other people didn't like?"

I dangle the bacon just beyond the cage bars, and she tries to poke her beak through but can't.

"Well?" I press.

Maggie jerks her head back, turns around, and shows me her tail. Grandmothers, it turns out, are just as fussy as cockatoos. I hate that she's my only source of information—

Or is she?

I fetch my *Little Webster* dictionary, which has been sitting on the bedside table. I haven't used it since I stood in front of the video store, trying to see past the bleached-out King Ralph stand-up and into a better future, but, well, if my magical grandmother can't help me, maybe I can skip the grandmother bit and go straight to the magic.

"What was Maggie's decision that made folks mad?" I say out loud, in case that helps.

I flip through the book and put down a finger.

"Grimoire," it says.

I stare at the cage. Her back is still to me.

"Maggie, where is your grimoire?"

In true parrot style, she raises her rump and poops.

"Quit being undignified and answer the question."

She turns around and sways angrily from side to side. "How should I know? I died. Do you know what that's like? One minute, you're driving along in the car, laughing with your friend, and the next minute, everything hurts, and people are shattering your ribs—"

"*I don't know* would've been answer enough," I say. "Was it in the car that day?"

"Again, I don't remember. I try not to think about it."

"So what decision did you make that affected other people and had to do with a grimoire?"

She draws herself up with as much chilly hauteur as a pink parrot can accomplish. "I do not answer to you, child. In our current relationship, you have far more power over me than I would prefer, but even if you restrict my freedom or threaten me, you can't make me tell you anything. I would suggest you worry more about your own problems than about what happened in the past. What's done is done."

I look her directly in the eye and pop the tidbit of bacon in my mouth, followed by a big bite of the biscuit. She watches me chew with great longing. I should've known my grandmother would be as stubborn as all the other women of her lineage. She's right, though. I'm not going to threaten her; even if I don't like my grandmother right now, I'm not the kind of person who would harm an animal under any circumstances.

"Then maybe we just don't need to talk as much. You can go back to singing musicals, and I'll figure things out on my own." I turn my back to her and pick up my dictionary. "Where is Maggie's grimoire?"

Flip pages, put down my finger. The word?

Below.

Well, that's not helpful.

Below what?

I look around the kitchen. The only thing below it is the video store. Still, there are several doors I haven't opened that I've just assumed are closets, so I might as well take stock of my new home. Maybe it's below the fridge, or below the bed, or below a big pile of broomstick skirts—or brooms—in her closet.

I start by opening all the kitchen cabinets, and I'm surprised at how normal everything is, outside of the tea selection, which is truly disturbing.

"Oh my God, did you rob a British grandmother? How many teas do you have?" I ask, holding up a box of Sleepytime tea—one of dozens of such boxes.

"As many as I wanted," she snaps. "You know, it's very rude to go through a person's belongings."

"First of all, you're technically not a person. Secondly, everything in here is legally mine. And third, did you think I would move in and not use your cabinets? You need to make the mental leap, Meemaw."

"I'm not a Meemaw, goddammit!" she squawks. "If you won't call me Grammy, just call me Maggie, for Pete's sake." She sighs. "This isn't easy. Dying, being a bird, watching someone take over my life. I'm glad you're here, honey, I am, but it's hard."

"Then help me! Give me the information I need to thrive here. If I had your grimoire, I could do magic. If I knew why people didn't like you, I could get them to like *me*. You're setting me up for failure. You told me I was a witch, showed me one simple spell, and then zipped your sharp little beak."

"It's for your own good, I promise."

I give an exaggerated shrug. "Then I guess I'll go back to ransacking."

I open every drawer and cabinet in the kitchen but don't find anything that looks like a grimoire. Maggie watches me silently, seething. I open a closet and find cleaning products and boxes and cans of food. There's a stick vacuum and a broom, but not a cool, witchy broom. It doesn't even smell like cinnamon. I hold it up.

"Is this a witch thing? Can I ride it and fly around?"

She snorts. "A green plastic broom? No. Why would you want to ride a broom, anyway?"

Finally, we're on the same page. "Right? Like, wouldn't it feel like the wedgie you get from a bad thong? If you sat sidesaddle, you'd hurt your back. And in the olden days, with wooden brooms? Splinters for days."

I move on to the bedroom.

"There's nothing hidden in there," Maggie shouts from the cage with the kind of nervous edge that suggests there is definitely something hidden here.

"Cool, then I guess I won't find anything."

I start with her tall dresser and am unfortunately brought face to face with my grandmother's undergarments. I swiftly close that one and attempt to erase it from my memory. In each drawer that does not contain underwear, I sift through the neatly folded shirts and pajamas, hunting for the telltale shape of a book. I don't find it, which forces me to again confront the top drawer.

"Let's go ahead and take care of this now," I murmur. I head to the kitchen for a garbage bag and fill it with handfuls of sturdy grandma-style, over-the-shoulder boulder holders and actual granny panties. Finally the drawer is empty, even if I didn't find the grimoire.

"What are you doing in there?" Maggie shouts.

"Throwing away your unmentionables. Which absolutely cannot be donated," I add before she can argue.

While I'm in here, I realize I might as well arrange the room the way I'd like it. I think the bed would go better against the other wall, and I'd like to feel like I accomplished something. I move the chair and mirror to the side and am surprised to see that there's no dust.

"Maggie?" I call. "If you've been dead for weeks and no one has been here, why isn't there any dust?"

After a long pause, she says, "Because there's a spell to repel dust, of course."

"Will you teach it to me?"

"You don't need it. It's already been cast. Do you see any dust?"

I already know she's hiding things from me, but I'm beginning to see the shape of it. Her grimoire is the key to casting spells, and she doesn't want me to know where it is.

Which is why I'm going to keep looking.

I grab a corner of the big brass bed and tug it across the floor. The cozy rag rug on the floor shifts, and I see a bumpy white line.

When I pull the rug away completely, I find a strange design on the bare wood boards. A star within a circle, surrounded by squiggles and dots, a strange language that reminds me of tarot cards.

The pentagram—or pentacle—or whatever—is painted on the old wood. I drag a finger over the rough texture, and call, "Meemaw, have you been summoning demons?"

"Of course not, you goose! There's no such thing as dark magic or demons." A pause. "So I'm guessing you moved the rug."

I head into the kitchen and open the door to the cage. "Explain."

She immediately hops out and flaps her wings. "It's a casting circle. It concentrates your power. It's a totally normal thing. Just put the rug back over it before Hunter gets here."

"But he's a witch, too, right? So why—"

"Witches don't talk about witch things outside of families and very close relationships. It's considered rude."

"So how am I ever supposed to learn anything?"

There's a knock on the door.

I briefly ponder the casting circle before covering it with the rug, dragging the bed back to where it was, and heading for the door.

I know Maggie is keeping something from me. I know Joyce Blakely and several of the other witch families hated her.

But what I don't know yet is whether she deserved that hate.

Maybe Maggie is the bad guy . . . or maybe she was protecting Arcadia Falls from something even worse.

22

I open the door right as Hunter is turning to leave.

"Got somewhere else to be?" I ask playfully.

He frowns in the least flirty way possible. "No, I just don't like to be kept waiting. My schedule stays busy." His jaw is tight, and he won't quite meet my eyes.

Something has definitely changed since last night.

"Then I won't keep you. Come on in." I stand back, holding the door open.

Hunter cocks his head but doesn't enter. "Upstairs? I thought we were talking about the store today."

"Yeah, I guess I was hoping to cut open the door in the apartment first so I wouldn't have to go around the building constantly. Like you said, the alley doesn't always feel safe."

He nods and enters, nearly stepping on my grandmother as he makes a beeline to the smooth walls of the kitchen corner. He raps his knuckles along the wall, *thunk-thunk-THUNK*. The last *thunk* sounds obviously hollow.

"Empty space," he says. "That's the door. I can cut it now, but it'll be rough and ugly. I can get supplies to finish it out tomorrow."

"If you wouldn't mind, I'd like to be able to move between the two spaces without passing by the Raccoon Disco Dumpster."

Hunter considers me. "You and Maggie are very different women."

I stare at the cockatoo watching nervously from her perch on the back of a kitchen chair. "Yeah, it's looking that way. But I never met her, so I wouldn't know."

I want him to see that whatever grudge his family holds against Maggie—

It's got nothing to do with me.

Especially if that's why he's suddenly being so frosty.

Hunter hurries out to his truck and returns with an electric saw that looks like something used to carve particularly thick-skinned Thanksgiving turkeys. After a few minutes of knocking and buzzing, there's a hole in the wall and a rough rectangle of drywall on the floor.

"Pretty sure the actual door is in the storage room," Hunter says, inspecting his work. "I can get that set up soon, too. The downstairs door locks from inside the stairwell, so if you're worried about safety tonight, you're covered."

The newly reopened doorway yawns dark and cavernous in the cheery kitchen. There's a light switch, so I flick it and find lots of dust on the stairs heading down into the store; I guess Maggie's spell ends at the wall. Of course, I now know that when I reach the landing and the stairs change direction, I will find a pile of old blankets and pillows at the bottom, but cleaning that up won't take long.

"Any work you need done up here?" Hunter asks, looking around. "I see you took down the blinds."

"One good yank is all it took, but I can handle window treatments. Everything else is in order."

Hunter heads for the newly cut door. Maggie bustles after him, but I snatch her up and swiftly slip her into the cage.

"Don't you dare—"

"Good girl," I tell her soothingly. "Wouldn't want you to get hurt while we're working."

I'm sure I'll pay for this later, if being yelled at by a telepathic parrot can be considered payment, but I want to talk to Hunter without a Regency-era chaperone squawking insults and anxieties in the background. As long as she's a bird, this is the equivalent of keeping a toddler in a playpen so they won't accidentally blow up the house.

Hunter leads the way downstairs, and even though it's a perfectly normal, if narrow, stairwell with enough light to see, it still feels like we're descending into some sort of mummy tomb. He turns on the landing first, and as I follow, I hear him moving the blankets aside to make room for me. Once the door to the store is open, the stairwell seems a much friendlier place.

I don't feel at home down here yet the way I do in the apartment, but I know where the lights are now, so I turn everything on. Those long fluorescent tubes will have to go, and soon. Their buzzing gnaws at my brain like a mosquito. The space feels emptier without Abraham, but the scent of boiled peanuts lingers.

Hunter leans against the counter, which is just a wooden box with some shelves on the back. His general uniform seems to be some sort of plaid shirt over a white undershirt, well-fitting jeans, and work boots. His hair is dry today with waves, shiny enough to suggest he takes nice care of it.

"So do you know what you want?" he asks. "I have some ideas, but it's your space and your money."

I take a deep breath and look around. I feel like a little kid making a Christmas list, about to ask for a pony.

"For one thing, better lighting. Probably a funky chandelier or two in front, some basic cans farther back. Whatever will look classy but be cost-efficient and easy to change out."

"There are actually a couple of old chandeliers in the antiques market," he points out. "Lots of inventory just sitting around that you might like, if you're into funky—and it all belonged to Maggie, once the store owner went to jail and stopped paying rent." He looks down and chuckles. "But—full disclosure—I'm pretty sure the dumpster raccoons have a nest in there, so we might need riot gear."

"Okay, so it comes with free pets. If you have time and a rabies vaccination, maybe we can check that out later?"

He nods. "If you like."

Well, don't sound so excited about it, I want to say.

I walk to the front door and turn to regard the store, imagining the possibilities. In my mind, the sad particle-board shelves fall away, their dull movie boxes banished to a corner. Hunter joins me, notebook ready.

"In an ideal world," I say slowly, like I'm casting a spell, "I'd have bookshelves all around the walls. Built-ins."

"And a rolling ladder, right? Like in *Beauty and the Beast*."

I blush. "I said an ideal world, but yeah. A girl can hope, right?"

"The great thing about being a carpenter is that I can turn those hopes into reality. Especially if you already have all the materials in the hardware store." He talks as he sketches. "Pretty lucky that you inherited two more stores that have most of the supplies you need, right?"

I find the little dictionary in my pocket, rub my finger over the snap. "Yeah, very lucky." Then I refocus on the task at hand. "So that's a side wall and a back wall of built-ins. Then I need freestanding shelves at regular intervals. Starting about here"—I move to a place that would offer lots of room for displays up front—"and ending here." I walk along the line the shelves would take, following the run of the wooden boards to where the shelves would end, toward the back wall. "So that's probably four sets of shelves."

"You know, if I built them on casters, you could move them around if you hold events or if you just wanted to change the store up a bit," Hunter says. He runs his measuring tape along the floor. "If they were nailed down, they'd be twelve feet, but if we wanted them to move, we'd do six-foot shelves and put them together. The casters would lock, though, so it's not like the shelves would be drifting around and knocking over customers."

It does not escape me that he said *we*, and I like that. It makes it feel less like I'm a prima donna demanding work and more like we're doing something together, building something new and exciting from the wreckage of Maggie's old life. Like we're dreaming this store into existence. I need to keep him in that mode, the one where we're a team—not the one where I'm the scion of his family's worst enemy.

"That's a great idea! I would love to be able to reconfigure things."

"And where will the movies go? I know the locals depend on this place. The nearest movie theater is twenty miles away, and the population skews older and less tech-friendly." The look he's giving me suggests there's more at risk than just where to put some moldering VHS boxes. This . . . is important to him.

"Of course. I honestly think they could be shelved spine-out like books and just take up a corner. Maybe get some newer releases, too." As I walk the perimeter of the store,

I realize that there's one cheap white particleboard shelf against the wall that's out of alignment with all the others. It has only four VHS boxes on it, so I grab it by both sides and try to rock it away from the wall. "What's this?"

Hunter walks over and considers it. Biceps straining in his flannel, he picks up the whole damn shelf and pulls it away from the wall to reveal . . .

A door.

My curiosity skyrockets, and I immediately go for the doorknob. It's locked, but I have Maggie's big key ring, so I pick the keys that look most likely to fit the brass knob and go through them one by one.

"Did you know about this?" I ask.

"Nope. I did a little work for Maggie, but she was very private and never seemed to want to do any upgrades. She had me stop by to replace the light tubes when they blew out, and she had me drywall over that door upstairs, but otherwise, I got the feeling she didn't want me in here."

Finally the key turns, and I open the door like a kid hunting for Narnia. It's an office—and it looks like it hasn't been used in a century. The dust spell is definitely not in force here. There's a heavy old wooden desk, several file cabinets, a dozen cardboard boxes, and a rolling chair that's got to be from the sixties.

And sitting in that rolling chair, coated in dust, is a human skeleton.

23

I don't scream, but I do make an unflattering *eep* noise and jump backward, directly into Hunter's chest. He immediately moves so that we're not touching.

"Is that what I think it is?" I ask.

"It's a skeleton," he confirms. "But I don't think it's real. If it were real, wouldn't there be junk on it? Or at least a puddle of gunk underneath it? Or a stain on the carpet?"

I take another step back.

We're not touching, but . . . we're almost touching. His body is warm and solid behind me.

I do not mind it.

And he's right.

If there had been a dead body in here, it would be gooey. Chunky. Probably clothed, as most people don't die naked in the office.

Probably not sitting in a rolling chair, coated in dust.

With one leg crossed over the other like we're about to have a performance review.

And there would definitely be a smell.

I step forward and prod the skull. It's obviously plastic.

"... Why?" is all I can say, looking at the mess.

"Your grandmother was a weird bird."

Still is, I almost say. *More than you know.*

I will be asking her about this later.

"I guess she thought it was a funny joke, or maybe it was left over from Halloween?"

"Your grandmother never struck me as a prankster, but I would imagine that if she had a place hidden and locked up to keep folks out, she'd enjoy the thought of scaring anyone rude enough to sneak in."

Hunter joins me in the small room and reaches for the skeleton's arm bones. From up close, it's pretty clear that this particular skeleton is on a smaller scale than an average human, like a Hobbit skeleton, and I can see the plastic seams. I can't believe I spent a solid minute thinking I'd just discovered another corpse. I guess when you learn that magic is real, you assume lots of other improbable things are real, too.

The door slams with such suddenness and ferocity that I jump.

We both stare at it, and Hunter walks over and opens it.

"Well, that was weird," I say. I suddenly want to get out of this room, but I don't want to seem like I'm freaked out by a slamming door.

Hunter looks toward the back of the store, his brow drawn adorably down. "Must be some sort of suction caused by the AC. At least the lock isn't sticky."

He's right. The AC is definitely on. I'm freezing. And I want to know more about this office. I am desperate to get out of it and go upstairs and ask my grandmother a million questions, but being alone with Hunter is a lot more fun, even if the vibes are off and he's currently not my biggest fan. Plus, he's here to give me an estimate, not sit around while I interrogate a cockatoo about a Hobbit skeleton.

"Shouldn't be too hard to get all this cleaned out," Hunter says, still standing in the door. "The dumpster is right out the back, and since there are only two active businesses on the alley, there's always plenty of room for trash. I can bring a dolly, and we can get it done in an afternoon. And I've got a door stopper in the truck. Don't want you startled again."

I'm excited to get things cleaned out until I remember that I have to pay this guy. "So do you have an hourly rate, or do you give me an estimate? I don't want to waste your time rolling boxes of dusty paper out to the dumpster when you could be building the bookshelves of my dreams."

A raised eyebrow. I didn't know he could do that.

"You dream about bookshelves?"

"You don't?"

That gets a chuckle.

"I already built the bookshelves I wanted for my own house," he says. "But I see your point." He turns back to the store and looks around, hands on his hips as he considers it. "My typical rate is forty an hour plus materials, but I do thirty for downtown businesses not owned by the Coves. Now, that rate is for incidentals, for your honey-do list. For the shelving project, let me measure out and give you a solid estimate. That way, you don't see me taking the time to drink some water and think you're paying for it."

"I wouldn't—"

A wry grin. "Plenty of people do." He pulls out his notebook again, takes it over to the counter, and draws as he talks. "So I'm going to show you a sketch of what I would do, given my druthers—what I think would be the most useful to you and the most beautiful. Then you can tell me if you love it, if you hate it, if you envision something else. Once we have a design we both like, I'll take the measurements and price out the wood." He looks up, meets my eyes. "This is going to be the most expensive part of this endeavor. Wood ain't cheap."

I nod. "Which is ironic, as it grows on trees."

He pins his lips to avoid smiling; he can't seem to stay annoyed with me for very long, as much as he'd like to. "But there are options. There are cheaper ways to start, just to get the doors open, and then, if you're successful, I can make improvements. Basically, you can have your Beast library, but it might be on layaway."

As he sketches, I look around the store before decisively tromping over to the front window and plucking up the cardboard displays one by one, tossing them in a pile on the ground.

"That *Terminator* stand-up is probably worth five hundred dollars," Hunter calls.

I stare down at Arnold's sun-faded face. "Are you kidding me?"

"Nope. Before you throw them out, check eBay. That's all I'm saying. If you can find buyers for all those displays, that money can go toward wood for the bookshelves."

I was going to drop all this junk in the dumpster, but if he's right, this pile of supposed tinder could be worth a few thousand dollars. The vintage posters on the walls, maybe, too. But I have a sense of energy right this moment. I want to start making visible changes here. I head back to the office and open the first box I find. It's nothing but empty VHS boxes, and now I'm wondering if they have any resell value. I'd love any way to squeeze more money out of this monstrosity, but I'm also desperate to clear out the musty space and make it my own.

The next box is receipts, and then tax documents and forms from the late eighties. I methodically go through all the boxes looking for anything that can get tossed without too much thought, but . . . everything requires thought. Hunter isn't around when I head up the newly cleared stairwell to my apartment. The pile of crusty blankets is gone. He must've moved them while I was in the office. It's so gentlemanly and thoughtful I could just melt into the floor. I add Febreze to the grocery list on my phone.

Upstairs, Maggie, still in the cage, tugs at the door with her beak, angrily growling, "You'd better let me out of here, so help me God!"

I unlatch the cage door, and she flutters through it and shakes herself. "I have the strangest urge to sing 'How Do You Solve a Problem Like Maria,'" she says. "Or just scream a lot. But then I also want to consult my lawyer."

"If you're done pondering the intricacies of bird law, I've got questions."

"Seems to be all you have," she grumbles.

"First of all: Why is there a skeleton in the office, and why is the office hidden?"

She cackles. "Found that, did you? Just a fun little surprise for whoever went poking around in my things. Left over from the Halloween scarecrow contest one year. That's my personal space, and I don't want anyone in there."

"Thanks for the heart attack. But it's my space now, and I plan to use it."

"Can't you just leave well enough alone? Is nothing sacred?"

"Sacred? No. Not the janky little office in a defunct video store and not Bilbo Bagbones. Next question: Is there anything in the office that needs to be kept, or can I toss it all in the dumpster?"

Maggie paces around the kitchen, chirping her frustration. "It should all be kept and left just like it is. It's none of your damn business!"

"It is absolutely my business." She's got me mad now, too. "Because you're either a ghost or a parrot, and neither of those things is a taxpaying entity."

"It's all important. Tina McGowan does all my accounting and taxes—"

I snort. "If Tina McGowan still hasn't done your taxes from 1988, she's a pretty bad accountant."

"She's an amazing accountant! I set up that business in 1987, and every year I pay Tina to just do whatever needs doing. The store made good money back in the day. And then it faded out and became more like a bad habit I couldn't quit. People seemed to need it. Uncle Abraham needed it. And as I got older, I got tired."

"But it's still legally a business and all that?"

Maggie fluffs herself. "Yeah, but I don't know much about the paperwork, honestly. Don't trust Joyce, but Tina and Colonel will take care of you."

I huff a sigh. All this sounds great, but the paperwork will have to wait. I want to get to work *now*, want to feel the satisfaction of a clean room and knowing I've made my mark. I want to Marie Kondo some shit, get that *Hoarders* satisfaction of scraping up the flat cats and putting down new rugs.

"So can I toss the junk that's in the office or not? I want that room cleaned out. Today."

Maggie looks up at me, cocking her head side to side. "It's done just fine locked up for ten years, but if you've got that much of a bug up your behind, put the boxes in the storage room. You know, the one between the video store and the hardware store? All that's your space. Why worry about something today if you can worry about it later?"

Yeah, that feels about right.

"Now just take me downstairs—"

I bark a laugh. "No way. I can't think with you shouting in my head." I go to scoop her up—

"Not the cage!"

She sounds so desperate that I stop.

"You don't know what it's like, being an animal."

She's panting, so I stop and stroke her head, trying to calm her.

"I'm helpless. No hands. No phone. No one else can hear me. If something happened to you, I would die in that box. At least if I'm loose, I have a chance."

She's acting Very Cockatoo, bobbing her head and generally acting skittish. She really is frightened. And I don't actually want to give my grandmother trauma. "Fair enough. But don't come downstairs. It's going to get dangerous once Hunter starts work. And don't do that thing where you freak out and splatter against the window."

"I will if I see you making eyes at Hunter Blakely."

"Did you ever consider that maybe he's very different from his grandmother? Kinda like how I'm very different from you?"

"Hmph. Doesn't matter. A Blakely is a Blakely."

"I'm beginning to see why people don't like you, GamGam."

I'm out the door before she can protest. It's a quick jaunt down the stairs to the store, and I'm already pleased with my decision to reintroduce the secret stairwell.

Hunter looks up as soon as I'm visible. "Want to see what I've got?"

His notebook is laid out on the counter, open to show a neat drawing of the store's layout. I'm honestly impressed with his work.

"So if we take out all the shelves you have now, we can move the counter over here, right by the restroom door, which would make it harder to steal from and also leave these two main walls free for shelves. We'd do built-ins around this entire corner, with the rolling shelves in the middle and display tables in front. That's what they usually do in bookstores, right?"

"Right. But maybe we could have some smaller shelves up here for cards and stickers? Gotta have gifties. And what's this?"

I point to a rectangle to the side of the front door.

"Display area. Like the department stores in New York."

I can feel my eyes getting hot and my throat closing up a little. "It's perfect," I say, my voice breaking a little. "Like you read my mind. But . . . how much is it going to cost?"

He points to neat figures, lines of numbers that seem to indicate lengths of wood. "I'll go home, price things out, and let you know. I think we can look at two options. Really nice built-ins that would last a lifetime, or basically just boards on brackets with bookends. It would look more modern but cost considerably less without baseboards and trim. You'll have to wait on that rolling ladder, though."

"And what's this circle?" I point to the drawing.

"The chandelier you wanted. We can go look in the antiques market, see if anything in there works for you. And I want to check the hardware store. Do you have those keys?"

I fetch the massive key ring out of my bag. "Hopefully. I also want to see the storage room. I'm not sure yet what can be tossed from the office, so I'm going to store the questionable boxes in there."

He nods, all business. "Let's go take a look. The storage room should be unlocked; I put Abraham's things in there in case you wanted to go through them. Just don't get your hopes up about the antiques—I don't know what the raccoons have gotten into."

"Well, for me, raccoons are a plus."

I reach for the handle, but the storage room door won't budge.

"That's weird," Hunter says. "It was fine ten minutes ago."

Undeterred, I start trying different keys. Unfortunately, Maggie only marked the key to the apartment, so it's just another guessing game. As I go through them, I am aware of Hunter standing beside me, watching me. His body is taut, on edge. I wonder if he is as aware of my physicality as I am of his. It makes me feel shy, to think he might be. It's been so long since I've been attracted to someone new that everything about it feels like fumbling in the dark. And yet he is keeping an annoying distance between us because of—

I don't even know! Something my grandmother did before I'd ever met her.

"Aha!"

I feel the key turn in the lock, but when I push the door, it doesn't budge.

"That's *really* weird."

I turn the key back and forth a few times. It's the only one that's worked at all, but the door absolutely refuses to move.

"Can I try?"

I leave the key in the knob and step back to let Hunter take a turn. He shoves the door, nudges it with a hip, pulls it toward him, all the usual ways of getting a sticky door to behave, but the door might as well be cemented in place.

He pulls out the key and stares at it; it's not unusual

in any way and looks just as old and boring as one might expect. "It shouldn't be doing that."

"Well, I've got like a hundred more keys. Let's go open the hardware store and see what's going on from the other side."

He hands me the key ring, which I appreciate. I can well imagine what Billy Wayne would do in this situation, which is take charge and establish dominance. But Hunter seems to understand that I feel ownership of this place. It's nice.

We open the back emergency door, and there's the alley. Hunter props it wide with a concrete block sitting conveniently outside. "Abraham used to open it up for a cross breeze when things got too warm," he explains.

The hardware store's back door is maybe ten feet away, and we go through every key in the ring without finding a single one that works.

"Is there another key ring?" Hunter asks. "Because this door is pretty heavy." He grabs the handle, and . . . the door pulls open.

We share a look.

"It shouldn't be doing that, right?" I ask.

He silently shakes his head and holds a finger to his lips as he gently, gently closes the door. His truck is right across the alley from us, so he jogs over there and returns with a metal baseball bat. I move out of the way to let him go first, and he gives me a nod of acknowledgment before opening the door again, reaching inside, and flicking on a light switch, all the while holding the bat like a club in his right hand.

Maybe I should be scared and staying out of the way, but it's my hardware store, damn it, and I want to see it. The door has a stopper, so I kick it into place and follow Hunter inside.

There's not as much light as there is in the video store,

Books and Bewitchment

as the shop is full of tall shelving and peg racks, one big open room. The front windows are papered over with yellowed newspapers and plywood, so it almost feels like something from a zombie movie, the light warm and blurry and glittering with dancing motes of dust. This back part is filled with pallets of wood and large boxes that haven't been unloaded. Everything looks untouched but older. Wire racks and hangers dangle from the cobwebbed pegboards, and somewhere, up ahead, a small creature has a heart attack and scurries away.

Hunter follows an aisle to the front of the store, and the little homey touches make me feel nostalgic for a place I never saw in action. There's a calendar on the wall, forever stuck in 2008, plus plastic toys and a TAKE A PENNY, LEAVE A PENNY dish bereft of coins. Some of the inventory has been cleaned out, but plenty of random things have been left behind, their plastic bags now brittle and stained yellow.

Satisfied that there's nothing weird going on in the store, Hunter points to the door that will lead to the storage room. I nod, slide a dusty hammer off the pegboard, and follow him.

My senses are all on alert, my ears straining to hear anything that shouldn't be expected in a building that's supposedly been untouched for almost twenty years. The wood boards squeak and complain with every step. I smell sawdust, regular dust, oil, and age.

As Hunter reaches for the storage room door, I tighten my fingers on my hammer, hoping I don't have to use it, because it's just now occurring to me how very close you have to be to someone to hit them with a hammer, and how very gross that would feel when and if it happened. The door swings open with a long, whining creak. It's pitch-black inside, and Hunter fumbles for the light switch.

Isla Jewell

The lights flicker on, and my heart just about falls out of my butt.

I guess now I know why the storage room door won't open from the video store.

Someone has piled dozens of chairs in front of it, an impossible and strangely intricate barricade of white folding chairs that reaches all the way to the ceiling like some sort of modern art. I look to Hunter, who appears just as confused as I am.

"What is this?" I ask.

And then one of the chairs detaches and flies directly at me.

24

Before I can react, Hunter steps in front of me and swings his bat. It connects with the flimsy white chair, which explodes with a meaty crunch. The chunks fall to the ground and go still. All I can do is stand there and boggle.

There is no one else here.

Chairs should not just be throwing themselves across the room.

They should not be stacked like a house of cards.

Another chair wiggles free of the clot, and Hunter grabs my arm, but gently. Still I don't move. I can't stop staring at the chair, watching it shimmy like a giant is playing Chair Jenga and doesn't want to topple the tower. Hunter tugs at me, but I am frozen in place.

"We've got to get out of here," he murmurs quietly, as if trying not to spook a wild animal.

When I don't respond, he picks me up with one arm, tucks me against his body, and carries me toward the door.

As I am pulled out of danger, I notice a cascade of strange little details. The storage room runs the full length of the building and is maybe twenty feet wide. Other than the Chair Jenga, there are boxes, a mop bucket, a broken fan, the kind of detritus anyone might expect. As I watch, the mop bucket's wheels twitch, and then it zooms directly toward us. The mop flies out of it and skitters along behind it like an uptight snake.

And that's when I remember I have feet and start moving on my own.

We all but dive into the hardware store, and Hunter slams the door and puts his back against it. The loud clatter that makes him jump suggests the mop bucket is apoplectic at the fact that it hasn't murdered us.

"What is happening?" I ask.

Hunter's face looks like a very sexy thunderstorm, dark and determined with a promise of violence. "What's happening is that you have a poltergeist."

I pause, waiting for more.

Waiting for him to burst out laughing at how ridiculous that sounds.

Then I remember . . .

Magic.

"A poltergeist," I say carefully, doubtfully.

He nods, slow and certain. "In a town this old, they happen. We've got plenty of ghosts, and sometimes they get mad and act out. Like toddlers."

"Poltergeists," I say to myself. "Ghosts. Yes. This is all very normal and fine."

He sighs heavily as the mop bucket jumps against the door like a nervous dog. "We don't have to beat around the bush. I'm a Blakely, you're a Kirkwood. You have to know about magic."

The fact that he doesn't choke tells us both everything we need to know, and yet this one word changes everything between us.

How much does he really know?

About me, about Maggie, about my family? And this thing Maggie did, whatever made people angry—was it magical?

It had to be.

That would explain why only some of the locals hold a grudge—

Because the rest of them don't know about magic and thus have no idea what really happened.

Just like me. I still don't know, either.

"Magic," I say cautiously, grateful for the calm in my trachea. "Okay, so poltergeists are real, and there's one in the storage room, and it likes chairs and hates me. How do we get rid of it?"

"We could use a spell." His face suggests that I know something I do not. Sarcastic, annoyed, pinched.

"Okay, let's use a spell. Do you have one?"

His hands are on his hips now, the dust dancing around him as the mop bucket, or something, plays the door like a tambourine. "No, Rhea, I don't have a spell. I was hoping you did. Because your grandmother stole them all."

My jaw drops.

I don't know how to respond to that.

"Maggie stole all the spells? From whom? How? Why?"

His lips twist as he regards me with more curiosity than anger now. "You really don't know?"

"I really don't. I felt the temperature in the room drop when Joyce revealed that I was a Kirkwood. A few people went colder than a Wendy's Frosty, including you. But I had no idea why, and no way to find out. I don't know anyone, remember? I'm brand-new."

He nods, clearly fighting with himself. "You never met Maggie? How does someone never meet their grandmother?"

Oh, I am not a good liar. I choose my words carefully. "I knew she existed, but I absolutely never had any contact with her before she died. She—"

Won't tell me what she did wrong, I almost say.

"Well, she just sounds like a mess. Mama hated her enough to run away, and now you're saying she stole spells. What does that even mean? Did she burgle you?"

Hunter looks around the hardware store. This conversation, and my conversational partner, is so interesting that I kinda forgot about the mop bucket—ghost—poltergeist—on the other side of the storage room door. It has not forgotten about me. It sounds like a horse trying to kick down a barn door.

"Let's go upstairs," he says. "It's best to give them space before they get too dangerous."

He heads for the door to the alley. Before I join him, I put a hand to the storage room door and say, overly loud, "Ghost, I hear you. Whatever's got you riled up, I'm sorry." The pounding on the door stops for one moment, like it's thinking, and then resumes twice as loud.

Not forgiven, then.

Once we're out in the alley, I realize that upstairs is exactly the wrong place to go. If Hunter is finally going to tell me the truth about Maggie, I don't need her trying to chew his nose off while screaming at me telepathically. I don't know if she knows the true bite force of that beak, but I do, and giving Hunter stitches is not going to make him thaw toward me.

"Let's go back to the video store if you don't mind. Maybe I can start carrying out the office trash while we talk. My mama always said talking's easier when your hands are busy, especially when you aren't going to like what you hear."

Hunter nods and we head for the video store. The mop bucket doesn't seem to mind us being over here at least, and it doesn't sound like the Angry Chair Barricade is budging. From this side of the door, all is silent, and I could almost believe that there's nothing wrong and I have not been targeted by a supernatural entity. I motion for him to talk, and we each pick up a box of old receipts and head for the dumpster.

"Well, I guess I should ask: How much do you know about magic? Were you raised with it?" he asks.

I don't want to lie to him, but it's sure hard to talk around the Maggie of it all. "Nope. But I had to put Maggie's ashes in the falls, and then Doris bit me, and suddenly I could hear her in my head. And Shelby and Tina have helped me a little, but not much. I'm floundering."

He nods. "Okay, so doing magic without a grimoire is almost impossible. The spells are extremely exact. This isn't like cooking or even baking, where too little baking powder leaves you with a cake that's ugly and flat but still edible. You have to get the ingredients just right. The ratio of blood to water is very specific, and the incantation—well, it's hard enough even when you're staring at the phonetic pronunciation. So grimoires are precious, and spells are passed down among families and carefully guarded. Nobody really talks about magic outside of their family. It's not forbidden, but the old folks act like it is."

We toss our boxes over the side of the dumpster and head back inside. "So did Maggie actually steal everyone's grimoires?"

A soft snort. "Kind of. Listen, you know how sometimes old Southern women get really protective about their famous recipes? When they 'share' them"—he makes air quotes—"they leave out a few ingredients so that no one else can ever make Mildred's Chocolate Dump Cake exactly the way she does."

I nod. I definitely know the truth of that.

"Your grandmother cast a spell that did that to all the grimoires. She brought all the witches together for a potluck, and even though magic is generally a private family thing, she said she wanted everyone to join together to cast a spell of prosperity over Arcadia Falls after the big storm. Everybody trusted her. Why wouldn't they? Up until then, she was beloved around here."

I sneeze as I open the next box, which is full of old-timey credit card slips. I wonder if he knows that Maggie's knack was influence. "How long ago was this?"

Hunter leans against the doorjamb. "A few years before I was born, as my grandmother tells it."

He picks up the box I offer him, and I pick up a box of ancient lollipops, wondering if the raccoons are going to go into diabetic comas when they find tonight's bounty. "So probably . . . not too long after my mom ran away."

"Maybe? I don't know the timeline. Anyway, since the storm destroyed your family's old place, everyone got together at my grandmother's farm and did this big ritual they were told would make Arcadia Falls prosperous and safe, protected from further storms. But instead, their grimoires became useless. Ingredients missing, words smudged. They didn't notice for a couple of days. Knacks still helped with little things, and if someone had memorized a spell perfectly, it would still work, but the rest of the magic was out of reach. Maggie said it was an accident, but everyone knew that was a lie."

We toss the boxes in the dumpster and return to the office for more.

"Folks started moving away, once they realized what had

happened. My grandmother, aunt, and mother confronted Maggie, but she swore that she hadn't done it on purpose and that there was no counterspell. Nothing she could do."

"Did Maggie still have magic?" I ask as I quickly close a box over a rat skeleton nestled among stained VHS boxes that no one will want on eBay now.

Hunter steps back and holds up his arms. "Look at this place. A dying video store. Do you feel any magic here? The ritual must've hit her grimoire, too."

I'm pretty sure Maggie did still have her magic, but I don't mention that to Hunter because I don't want to break the spell, pun intended. Hunter isn't being cold. He's not looking at me with age-old anger and conflicted emotions. He's giving me exactly the information I've been trying to pry out of my grandmother. He's finally telling me the secret she's been so desperate to conceal.

"So why didn't the families—I don't know—threaten her? Or contact other witches somewhere else in the world to see if there's a counterspell?"

Hunter peeks at the rat skeleton and gallantly picks up the box, while I pick up one with rolls of old-timey register paper for our next dumpster run.

"Witches are very private," he tells me. "Grimoires are never shared. When parents teach a spell to their children, they write it down only when the child can perform it perfectly. It's not like there's a secret map of witches or a subreddit where we can exchange tips and tricks. Just like it won't be spoken to non-witches, magic won't appear on the internet; someone must've cast a very powerful spell to prevent any kind of communication. That's why what Maggie did was especially terrible. Because sharing magic, doing a spell all together, was a new idea that she convinced everyone to try, and then she used it to take advantage of them."

Our boxes tumble into the dumpster in a puff of dust.

"But why? Why would she steal the spells? Did she not like magic?"

She does like magic. I know this. Even in cockatoo form, she taught me a spell. She was still using an anti-dust spell, and I bet her grimoire is somewhere around here and more functional than Hunter believes. But I just don't understand the why of it all.

Below.

Her grimoire is hidden *below.*

Damn it, magical dictionary, below what?

"Like I said, she claimed innocence, according to my grandmother. She was stubborn as a mule. I saw her at Chamber, I gave her estimates when she asked, I wished her good morning if I passed her on the street. But most of the witches in the area acted like she didn't exist. Since the magic was stolen, Diana was the only person who really knew her, and Diana died with her."

Back in the office, I realize that the rest of the boxes are in the "maybe" category. I wish I could put them in the storage room that is currently being used as a poltergeist playground, but I'm not trying that door again.

"There's got to be some way to get the magic back," I say, thinking out loud. "Has anyone tried—I don't know—the library? Oh, it's closed. Or what about inventing a new spell?"

At that, Hunter stiffens and looks away. "Let's get these boxes out to the dumpster," he says, not meeting my eye.

"But—"

"You don't need any of this shit, Rhea. Nobody does."

He picks up a box and hurries out the door. I don't have much choice but to pick up my own box and join him. I try my question one more time, but he pins his lips and shakes his head. It feels like a warning. If I thought he was stormy before, this feels like when the sky goes green and sick before a tornado. The anger seems to motivate him, though. Soon all the boxes are gone, leaving the office . . .

Well, not clean. Definitely not that. But far less cluttered.

When we're done, all that's left are a heavy desk, three chairs, a credenza, and a file cabinet, plus approximately seven pounds of dust. It's stuffy and lightless, but I'm starting to have hope that I can make this place my own—once I find a vacuum and give the room a glow up.

At some point in our work, Hunter tied his flannel around his waist, revealing his tattoos. One arm swirls with koi, while the other has a mountain sunset. I want to ask him about his art, but now is not the time. He feels like a barely restrained tempest.

"I'll be by tomorrow at nine," he says. With a brief nod, he's gone.

Frustrated by the way he suddenly shut down, I pace around the video store, looking for something to do. An old man is standing at the glass door, hand cupped over his eyes as he stares inside. I head back into the office, pull a piece of brittle printer paper from an extremely old dot matrix printer, find a marker, and write CLOSED FOR RENOVATIONS. The tape I find in a drawer is probably from the eighties, but it works well enough to stick the sign on the front door.

The old man squints as he reads it and shouts, "What about the peanuts?"

I pull the sign down and write: (WE WILL STILL HAVE BOILED P-NUTS). He smiles and gives me a thumbs-up.

So I guess I need to add "learn how to make boiled peanuts" to my massive to-do list.

I make sure all the doors are locked and head upstairs. Maggie is waiting for me in the kitchen, right inside the newly revealed doorway.

"How'd it go?" she asks.

"We found a poltergeist in the storage area and cleaned out the office, and I spent the entire time trying to figure out what Hunter is thinking. I swear, it's like one moment we're on the same page of the same book, and then I say the wrong thing and he's in a whole other genre. I don't smell, do I?"

"I'm the wrong person to ask." She clicks her beak. "Because I'm not a person anymore, and my sense of smell is all messed up. Like I told you, Blakelys are trouble. You're better off keeping your distance."

I gaze down at her, this pretty pink-and-gray bird, and head to the fridge. I need to get her some fruit and vegetables, but I haven't made it to the store yet. Instead, I take out one of her Diet Cokes and sit at the table with what's left of Shelby's box of goodies. I take out a cookie and consider it.

"So I know why everybody is mad at you," I say before taking a bite.

"You don't know anything." Her eyes focus on the cookie.

"Why'd you mess up everyone's grimoires?" I tear off a piece of cookie and hold it up.

Maggie snorts and turns away. "You can't bribe me with Shelby's cookies."

"Oh, so you're enjoying your pellets?"

"Not particularly, but I still have self-control. I'm not a fool."

My gambit failed, I put down the cookie. "Okay, here's what I don't get. Maggie Kirkwood is dead to everyone but me. You're a bird. You poop in a cage. You should be beyond shame. Why do you care more about the past than you do about me? Why won't you just tell me the truth? Why'd you do it? Why'd you steal the magic?"

After a long, charged, silent moment, she turns around to face me.

"I'll tell you if you'll go to the store and buy me some fruit. You're right. I'm sick of pellets."

I stand up immediately. "It's that simple? A few berries is all it takes?"

"Well, like you said, if I eat too much cookie, I die a painful death, and I don't think I get to come back after that. So, yes, I'd like to taste some actual food."

"You got it, Grandma Cockatoo!" I grab my bag and keys and head for the door. This is too easy. I needed to go to the store anyway. There's not much toilet paper left, and we need Band-Aids in case she gets mad again, and, well, this is my home now. I'm ready to start making it feel like mine.

But the second I open that door, Maggie is ready. She launches herself outside and off the balcony, fluttering to the ground.

"Oh, you ornery idiot!" I bark. "Something's going to kill you!"

"It's got to catch me first!"

I guess she's been practicing with her wings, as she's getting more air than I'd prefer. Although one of her wings is clipped, preventing her from bursting up into the clouds, she can get some good distance as is, fluttering for ten feet or so, and she's already got the lead on me, as I have to go down the stairs. She's hopscotching down the alley, much faster than I thought she could go.

Damn a stubborn human brain in a bird's body!

I trip on the stairs and almost fall, barely catching myself on the railing.

As my feet hit the concrete, she flutters over a tall wooden fence and disappears.

25

I walk around for half an hour trying to find my grandmother, but she has truly flown the coop. Thank goodness the alley is relatively private, as I mutter quite a few expletives trying to find some way past that wooden fence, which I'm assuming is Hunter's handiwork. It's annoyingly sturdy, so I finally have to give up and leave my stupid grandmother to suffer the consequences of her own actions. As angry as I am, I don't want her to get captured by an alley cat or trapped in a thorn bush. Even if she deserves it. A little.

I'd love to go to the grocery store, but I want to stay close to downtown in case she turns up or flies back home to peck miserably at my door and beg for forgiveness. I walk down the street for a slice of pizza and settle in for a sulky soak in Maggie's tub—no. *My* tub. Normally, I'd be totally absorbed in a book, but instead I'm catastrophizing about the many horrible things that can happen to a rogue parrot. I give up on reading and work on the grocery list on my phone.

Books and Bewitchment

It takes forever to fall asleep, and then my phone alarm is going off, and then I'm staring up into the trees as I walk down the street, hunting for a flash of pink, and then I'm accepting a hazelnut latte from Nathan and making my biscuit, and then I hear Hunter's footsteps on the stairs outside my apartment.

As usual, he looks annoyed. "I thought we were working on the video store."

"Oh. Sorry." I look at my phone. "You're ten minutes early."

His face might as well be made of granite. "My grandmother taught me that on time is late."

I gaze wistfully at the empty bird cage. "I have two messy sisters and a pet parrot, and I used to get pulled over at least once a week by my ex-boyfriend's grudge-holding brother, so I haven't developed that kind of discipline. I won't be late on you again, though."

He tries not to smile, his jaw gone tight; I'm getting accustomed to this look on him. "I have some prices on the wood for your shelves, if you'd like to get down to business." He gestures to the open doorway, and we head downstairs. I turn on the lights, and he lays out his notebook. It's covered in tidy rows of numbers. I didn't realize before now that good handwriting is apparently one of my turn-ons.

"Here's the cost of the wood." He points at a number that frightens me. "This lumberyard is usually cheapest, but I can call around if you want to try something else. Now, that's for the cheapest option, as bare-bones as I can build your shelves. Here's the Full Beast Library option." The number he points to gives me heart palpitations, and my dream bookshelves have never been so far away.

The dictionary sits heavily in my pocket, but it can't offer the help I need. It's odd—I don't actually know the shape and parameters of my magic yet, but I feel a pull to use it.

Like it *wants* to be used, an itch waiting to be scratched.

"Let's try something." I poke around under the cabinet until I find what I'm looking for.

A phone book.

I know they don't even make them in more cosmopolitan parts of the world nowadays, but I had a hunch that Arcadia Falls was still a Yellow Pages kind of place. I drop the heavy old book on the cabinet, noting that it's six years old.

Hunter can no longer contain his amusement. "Of all the ways people respond to high quotes, I have never seen someone whip out a phone book like that. You're not going to hit me with it, are you? I'm just the messenger here."

I close my eyes, flip through the pages until I'm compelled to stop, and put my finger down. When I open my eyes, I'm not surprised to see that I've selected a lumberyard. "Is this place still open?"

Hunter squints at the tiny words. "I don't know. I've never heard of them. But if you think it's worth a quote, I'll give them a call." He eyes me with curiosity. "What's your knack?"

"Books. They help me figure things out. They kind of did, even before"—I gesture wildly—"all this."

He chuckles as he dials his phone. "No wonder you dream of shelves. I've never heard of that one before, but let's see how it plays out."

Someone answers, and Hunter's voice goes into Classic Good Ol' Boy mode as he asks questions that make no sense to me. Needing something to keep me busy as he writes new rows of sexy figures in his notebook, I go through the shelves under the counter, hunting for things I can throw away. There's a stack of mail dating back so far that they've changed the stamps. I think about going through every envelope, but why? If it's important, they'll resend it. Out with the old, in with the new and clean.

"Okay, thanks. Yeah, please hold it for me. I'll be by this afternoon."

The look on Hunter's face as he hangs up is one I haven't yet seen.

Pure delight.

"That's one helpful goddamn knack you've got there," he says.

My smile reflects his. "Oh?"

"Well, it turns out someone ordered a very specific load of wood, gave a down payment, and decided not to pick it up. They need it out of the yard, so it's crazy cheap. Look at this number."

I do.

It is a very, very good number.

I am not scared of this number.

"So this will make my Beast Bookshelves?"

He nods, grinning. "And I have to admit, it's going to be a lot more fun for me. How about this for the total?"

He writes down another number.

"That's not enough," I say.

"I told you, the wood is cheap. And you already have all the fittings I need in the hardware store. Provided you don't want a bunch of really intricate molding—"

"I don't."

"Then it's honestly a pretty simple job. Although there won't be enough for the center rolling shelves . . ." He trails off, and his eyes fly wide. His teeth flash in a feral grin. "Hot damn! It just occurred to me—the antiques market already has them!"

"Has what?"

Hunter pumps his fist. "Grab your big key ring and come on. I can't believe I didn't think of this before."

Once I've got the keys, we exit out the front door and head to the antiques market. There's plywood completely covering the glass storefront, so I have no idea what's in there, but now I'm starting to get excited. It takes me several tries to find the right key, and then I'm smacked in the face with the smell of old mothballs and something animalistic and musky. In the darkness behind the plywood, everything is a monstrous jumble, and something furtively skitters in the back corner.

"Raccoons," Hunter says. "I think. Not a bear, though."

"As long as it's not turkeys."

The air is dead and still, and a thick layer of dust shifts under my shoes. When Hunter finds the switch, the old fluorescents flicker to life, and the penny pincher in me wonders how much I'm paying to keep the electricity running here. Once I can see, however, my tune changes. This place is . . .

The most glorious trash heap I've ever seen.

The space is bigger than the video store. There are tables and chairs, armoires, saddles, chandeliers, glassware galore, some weird mannequins, a dress form, a carousel horse, several moth-eaten deer heads, and one very perky taxidermy squirrel staring down at me from the cobwebbed walls—and that's just what I can see on this side of several dividers.

"How?" I mumble.

"The little old lady who rented the building used it as a front for selling the meth her grandsons made in her barn. They all went to jail and quit paying. Maggie was too old and tired to do much by then, so she had me put the plywood over the glass and just let it sit. But look!" The space is chopped up into booths, and he leads me around a corner. There are two rolling shelves, double-sided, filled with old books. "So that's two shelves. I think there's another one somewhere...."

"There's got to be two hundred books here," I say, carefully and lovingly picking up a yellowed Terry Brooks paperback.

"We're not done."

My heart lifting, I keep walking, seeing more possibilities with every step. I find lamps, tables, lots of smaller shelves, and a wooden bench painted with flowers that would be great for a children's corner.

Hunter points at a huge chandelier. Most of the bulbs on it are glowing, and the area around it smells of singed moth. "How about that one?"

"It's perfect," I say, followed by a sneeze. "Or it will be, after a good dusting." I point to a smaller chandelier. "That one, too. It just needs a coat of spray paint. I can pretty much decorate the entire bookstore this way, can't I?"

Hunter chuckles and leads me to another freestanding shelf crammed with books. "Are you sure your knack isn't luck?"

"If it was, would you chop off my foot and make a keychain out of it?"

"Too big for my pocket."

"Well, if it should come to that, please take the left. I'm a righty."

"That would be quite the—"

He stops himself and looks away. I know this look now. He's caught himself flirting with me when he's actually angry with me for some reason that has nothing to do with me.

And I'm sick of it.

"What is this?" I ask. "You're running hot and cold. Did I do something wrong?"

He squats and fiddles with the casters on a rolling bookshelf, avoiding my eyes. "No."

"Then why do I feel like we're dancing around something? Sometimes you flirt with me, and then you go quiet. Your jaw gets all tight. I'm worried you're going to break a filling."

At that, he looks up, his jaw tighter than ever. "I'm allowed to be quiet."

"Sure you are. But you're not allowed to be secretly angry at me. We just met. You seem really nice. I know *I'm* nice. We even made tentative plans to go out. But then you found out I'm a Kirkwood—which is not my choice!—and now you're mad. What's the real problem?"

He doesn't answer; he's back at it with that caster. I squat down next to him and flick the switch that gets it moving. "There. Now you can't pretend you don't know how casters work. Stop avoiding me. Tell me what's going on. Either we like each other, and something is standing between us, or maybe we just have to figure out how to get along while you fix my building. But I prefer honesty to shuffling around a big ol' invisible elephant in the room."

Hunter stands and takes a few steps away. He's taut as a hunting dog, and I can tell he'd love nothing more than to hightail it out of here and away from me and my questions. But I'm also guessing he's not a coward, and he knows that only cowards run.

"Is it because I'm a Kirkwood?" I ask again.

"Yes!" he practically shouts before reining himself back in. He paces back and forth, runs his hands through his hair. "I didn't know the full story about what happened between our families, so I asked my grandmother. She and my grandfather raised me—because my mother is dead." He looks up, his eyes piercing my heart with their anguish. "My mother died trying to fix your grandmother's spell. She died because she tried to return the magic."

The air goes still and cold. I glance up toward the apartment as if Maggie is still there and I can go ask her if this is true. But she's gone, and even if she weren't, she hasn't exactly been forthcoming on topics related to her past crimes.

I'm beginning to see why.

"Your mom died because of my grandmother?"

He nods slowly. "That's the story. Apparently, after the potluck and the destroyed grimoires, people were still trying to remember the spells they knew best. If they worked, they wrote them down in new grimoires, but those spells were few and far between. There was a lot of distrust, and nobody shared those spells, sometimes even within families. All that experimentation caused some damage. We were in our first drought in ages, and the littlest part of a spell going wrong could start a fire or an explosion. That's what happened to my mom. She was good at coming up with spells, which is a very rare talent, and she was trying to restore her grimoire. Something went wrong, and she died. Burned down the barn, too. I was maybe two, and my sister, Edie, was still a baby. I—" His voice breaks. "I remember the flames, but I don't even remember my mom. And she would still be here if not for Maggie."

The unfairness of it rises in my throat, but I swallow it down. Defensiveness isn't going to get me anywhere right now. This man has lost his mother. That's a tragedy I understand all too well.

I move toward him slowly, put a hand on his arm. "I'm so sorry, Hunter." When he doesn't pull away, I edge closer, like I'm approaching a wild dog. I slide my arms around his sides and pull him close into a hug. "I'm so sorry. No one deserves that."

At first, he holds himself stiffly, but then I feel him soften, almost melt into me. His head falls, his cheek against my hair.

"You're very small," he says, his voice soft and husky.

"'And though she be but little, she is fierce,'" I whisper back.

"Do you have a book quote or pun for everything?"

"Pretty much. It makes me good at party games."

We go quiet, and I rub his back like I used to do for Cait and Jemma when they were young and crying. In between sisters and parrots I have gotten very good at calming down upset creatures.

"It's not your fault." Hunter's voice is soft. "I know it's not your fault. You didn't even know Maggie. I've been so mad for so long, but my grandma didn't tell me the full story about my mom's death until recently. I knew Maggie was the enemy and that I was supposed to stay away from you, but I didn't know the full extent of it. I guess with Maggie gone, my anger transferred to you." He pulls away a little and looks down at me. His arms are around me now. "But you didn't do anything wrong. And you're impossible to hate. You've got this . . . unsinkable optimism." He shakes his head and dashes at his eyes with one hand. "I was not expecting to have emotions today."

"Me neither. I'm all out of ice cream and tissues."

He chuckles, and I feel it pleasantly against my chest.

"Anything else you want to get out? Old grudges? New complaints? Are you actually going to text me now?"

"Just one thing."

I look up.

He looks down.

I've only known this man for a few days, but there's just something so comfortable about him, so competent and kind. And his lips are just so kissable. They curl up at the corners. He leans in.

And then—

26

There's a knock on the door.

We break apart, though not guiltily. Personally, I'm annoyed and disappointed, and I'd like to give the person on the other side of the door a kick in the shins. Hunter doesn't look too pleased, either, and it's nice to see that thunder aimed at someone besides me.

"Hasn't this place been closed forever?" I ask.

Hunter looks longingly at my lips. "At least two years."

"Well, you'd think the massive sheets of plywood and large CLOSED sign would set the tone."

He rubs his stubble, which I almost got to feel rasping against my cheek. "Probably not a shopper. Must be one of the Chamber people."

"Well, I hate them."

I head for the door and pull back the newspaper plastered over the glass.

To my even greater annoyance, it's Joyce Blakely, Hunter's grandmother.

And she has seen me.

She gives me a tight smile—so like her grandson!—and points at the lock.

I have no choice but to open the door or further cement her hatred of me.

"Hi, Joyce," I say, grateful at least that I don't look like I've just been kissed into oblivion, because I'm pretty sure that's where things were headed next, at least if I had anything to do with it. "Can I help you?"

"I just wanted to stop by and see how things are going," Joyce says. She steps inside, politely shoving past me and looking around. "Poor girl. Left with such a mess. Maggie just sort of let things go, didn't she?"

Time to show Hunter that unsinkable optimism. "Maybe so, but I have faith I can get things back in order."

She walks around the antiques market, one hand on her purse, as if she's shopping—for something specific. "Have you explored the other properties much? The video store's been open forever, but the hardware store's been closed almost two decades, and this place has been shut up for two years, and the theater's been out of commission for, oh, at least ten years. And who knows what's upstairs."

I do not tell Joyce about the storage room she failed to mention, including the poltergeist with a passion for percussion.

"One property at a time," I say. "If you're going to eat an elephant, might as well start with a little nibble and not go for the whole trunk."

She beams at me like I've surprised her. "I swear, when I look at you, it's like seeing Miranda again. She was a bright girl, which I know because she and Maggie never did get along. I guess if you're here, your mama made a life somewhere else?"

Books and Bewitchment

I don't know how I feel about Joyce. She has a right to be mad at my grandmother—more so than most. The spell theft occurred at her farm, and her daughter died trying to fix it. And I know it's easy to transfer that anger to me, even if I don't deserve it. But as things stand, I like her grandson. And I'm realizing I want her to like me.

"Yes, ma'am, she did. She met my dad at college, and they were very happy together. I have two sisters back in Alabama. My mama hated Maggie, and she made me promise to never come to Arcadia Falls, but . . ." I look around. This shop, this downtown, this whole town, is magical. "I figured with both my mama and Maggie gone, it would be okay. So I hope I can make it work."

"Oh no. We lost Miranda, too? You poor thing." Joyce pulls me into a hug much like the one I gave Hunter recently, and I'm enveloped in soft grandma, wrapped in the scent of baking and baby powder and hairspray. This is what it should be like to hug a grandma. All I get is claws and beak, these days, and that's when I actually know where Maggie is. This is almost healing.

"Joyce?" I ask her hair.

"Yes, honey?"

I pull away and rub my eyes a little. "Can I be frank? There's something I need to know."

She cocks her head, confused. "Of course. I'll help if I can."

"I need to know more about how and why my grandmother messed with the spells. Why she took the magic."

Joyce dusts some cobwebs off my shoulder. "Your generation. So bold. We would've danced around it for hours back in my day, offering each other sweet tea and cookies and smiling through lying teeth." She sighs heavily. "Can I ask why you're asking?"

I take a deep breath. "Because I want to find a way to restore it."

She looks to Hunter and then back at me. "Oh, honey, I don't think that's a good idea." There's a note of panic in her voice. "You shouldn't . . . No. It's not worth it."

I steady myself. I know this is a very sensitive topic for the Blakelys, but . . .

I don't want to be on the outside anymore.

My family is from here. I belong here just as much as they do.

My grandmother betrayed them, and I want to set things right.

I want to give the magic back to Arcadia Falls.

"I don't want to make up a spell," I say, looking between grandmother and grandson. "I want to find Maggie's grimoire. I think it's still functional." A deep breath. "I think she kept her magic when she stole yours. There might be something in that book that could help."

Joyce puts a hand to her chest as emotions flit across her face. Fear, worry, hope, more fear. She closes her eyes as if seeking an answer within and then grabs my hands in both of hers. "Rhea, Hunter told me you were different, and he must be right. What you want to do—I appreciate it. It's the right thing. So I'm going to tell you something I haven't told anyone." She looks around the antiques market again. "I've been wondering for years if Maggie kept her magic. There were little things, little things that could be explained away, but . . . that's why I've been so mad at her. She used me, she lied to me, and then she denied my family advantages I thought she'd kept for herself. I think we'd learn a lot if we could find that grimoire. But it could be anywhere. It could be somewhere in here, or it could be at the junkyard in her crushed car. With Maggie gone, we just don't know."

I almost tell Joyce and Hunter that Maggie isn't truly gone, that for the moment she's simply missing. And yet something holds me back. We've just reached a new level of trust, but it's dangerous for other people to know that Maggie is still around. In her bird body, she's relatively helpless. I'm furious with her, and I know she's been lying to me, but I can't stand the thought of someone capturing her and threatening her to get what they want. I don't think Joyce would do that, but then nobody thought Maggie would do what she did, either.

Hunter's been giving us space, but now he steps forward. "We can look for it as we renovate the video store. Rhea, you can check around her apartment. Use your knack to find it, maybe? And you haven't even been in the other two apartments or the theater. All sorts of places where a book could be hidden."

Joyce releases my hands and nods. "I'll talk to some of the other folks. Quietly, of course. See if maybe they know of a place she might have hidden something. Rhea, have you met Tina McGowan? She's Diana's daughter, and there's a possibility that some of Maggie's things might've ended up with her, since she and Diana were together when they passed."

I have to laugh. "So it could be anywhere in three apartments, a video store, a theater, a hardware store, Tina McGowan's house, or the junkyard. Lordy, my grandmother was a piece of work."

"That book's been missing for decades. It'll keep a while longer," Joyce says. "But it's nice to know that you want to help. I miss the days when witches helped each other." She walks over to Hunter for a hug. "I won't keep you young people any longer. I'll be at Marla's for lunch. You know where to find me." She stops at the door and looks back. "You're a sweet girl, Rhea. Maggie didn't deserve you."

And then she's gone and I'm locking the door behind

her before the usual downtown shoppers try to rush in despite the plywood. Part of me hopes Hunter will corner me against the door and try for another kiss, but I guess nothing kills the mood like an interrupting grandmother. He's keeping his distance. Of course, he's also inspecting the bookshelves we came here to find, so I can't really complain about that. He plucks a paperback off the shelf and flips through it, making my heart flip, too.

"Can I keep this one?" he asks. "Bongo ate my copy of *The Shining* when he was a puppy."

I can't help grinning. Nothing makes a guy as cute as holding a book he loves. "*Cujo* would've been a more appropriate choice, but I guess puppies don't know any better. Please, take anything you like."

"Even the set of armor?"

I look back into the corner, where I see a life-size suit of armor. "Am I that scary?"

He laughs. "No, but some of my clients remind me of fire-breathing dragons."

I wait, my back against the door. I'll come over here again, once we're further along, and see what else I need, but for now . . .

"So what's the next step for the video store?" I ask. "I don't mean to seem impatient, but . . ."

"Closed businesses aren't good for business. I get it." He meets me at the door. "If we get the walls stripped and painted and the carpet torn up, I can get started as soon as I have the wood. The shelves will only take me a couple of days. Oh, and I'll need a card to pay the lumberyard. Sound good?"

Maybe it's not a kiss, but it's just as sweet. "Yes, building my bookstore sounds good."

It's a relief to be back in the open air of the video store. I give him Maggie's debit card for the wood, and we both

Books and Bewitchment

breathe a sigh of relief when it goes through and the lumber is officially mine. As he moves around the room, I watch him, wondering if he feels the same constant pull toward me that I do toward him. He has to; I catch him glancing at me, then looking down and smiling. There's something sweet and shy about him, something so different from the swagger of my only other boyfriend, back in Alabama.

"I feel so useless," I say. "How can I help?"

"Maybe you could pack up all the movies and take down the posters? And if you want the walls a different color, we'll need to clean and paint them before I start the build. Three gallons of interior latex eggshell should do it. I know that's short notice for big design decisions, but I feel like you want this done fast."

"Tidy up and buy paint," I repeat. "Sounds like a fun afternoon."

"Then I'm off to patch a hole in Marla's wall. When I asked her how a cast-iron skillet ended up in the drywall, she told me she didn't pay me to ask questions."

"Well, just don't give her a reason to throw a skillet at your head, and you should be fine."

Hunter leaves, and then I'm alone in the store.

My store.

All I have to do is select a paint color.

And maybe that should intimidate me, but instead, I feel empowered. Hopeful. Excited. I have never had such freedom in my entire life, and I don't have to ask for anyone's opinion before I go buy paint. I know exactly what I want, and it feels amazing.

I fetch a couple of empty boxes from the hardware store and start carefully packing up the movies by genre. Perhaps it didn't seem like there were a lot of movies earlier, but now that I'm responsible for putting away every single box, there are way, way too many movies. As I pull them from their shelves, I get accustomed to their weight and pay attention to see if anything is perhaps a little too heavy—as heavy as a grimoire. None are.

It takes me two hours before I've got all the boxes and cardboard stand-ups stashed by the alley door and I'm dragging a chair around to carefully unhook thirty-year-old tape from the peeling walls. I roll up each poster and rubber band it, then put them all in a box. When I've got more time, I'll learn how to use eBay and see if Hunter is right about the street value of elderly Terminators and middle-aged Ninja Turtles. Once that's accomplished and I'm quite certain Hunter won't be disappointed with me in the morning, I double-check that all the doors are locked and look at the stuffy little office with new eyes.

Maggie doesn't want me in here. She doesn't want anybody in here.

But why?

I go through the desk and the filing cabinets but don't find anything resembling a grimoire. I feel around the walls, wondering if there's a secret door, but there's nothing. The ground is solid carpet, old and flat, a less-faded version of the eighties neon designs outside.

I take the dictionary out of my pocket.

"What is Maggie hiding in here?"

I flip through the pages, and my finger lands on one word: *Secret.*

That is extremely unhelpful.

And yet . . .

There's something here. I can feel it, like a TV left on in the background or the electric thrill of lightning in the air. It's here, but I can't find it.

And I don't know what it is.

27

It's easy for me to select the right paint color for my bookstore. I want this place to be welcoming and full of sunlight, so I choose the brightest white they have, a perfect backdrop for whatever motif I eventually decide on. Once all the paint is mixed up—because white apparently includes tons of other colors, somehow—I do a full shop at Walmart for the first time since arriving in Arcadia Falls. I have a long list: cleaning products, home décor, food, and a ball of yarn and a crochet hook so I have something to do at Craft Night. Seeing the total for that full shopping cart makes me wince, but I'm basically starting from nothing, and Mr. Buckley will reimburse me for the parrot supplies. The curtains and curtain rods are a onetime thing, and life isn't worth living without a coffee maker.

Back at the apartment, I carry up all my groceries and dump them on the kitchen counter. My heart sinks again when I remember the bird cage is empty. I want Maggie to be here, fussing at me, and failing that, regular Doris. For three years, I've come home to a perky pink-and-gray cockatoo who's always happy to see me no matter what. I've had someone to share a salad with at dinner, someone to snuggle with on the couch while I read. She especially liked medical dramas on TV for some reason and would whistle whenever a handsome doctor appeared on the screen. Yes, even for Hannibal. Doris was a weird bird, and maybe Maggie is weirder, but I want that parrot safe and back in my life. I put up the groceries, including the fruit and veg I got in case she returns. If I think about her too much, I'm going to start crying.

Now that I'm anxious and full of energy and eager to avoid staring at an empty cage, I decide it's time to unload the Explorer. The big plastic tubs full of my life were easy to carry the ten feet from my old front door to my car, but lugging them up the stairs is a lot harder. I begin to wonder why people have things and if perhaps I should just upend everything into the dumpster and give the raccoons the coziest night of their lives. But no. It's just time on task, so I put in earbuds and a thriller audiobook and keep hauling until the car is empty. I finish around dusk and fix myself a girl dinner of cheeses, pepperoni, crackers, and fruit. I've added my own Diet Coke to Maggie's supply, and now the cans are intermingled. I don't know if the one I drank with dinner was hers or mine.

"Idiot bird," I mutter. I open the door and shout, "Hey, Grandma Cockatoo! If you're out there, holler!" I'm met by silence. "If you're in trouble, scream!" Still more silence. "Please come back! Let's talk it out! I have bananas!"

"You *are* bananas! Quit making all that noise!" someone shouts from somewhere nearby, and I sheepishly close the door.

If she's out there, she doesn't want to be found. Not that it stops me from looking. I head down the stairs and walk the streets of Arcadia Falls jiggling a can of pistachios and singing "My Favorite Things" from *The Sound of Music,* but I don't see even a single flash of pink. At least I don't see any pink smears in the road. This time, when I hear the turkey bell go off, I dart into the nearest store, which happens to be Barb's boutique, and watch from behind the glass as the gobblers strut down the street like they own it. There is not a pink bird among them, so at least I can rest easier knowing Maggie hasn't turned the lovesick turkeys into her personal Brute Squad.

Eventually, I head back to the apartment sadly parrotless.

Although Hunter has been attending to other commitments, he does stop by in the afternoon with an unexpected offering: a tub of books.

"You said you might want to sell used books," he tells me.

I squat down and sniff, inhaling that very particular and unique odor of old paperbacks. "Seems like it might be of value to the community. I was thinking more cheap romance, but the folks who appreciate VHS might like fifty-cent Heinlein." I pick up an ancient Danielle Steel mass market—*The Gift.* "Where'd you get these? You didn't rob a library for me, did you?"

"I would never. They might take away my card." He frowns. "If the library ever opens again, that is. But no. I was trapping a possum in Marla's attic and saw that she had a lot of stuff piled up. Tons of books. She's always complaining that she'd love to clean out her attic, so I asked if I could cart the books away for a good cause. She said to tell you to find them good homes. There are three more boxes in my truck if you want them."

I try to imagine a world in which I do not want four

boxes of free books. "Oh, I want them. And I promise to find them good homes."

The book feels so cozy in my hands; I miss these old, blocky paperbacks that still fit in a purse. I open it to check the inside cover, and a shiver ripples over my entire body.

"Arcadia Falls Gift Swap 1994. Merry Christmas, Marla! Love, Miranda and Maggie."

It's my mom's handwriting.

My mom—

She held this book in her hands, wrote in it, even drew a goofy little wreath with a loopy bow.

Out of all the books in Marla's attic, this is the one that I picked up.

Magic is just so . . . magical, isn't it?

My eyes fill up with tears as I show him the open book.

"Whoa." His face softens as he looks back at me. "I had no idea."

"Me neither." I gently put the book on top of the pile and stand, overwhelmed with emotion. "Thank you." When I throw myself into his arms, he catches me.

"Rhea, are you . . . crying?"

He rubs circles on my back as I give a small sniffle. He knows that my mom's writing is in this book, but he doesn't know that Maggie has this same Danielle Steel book on her shelf, probably purchased at the same time, and that she is still missing. And he doesn't know that a man has never done anything this thoughtful for me in my entire life and that I'm slightly overwhelmed.

"Crying? No. It's just the dust."

He swipes a thumb sweetly over my cheek, wiping away the tears. "Sounds like somebody needs a vacuum. And some Benadryl."

That gets me laughing again, and then he deposits all the

used books downstairs and heads off to his next job. I pick up the Danielle Steel and hold it to my chest as I watch him pull away. Bongo barks once from the back of the truck and smiles at me, his tongue lolling. I realize that Hunter has been parking in my other sacred parking spot. And I like it.

The next morning, I watch from the apartment as Hunter and Cisco arrive with a hefty load of wood. They unload it and set up a circular saw in the alley, then Cisco heads on out. Hunter begins his work, and I am fascinated by how serious and immersed he is. His face shines with the joy and intensity of a conductor mid-symphony, and the cut wood stacks up at an inhuman speed. Any hope I had of flirting is gone; the man is in love with his art. I'm aware that just staring at him in awe is not a feasible way to spend the day, so I focus on fixing up the apartment—and looking for Maggie's grimoire.

Once I've got my audiobook blasting, the work goes smoothly. I begin with the absolute wreck of Maggie's closet. It's so stuffed with her Stevie Nicks wardrobe that I haven't yet unpacked my own things; it's just easier to live out of suitcases. Now I'm faced with the grim task of picking up each dress and broomstick skirt and shawl, folding it reverently, and placing it on the bed to give to charity. I miss Maggie, but it's better if I do this part alone. Things are already Landslide-y enough.

I am momentarily faced with the strangest feeling, the sort of sensation for which there is probably an exceedingly long word in German with lots of umlauts: As I fold a slinky satin-and-lace dress, I realize that my grandmother, now a cockatoo, was once a vibrant young woman with a love life of her own, which is how, I assume, my mother came to be.

This feeling is not one I wish to explore any further. I shove the dress deeper into the stack, which keeps falling over because all the fabrics are slippery, and focus on the work at hand. I end up with three full bags of clothes and one of shoes and not one single grimoire to be found. There are no secret doors, no loose floorboards, no telltale rectangular lump in a cozy cardigan. Still, it's enormously satisfying, staring at the empty closet, and it feels even better once I have all my own clothes neatly hanging on Maggie's nice wooden hangers and my shoes lined up on her shelf on the floor.

While I'm in closet mode, I head to the door in the living room that I assumed was a coat closet, but when I open it up, I do not find a bunch of swoopy hippie coats and shawls to donate.

Before me sits the most glorious apothecary chest I've ever seen.

Almost like a card catalog on steroids.

"Oh, lordy," I whisper to myself. "Is this a built-in?" I run my fingertips over the glossy wood, fully aware that a phalanx of people on the Old House Lovers Facebook page I follow would freak out if they could see this treasure.

The drawers range in size from small to large and have hand-painted labels. Flowers and herbs in one section, feathers and claws in another, stones and crystals in yet another. I can't help myself. I have to pull open every drawer, run my fingers through rivers of petals and shifting sands of spices and bins of tiny seeds that I am fairly certain are not actually the eyes of newts.

If this is what being a witch is, I am very much onboard.

Why didn't Maggie show me this?

If she wanted me to stay, this cabinet would've helped turn the tide.

I have never been so enamored of an object in my entire life except an actual card catalog I once saw for sale at an antiques shop back in Cumberville. Even in our Podunk town it was so expensive I couldn't afford a single drawer.

As I methodically peruse the magical offerings on hand, I keep an eye out for that grimoire. There could be no more fitting resting place for a book of magic spells than a cabinet of magic ingredients. But even when I get to the bigger cubbies, I don't find a single book. Folded fabric, perfectly clean animal skulls, and even some ornamental (I hope) knives, but no book. I press places on the interior walls, hoping to find a secret door or drawer, but the cabinet does not relent.

It goes all the way down to the floor, so I fetch a stool and look on top, but all I find there are jugs of water like the one in the bathroom.

Water from the falls, I suppose.

"Knock, knock," Hunter calls, and I gently close the closet door and hurry into the kitchen to find him standing on the stairs, just outside the raggedly cut doorway. I'm pretty sure he couldn't see from here to there, but I don't mention the cabinet. I'm not even sure why. It feels special and personal, and at least for a while, I want to keep it all to myself, treasure it like a kid with a shiny new doll who doesn't want to share.

"What's up?"

He points at the cage. "Where's Doris?"

And it's funny, but I feel guilty for admitting what happened.

Like I'm her owner instead of her granddaughter.

It's not that I'm negligent; she has a fully functional human brain and has chosen to put herself in grave danger all by herself and against my wishes. But I can't tell him that.

"I don't know. She flew out the door the other night. I couldn't catch her. I've been calling for her, but . . ." I trail off.

And admit the truth.

Or some of it.

"I'm really worried about her."

He steps closer to the cage and looks inside like she might inexplicably be hiding within. "I don't know much about birds, but we could make some signs? You certainly have plenty of window space. This is the kind of town where handmade signs still work. And you should use the Chamber group text. Obviously, if anyone notices a pink pigeon flying around, they're going to tell somebody. And we could call the police and animal control. I'm so sorry." He pauses. "I know we're not supposed to talk about it, but is she your familiar?"

He's still standing on the stairs like a vampire waiting for an invitation. I motion him up, but I'm not sure how to answer.

Is she my familiar?

Yes.

And also very much no.

For a moment, I ignore the question and fill in the silence with hospitality.

"You've got to be thirsty. Want some water? Or a Diet Coke? I was going to make some sweet tea, but I haven't yet. It's on my to-do list. My very long to-do list."

"Water's fine." He sits on a kitchen stool in that way handsome men have, one leg on the ground and one hooked on the footrest. I put ice in a glass and run water from the tap, and as he drinks, I enjoy watching his Adam's apple bob like some hunk from a soda commercial.

"I don't know much about witchy things, but I can hear her talking in my mind," I finally say, opting for a little bit more of the truth. "If that's what a familiar is."

He cocks his head. "That's weird, then, that she would fly away. Familiars are generally bonded to you. They want to be near you."

I stare at the door and think about how she bounced

and splatted across the parking lot, desperate to escape my many questions. "I guess she didn't like what I had to say. We were arguing. But she doesn't know how to survive on her own. She—"

I stop myself before I can say too much.

"Did you have a construction question for me, or were you just craving sink water?"

He rattles the water in the glass and tips it toward me in cheers. "I know it's a little early, but I've got to head out. I'm finished up for the day, and I thought you might like to see the wood that will become your bookshelves."

I jump up and down a little. "'Yes! A thousand times yes!'"

He stands, grinning. "If you're quoting a Jane Austen movie, does that mean you're happy?"

"I'm talking to a man who knows I'm quoting a Jane Austen movie. I'm ecstatic!"

He leads me downstairs, and holy crap. It doesn't look like a bookstore yet, but it doesn't look like a video store. Wood is stacked in a honey-gold pile, the ground drifting with shavings. He's marked off the walls and started pulling up the carpet.

"How are you this fast?" I ask.

"When most people ask that, I can't tell them it's magic or I'd cough up a furball. But I can actually tell you. It's magic. My knack. You know how they say 'Measure twice, cut once'? I only have to measure once, and I'm always correct. It makes building a breeze."

I run my fingers over a wood board. "What kind of wood is it?"

"Cherry. Normally, I'd consider it a luxury wood, but you found a fantastic deal." He steps closer, so close I can see the sawdust caught in his hair. "Books and building. We make a good team."

As much as I love the wood, the man who shaped it is more captivating by far. I turn to face him. We're standing close now. And for once, he doesn't seem conflicted at all. I look up, and he looks down. I reach to pull a little curl of wood shaving from behind his ear and toss it on the floor.

"Hey, isn't the guy supposed to do that?" he asks playfully.

"Well, there's nothing in my hair."

"I'll be the judge of that. Actually, I think there might be something in your ear. . . ." He reaches up and strokes my ear, sending shivers down my spine, before holding up a quarter.

"You do close-up magic?" I ask.

"What can I say? I was a weird kid."

"Me too. I wonder if it's a witch thing or an us thing?"

"Probably both." He turns the quarter back and forth. "Now, most magicians would say you need to clean behind your ears, but I think that might kill the vibe."

"What vibe is that?"

He reaches toward me—

And past me, running his finger along a board leaning against the wall. "The scent of freshly cut cherry, the crunch of sawdust under your feet, the silvery gleam of dropped nails in the golden-hour sun. It's romantic."

I nod and look at his lips. "A tale as old as time. Beauty and the *Birch*."

He chuckles. "How do you do that?"

"Make terrible wood puns? I just *teak* about it real hard."

His eyes crinkle up, and he reaches for my face, his calloused fingers gentle on my jaw. "It's adorable."

And then his lips are on mine, soft and tender, and I close my eyes and melt.

But he pulls away.

His hands are still on my face, and I open my eyes to find him hovering there.

"Is this okay?" he asks.

"I will literally die if you stop," I tell him, because it's true.

He kisses me again, still gentle but firm, determined. He approaches kissing me like he does building: thorough and serious. I have never been kissed this way before. Like it matters. Like every touch is a stamp that will live forever on my skin. I let him lead, wait for him to change his angle and run his tongue across the seal of my lips, gently begging entry. My middle goes hot and dizzy, every atom of my body fizzing and alive. My hands trace up his sides, the soft warmth of his ribs through his flannel, the hard ridge of his spine. I am filled with fire and longing, and I almost want to step away from the pile of wood so it won't catch and burn.

His phone beeps in his pocket, and he reluctantly pulls away.

"Did I mention I'm leaving because I need to give someone an estimate? I don't think I've ever been late for that before, but I mind it a lot less than I thought I *wood*."

I laugh and lick my lips. "Still with the wood puns."

"Well, when you've *got wood* . . ." He looks down briefly and smiles. "Not complaining. But I do need to go. I'll be back tomorrow morning, if that works?"

"*Fir* sure."

He caresses my face and plants a kiss on my forehead. Right before closing the door, he says, "*Pine* for me."

And then he's gone, the first person to best me when it comes to puns.

I have never minded anything less.

28

As I lock up the video store, I'm absolutely giddy.

Finally, he's not running hot and cold.

Just hot.

Very hot.

Hopefully talking through the magic issues and coming clean with Joyce means there's no more reason for the Blakelys to associate me with Maggie's foul deeds. Maybe I'll get more eye crinkles and fewer tightened jaws, more wood puns and fewer tempests. A girl can dream.

It's almost five, and I have an idea, but I'll need help. And maybe on the way to my destination, I'll catch a flutter of pink amid the changing leaves and get the chance to talk Maggie into coming back home.

The downtown streets are beginning to feel like a place where I belong. Lindy waves as I walk past the restaurant, and Barb stops adjusting a scarf on a mannequin outside her boutique's open door to ask me when my store will have peanuts again.

"When I learn how to make them right!" I tell her.

"Well, hurry up, then," she huffs, like she has a peanut deficiency.

I haven't been to Shelby's bakery before, and I smell it before I see it. It's very cute, with a white-and-silver striped awning and white iron tables out front. The lady at the counter calls for Shelby, who appears in an apron with colorful dye staining her hands.

"I do all the cake decorating," she tells me. "Are you here for a snack or girl talk?"

"Can't it be both?"

She won't take my money for a donut, so I put a five in the tip jar and we sit outside at one of the sunny tables.

"What's up?" she asks. "Is it Hunter?"

Part of him was up when he kissed me earlier, but that's none of her business.

"Hunter's fine," I say, meaning it both ways. "But no. Do you have a printer? My cockatoo flew away, and Hunter said I might have better luck finding her if I put up signs."

Her eyes fly wide in worry. "Oh, honey, no! I'm so sorry! That's got to be so scary for you. I do have a printer, so if you just send me a doc, I'll get a stack ready to go. What's your number?" She pulls out her phone, puts in my number, and sends a text, and my phone pings in response.

> Chamber emergency: Rhea Wolfe's bird got lost. Please report any sightings.

She looks up. "A group text is honestly the quickest way to get anything done in town." Our phones both immediately report several text messages as Chamber members express their concern and Colonel claims he saw a turkey pecking at something pink in the middle of the road today, but it turns out it was just an old sock.

"I wish we still had sp— *Gurk!*" I sputter.

Shelby waves as a pair of tourists exits the bakery. I feel like I'm choking on a live frog. They head up the sidewalk and out of earshot, and my throat is finally empty again.

"I wish we still had spells," I say, much softer this time. "I bet there used to be a finding spell or something."

Shelby looks at me like I've gone insane. "We still have spells. What are you talking about?"

That stops me. "Wait. What? Who still has spells?"

"Um, everyone? As far as I know?"

I am shocked, and the plot has thickened.

"But the Blakelys told me all the magic families had their grimoires ruined back in the nineties and nobody can do spells anymore."

Her mouth snaps shut as she blinks ferociously. "Oh my God, that's crazy! My mom and I still have our grimoires. My grandma did, too. We do spells all the time. I'd heard the magic was dying out, but . . . not like that."

Mentally, I connect the dots and realize that Maggie must've told her best friend, Diana, what she was going to do at her ritual, thus allowing the McGowans to avoid the same predicament as the rest of the witches of Arcadia Falls. I had suspected that Maggie's grimoire was intact somewhere, and now I know that at least three other grimoires remain functional: Shelby's, Tina's, and Diana's.

"How did you not know about this?" I ask. "About what happened to everyone else?"

She shrugs. "Witches are secretive. We never get together or talk about anything, outside the family. The only reason you and I are having this discussion is because you're tacky enough to ask—no, I don't mind, but it *is* tacky!—and because all the women in our families have been best friends for generations. It would just feel wrong not to be there for you with your mom and grandma gone, you know?"

I'm half annoyed and half ashamed, and I don't enjoy either emotion. "I don't mean to be tacky. There's just so much I don't know."

Especially with Maggie avoiding me.

"But I don't have a sp—" Shelby smiles as some teenagers walk by. "That thing that might help you. I haven't heard of that sort of thing before, but it sure would be useful. I lost my keys one day and it turns out I'd baked 'em into a wedding cake. At least it was a bottom tier and not the one they'd put in the freezer to eat on their anniversary." She leans in. "Even a spell can't make me less forgetful. It still rose beautifully."

I shake my head. "It's just bizarre to me. The whole thing. Each family hoarding their books. My grandmother trying to destroy them. Why wouldn't people want to share ways to make their lives better?"

Shelby cocks her head. "I guess so nobody gets too powerful? Or maybe it's like . . . specialization. Like, Edie can sell anything to anybody—that's her knack—but she didn't start another bakery to compete with me, you know? She started a soap and candle shop. We all do different things."

"Well . . ." I'm thinking out loud now, trying to work through my feelings. "It seems to me, as someone new to all this, that the old ways aren't exactly working. The magic is disappearing, the young people are leaving town. One person tried to take control instead of spreading the wealth, and it caused ripples. Wouldn't it be better if people helped each other and shared resources?"

Shelby looks utterly scandalized but also compelled. "Yeah, it doesn't really make sense, does it? The only reason you wouldn't want to share with me is because you want power over me, which would suggest you're not that great a person." She leans in. "So you don't have a grimoire? Or any spells?"

I shake my head, because even if I did one spell, I didn't write it down, and I forgot the details, and Maggie isn't around to remind me. And she didn't even tell me to write it down in the first place!

"Then," Shelby says, "I'll give you a spell for your toaster that ensures your toast is always perfect. How about that?"

Having lived with a terrible toaster for many years, I appreciate the bounty of this gift. "That's really kind. I wish there was something I could do for you in return."

She rubs her hands together. "You just keep those shelves stocked with rom-coms and have a generous used book return policy, and we'll call it even."

I hold out my hand, and we shake. "Deal!"

The cashier appears in the door to ask Shelby something about frosting, and she excuses herself to go fix the latest batch of cupcakes before an absolute baketastrophe can occur. I finish my donut and make a proper purchase at the counter, and Shelby reminds me that I absolutely can't miss Craft Night. When I tell her I bought yarn just so everyone can see what a terrible crocheter I am, she squeals and does a little dance.

My phone pings again, and I look, hoping that maybe someone in the Chamber has found Maggie. But instead it's a number I don't know.

> Rhea, this is Jemma on someone else's phone because either you're dead or you put us on DND again, and if you don't text me back, I will send Officer Jimmy Wayne after you.

Not dead, I text back. Doing really well! But things are getting interesting. I'll FaceTime you in an hour. Promise. Tell Cait.

She texts back a dozen exclamation marks and a skull.

Message received.

"Gotta run. Sister emergency," I tell Shelby.

Back home, I make a salad using Maggie's veggies and put together a LOST BIRD flyer. It's pretty simple—just a picture of Doris, some quick facts, and my name and number—but it's not like she's going to be confused for any other random rose-breasted cockatoo running feral in the north Georgia mountains. I text Shelby for her email and send the flyer over with my thanks for printing it. I know I could ask Cait for help, since she's a design whiz, but then I would have to tell her I lost my cockatoo. I don't need to give my sisters any more reason to freak out.

And that's why I have to call them.

I went too long, and now I know . . . I'm going to pay.

29

My sisters pick up the moment I FaceTime them, and I'm already bracing myself.

"Thank God!" Cait wails. "No texts! No nothing! We thought you fell off the mountain! We thought you died in a mountain murder cult!"

"Phone signal is spotty," I begin weakly. Which isn't true, but it's not like she's just going to show up and call me on it. "And I don't always get notifications since that last update. But I'm fine!"

"We didn't know that!" She throws up her hands. "Jemma said you might've gotten abducted by Bigfoot. Or eaten by bears."

"There is a startling lack of Bigfoot around here, although there are several helpful books on the subject in the video store. And I haven't seen a bear yet. It's the turkeys that worry me."

Cait's in her home office, and Jemma is in her Instagram-ready studio apartment, surrounded by dying plants in cute little pots. I want to hug my sisters so badly it hurts.

"So what's kept you so busy that you had us about to file a missing person report?" Cait asks. Her eyes are elsewhere, and I know that she's probably using this time to zoom through her never-ending inbox.

"Let's see. I've got someone building shelves for the bookstore. I joined the Chamber of Commerce. And I went to Walmart and started getting the apartment up to my standards. . ."

"So you bought a coffee maker," Cait fills in, and I point at her and wink.

Jemma leans in. "Have you met anybody?"

"So many people! The couple who owns the inn, the entire Chamber of Commerce, the folks at the bar, the daughter and granddaughter of our grandmother's best friend. Everyone has been very welcoming."

"That's not what I mean. Have you met any cute guys? Or girls?"

"Or local cryptids?" Cait adds.

"There aren't a ton of young people in town," I say, realizing how far I'm having to go not to lie to people when I'm avoiding the truth these days. "Or cryptids. We're too far south for Mothman, unfortunately."

"But you're really opening a bookstore?" Cait asks. She finally focuses on me. "I bet you're neglecting all the important stuff. You're going to need a logo and a website. A color palette. A brand. What're you going to call it?"

I take a deep breath. I've been going back and forth on this very topic in my head. Upscale or homey? Whimsical or serious? What kind of bookstore do I want? But the answer I've come up with is the simplest one.

"The Arcadia Falls Bookshop and Boiled P-Nut Emporium," I say.

After a long pause, they both burst out laughing.

"Oh my God, Rhea, you cannot call it that. I won't let you," Jemma wheezes. "How would I even tell people? That's mortifying."

"More important, how would I fit all that on a business card?" Cait asks.

Judging by the reflections in her eyes and the click of her keyboard, I can tell that she's already trying.

"Maybe Downtown Books? Or Mountain Books and Peanuts?" she suggests.

"Or even just drop the part about the peanuts." Jemma's nose wrinkles up. "Maybe drop the peanuts entirely."

"The peanuts are nonnegotiable. The town would riot," I tell my sisters, using my Big Sister Voice. "For the past decade, the peanuts have been the real moneymaker. So maybe if people keep coming in for peanuts, they'll get comfortable enough to come in for more."

"Booknuts," Jemma mumbles to herself. "Shells 'n' Shelves. B's and P's. Wait. No." She grins, eyes alight. "Nuts for Books!"

And honestly, my jaw drops.

I . . . kind of love it?

"Short, simple, does twice the work," Cait agrees. "And gives it a playful feel. Kinda homey. Very approachable."

"Maybe I could have a squirrel mascot, or collect squirrel art," I say. "Oh my God. I just remembered—there's literally a taxidermy squirrel in the antiques market. You guys, I already have a squirrel."

I don't even realize that I'm doing it, but the little dictionary is in my hands, and I'm turning it over and over as the possibilities mount up. This all just feels so perfect.

"Now, Cait, I'm gonna need a logo. Classy but whimsical. Inviting. Don't want to scare off the locals or make the tourists turn up their noses. It should be child-friendly, but like there's stuff for the whole family. For everyone."

"Nutsforbooks.com is available." Cait looks up, very serious now. "Pretty cheap, too. Nine bucks per year. Buy it?"

"Buy it." I chuckle, tingling with delight. "Man, it sure is nice when one sister is an advertising genius and the other one is an influencer with great ideas."

"I dunno," Cait mutters as she works her magic. "Jemma did also suggest Booknuts, which is not great."

"I meant people who were nuts for books not, like, books with, um, bits," Jemma says. "Obviously."

"Well, you know, Jem, the guy who came up with truck nuts is certainly raking it in. Maybe we have someone 3D-print book nuts, and—"

"I withdraw my support if testicles are involved," Jemma says prissily.

"We're getting off track. When's the grand opening?" Cait asks.

I grimace. This is the not-so-fun part. "I'm not sure. Now that shelves are going up and we've got a name, I guess I'll go talk to Tina and Colonel about business stuff. Hopefully a couple of weeks?"

"Halloween," Jemma says, as if it's already decided. "With a party. It's the perfect theme."

"I'll have some logo ideas over to you tonight. Do you have colors? Any kind of style? A favorite font?" Cait is grinning, a sure sign that my business, for at least a little while, will be her hyperfixation.

"The walls are bright white, and the wood will be honey gold. I want things to feel light and airy. Pastel rainbows, maybe. A mural. Quirky but aesthetic. But not too dull—no sad beige books for sad beige children. And not too old or frumpy or country. Like, the kind of Etsy store that makes you want to pay extra for pretty gift wrapping, you know?"

"Oh, Rhea, you have to let me come up and help style things, once you have stock!"

"I know, Jem."

"And then you have to let me fix whatever Jemma does."

"I know, Cait."

"Rude!" Jemma complains.

"You guys . . ." I stare down at the tiny dictionary in my hands. "I have a really good feeling about this. For the first time, it's like I can see the future I want. Like I'm finally the main character."

"As long as the book isn't horror or true crime, that's great," Cait says. "Just watch out for—"

"Shush!"

My sister goes silent as I turn to listen.

There it is again.

A knocking noise from downstairs. It doesn't sound like a fist on the glass door of the video store, though. All the little hairs on my arms rise, and I pick up my phone and fetch the flashlight I bought at Walmart.

The knocking grows more insistent.

I hope it's Hunter, but I know it isn't.

"What's wrong?" Cait asks.

"There's someone knocking downstairs," I say. With my sisters still on FaceTime, I sidle down the darkened stairs. I could turn on the light, but that would just reveal my position to whoever is down there. When I step off on the bottom floor, the lights are off in the video store, with just a scant orange glow near the front window, the streetlamps casting their light through the dirty glass.

"Hello?" I call.

"Oh my God, we're about to watch her get murdered," Jemma whispers. "We're witnesses!"

"I don't think murderers knock," I say. "It's probably some crazy old coot looking for their nightly peanut fix. This place used to be open until ten, and as long as the door was open, it was on the honor system."

"That's a horrible way to run a business!"

"I know, Cait. Now shush."

I shine the flashlight around the room, but it's mostly empty now, other than piles of wood. All the tall, cheap shelves that used to divide the space are gone, either donated or tossed. There's not really anywhere to hide, except under the counter or behind one of the closed doors.

When the knock happens again, I jump, and my sisters scream.

"What is it?" Jemma barks.

And I know, but I don't tell her.

Because for one thing, I don't want to get that awful choking feeling, and for another, she would think I had lost my mind.

Oh, it's just the poltergeist in the storage room. No big deal. It just likes stacking chairs and mopping badly, but I don't think it can open doors.

Yet.

That is what I absolutely do not say.

"Uh, we're closed!" I call for my sisters' benefit. "Sorry. Our grand reopening will be on Halloween."

I'm not shouting at anyone, because there's no one there, but it seems to work.

"Man, those people are nuts for nuts," Cait says.

I take one last look at the door to the storage room. The doorknob twitches.

"No!" I say firmly, like I'm talking to a naughty dog.

Cait looks confused. "No?"

"He was shaking the door handle. Guess I need a bigger

sign. And speaking of peanuts, do y'all know how that works? Do they come wet or dry, and how long do I boil them? Do I have to wash them first?"

I head back upstairs, and our conversation returns to more mundane topics before we wish each other a bushel and a peck and a hug around the neck and end the call. The knocking has stopped—I guess poltergeists respond to firmness—but I'm on edge for the rest of the night. I was so busy asking Shelby about finding spells that I forgot to ask how to get rid of unwanted ghosts. I add that to my to-do list, which seems to constantly grow despite how efficacious I've been so far.

As I lie in bed, waiting for the knocking to start up again, I know what has to happen next: I need Hunter to put the upstairs door back on its hinges. I am well aware that the whole point of a ghost is that it's incorporeal, but I'd feel better with at least two layers of protection between myself and anything that finds its way into the empty store down below. I won't go in the storage room again, and hopefully that means the poltergeist won't creep up the stairs and bop me with a mop while I'm asleep.

If Maggie were here, I could ask her about it. How ghosts work, if it was here when she was alive, if it can hurt me, if I can get rid of it.

But Maggie is gone, and I am haunted in more ways than one.

30

The next morning, I'm up bright and early to visit the bakery for the promised LOST BIRD flyers and maybe a chocolate croissant to soothe my fragile nerves. The poltergeist didn't bother me again last night, but I was constantly expecting to hear knocks in the stairwell or see a folding chair flying at my face. Waiting for something scary to happen is almost worse than it actually happening.

The video store is fine, at least, and—

You know what?

I'm going to stop calling it the video store.

There are no more videos on display. No more Arnold, no more *Short Circuit 2* poster.

It's a bookstore.

Maybe it's just *starting* to be a bookstore, but that's worth something.

The bookstore is fine—gosh, that feels good to think—with no poltergeisty games like Cherry Plank Pick-Up Sticks or Boxed Video LEGO-splosion. Everything is exactly like Hunter left it. I head out the front door, leaving it unlocked in case he gets here before me. I can't believe I've become the kind of person who would leave the door to their business and apartment unlocked, but, well, it's Arcadia Falls. The most expensive thing I own is a parrot cage, and I'm fresh out of parrots. The Unsafe Safe is stuffed with cash, but it just looks like an old table under a tablecloth. And if anyone tries to steal anything else, maybe the poltergeist will scare them away.

As soon as I'm on the street, I see it:

My flyer, plastered everywhere. There's one taped to every Chamber business, the backs of stop signs, and the blue metal mailbox, which I think might actually be a federal crime. There must be dozens of them. Shelby really is magical.

The bakery is still closed when I get there, but there's a light on in back and the scent of warm bread fills the air. I knock on the door, and an employee tells me Shelby isn't in yet. I don't know her well enough to burst into her apartment before I know she's awake, so I shoot her a thankful text with lots of prayer hands and head back to the store. As a family friend, I am allowed to buy two hot ham-and-cheese croissants before they open. I owe this girl more than I can express.

My next task is the sort of thing I've been dreading. It's not difficult, and it will yield excellent dividends, but it's going to take some work.

I grab a trash bag in the apartment and make a beeline for the Unsafe Safe. I feel like a cartoon character as I sweep armfuls of crumpled bills into the trash bag. There are so many I have to shove them down to make enough room. I briefly wonder why there are no coins, and then I remember the huge jug upstairs in a corner of the apartment, filled with silver and topped with feathery plant fronds, and wonder how hard it will be to roll up all those coins.

Let's just start with paper.

Back upstairs, I put on my audiobook and sit at the kitchen table, pulling out the dollars one by one and straightening them as best as I can. It's tedious work, flattening bills that have likely been crumpled for months or years and counting them out into stacks, which I wrap with rubber bands from Maggie's junk drawer. I'm somewhere above twelve hundred dollars when I hear a bang from downstairs.

"Hunter?" I call.

There's no answer.

"Ghost?"

Still no answer, but that makes a lot more sense.

I creep downstairs with 911 pressed into my phone, hoping I'm not about to find an actual problem. Instead, I find . . . the opposite of a problem.

The office door is open, and sitting on the floor is the fishbowl full of cash that until recently sat by the boiled peanuts. I'd actually looked for it earlier and couldn't find it.

"Thank you?" I say to the empty room.

This ghost must've inherited Hunter's former tendency to run hot and cold.

I kneel and pick up the fishbowl. It's icy cold—the whole room is, actually.

It becomes even colder when the door slams shut.

"Not again!" I put down the fishbowl and hurry to the door, twisting and tugging the knob. It doesn't budge. "Ghost, did you just catfish me into my own office? What do you want?"

The chair in front of the desk slowly, creakily rolls to the side of the room.

"You want me to sit?"

The chair falls over.

"Okay, no, then. Do you know charades?"

There's a loud thump on the floor, like someone has stomped their foot.

"Are you angry?"

Another stomp.

"Is . . . is one stomp *yes*?"

Another stomp.

"Do you want me to go away?"

Two stomps.

Interesting.

"So you don't mind me here?"

Two stomps.

I guess two stomps is *no*.

I realize I am playing a party game with a ghost.

"So what are you angry about?"

Multiple stomps on the floor like a child having a tantrum.

"I don't understand. Maybe I can leave and get a Ouija board?"

Two hard stomps on the floor.

"Well, then write on the wall in blood or something! It's cold in here and I left a lot of cash upstairs and—"

"Rhea?"

My whole body sags in relief when I hear Hunter outside.

"In here!" I call, slamming the flat of my hand against the door.

It opens, and I tumble out and directly into Hunter's chest. He catches me, and I wrap my arms around him and shove my face into his shirt, clinging to him like he's a life preserver.

He pulls away to look down at me, puts a hand against my cheek. "You're freezing. What's going on?"

"The ghost. Poltergeist. It tricked me into going in there and locked me in. It was trying to communicate with me, but we didn't get very far." The door is still open, the money sitting enticingly on the floor. "Hold the door for me, will you? I want this done."

Hunter reluctantly releases me and braces himself as he stands against the door. I dart into the office, grab the fishbowl, and dart out again, my heart hammering like crazy. It's not cold anymore—the room or the glass. I guess the ghost has gone back to wherever ghosts go when they're not scaring the bejesus out of people.

"Let's go upstairs," I say. I don't want to be anywhere near the office right now. "And if you found the door to the stairwell, I'd love to get that put back on so I'll have some privacy. From the ghost." Which sounds deranged, but I'm way past worrying about that sort of thing.

Hunter follows me upstairs, and I give him a ham-and-cheese croissant and offer him coffee from my brand-new coffee maker. We sit at the table, surrounded by stained cash, and I gulp down my coffee like it's ghost repellent.

"Has the ghost been bothering you?" Hunter asks me. "Have you seen it?"

I stare at the opening to the stairs, startled. "No. *Can* witches see ghosts?"

"Some can, apparently. But what happened just now?"

I swallow a lump of croissant. It's so good—it doesn't deserve to be choked down this desperately. "Just noises. A bang last night, thumps today. The room went cold when we were talking—or when I was talking and it was stomping. One stomp for *yes*, two for *no*. I accidentally asked it an open-ended question and it had a temper tantrum." I shake my head. "I thought being a witch would involve more cauldrons and brooms and fewer hauntings."

"Magic shit is magic shit," Hunter says. He finishes his croissant and dusts the crumbs off his fingers and onto the waxed paper. "Can't have the good without the bad. Are you hurt? Or just scared?"

"More annoyed, really. I finally get a place of my own and I've got an incorporeal roommate with communication issues." I take a sip of coffee, searing my esophagus. "Oh God. I hope I can get rid of it before opening day. I do not need books flying off the shelves. At least, not *Ghostbusters*-style. More like what *Fifty Shades* did in 2012."

He raises an eyebrow. I melt.

"I'll have to trust you on that," he says. "But I'll ask my grandmother. Maybe she knows something."

"And I'll ask Tina McGowan about anti-ghost spells when I take all this cash to the bank. I'll feel a lot better when there's nothing in here worth stealing. Every time the ghost thumps, I think I'm getting robbed, and then I don't know which is scarier: a person with bad intentions or a clumsy-ass ghost."

He sits up straighter, and suddenly he's all business. "Speaking of opening day, I have a few questions, if you have a moment?"

"What's up?"

Thus begins a process in which he asks me construction questions I don't know how to answer and then makes suggestions that I immediately accept.

"I trust you," I finally say. "You know what I want, you know I'm on a budget, and I know you'll make the best decision for me. I'd like to open on Halloween, if you think that's possible."

Hunter leans back in his chair and laughs. "Oh, I'll be done way before then, don't worry. You just order your books and do your decorating and advertising—you know, the hard part. These shelves will be done within the week."

He stands and stretches, showing me an enticing strip of belly. I want to nestle into him, but I'm not quite sure about the parameters of . . . whatever we're doing. The first time I kissed Billy Wayne, I was fifteen, and we were all over each other like bonobos. But now I'm an adult, and there are all these weird rules I never learned about dating. I stand up, too, hoping he'll make the first move. But he doesn't.

"I'll be downstairs building your dreams. Holler if you need me."

I put on my big-girl panties and take a chance. "Uh, holler."

He laughs and pulls me in for a hug and a quick peck on the lips. Nothing like the passion of our last encounter, just light and friendly and fun. "Cisco's on his way to help me, or I'd take you up on that holler." His eyes crinkle and he slips his fingers down my sides and into my belt loops, pulling me toward him. "But maybe you'd like to join me for dinner at my place? I make a mean steak au poivre."

I put my hands on his chest, liking where this is going. "You can cook?"

His grin is knowing and pleased and . . . devastating. "I just follow the recipe. It's not that hard. I don't know why men pretend they're so helpless."

My knees literally go weak. "Are you sure you're real?"

He leans in to kiss me. "Pretty sure. We'll see how much you like your bookshelves before you decide. Is that a yes?"

"A thousand times."

He winks and heads downstairs, and I try to convince my knees to stop wobbling and my heart to stop bouncing around like a freakin' Gummi Bear. I finish flattening and bundling the rest of the cash, including the Poltergeist Fishbowl dollars, and try to figure out the best way to carry $1,223 to the bank without looking immensely robbable.

Isla Jewell

I end up just shoving everything in Doris's bird backpack and zipping down the privacy panel. Oddly, it weighs about the same as my missing bird. I wave to Hunter and Cisco as I push out the front door.

But the strangest thing has happened outside.

Much to my surprise, all the LOST BIRD flyers are gone.

31

Just an hour ago, there were dozens of flyers everywhere. Now there are none.

I stop at the blue mailbox, where I know I saw a flyer—and internally questioned its legality. Only a few torn shreds of tape remain, which means I did not hallucinate that moment.

Someone took the flyers down.

This is very strange. I shoot off my first group text to the Chamber, asking if anyone has seen the missing flyers or knows what happened to them. The response is immediate: a string of confusion and lots of emojis, plus rage from Shelby for the time, paper, and precious printer ink. No one has any clue, but the flyers were definitely here an hour ago.

I arrive at the bank and walk inside, looking for Tina. She's not in view, so I go to the teller and apologize before sliding stack after stack of cash across the counter. A few minutes later, I am handed a deposit slip, pleased to find I was only ten dollars off in my counting.

After half an hour of me loitering around with an empty neon-pink bird backpack like an absolute weirdo, waiting for Tina McGowan, people start looking at me funny, so I head back home and grab my laptop. I need to set up Wi-Fi, which is annoying because I need Wi-Fi to set up my Wi-Fi. There's no coffee shop downtown, so I kill two birds with one stone (phrasing; sorry Maggie!) by putting five bucks in Nathan's fishbowl for a lavender oat milk latte and some quality internet time. The first thing I do is schedule my own Wi-Fi service, which will be installed next week. The second thing I do is search *how to open a bookstore,* and much to my surprise I discover a treasure trove of resources online. There's even a forum that seems to have every answer, link, and checklist I've ever needed. I sink into a squishy chair and take notes, making a to-do list and a to-buy list. They are both intimidatingly long lists. This is starting to feel very real. I have never been so excited about owning one of those chalkboards that you put out on the sidewalk.

When I check my inbox, Jemma is already sending me links to a sign shop that can turn around a reasonably priced vinyl sign in two days and an Etsy shop that makes those neon signs that everyone uses at weddings. Cait has already created three very different logos, and one of them is so perfect that my eyes well up with tears. The font, the colors—it even has a perfect little squirrel holding a peanut.

I am so lucky, I think, to have so much support.

When I moved up here, I felt like I was going to be all alone, but now I'm surrounded by generous, talented people who are willing to give their time and thoughts to help me realize what has only recently surfaced as my life's dream. Not only my sisters back home, but Nick and Nathan and everyone in the Chamber. Emboldened, I make several purchases with Maggie's card. Each time I add something to a cart, I'm giddy. Each time I click the BUY button, I hold my breath and nearly chicken out. I'm not used to spending money. It's . . . a lot.

But it's happening.

It's really happening.

I know Colonel will reimburse me from the trust, so I keep a spreadsheet of expenditures and start a folder in my brand-new NutsforBooks inbox for receipts so I don't have to watch them pile up. I'm being as frugal and reasonable as I can be, but it's just really, really fun selecting your own book cart and thinking about pushing it around your own bookstore. I was the kind of kid who once asked for office supplies for Christmas, so this is pretty much the best day of my life.

And then I have to do the hard part: I have to set up accounts and learn how to buy books and choose a POS system and and and . . .

Opening a bookstore is not for the faint of heart.

When my latte is nothing but lavender foam with crunchy bits and I have online shopping fatigue, I feel an immense sense of satisfaction. Nathan is in the kitchen working on hors d'oeuvres for a bachelorette while Nick gets the rooms ready, so I toss my cup and call out my thanks and goodbyes.

"You'll be at Craft Night, right?" Nathan calls back.

And I promise I will be.

When I enter the bookstore, I'm floored by how much work has been done. The skeletons of shelves line the two main walls. Even more impressive, Hunter is carrying a board, his flannel tied around his waist and his muscles bulging. I watch him slide the board into place, where it fits perfectly. I can already imagine lining up the books on these shelves, making little labels to designate genre, dusting them every day before I flip over the OPEN sign in the window.

He turns and sees me, and his eyes light up.

"Everything good so far?"

I look him up and down. "Oh, yeah. Everything is amazing."

I can't help running a hand over the marzipan-colored wood. It's a little rough, but the whole room smells like progress and hope. Hunter is watching me inspect his handiwork, his arms crossed, a few blond hairs falling over his eyes. I turn to him and go up on tiptoe to tuck the hairs behind his ear.

"You really are building my dreams. I kind of can't believe it."

Oh.

Oh, it's happening again.

He's looking down, I'm looking up. I'm drawn to him, like being around him makes me feel light and floaty. My lips part, I hold my breath—

And he knows what to do.

He kisses me.

And my God, what a kiss.

Strong hands grasp my jaw tenderly as he steps into me, his lips landing on mine, soft but with a desperate intensity. I tense up momentarily at the suddenness of it, the certainty. This man knows what he's doing, and he does not waver. His mouth is warm, firm, hungry, and my hands are suddenly determined to touch him. I trail my fingertips down his sides, feeling the curve of ribs, the hardness of muscle. Hunter Blakely is a sturdy, powerful man accustomed to molding reality with his calloused hands, and he is making a different kind of magic bloom in my blood as he kisses me with his entire body.

I answer in kind, meet him eagerly. He's pressed against me, and he walks me backward three steps until my butt hits the wall, pinning me there in the most delicious way. I follow his lead; this man can move me any way he wants to as long as his lips keep working against mine, his tongue sliding along until I open my mouth enough to grant him access.

Somewhere—light-years beyond the cage made of our bodies, the warmth pooling between us, the hot breath passing from him to me and back again—something bangs against the wall.

He pulls away, dragging his thumbs along my jaw.

"I think your ghost doesn't approve of me," he says, voice low and teasing.

I look up into his eyes, and it's like he really sees me, more than anyone ever has.

"It doesn't like anything but fishbowls and charades," I answer, a little breathless.

His fingers reluctantly leave my face. "So I . . . should've asked if that was okay."

"If it wasn't okay, I would've pushed you away."

"You shouldn't have to push a man away."

I let my head fall back against the wall, put a hand on his chest, right over his heart. "I don't want to push you away." I curl my fingers into his shirt and give it a tug. "I . . . kinda want to pull you back for more. So let's just say, from here on out, I'll let you know if something isn't okay, but until then, don't stop."

A devastating grin. "Yes, ma'am."

"A boy with manners, I like that."

There's another annoyed knock on the storage room door, and Hunter snorts and rolls his eyes. With deliberate rebellion, he puts a hand on the wall and leans in with slow purpose, searing my lips with his own. It's brief but so hot I'm surprised smoke isn't curling up from between us.

"I'm almost done for the day, and then I need to head to the store for supplies. Come over around seven? I'll text you the address."

I'm dazed from his kiss. "I'll be there."

There's something formal and almost giddy about our goodbyes, as crush-drunk as two kids leaving school who will later meet up at prom. This will be my first first date in over ten years, my only date that hasn't been with Billy Wayne. I scurry upstairs to begin my beauty rituals, all the while thinking about Hunter moving around downstairs, knowing he's thinking about me, too. I'm beginning to realize that before I arrived in Arcadia Falls, I had forgotten how to dream. I knew everything about my hometown and the only boy I'd ever dated, but now my life is full of firsts again, like I'm just waking up from a long hibernation. I'm full of energy, and every day brings exciting new ventures. If I can just find Maggie and get rid of this troublesome ghost, maybe I can stop worrying for once in my life.

Well, something tells me bookstore owners never stop worrying, but at least I'll be worrying about different things. Normal things. Bookish things.

There's one more item on today's to-do list, other than go to Hunter's house and apparently sup upon steak au poivre. I take my key ring and find the key for the antiques market. The square is mostly quiet, other than the restaurants, which are just gearing up for the night. I open the glass door and make a beeline for the taxidermy squirrel I remember seeing earlier and easily unhook him from the wall. He's mounted on a chunk of wood, vertical and looking over his fluffy shoulder with curiosity.

"How'd you like to be my new mascot?" I ask him.

32

On the way to Hunter's place, I pick up a bottle of wine. His address is in my phone, and I enjoy the drive through the mountains with the windows down and my music flowing. The leaves are glorious in their transformation, bright pops of yellow and orange standing out like nature's confetti among the darker green forest. Whatever is blooming down in the glossy green hollers smells amazing, and even though it's only three miles from downtown, I feel like I'm in the middle of the primordial wilderness. I'm beyond curious to see what his house looks like and am stunned when faced with the reality.

Maggie made it sound like our magic was typically quite small, the equivalent of being good at math. Hunter said he only has to measure once, and his bookshelves are definitely delicious, but now I know he was being humble. If he built this place, he's a Mozart of construction.

His house isn't large or ostentatious, but it is beautiful like the homes on the covers on magazines, the sort of place that takes your breath away. Gleaming woods, hand-built stone walkways and chimney, crystal-clear windows with glowing stained-glass accents, a symphony of sights that fits perfectly into the forest. The front door is open, and the black Lab that slurped me during the turkey fiasco bounds out to greet me. I walk up the stone path, wine in hand, feeling like those kids who eagerly ran into the witch's house because it was plastered with candy and they were starving. This man, this house—is it too good to be true?

"Hi, Bongo," I say, holding out my hand. The dog sniffs and licks it, then trots back toward the house, looking over his shoulder as if urging me to hurry up. I pause on the doorstep. "Knock, knock?"

"Come on in!" Hunter calls. "I'm in the kitchen. Bongo will show you the way."

I follow Bongo through the soaring foyer and into a living room with a back wall of solid glass that looks out onto a creek. The sofas are low and soft, and a fire burns prettily in a modern fireplace. My favorite part, of course, is the wall of built-in bookshelves, and I can't wait to run my fingers over the spines of all those books. A bookshelf is basically a person's heart on display—the words that made them who they are, that brought them comfort during dark times, that inspired them or bewitched them. These shelves aren't totally full yet; there are family photos, knickknacks, and small wooden sculptures of birds. It's homey but not cluttered, and I wonder if he carved the birds himself. Inoffensive jazz plays quietly from a hidden speaker, adding ambiance as I look around. I'm so busy gazing out the window at the gorgeous vista that I don't realize Hunter is in the room until he's right behind me.

"So you like the view," he teases.

"It's incredible."

"The entire back side of the house is pretty much all windows for exactly that reason. Come on into the kitchen. Dinner is almost ready."

I can smell it now—the sizzle of steak riding the air.

"You built this whole place, didn't you?" I ask.

He chuckles, gray eyes glowing with pride. "Of course. That's the only way to get things just the way I want."

The house is open concept, and the kitchen is sleek and masculine but thoughtful. It's clear he planned a space that would be easy to cook in and didn't just throw things together for the sake of calling it a kitchen. He takes the wine from me, puts it in the fridge, and pours me a glass of already chilled white. I sip it, enjoying the crisp sweetness and grateful that I finally have something to do with my hands, other than petting Bongo.

"You didn't need to bring anything," he tells me.

"I'm Southern," I remind him. "I always have to bring something."

Earlier today, Hunter approached me with hungry confidence, but now we're shy again. Not that I mind. The fanciest place Billy ever took me for dinner was Applebee's, and he always expected me to split the check. And of course the one time he tried to help me when I had the flu, he made a stale sandwich with no mayo or mustard and left it on a paper plate on the doormat so he wouldn't get sick himself. That sandwich scratched my already sore throat going down, but I told myself I was lucky to have him.

Now that I see the table set on the back deck, the candles glowing, the bouquet of hydrangeas sitting in a clear vase, the actual cloth napkins, I can only view Billy as a little boy playing at being a man. He couldn't even unclog his own toilet or hang his own taxidermy deer mount without my help. Hunter Blakely, on the other hand, has actual fresh chives sprinkled over his buttery mashed potatoes, which definitely didn't come in powder form.

It's a little chilly outside, but it only makes me feel more alive, my nerves awake for the first time in years. We sit and clink our glasses, and I cut into a perfectly medium-rare steak. As we eat, Hunter asks me about my sisters and the town I grew up in, tells me stories about growing up in Arcadia Falls and getting in trouble with his sister, Edie. I learn that his dad ran off even before his mother died, and he felt like he had to be the man of the house at an early age, a job he took very seriously. I shyly tell him about my experience at the falls, and he laughs the appropriate and respectful amount. Then he tells me about how his grandfather unceremoniously pushed him into the falls without telling him anything when he was eight and he thought it was an attempt to drown him. "Joyce gave him hell for that," he says fondly.

"Did you already like building things?" I ask.

He finishes his bite and looks out into the forest for a moment. "I was a shy kid. I liked books and math more than sports. I loved animals. Thought I might be a vet." Bongo's tail thumps supportively from a dog bed placed nearby. "But after the falls, it was like finding a new, secret room in a house you'd lived in forever. I can see what wood wants to be, see how the pieces of a house or a shelf fit together in my head. I crave the feeling of getting lost in the work, you know?"

"Not really," I admit. "I mean, I'd like to, but flipping through a book isn't the same as dreaming up something amazing like this house. My knack seems more like a boost than a calling. Not that I mind. So far, it's been really helpful. Although . . . I guess I've always found my way in books. Some of my first memories are of helping my mom with my sisters, and I never really got time to myself. But when I read a book, I go somewhere else, somewhere special and private where the story is mine alone." I feel a blush in my cheeks, and it's not just the wine. "I've never told anyone that. I don't even think I've ever had the thought before."

"There's something about the mountain air that makes things clear." Hunter stands and looks down into the trees like a benevolent king surveying his domain. "But I've never really given it much thought before now, either—how the magic is part of you. For Edie, it was like finding her confidence, her voice. She was so shy when we were little, even more than me. Before the falls, I always felt like something was missing in my life, but I didn't know what."

I'm grinning so wide it hurts my face. "Yes, that's it exactly! A missing piece, but you didn't even know you were doing a puzzle."

Bongo stands and trots over to lean against Hunter's leg. "It's nice to have someone who can actually talk about magic with me, someone who's not related to me. I've only ever dated non-witches, and it never really lasted because I couldn't fully be myself. It's always just been me and Bongo. But I'm glad Grandma told me to bring him along the day she and Grandpa took me to the falls."

Oh.

I should've guessed this was his familiar.

"So you and Bongo can talk? Or—am I not supposed to ask that? Shelby said it was tacky. I don't know all the witchy faux pas."

Hunter looks at me, his eyes soft. "You can talk to me about anything, faux pas be damned." He strokes Bongo's silky head. "But yeah. He sounds a lot like Matthew McConaughey, actually. Very chill and positive. I'm lucky, considering how long familiars live. Some people get stuck with far more annoying sidekicks. Is your cockatoo—"

"Annoying? Yes. She's very annoying when she deigns to remain in my company. But at least she goes to sleep at sunset."

"Any luck finding her?"

I deflate a little. "No. Shelby printed up some flyers for me and taped them all over downtown, but someone took them all."

His jaw drops. "In Arcadia Falls? Wow. I didn't know there were folks that mean-spirited here. If you want, I'll print some more. We can put 'em inside the businesses, facing out through the glass. Then somebody taking them would be really noticeable."

I honestly can't believe someone taking them from the outside wasn't noticeable, but there's nothing I can do about it tonight, so I might as well stop worrying.

The food is so good that I could keep eating until I was sick, but I don't want to be sick just now. Steak, potatoes, green beans, all perfectly delicious—if Hunter were anyone else, I would ask where he ordered the takeout from. But this is Hunter, and I saw the cast-iron skillet sitting beside the sink. When we're done, he takes our plates inside and brings out delicate cups of chocolate mousse.

"Are you sure your knack isn't stopping time? You've only been gone a few hours, and this is a feast!" I say. My eyes roll back in my head when I taste it.

"Chocolate mousse takes literally five minutes," he informs me, although he looks pleased at my reaction. "Three ingredients. The recipe is online. It's not rocket science."

But he went to the trouble of gathering the ingredients and learning how to make it. This man is so startlingly competent that I fear two hours on his (handmade) back deck will forever change how I judge other men.

Three ingredients or forty, the mousse is a lovely treat,

and the serving size isn't enough to weigh me down, which I appreciate. For a long moment, we sip our wine, and I tip my head back to look at the clear indigo sky fringed with shifting gold-tinged leaves. The stars are so close I want to reach out and boop one with a finger. I realize that perhaps the wine has gone to my head. Not that I mind. I'm nervous and excited and desperately worried I'll make a fool out of myself.

Hunter stands. "Can I take your plate?"

I stand, too; I don't know what to do with myself, so I grab my plate and say, "Let me help with the dishes."

The candlelight flickers in his eyes; he's amused, but he looks so earnest. "I didn't invite you over to stand at the sink."

"Well, I wasn't raised to watch other folks do all the work."

He steps in and takes the dish from my hand, putting it right back on the table. We're close now, and there's a light chill in the air, and goose bumps rise along my upper arms.

"Have you ever considered laying down that burden and letting someone take care of you for once? What if I want to do all the work?" His big, warm hands rub my arms, and I shiver. He pulls me close, wraps his arms around me.

"Is that what you want?" My voice is quiet, husky, as if the valley below can hear every word.

He pushes my hair back, and his lips brush my ear. "Let's just see if you like my performance."

Bongo stands and trots inside, and I lift my face up and see stars in Hunter Blakely's eyes. His lips land on mine, and there's this slow, building sensuality about it. He's kissed me as an exploration, he's kissed me with sweetness, and now he's kissing me like a good prologue, teasing what's to come. His tongue slides between my lips, and I breathlessly open to him, up on my toes with need. He tastes of wine and wildness, exploring my mouth with leisurely demand. The way he laps at me, explores every corner of my mouth—it makes me melt.

His fingers stroke my cheek, my jaw, the line of my neck, and his lips follow, leaving a trail of fire down my throat and along the tender hollow of my clavicles, kissing both sides like a benediction. I wore a button-down shirt for this very reason. There is nothing more erotic than the purposeful flick of a button, of sensitive flesh newly exposed against a backdrop of late summer stars. The first button goes, and he places hot kisses down the line he's forging. I'm glad I wore a cute, lacy bra—and that we already established my willingness to accept whatever comes next.

"I like this," he says, tracing the underwire.

"I wore it for you."

He bends his head, reverently kissing just above the lace. "I'm glad."

When he straightens, I can tell he's thinking. His lips curve into a wicked smile, one that I haven't seen before but that nearly brings me to my knees. He draws his index finger from my chin to my navel, making me shiver, and tucks it into my jeans, just behind the button.

"I'd like to get you somewhere more comfortable," he says.

Out in the forest, an owl calls. The leaves rustle all around us as the soft breeze ruffles my hair.

"Just tell me where."

He walks backward, tugging me across the deck by my jeans, toward a rope hammock strung between two solid posts. I noticed it on my way in, mainly because it looks like an absolutely perfect spot to curl up with a book. I honestly thought we were going to his bedroom, or at least the couch, but I'm curious what he has in mind. I'm pretty shy about this sort of thing and I'm not into PDA, but . . . well, it's just us and the owls, out here. The nearest house is at least half a mile off, and if Bigfoot is around, he's being quiet.

At the hammock, Hunter stops and turns on a heater, the kind you see at outdoor restaurants sometimes. A cozy warmth radiates from it, and my shoulders relax. Hunter turns me around so that my back is to the hammock.

"Sit," he commands me.

And—oh, I like that.

I sit in the hammock, my feet on the ground.

"Lean back."

In general, I do not like being told what to do, but this is very, very different. I lean back, and the curve of the rope supports my back and head comfortably. I slide off my flats and feel the cold boards under my bare feet. My shirt is half open, my head muddled and spinning sweetly as Hunter kneels before me.

The hammock is slung low, and Hunter leans forward to wrap his arms around my waist, pulling me up off the hammock to kiss me again before hungrily nibbling and licking all the way down to my jeans, unbuttoning my shirt the rest of the way as he goes.

Never have I wanted one single button to disappear quite so badly. I want this man in a way I have never wanted anything, want to see what he will do next, knowing full well that I'm going to love it, but that he's definitely going to take his time and tease me until I'm begging him with my body to continue.

He undoes the button on my jeans with his teeth, and I let my head fall back, and the stars overhead become fireworks.

33

Some time later, I'm lying on my back, gazing up at the heavens. My body feels wrung out, emptied, echoing like the last note of a song. The stars twinkle their approval, although the moon is noticeably absent. An owl calls and is answered by a softer call from across the valley. I imagine silent wings brushing white across the blackness of the night as he follows her invitation.

Hunter lifts his face from my tummy and places a tender kiss by my navel. "See? It's not so bad letting someone else do all the work."

I swallow hard, feeling utterly laid bare. Hunter is nothing like the only other man I've dated, and I can't help thinking back to all the times I gave Billy honesty and got confusion, annoyance, or indifference in return. I had gotten so accustomed to pushing my feelings down, to living with my frustrations. What Hunter just did to me—

Billy tried it once when we were eighteen and swore he'd

never do it again. But Hunter looks as sated as I feel. "That was incredible," I say shyly.

Hunter stands and holds out a hand, and I fix my jeans and let him pull me to join him. It's a surprise when he picks me up, just swooping my legs out from under me in a cradle carry. He pecks me on the lips before taking me inside and depositing me carefully on the couch. I curl up with my legs under me, and he brings over two glasses of ice water. After handing me both glasses, he sits beside me and pulls my legs over his lap before taking his glass back and drinking in long, slow gulps.

"*You're* incredible." He gives me a lopsided smile, his eyes big and . . . vulnerable? "Can I tell you a secret? One I think you'll find particularly interesting."

"Always."

He puts down the glass and reaches to hold my hand, turning it over, tracing the lines of my fingers as if memorizing them.

"I . . . learned that from books."

I blink a few times.

"Are you sure? Because you, um, definitely seemed to know exactly what you were doing."

He focuses on my hand, stroking the soft skin of my wrist. "My sister has always loved romance novels—and vampire novels—and especially vampire romance novels. She told me once that there were no guys in Arcadia Falls who were anything like the guys in books, so I decided to read a few of her favorites to see what, exactly, a thinking woman wants out of a man. And I learned a lot."

"I'd say you did," I murmur appreciatively.

I see his dimples when he smiles. "I'm glad you think so."

"But what else did you learn?"

Because I really am curious. I felt the same way as his

sister. I read books about gentle Scottish Highland warriors and softhearted rakes and cowboys with hearts of gold, and I looked around my hometown and decided that maybe books were just aspirational. Now I'm beginning to wonder.

"First of all, I learned that she was right—none of the guys at our high school were anything like the dudes in those books. None of them were billionaires or owned Christmas tree farms. But mostly, I learned, or at least studied, what it seemed like women wanted. Confidence. Competence. Kindness. A man who knows how to be firm but gentle. I was also surprised that my sister was reading such racy books so young, but like I said, all the guys I knew were looking at magazines, so I guess what's good for the gander is good for the goose."

"Many would argue that dirty magazines are not great for ganders in regard to understanding geese."

He chuckles. "Point taken. Still, you rarely read a romance book where the guy is a cowardly, incompetent, passive buffoon. And there's never one where he's a pompous, selfish douchebag who ultimately only wants sex."

"Did you just use the word *buffoon*?"

"There was a lot of Regency romance on Edie's shelf."

I've gulped down all my water and rearranged my bra, so I move in to snuggle against him. He lifts his arm to welcome me, then settles me close.

"Your sister sounds pretty cool, if she let you borrow her books."

I feel his laugh this time, a rumble against my chest. "Oh, she didn't *let* me. I snuck them out one by one without telling her. When she did finally notice, she pitched a fit. But I'd learned enough by then to know that defending myself or shouting back would only make things worse, so I apologized and begged forgiveness."

"Smart man."

"We get along great now."

I realize that although I am fully sated for the first time in my life, I have barely gotten to touch him at all. He's wearing, as usual, a flannel over a white tee, and I put my hand over his heart, feel the heat of him seeping into my palm.

"So what about the women in romance novels?" I ask shyly. "Were the girls you grew up with anything like them?" We both know what I'm asking, really.

He holds my hand, pressing it into his chest. It's easy to talk this way, touching at multiple points but without the added anxiety of eye contact. "I'm not the kind of guy who badmouths the women who've been kind enough to date me. But most of the girls around here want a guy in camo who hunts. I don't hunt. Once Bongo started talking to me, I couldn't imagine taking an animal's life with my own hands. Those buffalo steaks at dinner were raised humanely. I got very picky about meat. Not that Bongo is. At all. And the magic thing makes it even harder. I've felt torn, these last few years. I love Arcadia Falls, but I wasn't finding what I needed." He picks up my hand and kisses the back of it. "I don't think I've ever been so honest with someone before. It's nice."

I take a deep breath.

He deserves the same honesty he gave me.

"I also have a secret..."

He squeezes me against his side. "Oh, no. I read a few of those novels, too. Is it the billionaire cowboy's secret baby?"

I playfully swat him. "No. I have an IUD. It's just that... what we just did. I've never actually *ended* with another person, if you get what I'm saying."

Hunter's fingers curl protectively around mine. I want to look at his face, but I feel so shy around this topic. The more time I spend with Hunter and away from Alabama, the more I'm realizing that I was caught in a horrible, vicious cycle of disappointment, all the while telling myself that it was perfectly normal.

"I'm sorry you never got the attention you deserve," Hunter finally says. "I can't imagine why someone wouldn't spend the time to give you what you need. Watching your face . . ."

I shy away, tucking my head against him.

"Rhea, you're so beautiful. You're beautiful when you let go."

My cheeks go hot, to think of how open I was to him and the sky and the world. I was so lost in sensation that I didn't even think about the fact that he could see everything while my eyes were closed.

"Sounds like we both learned something new tonight," I murmur.

I start buttoning my shirt, and Hunter says, "You know you don't have to hide from me. I don't ever want you to feel like you have to."

But I just smile and keep buttoning. "I'm not hiding from you. Hell, you've seen things I can't see without a mirror and really good lighting. But I thought maybe there was some more chocolate mousse, and I didn't want to scandalize Bongo."

Once I'm done buttoning up, I disentangle myself from Hunter and stand. I miss being so close to him, but I can sense that the intimacy I feel right now will stick around past the afterglow. And, honestly, girls who don't want UTIs have to pee after that sort of thing.

"You know a dog's sense of smell is a hundred thousand times better than that of a human, and they can hear things a quarter of a mile away?"

My eyes fly wide, and I button one more button than usual.

"It's okay." Hunter's eyes crinkle, and I'm treated to both dimples. "He likes you. And he's happy for me. And he says if you feel weird about it, just give him a chunk of steak and he'll go farther away next time."

The words *next time* ring in my head because I so, so want there to be a next time. I want to come back to this house, to the beautiful views and immaculate quiet of the mountain. I want to see Hunter's bedroom and find out what else he learned from his sister's books. I want to give Bongo half a steak, especially when he looks up from his bed, tongue lolling and eyes laughing knowingly, and licks his lips.

There is indeed more chocolate mousse, and Hunter and I take turns eating it out of a mixing bowl with teaspoons while Bongo slurps up the remains of my dinner—or the parts of it that Hunter deems dog-safe. I turn on the hot water and start doing dishes, and Hunter protests a few times before he understands that I will in fact be helping to clean up and yes, I know not to put soap on his cast iron and to oil it afterward. It's pleasantly homey, cleaning up together. We bump into each other with the friendly softness of pollen-heavy bumblebees colliding among the flowers. There's an ease here I didn't expect—that I didn't even know was really possible.

And then the kitchen is spotless, and I don't know what to do with myself. I've had half a bottle of wine, which means I shouldn't drive home, and to be honest I don't particularly want to go there, not with a poltergeist stomping and slamming and bumping around. But I don't want to be a burden, and even though tonight was absolutely wonderful, I don't want it to go any further just yet. I put my hands in my back pockets and lean my hip against the island.

"Sooo . . ." I start.

"I have a guest room, if you'd like to stay over," Hunter offers.

Relief melts in my chest. "Yeah, I probably shouldn't be driving. Thanks. Could I maybe borrow a tee and some shorts?"

He grins. "Of course. Come on up."

Hunter leads me up a set of stairs to the second floor and opens a door to show a room with a puffy white hotel comforter, a pile of white pillows, and a cozy white rug on the gleaming wood floors.

"I don't know much about decorating, but my sister says all white is easy. You just keep buying white shit, and it will always look like a fancy hotel," he says a little sheepishly.

"Good thing it's not that time of the month, or this place would look like a crime scene," I murmur before realizing what I've just said out loud to a man who would know—intimately.

Luckily, he bursts out laughing. "Yeah, well, some of my towels are black, so I'm sure we'd be okay. Back in a minute with some pajamas."

He leaves, and I turn back the comforter and desperately wish I'd brought a phone charger. Lo and behold, there is one—a couple, all white of course, attached to the white alarm clock.

When Hunter reappears, he puts a few folded items on the bed. The comforter is so fluffy that even a pile of clothes makes a dent. "So I went for soft stuff. Short-sleeve tee, long-sleeve tee, shorts, sweats. Take whatever you like. There's a bathroom down the hall. I set out a toothbrush and towels, if you want to shower."

"Do you have company often?" I ask nosily.

"Nope. Just my sister when her AC went out, and I shop at Costco, so there's always extra sitting around. My room is at the end of the hall if you need anything. I'm going to take Bongo out and lock up."

This is all so new for me that I'm waiting for him to waggle his eyebrows or straight-up ask for sex, but the vibe I'm getting is just that he's happy I'm here. Once he's gone, I take a quick shower and put on the tee and shorts, which are huge on me but deliciously soft, brush my teeth, and slide into the bed. It's cozy as hell, and yet . . .

It's not what I actually want. I tiptoe down the hall and softly knock on Hunter's cracked door.

"Come in."

The room is dark, but I can see the outlines of a king bed and the glimmer of another huge bank of windows. Hunter is just a shadow under the covers.

"You okay?"

"I . . ." I don't know what to say, how to ask for what I want. "I thought I heard a ghost."

He flips the covers back. "Well, we can't have that. Come over here, and I'll keep you safe."

I pad across the room and slide between the sheets, turning my back to Hunter. He pulls me close and tucks me into his chest, sighing like a happy dog. It's barely a few breaths before he falls asleep, so I do, too.

I sleep through the night, wake to birdsong and the sunrise, and learn that Hunter makes a mean omelet.

Soon, I'm driving home, and everything is right in the world.

Until I open the unlocked door to my apartment.

Someone, it seems, has broken in.

34

Whoever they are, the thief was . . . almost apologetic. A few things have been removed from their places, and some hastily and sloppily replaced, but I quickly realize that this was not a general robbery. I was burgled for one thing and one thing only.

Bird supplies.

Pellets, treats, toys, the pink bird backpack.

Those are the only things missing.

And since all the doors and windows are intact, I can only assume that the thief has a key.

Hmm. Someone with a key who needs bird supplies.

Someone Maggie would run to the moment she got away from me.

Someone who ultimately means well but is a hot mess.

Someone who was not at work yesterday.

Maybe I should be mad, but mostly I'm just relieved. If Maggie ran away to stay with Tina McGowan, her best friend's daughter, then she didn't end up as raccoon food or a turkey chew toy.

Plus, if Tina broke in to get Maggie's bird things, then Maggie clearly isn't suffering. I think about finding out where Tina McGowan lives and storming the place, but it's kind of peaceful without Maggie, now that I don't have to worry. Hunter will be over soon to get back to work, and I've got Craft Night later today. That's when I'll ask Shelby about her mom, and maybe she'll even go with me to look for my scofflaw grandmother. I don't want to scare poor Tina by bursting into her home and accusing her of aggravated bird theft. Maggie's probably figured out a way to talk to her, so let her terrorize someone else for a while. I have gone from panic to just being grateful that Maggie is alive and that she has a temporary babysitter.

I devote my morning to relaxing as Hunter works, feeling only slightly guilty that he's cleaning the walls and painting while I'm curled up, reading. Still, he's getting paid, and this is my favorite way to spend a Saturday. I've done good work this week, and I've decided that in my new life, I will prioritize self-care.

At lunch, I bring him a sandwich and sweet tea, and am rewarded with a chaste kiss, which is fine, as he's covered in white paint. Apparently, his knack only extends to building, as painting takes him nearly all day, which seems a pretty normal speed for such a task. At the very end, he appears holding a white wooden door and apologizing for taking so long, and I'm mesmerized by watching him neaten the hole and screw in the hinges; I have never before given a single moment's thought to how a door works, and it's more complicated than it seems. Once I have a sturdy, locking door between me and the ghost downstairs, Hunter heads home to wash off the paint and take his grandmother out for their weekly supper date.

I seriously don't know if this man is real or I conjured him up after reading Jane Austen books with a fever.

Before I walk over to MacGillicuddy's for Craft Night, I stop downstairs to admire Hunter's work. Gloriously bright white walls greet me, and the stacked wood shines like a jar of honey against its crisp backdrop. It is truly startling how fast he works. Magic has somehow become a part of my everyday life, and I wouldn't want to go back to a time without it. If I flipped through my *Little Webster* right now, I'm pretty sure my finger would land on the word *lucky*.

Well, except that *lucky* isn't in the miniature dictionary. I'd settle for *luck*. It's between *lubricate* and *lucre*, which are also applicable words to my current situation.

It's a beautiful, balmy evening, and when I show up at the tavern, Craft Night is already in session upstairs. Shelby saved a place for me on the couch, so I sit down with my crochet hook and try to remember how to make a magic circle. She's knitting, while Keelie and Colonel's assistant, Riley, are also crocheting, and Nathan is doing a saucy cross-stitch with a curse word and flowers. Hunter's sister, Edie, is at a table nearby making adorable animals out of some sort of clay. I haven't seen her since the Chamber meeting, when we never got a chance to speak and I thought she was just a pretty blonde sitting too close to my crush. I'm a little nervous about meeting her, but she gives me a smile and waves.

"So how long have you guys been doing Craft Night?" I ask the group at large.

"On and off for years," Shelby tells me. "Some of our moms used to do this, back in the late nineties, I think? Farrah, too. She still has her BeDazzler. That's why she lets us keep doing it."

"So it's always the same people?"

"People come and go," Nathan says with an eye roll. "But we're the lifers. Riley is pretty new. Lindy comes sometimes, but one of her cats is about to have kittens, so she's sitting by the nest. Emmy quit coming a while back after some nasty business where her boyfriend almost got thrown out of the bar."

"Speaking of crafty, how's it going with Hunter?" Shelby asks.

Nathan picks up his embroidery hoop and squishes on the couch between us. "Yes! Do tell. I am dying to hear."

"Um." I look over at Edie, who is studiously working with her clay and not looking up. "I do not kiss and tell."

"But that means you kissed!" Nathan crows. "I knew it."

"If y'all say another word about kissing my brother, I am going to leave," Edie says, but in a friendly way. "Unless you want me to show Rhea the mullet he had in eighth grade."

"I mean, I think we all want to see that," Keelie says.

Shelby giggles. "I saw it. It was hilarious."

"Mullets are back." Riley sighs. "Unfortunately."

They keep gossiping, but not about me, thank goodness. I learn about Lindy's cats, Colonel's problem with online slot machines, Keelie's crazy donkey, Barb's infatuation with the much younger UPS guy. It's so nice to just sit here and feel like part of a group, and when Farrah comes upstairs to take our orders herself because the bar is packed, I get the special and thank her for letting us hang out.

She looks around the room, her glittery blue eyes going misty. "When I was your age, we did the same thing. Me, Marla, Elizabeth, Shelby's mama, your mama, Cash and Keelie's mama. It's good to have young blood around. Kids have to get out and be kids, you know?"

I do not remind her we are all in our mid-twenties. I've been attending to business all week, from my grandmother's ashes to Abraham's death to all the aspects of starting a new store. I've had enough of adulthood. For tonight, at least, I'll be content to sit here and make crappy granny squares as Nathan reads tarot for Edie, and Keelie and Riley argue over what to get Cash for her birthday.

After snipping off my third square and finishing my second sweet tea, I need to hit the bathroom. The stairs are old and steep—the whole bar is ancient, the wood worn and wearing decades, maybe centuries, of carved initials and curse words. I trail my fingertips along the ancient boards, thinking about a younger version of Farrah sitting cross-legged with my mom and Tina McGowan, making their own crappy granny squares and sharing French fries.

On my way back up the stairs, I see a woman standing on the landing in a long dress, staring up toward the party room. I stop, not wanting to bother her. There's something so sad in her eyes. I wonder if maybe she used to date Riley or something. She looks down and sees me—

And dissolves.

"So you saw her, too, huh?"

I turn to find Farrah smirking as she stands there holding a tray piled with all of our food like it weighs nothing.

"The . . . ghost?"

If I didn't already know Farrah was a witch, I would feel like an idiot saying it.

She nods, her bangs bouncing. "She's been around since before I was born. My dad called her Mrs. Mac." Farrah shifts the tray. "You see ghosts a lot?"

There's something private about the landing, hiding us from the raucous people downstairs and the gossipers upstairs. And there's something about Farrah that makes me trust her, maybe because she was friends with my mom and didn't take shit off Maggie. "I didn't even know about magic until this week, but I think I've seen a couple of ghosts already. I saw a dog at the inn, but Shelby says there isn't one. And I've got a poltergeist in the storage room."

Farrah nods, looking serious now. "Let me go deliver this food, and then we'll have a little talk, you and me. Wait here."

I do what Farrah says because she is slightly terrifying, like a tornado of glitter that could either give you a makeover or ruin you if she wanted to. She's back in under a minute, and when she leans in, I lean in, too.

"If you just found out about magic, and your mama and grandma have both passed, I take that to mean you don't know about ghosts, either?"

"Nothing. And Shelby says witches don't talk about magic stuff, so I don't know what to do. I need my bookstore to do well, but nobody wants to shop with an angry poltergeist."

Her hand lands on my arm. "Oh, honey. All poltergeists are angry. If they weren't angry, they'd just be normal, harmless ghosts like Mrs. Mac." She huffs a breath like she's making a decision. "There's a spell to calm them down. It's not hard. Are you good at following directions?"

"Yes, ma'am. I used to get awards for coloring in the lines."

She barks a laugh. "Your mama hated coloring in the lines! But it definitely helps with the magic. I'll write the spell down and slip it in your bag on your way out. This building's had so many angry ghosts that I've got it memorized."

Farrah turns to leave, and I blurt out, "But I thought witches didn't share magic."

She raises her chin. "Good people help good people. I don't know what went wrong around here, but folks got real weird about magic a while back. Nobody'll talk about it, but I will. That's why I was always at odds with your grandmother. I swear, that woman could make a preacher cuss. Thought she knew everything! No disrespect, but I do things different. I'm not gonna let a sweet kid get run out of town by an ornery ghost. Hell, I'd cast the spell for you, but"—Farrah flashes a pageant grin—"it'll be good for you. Builds character." She pats me on the arm and bustles back downstairs.

So I eat my burger and make my granny squares and laugh and laugh and laugh, and as I'm heading out, Farrah stops to say goodbye and slips a piece of paper into my bag.

I get home, find an empty journal in one of my plastic tubs, and turn to the second page to write my very first spell in my grimoire.

Tomorrow, I'm gonna bust a ghost.

35

With so many non-witches around at Craft Night, I never got the chance to ask Shelby about her mom, so I text her first thing in the morning and ask her where her mom lives and if she's up for a visit. When she asks why, because who wouldn't ask why, I tell her: I think she has my cockatoo.

Soon we're in Shelby's electric car, zipping a few miles down the road to her parents' house.

"But why wouldn't she tell you?" Shelby asks for the hundredth time. "She knows you're the only person in town with a bird like that! Oh my God, do you think she took down the flyers, too? If so, that woman owes me ten dollars' worth of printer ink. What the hell is she doing with a bird, anyway? They make her sneeze. I had to rehome all her damn chickens."

Tina McGowan lives in an adorable ranch with a beautiful garden full of hummingbird feeders and sheet metal goats. An older man with a comb-over and mustache waves to us from the open garage door, where he's sitting in a lawn chair, smoking a cigar. "She's in the bedroom," he calls. "Bein' foolish."

"Thanks, Daddy."

Shelby bursts in the front door, shouting, "Mama, you'd better not be harboring a bird fugitive!" When Tina does not immediately enter the room, she mutters, "I know you're in there, soaking your feet after church."

The first thing I notice is my pink bird backpack sitting on the kitchen table, surrounded by bird supplies. The second thing is a loose stack of LOST BIRD flyers, a few of which have been shredded by a bored and enterprising parrot. The parrot, however, is not currently in attendance. Which is probably good, as a cat meows and rubs against my shins—a young tortie. A sleek black cat watches from the hearth, while a hefty tabby is curled on the couch. *So this should've been Maggie*, I think as I reach down to stroke the tortie's head. I'm not a cat person, but I'm glad Moon and Artemis found a good home with Tina. Judging by the number of cat trees, toys, and beds strewn around the space, they're happy enough here.

Shelby sighs dramatically and leads me down a hallway to a closed door. "I hope you're decent, because we're coming in!" she shouts. "And don't try to hide in the closet. I can smell your VapoRub."

There's no answer, so she reaches over the doorframe and pulls down a nail, which she uses to pop open the lock. The door opens, and I'm faced with a red-cheeked, puffy-eyed Tina McGowan sitting on a recliner in Minnie Mouse pajamas, her bare feet stuck in a bubbling footbath and her neck gooped with VapoRub. A rose-breasted cockatoo stands on the sky-blue carpet between us like a guard dog.

"This is trespassing!" Maggie shouts, making me wince.

"Mama, honestly, what the hell?" Shelby says.

Poor Tina sneezes violently and looks like she wants to throw up. "I . . . I just . . . wanted to take care of her."

I close the door, squat down, and look Maggie in the eye. "I know everything," I tell her. "So I'm not going to pester you for answers anymore."

"You don't know half of what you think you do," she grumbles.

I reach into my pocket and hold out a handful of pistachios, which were Doris's all-time favorite food. "Now, if you'll come along, you can have all these nice pistachios."

She clicks her beak as she thinks about it. "Well, I don't know. Tina's been an absolute pleasure."

"That's because she can't hear you and is thus free of your complaints, insults, and general meddling. I'll commit to trying to get along better if you will."

A sigh. "Fine. But no more closing the cage door."

"And no more calling me a hussy."

Shelby gasps. "She did not say that!"

I look up. "Absolutely she did."

She shakes her head. "I've never heard of a familiar that mouthy, but I guess parrots come with a built-in attitude, huh?"

My eyes meet Tina's. The guilt and terror on her face tell me she knows exactly where that attitude is coming from, and she knows it's not just the parrot talking. Maggie must've found some way to communicate with her. My eyes bounce around the room until I see a Scrabble board set up on the floor, the tiles strewn around in various words.

"Clever girl," I murmur.

I hold out the bird backpack, and Maggie hops in. "Pistache!" she barks in a voice that now makes me miss the old Doris. I obediently put the little pile of nuts in her food cup, and she starts gobbling them down.

"Please don't be mad, honey," Tina says. "I was trying to help."

I give her the best smile I can conjure, given the circumstances. "I know. Thanks for keeping her safe. But if I have a heart attack later in life due to the stress caused by the last few days, I'll send you a bill."

She laughs weakly and puts her fingers to her chest. "Nearly gave me a heart attack, too, if I'm honest. It ain't every day a pink bird lands on your windshield. I thought I was in *Psycho*."

"*The Birds*," Shelby corrects.

"Well, just the one."

I zip up the bird backpack and gather the rest of the stolen supplies. Shelby offers me a reusable grocery bag to carry everything. Tina doesn't budge from her recliner and footbath, but she calls, "I'd offer to fix y'all some lunch, but my feet. Help yourself to anything in the fridge. Leftovers are in the butter tub."

Shelby opens the fridge to show me that it's about fifty percent butter tubs. It reminds me so much of my mom's fridge that my chest goes tight. "Who needs real Tupperware, right?" she says. She pokes around until she finds some chocolate pie, and we sit at the table and eat our slices off china saucers while Maggie works through her pistachio pile and sings little bits of *The Music Man*, almost against her will.

On the way back to town, Maggie is quiet and Shelby is apologetic. "Sometimes my mama doesn't have the sense God gave a goose. I can imagine her taking in a stray—she tried to adopt a possum one time, for Pete's sake—but to find Doris and then decide to steal all the flyers and keep her? That's just beyond."

"Doris can be very stubborn," I tell her. "But I think we'll learn to compromise."

It's a sign of that compromise that Maggie does not argue with this statement.

Shelby drops us off, and I tote Maggie upstairs, where she settles back in with a decent enough attitude.

"So did you have a nice adventure?" I ask her.

She huffs and fluffs her feathers. "Tina's a sweet girl, but let's just say that her porch light is on but no one's home. She's a whiz with numbers, but that's pretty much it. I just about concussed myself trying to get her to pull down the Scrabble board so we could talk that first night. And that was after me screeching, 'No Rhea!' a hundred times, and every time, she said, 'I don't have Blu-ray, just VHS.' Anyway, I reckon it's good to be home." She flutters into her cage and drinks water like everything is back to normal.

I watch her for a moment, but I'm not interested in waiting around anymore. "So I know you messed up everybody's grimoires so they couldn't do magic—at least all the grimoires except yours and the McGowans'—but what I can't figure out is why."

A martyred sigh. "Do we have to do this?"

"Yes. Just tell me the truth, and I'll stop asking. You'll stop running away. No more secrets."

Maggie hops onto her perch and cleans her feathers. I give her time.

Finally, she says, "It's because of what happened with your mama."

It feels like being slapped in the face. "What do you mean?"

She keeps her back to me, her voice in my head soft with old regret. "After she caused the tornado, I felt responsible. I'd pushed her, and she nearly destroyed the whole town, the whole mountain. Our family farm—our home—was gone. And then she ran away. So I decided I needed to find a way to make the magic less easily abused. I couldn't let something like that happen again. I worked up from a small spell to a bigger one, practicing, and then I invited everyone over, and . . ." She runs a feather through her beak. "Sounds like you know what happened after that. It worked. No more catastrophes."

I want to argue, attack, blame, but I know that none of those things has worked so far.

"Why'd you let some people keep their magic, though?"

She briefly eyes me and returns to preening. "The people who kept their magic didn't have much power. The McGowans couldn't start a stiff breeze with all three of 'em working together. And Farrah . . ." She barks a parrot laugh. "She can talk to animals, but she can't do much harm with that sort of knack. And she never trusted me. She didn't come to the potluck, so I reckon her grimoire still works. Anyway, what's done is done, and it can't be undone."

"I think maybe it could be if I found your grimoire."

Maggie bobs her head in annoyance. "Well, it can't, and you won't. So let's put it behind us and move forward. I can give you a few spells that I remember. The dust spell, the light spell. I've got a good one that can help you fall asleep."

"But without your grimoire—" I start.

She blows a parrot raspberry. "I know a few by heart. You can write them down. Start a grimoire of your own. That's how it was for your mama and me, all the Kirkwoods down the line. Can't imagine how far back we must've learned those spells, and then they were taught, parent to child, for centuries. I always liked how they made me feel connected to our history. You're a part of that, you know. Our legacy."

It's a peace offering, but it's not nearly enough. Fortunately, she has accidentally confirmed that her grimoire still exists. That just means I need to find it. I've torn this apartment apart, and the old video store has been stripped to the bone, but that still leaves the hardware store, the theater, the antiques market, and the spaces above them. Plus the storage area, which is currently ghost country. Oh! And the candy store. Maggie told me the owner's name once, but I've forgotten it. He must've known Maggie, and she must've trusted him, if she sold property to him when she won't sell it to anyone else. The fact that there's candy involved only makes it sweeter.

"I'll definitely take you up on that later, but I've got some errands to run. You should have everything you need here. You want me to put on a movie for you?"

Maggie happily fluffs her crest. "Finally you're talking sense. That is very thoughtful. Please put in *9 to 5*. It's in the VHS stack."

I get her movie going and move the bird backpack directly in front of her old, cubical TV so she can sit on the perch if she likes. She has food and water and 109 minutes of Dolly, so it's time for my next fact-finding mission.

The candy store is just a few doors down from the bookstore. I haven't stopped in here before and don't know much about it, other than the fact that the owner probably loves the Grateful Dead. Most of the downtown businesses have a homey mountain vibe, brick and burgundy and gingham and bear paw prints, but this place looks like fairy folk raving at Woodstock. There are brightly painted concrete statues outside, bearded gnomes with sunglasses and frogs on red mushrooms with white spots, and the windows are nicely painted with spring flowers. BIG ROCK CANDY MOUNTAIN, the sign reads.

As I get up my gumption, Shelby appears as if by magic. "You got a hankering for candy, girl? Was my mama's chocolate pie not enough?"

"More like a hankering for information. What's up?"

She holds out a white paper bag. "I was bringing you goodies to apologize for my mama's deviant behavior. So, you know, more sugar."

"Apology unnecessary but happily accepted." My eyes rove over the candy store's magenta walls painted with rainbows. "Do you know who owns this place? Are they in the Chamber?"

Shelby rolls her eyes. "A crusty old hippie guy named Smokey. He's from here but not magic—I've known him all my life, and I don't even know his last name. He doesn't believe in government or taxes or civic responsibility, so he won't pay Chamber dues."

"So he's pretty chill?"

"Not when you want him to stop playing the damn drums at three in the morning. Seriously, everyone on the square hates it. What kind of information are you looking for?"

I'm not sure how much to tell her. "Oh, just more questions about Maggie."

She shakes her head in sympathy. "She sure left things a mess, huh?"

"Understatement of the year."

I push open the door with a jangle of bells, and the dreamy scent of chocolate and caramel envelops me.

"Welcome to Big Rock Candy Mountain!" calls a big guy who looks like Santa Claus on an acid trip. His tie-dye shirt is printed with the shop's gnome logo, and his eyes are red and jolly.

"Hey, Smokey!" Shelby says. "This is your new neighbor, Rhea Wolfe. Rhea *Kirkwood* Wolfe."

At that second part, his eyes twinkle. "Maggie's kin?"

"Her granddaughter. Hi." I hold out my hand to shake, and he squeezes around the counter and pulls me into a patchouli-fueled hug that reminds me why deodorant exists.

"Welcome to town, honeypot," he booms. "Your granny was a pistol, I tell you what."

I extricate myself gently. "So they say."

"Now, Rhea, are you interested in selling? Because I would love to expand. Start an ice cream shop next door, maybe." He gazes past me to the wall like he can see through it. Which, judging by the scent of skunk on him, maybe he can.

"My grandmother's trust won't let me sell, I'm afraid, but renting is always an option."

Smokey grimaces. "I bow to no landlord. Rent's due, blah blah blah. Let me know if you can get out of it."

"I'll let you know," I say. "But until then, I hear your caramel apples are to die for."

He turns, throwing out an arm like Willy Wonka. "Come with me and you'll see—"

"A world of pure imagination?" I ask.

"That, and fudge, thirty-two flavors! Nora, sugarplum, it's on the house for our new neighbor."

I step up to the counter, and the college-aged woman at the cash register smiles at me politely. She's wearing a much smaller version of Smokey's tie-dye gnome shirt and has glass gauges in her ears and a silver hoop in her nose. Her pixie has grown out to an uneven shag.

"What can I get you?" she asks.

I point to a huge apple rolled in caramel, chocolate, nuts, and God only knows what else. "Just one of those, please."

"And you've got to try some fudge," Smokey says. "I'll fix you up a box. Good fudges make good neighbors!"

He starts plucking up pieces of fudge with waxed paper, singing, "Here comes the fudge . . ."

"Nora, how've you been?" Shelby asks.

And that's when I remember—this must be Nora Cove, the daughter of the awful Coves who were jerks at Chamber and wouldn't let us in when the turkeys attacked.

"Not bad," Nora says, but she sure doesn't look thrilled about it.

"Say, Smokey," I ask. "Did you know Maggie well?"

"Not in a biblical way, but we were neighbors for a long time, and she sold me the shop. Got along pretty well, although she sure could shout louder than anybody I ever knew. Didn't like drums. Wicked fast arm with an egg, too. Hit me right in the back of the head once."

"I heard that was because you threw too much chocolate in the dumpster and it made the raccoons go nuts," Shelby says.

Smokey throws back his head and laughs. "I didn't mean to start a raccoon orgy, but life finds a way."

"Did she ever give you something to hold for her?" I ask.

His red eyes blink in confusion. "Was I holding? For your grandma?"

I put up my hands. "No. Just . . . I'm looking for something that's missing from her apartment. A book. It was important. I think maybe she hid it somewhere to keep it safe."

He shakes his head. "Little mama, nobody who wants to keep track of something gives it to ol' Smokey." He knocks his knuckles against his head. "I got the memory of a goldfish."

Nora hands over a white paper bag with the apple and more fudge than I'll be able to eat in a month. "Hey, Smokey, can I take my break?" she asks.

He nods and points at her with a nicotine-stained finger. "Ten minutes. Candy doesn't wait."

It sure seems like it does to me, but that's not my problem.

Shelby and I give our thanks and goodbyes, and Nora comes out from behind the counter and follows us outside, immediately looking around like the turkeys might arrive en masse and trample us to death. She walks around the corner to the back door of the candy store, and we follow.

"What's up?" Shelby says. "Is it your folks—"

Nora grimaces and looks away. Her parents are obviously a sore spot. "No. I mean, yeah, always, but it's just . . . Smokey doesn't want anybody to know, but when we had a leak last year, he had to pull up the floor, and he found a hidden cellar below the candy store. It wasn't in the survey or whatever when he bought it, and he doesn't want to pay taxes on it or have the survey redrawn or tell the health inspector, because he's Smokey. Anyway, if you're looking around these properties for something hidden, I think you should know that they might have basements."

It hits me like a ton of bricks—or a ton of fudge.

A basement.

Below.

The way the poltergeist kept stomping on the floor in the office and moving chairs around. The ice-cold fishbowl sitting in the middle of the carpet. The fact that Maggie told me to stay out of the office and took great pains to hide it for years.

"Nora, you're a genius," I say. "I really owe you one."

She beams and nervously tucks her hair behind her ears. "Then maybe you'll consider hiring me, when your bookstore gets going?"

I'm not going to have money to pay for an employee for a while. But I'm suddenly forced to face the fact that yes, even in a small town, one person cannot run a bookstore alone.

"Well, I mean, do you like books?"

Her face lights up. "Omigod, are you kidding? I love

books. Especially comics and graphic novels. And kids' books. And poetry. My parents threw away all my comics. Said they were sinful. But a whole bookstore..." When she smiles—when it's genuine—Nora Cove looks like an entirely different person.

"Then I'll think about it, but honestly, I don't even know if I'm going to make any money opening a bookstore. So it's not like I can offer you full-time with benefits."

Nora narrows her eyes in the direction of the candy store. "I am currently making under minimum wage paid in fudge-stained cash from a guy who calls me Nora Bora and needs at least five hugs a day. Actual minimum wage and no sexual harassment is fine." Her phone buzzes, and she checks it and frowns. "Break's over. Smokey does not know the meaning of time unless it belongs to someone else. Will you think about it? Please? It's my dream job."

"She was great at the toy store," Shelby assures me excitedly. "So good with kids, she knows about inventory, POS systems, helping customers, accounting, all that. And she painted Christmas murals on the glass, too!"

"I did the flowers. I can paint anything on glass."

I can't help smiling. "Then I will definitely think about it."

As we wave goodbye to Nora, Shelby says, "That went well. Plus, free candy!"

She's right. I've got a caramel apple and five pounds of fudge in one hand and a bag of baked goods in the other. I'm already hoping Arcadia Falls has a good dentist. But sugar aside, now I have to do three things that scare me:

1. Get rid of that pesky poltergeist with a spell from a near stranger when everyone is telling me not to trust other witches or their spells.

2. Figure out how to get into the basement that I'm now certain is lurking under my bookstore.

3. And scariest of all, figure out how to navigate the hiring process.

36

It's Sunday, so Hunter isn't working. The bookstore is absolutely silent, everything exactly where and as it should be. The office door is open, and I almost walk inside, but . . .

I don't want that door to slam closed again, not while I'm in there alone and not expecting anyone to stop by until tomorrow morning.

"Not today, poltergeist," I say, gazing into the enticingly empty room.

In response, all the drawers pop out of the desk and land on the floor as if daring me to come inside and fix it.

"Not today," I repeat. "But nice try."

This pretty much clinches it for me: I have to get rid of the ghost, or at least calm it back down. I wouldn't mind a nice Mrs. Mac floating around or a friendly see-through dog curled up by the door, but this ghost threw a chair at me, and only one of us has anything left to lose. I know Hunter is helping his grandmother on the farm today, so I guess I'll just hang out in my apartment with Maggie and wait until I can talk with him tomorrow. With him around, I'll be braver.

My grandmother and I curl up to watch *Drop Dead Gorgeous*, which is one of her favorites. It's calm and companionable, and we laugh at all the same things. She hops around and I scritch her head, and when it's over, she tells me all the silly things Tina said and did, and it's the best time we've ever spent together, mainly because we haven't crossed each other's boundaries or talked about anything serious. Sharing a salad with her at dinner reminds me so much of my old life with Doris, but Maggie seems like she's relaxed, like she's actually being herself around me.

"I still don't get it," I say as we munch on raspberries. I eat mine one by one with a fork, but she tears into them with her beak, smearing her face with gory red. She looks like a parrot serial killer, but I don't tell her that.

She looks up. "Get what?"

"Why did you make plans with Diana to become a cat? Did you just want a few more years? I could see Lindy planning her life in a cat body, but not you."

Maggie chews, red juice dripping. "I got some bad medical news a few months ago. Something terminal. I . . . I wasn't ready to go. So I figured I could cast my spell and get a few more years out of life. Diana had a little money, and we wanted to travel. It's a lot cheaper, when you're a cat. Wouldn't you want to hang around with your best friend just a little longer?"

I look at the parrot who used to be my best friend, Doris. "Yeah, I guess I get that. And it's pretty normal, fearing death."

"To be honest, I didn't even know if the spell would work. But, well, if you're dead, it's not like you know any different.

Getting to come back and meet you is . . ." She looks at me, her red eyes dilating. "Honey, it's better than anything I could've hoped for. I loved Diana like a sister, but it hurt knowing I might have grandkids out there and I'd never get to meet 'em. And here you are, just as strong and smart and beautiful a child as anybody could hope for. A little pushy and nosy, but—"

"No, don't say anything else. I preferred the first part, when it was complimentary."

"But you're just perfect, is what I was going to say. I can't wait to meet your sisters, even if they can't know who I am. When are they coming to visit?"

I take a deep breath. "I told them to come up for the grand opening on Halloween. If they showed up now, they'd want to rearrange everything, and I need to do this myself. For me. Exactly the way I want things done."

Maggie bobs her head. "It's empowering, owning a business. I remember what it felt like when I opened the video store. Everybody thought I was crazy. But back in the eighties, that shop was the place to be on a Saturday night. Kids would cruise by with the windows down and music playing, waiting for a parking space. I would decorate for Halloween and have a movie character costume contest. At Easter, I would hide little egg tickets in the movie cases, and the winner got free candy." She sighs. "It was hard, watching my store die. And not just because I got slow—but because movies changed. People used to love the feeling of coming to a movie rental place. It was part of every date or party. Netflix and chill, my fanny."

"I know it's hard to watch things you love change," I say carefully. "But maybe that's just part of the natural life cycle. I'm keeping some movies, but I think . . . I think the store could go back to being a destination, you know?

People will come here for dates. Kids will come to study. Maybe we can do a book-character costume contest. Or use your Easter egg tickets in the books."

Maggie's crest goes up. "Oh, honey. I'd like that."

"Witchiness doesn't have to be the only legacy, Meemaw. I'm going to give Arcadia Falls a new destination, a new place to gather, just like you did."

"But you'll still have the peanuts, right?"

That makes me chuckle. "Yes. Or else I think Barb would put out a hit on me."

"The peanuts are a real moneymaker," she agrees.

Before I settle in for bed and long after Maggie has fallen asleep, I read the spell Farrah gave me and gather all the ingredients from the apothecary cabinet. I'm glad Maggie is back, and we're getting along well, but I still don't exactly trust her. We haven't mentioned it again, but she doesn't want me to find that grimoire, which makes me want to find it all the more.

The next day, I greet Hunter with a kiss on the cheek and a cup of coffee made the way he likes it.

"I could get used to this," he rumbles. He drinks it standing up, too full of energy to settle down at all. I wish I had a better segue into what I want to discuss, but I'm sick of cohabitating with a poltergeist who doesn't even pay rent.

"While you've been working on the shelves, has that poltergeist bothered you at all?" I ask innocently.

His brows draw down, and he uncrosses his feet like he might have to fight. "No. Why? Has it been bothering *you*? Is it riled up again?"

I almost feel guilty burdening him with my problems, but isn't that what a partnership is? Two people who solve their problems together?

"It had a little fit yesterday. It tossed all the drawers out of the desk. I'd like to do something about it." Before he can interrupt, I barrel on. "I have this spell—"

"No!" he barks.

It's the loudest I've ever heard his voice, and I jump.

He closes his eyes, pulling himself together. "Rhea, I told you about my mom. Spells can be dangerous. If any part of it is wrong, if an ingredient is missing, things can get deadly."

"It's the whole spell," I say. "From someone who's used it a bunch."

He carefully puts down the coffee mug and sits beside me at the table. "How can you know that for sure? Where did the spell come from?"

"Farrah gave it to me. She was friends with my mom. I think I trust her."

"You think?"

I look down, feeling silly. "Why would she lie to me? She didn't go to Joyce's farm that day. Her grimoire is fine. You can ask your grandmother. Wait." I sit up. "Maybe your grandmother can help. If we call her and Tina and Shelby, people who've been doing spells all along, who know the magic—"

"They'll never trust you. Not after Maggie."

"The McGowans still have their grimoires. They can do spells. They weren't there, either."

His head is in his hands. "God, I didn't know that. I thought it hit everybody. But they've just had their spells, all this time? No wonder they didn't hate Maggie like my folks did."

"Please, Hunter. I need this ghost gone. It's terrorizing me, and I can't open a business with it—I don't know—throwing dictionaries at people, as much as they might need it. Just talk to your grandmother. Let's at least meet and discuss it. I get why it's not smart for me, a brand-new witch who knows nothing, to do big spells, but if we bring together several people who know better—"

"This is a bad idea," Maggie warns in my head. "He's right. They'll never trust you."

"I trust these people," I say firmly, for both of them to hear. "I trust that they want the best for me, and that they want the best for Arcadia Falls." I don't tell Hunter that part of my reasoning behind the ghost banishment is that I need to be totally safe while I search for the grimoire. I can't. Maggie is listening.

And that's how it comes to pass that at noon, I'm opening the bookstore door for Farrah, Joyce, Tina, and Shelby, who called them all together. I already owe Shelby so much that I don't know how I'll ever repay it. I lead everyone to the office, with Hunter trailing along behind and Maggie sitting on my shoulder, muttering negativity directly into my brain. Hunter is wary, but he's willing to listen. I wanted to call it a parley, but we both agreed that sounded too much like a pirate party.

"We first encountered the poltergeist in the storage room." I point to the door but have no interest in touching it. "There was a big pile of chairs against that door, and it threw a mop bucket at us. But now it seems focused on the office. It's locked me in there, banged on the floor, tore up the desk, moved the chair. Even tried to lure me in with money. It was almost . . . talking to me one day, knock once for *yes* and twice for *no*. But I can't open a business with something like that around."

"Have you tried the spell?" Farrah asks me.

"Not yet. To be perfectly honest with you, I'm a little scared. I know that bad things can happen if a spell goes wrong."

Joyce's eyes flick around the circle. "How do we know this isn't a trick?"

"Because I'm not behind it," Maggie says in my head.

"Because it's my spell," Farrah says so that everyone can hear. "And I wouldn't be here doing it if I didn't believe it was one hundred percent safe." She's got that no-nonsense, no-BS way about her, such that doubting her almost feels like a sin.

I hold out the paper she gave me, and Joyce snatches it from my hand. She puts on a pair of readers that have been nestled in her hair, and when she's done, she passes it to Tina. Shelby reads it over her shoulder.

"I don't see anything dangerous," Joyce allows. "But that doesn't mean it's safe."

"How do you know—" Hunter begins, but he can't go on.

"You get a feel for spells," Tina explains. "The ratios just make sense. That's how people come up with things—they get good at guessing." She smiles softly. "Like your mama."

"I'm willing to try if y'all are." Shelby looks to me. "Rhea, do you have the ingredients? And some water from the falls?"

I draw in a gasp. "Y'all are willing to help me? Right now? Just like that? We can do the spell together?"

"We can't . . . We shouldn't . . ." Hunter trails off and looks helplessly from me to Joyce. "I don't know if I can. Maybe the more experienced people can do it and Rhea and I can go somewhere else, somewhere out of—"

"Blast range?" I say. "No way. This is my store. My home. I need to be part of it." I put a hand on his arm. "This isn't like what happened to your mom. Farrah has used this spell, and she's here to help cast it. We're going to be fine. But if you don't want to be here, I understand. I want you to do what you need to do." I give him an encouraging smile. "Hunter, this is what we were born to do. Spells. Magic. We're witches. This is our legacy."

"Damn right!" Maggie crows in my head. "That's my girl!"

Hunter looks to Joyce, and she nods encouragement. "I trust Farrah. It looks sound."

"I've done this spell before," Farrah says firmly. "Several times. Or else I wouldn't suggest it."

Poor Hunter is going through some real internal shit, but the women around me are comfortable with each other and the silence. As we wait, there's a heavy stomp on the floor inside the office as if the poltergeist is urging us to hurry up and get on with it. I briefly wonder if it knows that it's hastening its own end, but maybe it's not that intelligent.

Finally, Hunter nods.

"If I can't trust the people in this room, I can't trust anybody. And I'm not leaving Rhea. Or Grandma."

I hold out my grocery tote, which includes all the ingredients, plus a jar full of falls water and a safety pin. My Doris bite has healed, but I'm ready to sacrifice the ten drops of blood the spell wants.

"Is there a casting circle down here?" Farrah asks.

"There's one upstairs. Almost exactly over this spot, now that I think about it."

Farrah looks up, considering. "Do you have enough salt to draw a circle that could fit us all?"

I hand Maggie over to Tina and hurry upstairs, and whatever happens while I'm fetching my brand-new canister of iodized salt, everyone is laughing together and hugging when I get back down. Farrah takes the salt and pours out a near-perfect circle on the wooden boards that were revealed when Hunter ripped out the hideous old carpet between the storage room and the office. The other women step over it and take their places within, urging me to join them. Hunter is the last outside the circle, and I can see that he's still worried.

"You don't have to do this," I remind him.

"Well, maybe I want to. No point in wishing for magic

if you're not going to use it, right? And Farrah said that the more people involved, the more smoothly it's likely to go. I'm not gonna chicken out and leave you to do all the heavy lifting." He steps inside the circle and takes my hand.

"It would be best if Rhea did this part," Farrah says. "This ghost seems to have some connection with you, or something it wants to communicate." She guides me as I fill a small bowl with the falls water, add the ingredients, and prick my finger. After the tenth drop falls, she gently moves my hand away from the bowl. I look down, watching the red drops swirl over an amalgam of herbs and flowers and little stones.

"Now join hands."

I follow Farrah's directions, holding her hand on one side and Hunter's on the other. Six witches, hand in hand to close the circle. Maggie sits on Tina's shoulder still, but she's keeping quiet. I would imagine that, like Hunter, she's having some big emotions right now.

The spell sits on the floor by the bowl, and when Farrah nods to me, I begin reading. The incantation is spelled out phonetically, the unfamiliar syllables as slick as oil on water. With each word, I speak clearly, terrified that one wrong sound or intonation will start a tornado or an explosion. Hunter's hand is tight around mine, and if I pay too much attention to his wide, worried eyes or the sweat beading his forehead, I won't be able to continue. There are more words than there were for the light spell, and Maggie isn't helpfully pronouncing them for me. I feel like a kindergartner sounding out unfamiliar sentences, or like a kid riding a bike without training wheels for the first time. I pause, and Farrah squeezes my hand in assurance. I continue.

As I reach the final line, the storage door slams open, banging against the wall as a fierce wind rushes out.

The poltergeist, it seems, has taken notice.

37

A sudden wind gusts around the room, whipping our hair into a frenzy, although the salt on the floor doesn't budge. The desk drawers, already on the floor, dance a jig, and that loud thumping starts up again, right where the two chairs once sat. The temperature drops, raising goose bumps along my arms. It's like being plunged into ice water, the cold seeping into my veins.

"You have to finish it," Farrah whispers. "Ignore what's happening outside."

I refocus on the paper, but the wind yanks it out of the circle and toward the open storage room door. I try to step on it, but it's out of range.

"Don't let go!" Farrah shouts, and I don't know how to proceed, because even if I had memorized the last words, I don't remember how to pronounce them.

With a loud squawk, Maggie flaps to the ground outside the salt circle and waddles after the paper. She catches it in her beak right before it slips through the open doorway. She has to fight the wind on her way back, her head jutting forward and her feathers billowing in the gusts. I'm worried it's going to blow her away since she weighs just about nothing, but she makes it into the circle and uses her feet to flatten down the spell. The words come up slowly, like they're fighting to stay inside me. Hunter squeezes my hand hard, and I finish the spell as Maggie gets blown backward into the wall.

The air immediately goes still as all the banging and stomping cease.

There in the middle of our circle stands—

A ghost.

Gently glowing, a shape takes form.

A bent old man.

Abraham.

"It ain't right," he says in a voice like twinkling stars. "Let the girl undo it."

"Abraham, are you ready to move on?" Farrah asks, her voice solemn.

The ghost turns toward her and blinks. "This is my home," he says as if surprised to be asked such a ridiculous question. "She'll need me. I didn't mean to raise a fuss, but she wouldn't listen." He steps in front of me, leans in, and whispers, "It's under the office. Go give 'em hell, kid."

And then he dissolves like fog burned off by the morning sun.

I look down, expecting Maggie to start screeching in my head at this truth bomb, but she's lying on the floor, still as a stone.

38

"Can I leave the circle now?" I ask. I've read way too many books and watched way too many movies in which the heroine thinks she has completed her task and then fumbles it at the last minute.

Farrah nods, and I let go of Hunter's hand and hurry over to Maggie, gently picking her up. Her personality is so big that I forget how delicate she really is, how slight her body is under those feathers.

"You okay, honey?" I ask, gently stroking her. At least her neck isn't loose. I'm pretty sure I can feel her breathing. She's warm. But her eyes are firmly closed.

Until one opens and focuses on me. "Shipoopi!" she squawks.

She flaps her wings until she's perching on my arm, looking around the room in confusion.

"What on earth?" she says in my head in a voice that I've never heard before.

"Maggie?"

She blinks up at me. "Pretty sure my name is Doris, but I think I just got knocked ass over teakettle."

I stand, holding my cockatoo, my eyes burning.

"I . . . I think Maggie's really gone," I say.

"Maggie?" Joyce asks, confused.

And I guess I don't have to keep her secret anymore.

"Before now, that was her. My cockatoo. Maggie was . . . in her. She did some kind of spell so she could come back, and she ended up in the parrot's body. But now I think Doris is just Doris again." I look down at the smudged salt circle. "She was outside of the circle, at the end. The spell—it must've worked on her, too."

The hands that held mine now touch my shoulders as Hunter and the other witches gather around me.

"That's what's supposed to happen," Joyce says softly. "She was able to move beyond. To find peace. And I'm sure she was glad she got to meet you and get some time with the granddaughter she never knew."

"She sure loved you, honey." Tears are making a mess of Tina's mascara. "It took forever for her to move those Scrabble tiles into place with her little beak, but she wanted what was best for you."

I'm crying now, too. Maybe the only real peace Maggie and I ever knew was watching movies together for one single night, but I'll hold that memory fondly for all of my days. She brought magic into my life, and she brought me here, to Arcadia Falls, even if it was by accident. My grandmother gave me the choice to dream and the resources to help make that dream come true. I'm just sorry she won't get to see everything come to fruition and know that her legacy, that this land and our family, will carry on here in Arcadia Falls.

"Okay, now we really have to do a mural on the side of the bookstore." I sniffle. "Can we do, like, half Stevie Nicks and half cockatoo?"

"She always was a vain old thing," Tina says, shaking her head. "Had more lipsticks than anybody I ever met. Miranda and I borrowed one once, and she went on a rampage."

"Who died?" Doris asks in my head. "Where's the body? Because let me tell you, you don't want to let those things sit around. When my last owner died, I had to smell her for days." And then, out loud, "Lordy!"

The women tell me old stories about my grandmother as Hunter sweeps up the salt. I try to get used to this new voice in my head, try to remind myself that I got my old Doris back and that now I have a built-in friend who won't holler at me quite so much, hopefully. Doris has never called me a hussy, at least. And maybe she won't raise such a fuss if she catches me kissing Hunter, because I definitely plan on doing that at the earliest possible convenience.

But then I remember—calming the poltergeist was only one half of the plan.

"Tina, can you hold Doris?" I ask, and Tina holds out her arm. Doris steps over, murmuring, "She seems familiar. And a little scared? And she smells like VapoRub, just like Hilda used to. That's good. I won't bite her."

Now that the poltergeist isn't a threat, I kick at the office carpet and am not surprised to find that it isn't firmly stuck down. With a few rough jerks, I pull it back to reveal . . .

A trapdoor.

"Holy shit!" Hunter says.

"Language!" his grandmother admonishes.

"Shipoopi!" Doris adds.

The trapdoor looks just as old as the floors, which is to say, original to the building. There isn't a pull ring or rope like you see on an attic pull-down door, but there is a recessed area just the right size for Hunter to get his fingers under the edge and lift it. The darkness beyond is complete, and the scent of wet stone and minerals wafts out. Stone stairs lead downward, and I turn on my phone's flashlight and prepare myself to descend.

"Want me to go first?" Hunter asks.

The poor man must be absolutely frazzled after watching the people he cares about attempt a spell, and yet he's still offering to descend into the unknown depths first. But this is my store, my grandmother's transgression that needs to be made right, and honestly I'm such a seething cauldron of emotions that it's not like fear can really touch me. Adrenaline and grief are coursing through my veins like hot coffee, and I'm eager to see what Maggie tried so hard to keep hidden.

"I've got it, but thank you."

I have a hand out to catch myself as I take the steep stone steps deeper down. With each inch lower I get, the air grows colder, but not like ghost-cold. More like cave-cold. Back in middle school we went on a field trip to a historic home that had an ice house—basically a closet hollowed out of the underground stone to keep food cold. That's what this cellar feels like.

"She has nice manners," Joyce whispers when she thinks I'm out of range. "I like her."

I am unsurprised when I see ancient rock ledges lined with mason jars full of various gunk that I identify as pickles and jams and chowchow. My phone light plays over the thick glass, and I wonder if it was Maggie or another, older relative of mine who stood over a stove, stirring and stirring before putting away food for a rainy day. Maybe a whole line of Kirkwoods contributed to this cache of good food, always making sure the next generation would be cared for.

Books and Bewitchment

I step onto the uneven stone floor, and I'm in a room about the same size as the office. It's dominated by more filled mason jars, and I feel . . . weirdly at home here. As I shine my phone around every crevice, I finally see it.

Maggie's grimoire.

Several grimoires, actually, each tucked up in a gallon Ziploc bag, the nicer kind with the slider on top, decorated with a Christmas motif. I carefully gather all of them, the plastic chill against my arms, and carry them upstairs, out of the office, and over to the counter. Laid out in a line, there are four grimoires, the oldest of which looks like it might fall apart into dust at any moment. Maggie's grimoire is the youngest, with a faded green cloth cover. The other witches circle around but give me plenty of room. No one says anything. There's a reverence, an electricity in the air.

To think, all this time, Maggie's grimoire has been right beneath me. *Below* me. As I walked around my apartment, as I flirted with Hunter, as a surprisingly helpful poltergeist banged on the trapdoor repeatedly, trying to get my attention. A witch's ancient spell book being zipped into a modern plastic bag with snowflakes printed in light blue is a strange juxtaposition, but Maggie was clever and stubborn and knew full well the wet would destroy the pages otherwise. I wonder how long her grimoire has been down here. Did she hide it after casting her disruptive spell or more recently? And then I wonder what happened to my mother's grimoire. Did she leave it behind when she ran away from Arcadia Falls? Or is it hidden somewhere in those plastic tubs in the storage shed behind our old house, just some random old book I hastily tossed in among her college yearbooks and spiral-bound church cookbooks that carefully kept itself magically hidden from my then un-witchy senses?

I'm stalling, I know I am.

Because what happens if the answer isn't here?

What if I can't fix what Maggie destroyed, can't return what my grandmother stole?

Well, what if?

Hell, if I can face down a poltergeist, I can unzip a bag.

The book is cold in my hands but not wet, at least. The bag did its job; sometimes, the name brand really is best. I open the faded cover like it might fall apart in my hands, but it's sturdy enough. The spells at the beginning are in a wobbling, childish hand, then a loopy cursive, then the neat, slanted script that every Southern grandma uses when copying a recipe onto an index card.

"Do we know what we're looking for?" I ask the group.

"We'll know it when we see it," Farrah says grimly. "I'd guess it'll be somewhere toward the end."

I keep flipping until I find it.

Missing Ingredients.

But of course, to someone like me, who has done exactly two spells, it's like reading a different language. There isn't some highlighted part that tells me how to reverse it.

"Can we fix it?" I ask, worried.

Farrah leans in, running a French-manicured nail covered in tiny crystals down the long list of ingredients. "I don't know how," she finally says. "If there's a way to break it, it's not obvious. I'm so sorry, Rhea."

No one else steps forward.

The mood falls, all our former excitement drained away by the handwritten letters on a yellowing page.

"We appreciate you trying, honey," Joyce says, patting my arm before she turns to leave.

But then I realize . . . this isn't done.

"Wait."

The other witches stop and turn back, curious. I run my

palm over the line of books in freezer bags. "The problem isn't that some families have lost their magic. It's that they've lost their spells. And because of that, everyone has been too distrustful and scared to talk to each other. No one has been willing to share. Between my family's grimoires, Farrah's grimoire, and the McGowans' grimoires, if we can all just trust each other, the families whose spells were taken should be able to start new grimoires. Right?" No one speaks, so the words keep tumbling out of me. "I mean, I know it'll never be the same as it was before. That some things will be lost forever. But I'm happy to share whatever is useful from what's here."

They're being so quiet that it's freaking me out, but then Hunter's arms wrap around me and lift me off the ground in a twirling hug.

"Really?" Joyce is saying, shell-shocked. "Really, that's all it takes? After all this time?"

"If somebody had just asked for help, I would've helped." Farrah shakes her head, her bleached curls bouncing. "I didn't even know why everybody hated Maggie all of a sudden."

"Did you know?" Shelby asks Tina as Hunter sets me back down. My legs are weak for more than one reason.

"No, but I bet my mama did. She and Maggie were thick as thieves. I was taught to keep the family spells secret, like everybody else, but I remember feeling slighted, that we weren't invited to the farm that day." She looks at me with a shy smile. "And I missed Miranda something fierce, too. But after she left, things changed."

"Well, let's change 'em again," I say. "Wait! I've got something upstairs."

I run up to the apartment and dig through the books I've put on Maggie's old bookshelves until I find two nice journals.

Yes, I have several unused journals.

I know, I know. I can't help it. They're just so pretty.

I bring them back downstairs with a couple of pens and put them on the counter. "Hunter, Joyce, y'all can go through these grimoires and write down any spells you like. Or maybe you want to go upstairs and sit at the kitchen table? Or come back at a more convenient time? I just want you to know that you're welcome. The Kirkwoods owe y'all, and I want to make it up to you."

Joyce holds the blank journal against her chest like a little girl. "I—I don't know what to say."

"I think *thank you* will do," Hunter tells her, pulling me in with one arm.

Farrah puts her hands on her hips. "Just let me run home and get my family's books. We can have a little party. A real one, not like Maggie's."

"I'll run home and get mine, too," Shelby says. When Tina clears her throat, Shelby adds, "And I'll stop by the bakery."

Half an hour later, I've got a kitchen full of witches swapping stories and spells as they drink my sweet tea and eat monster cookies. Doris happily bobs her head from her cage.

"Oh, what a beautiful mornin'!" she sings.

And it is.

39

The next few weeks are kind of a blur. Hunter continues construction on the bookstore unencumbered by a cantankerous poltergeist. I flit about the space, painting the office and placing orders and accepting packages and unpacking boxes. Hunter watches nervously as I do the anti-dust spell I've already copied into my own grimoire, but it's successful, and we both sneeze a lot less. I order a sign, and Lindy brings me sketches for Maggie and Diana's memorial mural. Every day, it seems, a new family of witches shows up at the front door clutching empty journals and politely asking if it's true that I'm willing to share my family's *you-know-what*. I go through gallons of sweet tea keeping them hydrated while they sit at my kitchen table and copy down spells that the Kirkwood witches have handed down for generations. When they're done, they hug me and pat my shoulders and thank me, and it feels like I've suddenly got all those cousins and aunts and uncles I always wanted, a growing family of people who see me for who I am and accept me into their community.

They share their thanks in quiet ways—a basket of late-summer zucchini on the shop's doorstep, a well-memorized spell to keep bugs away, a permanent ten percent discount at Edie's store, where I will eventually have to buy soaps and candles of my own. At Craft Night, Edie teaches me how to make little animals out of clay. My first one is a lumpy squirrel holding an acorn, and I couldn't be more proud.

I do a better job of keeping my sisters informed of my progress, although Cait is annoyed that I just slapped her logo onto business cards and didn't let her do a full design with color coordination and rounded corners. Jemma begs to see how the store is coming along, but I tell her she has to wait until the grand opening, just like everyone else. I order cute vintage-looking Halloween decorations and place an order with Shelby's bakery for the ribbon cutting. A reporter from the local paper stops by to do a story on the store, and I tell them we'll be having a book-character costume contest on opening day.

All along, I keep expecting to hear Maggie's voice in my head, but the Maggie I briefly knew is gone. In her place, Doris reclaims her role as my sidekick. She doesn't have Maggie's knowledge, as she has only ever lived with Hilda, Horace—briefly, unhappily, and bloodily—and me, but she loves watching movies and begs me to put on show tunes so she can dance around the apartment. And she retains her cloaca control, which is nice for my cleaning efforts, as is Maggie's ongoing anti-dust spell, which makes the bird dander much more manageable.

The storage room gets a good cleaning out, and I can feel a difference in the vibe, now that Abraham is just a normal ghost instead of a poltergeist. Farrah was right—

Books and Bewitchment

Arcadia Falls is chock-full of ghosts. I see them occasionally, strolling along a balcony or staring down from a second story window. The dog at the inn even greets me sometimes, although I have to hide it from Nick and Nathan, who will never know all of the magic that swirls around them in our picturesque mountain town. They tell people the inn is haunted as a folksy gimmick, but it's probably better they don't know about the blood-soaked soldier in the Camellia Room who's always looking for his lost leg.

As the trees change color and the air turns bright and crisp, I really do feel like I'm living in a book as I stroll along the quaint downtown sidewalk after a bowl of butternut squash soup at Lindy's, my heart full and my boots crunching on leaves, to see Hunter's latest work. He finished the shelves quickly but still had light fixtures to hang, floors to refinish, a bathroom to sharpen up, and a shelving system to create in the storage room.

Then one day when I open the front door, I'm greeted by yet more boxes of freshly delivered books—and Hunter holding a bottle of champagne.

"It's done?" I ask.

He grins and nods. "Finally."

I playfully roll my eyes. It's looked fine to me for days, but he insists on getting every particular right.

"Here's what I've been waiting for." He points to the corner, where a rolling ladder waits with a big ribbon tied around a rung. "I've been working on it at home so you wouldn't sneak down at night and see it first. Do you like it?"

My heart does a swoop. "'I must learn to be content with being happier than I deserve,'" I tell him, running my hands greedily over the polished wood.

He laughs, his eyes doing that crinkly thing I love. "If you're quoting Jane Austen, I know you're truly happy."

I hug him, and his arms close around me, and he smells like hard work and sawdust and whatever it is they put in men's deodorant to make them smell like a mountain stream.

"Well, what are you waiting for?" he says. "Give it a try."

All the books aren't on the shelves yet, but he's right—I have to try it. I climb on the ladder, and he sets down the champagne and takes hold and pushes me across the longest wall of bookshelves. The wood glows like amber in the sunshine as I zoom past it, and I throw back my head and laugh with feverish delight. Hunter walks along beside me and catches me before the ladder reaches the end of its tracks. I hop down and turn to face him.

"I can't believe how quickly you did all this. It really is everything I ever dreamed of."

His chest rumbles against my cheek as he chuckles. "That's the magic."

I draw back to look up into his eyes. He has that tired-but-satisfied look people get when they're exhausted from doing what they love best. "I think it's also you."

His head tilts down toward mine. "And maybe a little bit you. From the moment I met you, I found myself wanting to impress you."

Warm lips land on mine, salty and sweet, and I forget about bookshelves and ladders and sweat as I lose myself in kissing him. We've been taking it slow, but, well, this is a celebration. All his hard work has come to fruition. Which gives me an idea. "Have you seen the office lately? I finished decorating. And did the anti-dust spell."

He knows exactly where I'm going with this. "Oh? So we should go check it out?"

I nod. "You should definitely take a look at my handiwork."

Hunter takes my hand, lacing our fingers together. He walks backward, pulling me along. "So tomorrow, I'll bring in the rolling shelves from the antiques market and get them cleaned up and in place."

"You really know how to get a girl hot. . ."

We turn the corner toward the office, now hidden from the big plate-glass window out front. "Might even install some new sockets so you don't get electrocuted making boiled peanuts. . ."

"Keep going, tiger."

The office is in sight now, the door open and the light on. It looks absolutely spotless, like a completely different room than when I saw it last. New paint, new carpet, new art on the walls, a sturdy new desk Hunter built from the excess wood, a desk that didn't exist at the same time as Herbert Hoover and that has not been denuded by a ghost.

"If you're a good girl, I might even build you some cabinets."

"Those might be the best words a man can utter, besides, 'I don't need a list, I just know what needs to be done and will do it,'" I murmur.

"I don't need a list—" he starts.

I put a finger against his lips, and his eyes crinkle up with amusement and . . . something else. Something more. Something I feel, too. He's just so perfect—for me. This man who loves books, his dog, his family, his town, who can dream up things and then make them happen with his hands. This man who is self-assured and self-sufficient, who cleans up after himself and cooks and—

I should stop thinking about how perfect he is and see what he looks like without his shirt.

Some time later, after I have discovered his first tattoo—of Smaug, no less—and likely scandalized the ghost of my great-uncle, I sit on the desk, dazed and sweaty. "So I guess we christened the office," I say. "Shall we go to the apartment and get cleaned up? After we find our clothes, because that is a very large glass window."

He stops, leaning against the door in a way that shows me all the muscles I've felt through his flannel but never actually seen before. "Oh, so the Terminator is good enough to be in that window for thirty years and I'm not?"

"I don't give a shit about Arnold, but I want to keep you all for myself," I tell him. "Actually, that's not true. I like Arnold, especially when he's hanging out with his miniature horse. But just as a friend."

Once we're both dressed, or at least Hunter has his jeans on, we head upstairs. He pauses at the top step and then laughs. "I keep waiting for a screaming cockatoo to fly at my face. I don't want to be around an angry parrot when I'm half dressed."

I hope he doesn't see the sadness in my smile. "Yeah, that beak is sharp, and she loves things that dangle. But Doris likes you, so you should be fine."

The kitchen is currently filled with boxes of business cards and stationery and manuals for my new cash register. There's also a bag of supplies for the bathroom downstairs, which I need to paint. . . .

"Good gravy, I still have a lot to do," I mutter.

"Make me a list. Not because I don't know what needs to be done, but because I don't know which things you want to do exactly your own way."

I go up on my tiptoes to peck him on the cheek, one hand on his chest. "One of these days, you're going to have to take another job. I know you're not charging me enough."

His arm wraps around my waist. "It's not my fault you get girlfriend prices."

My heart stutters, and I keep my hand on his chest. His eyes are shining, so earnest. "Amazing sex and lower prices? That sounds like a pretty good deal, honestly."

He puts his hand over mine, holding me to him. "To be clear, amazing sex and lower prices are in no way related. They're just bonuses to putting up with me."

I look directly into his eyes, and it's just as electric as it was the first time I met him. "It is a pleasure to put up with you."

He laughs, eyes dancing, and kisses me again. "I always hoped a woman would say something like that to me."

With a jolly jingle, the front door opens. "Delivery!" someone shouts.

I look to Hunter, who nods. "Go on. It's your bookstore," he says. "And you're the only one who's wearing shoes."

I want to dance as I run downstairs, calling, "A bookseller's work is never done!"

Two Weeks Later...

I'm standing at the counter by my brand-new cash register, my nerves jangling like crazy as I watch the clock count down the minutes.

It's almost time.

The bookshelves are covered in books—and one corner is jam-packed with old VHS and DVD boxes for the townies. Nutkin, the taxidermy squirrel, is hanging on the wall, and the chandeliers are glowing. Nora Cove—now freed from the tyranny of tie-dye and fudge stains—is standing by to help shoppers, while Hunter is on a ladder making sure the GRAND OPENING banner is perfectly centered. The whole Chamber is outside arguing over how to best cut the ribbon, while Farrah patrols the streets in her Glinda the Good Witch costume, ready to give the turkey flock a stern telepathic talking to if they should dare to show up on my big day.

Books and Bewitchment

The Arcadia Falls populace is milling about, excited about something new for a change and, if I'm honest, jonesing for boiled peanuts, which are simmering in their new twin slow cookers on a much sturdier table Hunter built to match the bookshelves. Although I've chosen a great POS system and have everything ready at the counter, we're still on an honor system for peanuts, and the fishbowl is shined and sparkling. Some things don't need to change.

"Oh, what a beautiful day!" Doris sings from the series of perches Hunter built into the wall behind the counter just for her. Then, in my head, "Are they almost here?"

"They're on the way, but they hit some traffic in Atlanta," I tell her. "Now come on. It's almost time."

I let her step onto the shoulder of my Elizabeth Bennet dress and head outside. Joyce Blakely, wearing an Alice in Wonderland costume, gives a speech on behalf of the Chamber, letting everyone know how wonderful it is to finally have a bookstore in Arcadia Falls and wishing me, the girlfriend of her grandson, a beautiful opening day. I can tell Nick wants to bang his gavel, but he'll have to settle for waving his fake Sweeney Todd cleaver.

My sisters are running late, but the show must go on before somebody throws a brick through the glass to get at the boiled peanuts. I use a comically large pair of scissors to cut a big yellow ribbon, and then the curious, costume-clad public is pouring into Nuts for Books, the first bookstore ever in Arcadia Falls. And sure, there's already a line for peanuts, but soon there's a line at the counter, too.

We have bestsellers and classics and used books and my personal favorites—mostly romances—and Nora's selection of graphic novels and lots of Georgia authors, plus a shelf for local indie authors who need a shot. The spinner rack is still chock-full of competing cookbooks, local ghost stories, and Bigfoot memoirs. The Squirrely Reading Nook is cozy with rugs and benches and a colorful mural of local birds and squirrels and flowers. We've got a big calendar on the wall with several book clubs already scheduled to meet here, and one crowded table up front for Sadie Rugg, a hugely successful author who happens to live five miles away in Scorpion Hollow and asked us to be her home store. Preorders for signed versions of her next book are already into four digits, and we had to open a second date for her launch party to make sure all her fans can get in the door. Everyone keeps telling me how lucky I am, and I can only rub the little dictionary in my pocket and agree that I am, indeed, very lucky.

"You know, Miss Wolfe, Maggie would be proud," Colonel says as he nibbles one of Shelby's cookies in his Long John Silver costume. "And the memorial mural is a touch of genius."

"She would've loved it," Tina agrees, dabbing at her eyes with a tissue.

I nod and wipe at my eyes. I'm not going to cry.

We mustn't dwell. No, not today. We can't.

Not on New Bookstore Day.

An hour into the grand opening, I've been so busy that I haven't had a chance to look up, much less check my phone. I've had to refill the peanuts and dump the cash register once already, and so many people have stopped to compliment us on the store and wish me well that my cheeks hurt from smiling.

"Rhea!"

When I hear Jemma's voice, I look up, tell my customer I'll be back in one second, and hurry out from behind the counter to hug my sisters. They look exactly the same, of course—it's only been a couple of months, even if literally everything about my life has changed.

Books and Bewitchment

"It looks amazing!" Cait says, and I can tell she means it.

"The sign! The neon! The floral selfie wall! It's perfect! You did exactly what I told you!" Jemma jumps up and down and squeals at me before hurrying off to grab photos for her Instagram. They're dressed as Peter Pan and Tinkerbell, and I can tell it's costing Cait her dignity to wear the pointy green hat and curly-toe shoe covers.

"So this is Arcadia Falls, huh?" Cait asks me. "The town from hell that we were never supposed to set foot in. You never told us it was so aggressively charming."

"You . . . kind of have to experience it for yourself."

I can see the customers growing impatient, so I pat Cait on the shoulder. "Here, take Doris with you. Look around. Go up the back stairs to the apartment if you need some quiet time."

"Is there a coffee shop nearby?" she asks.

"No, but there's a coffee maker upstairs."

With a thumbs-up, she's headed to my apartment's kitchen.

After that, time absolutely flies. The costume contest is a riot, and everyone agrees on the winner: Nathan, who used a cardboard box to make himself into the Arcadia Falls Video Emporium & Boiled P-Nut Palace, complete with little paintings of Arnold and Howard the Duck in the window. Barb argues that it's not a book character, but Joyce helpfully points out that the Video Emporium was included in *The 1996 Official Downtown Arcadia Falls Chamber of Commerce Atlanta Olympics Family Cookbook* on the spinner rack, so Nathan graciously accepts his trophy.

Our first day's sales are beyond what I ever dared to hope. People came from miles around to see the new store and buy books and gifts—and, again, yes, sup upon the peanuts they've apparently been missing like crazy for the past couple of months. The fishbowl is absolutely crammed for the third time when I close the front door, and I'm glad I taught Hunter how to refill the slow cookers. The Sadie Rugg table is picked clean. Edie's book-themed soaps and candles are almost entirely sold out, as are Shelby's book-themed macarons and Smokey's book-themed fudge. I go through the steps of closing out my drawer, put everything in the new, locking safe—the Safe Safe—bring in the sandwich board from the sidewalk, unplug the peanut pots, and turn out the lights on my first day as a bookstore owner and peanut monger.

I'm so, so glad I had Hunter open up these stairs. I'm exhausted as I head for my apartment, but the moment I hear the laughter and voices within, I catch a new wind. Here in my kitchen are the people—and bird—who helped make my dream happen. Cait and Jemma and Hunter and Shelby and Edie and Doris, all gathered around the remains of the gorgeous custom cake Shelby made for the grand opening, picking at it with forks.

The moment I'm through the door, Jemma screeches and Hunter pulls a bottle of champagne out of the fridge and pops the cork, careful not to get any on his Mr. Darcy breeches. He and I make eye contact, and I'm reminded of the last time he brought up the idea of champagne. The hunger in his gaze reminds me that once we convince Shelby and Edie to walk Cait and Jemma over to the Magnolia Inn, we'll have this place all to ourselves. Mostly.

Doris will thankfully be asleep instead of trying to keep us apart. But for now, she's on the table, bobbing her head, singing "Bali Ha'i."

Cait holds up her glass. "To Rhea! Sis, I'm so proud of you."

"To Nuts for Books!" Jemma adds. "And did I mention we have to get you some plants?"

"To the Kirkwoods!" Shelby says. "Arcadia Falls just wasn't the same without y'all."

"To books!" Edie says. "As long as Hunter doesn't steal mine anymore."

"To the future!" Hunter clinks his glass against mine, and I can see the future spread out before us, a story unfolding page by page, complete with a happily-ever-after.

"To magic," says a familiar voice, and I nearly burst out crying when I see the ghostly shapes behind Cait and Jemma. I'm used to Abraham by now and grateful that he seems to have boundaries, showing up in the bookstore rarely and only to be helpful.

But this is my first time seeing Maggie.

Her glowing form—her glowing, ghostly, human form—smiles at me.

I hold up my champagne.

"To magic," I say.

And I mean it with all my heart.

ACKNOWLEDGMENTS

Big thanks and two scoops of boiled peanuts to:

My agent, Stacia Decker, who is clearly a powerful witch with multiple knacks.

Editor Sarah Peed for taking a chance on the Arcadia Falls series.

Editor Emily Archbold for metaphorically turning a failing video store with flickering fluorescents into a thriving bookstore, and to the entire Del Rey team.

Eric Smith, Melanie Meadors, and Jennifer Morris for being my first readers and offering such helpful insight on a fast turnaround. Y'all are the best!

Everyone at Malaprop's Bookstore/Café in Asheville, North Carolina, including Gretchen, Katie, Justin, Bobby, Nate, Stephanie, Jennifer, James, Canda, Patricia, Layla, and Virginia. I can't recommend Malaprop's enough, whether you're in Asheville and looking to browse or an author looking for an amazing event space. And they even have an Instagram account where they take pics of the cute dogs that visit: @Malapups_Asheville. Thank you all for your time, kindness, and patience, and thank you for allowing me to borrow "the Unsafe Safe."

Kate and the crew at Poe & Company Bookstore in Milton, Georgia, where you can always order my signed and personalized books.

Alex White and the Smoky Writers for encouragement

and kind words after readings of the opening chapter of this book as well as the short story "A Midsummer Night's Scheme" in the *Paranormal Payback* anthology and the novella *The Bartender and the Beast* in the *Canines & Cocktails* anthology from Horned Lark Press.

Kevin Hearne and Chuck Wendig for being the most supportive buddies in the whole ding-dang world.

My husband, Craig, and my kids, Rhys and Rex, for putting up with me, even if my son often calls me Meemaw just to rile me up, like Rhea does to Maggie.

My wonderful friends: Cathy, Heidi, Whitney, Ericka, Christine, and Kathryn.

My longtime writing group: Ericka, Seth, Kevin, Jim, and Allison, who are often forced to read scenes of my books shoehorned into unrelated writing exercises. And to Reginald. He knows why.

My writing pal Molly Harper for a kind welcome into the world of witchy romance. If you haven't read her Starfall Point series, I recommend it!

Again, thank you to the booksellers. There is no place on this earth as magical as a bookstore, and you are the stewards of those enchanted shelves, and you make the world a better place.

Always, and especially, thank you to the readers. Whether you're reading paper books, e-books, or audiobooks, whether you're buying books or borrowing from the library, you are graciously supporting authors like me as we pursue our craft and our dream. I see every tag on Instagram and am so grateful when you take the time to post about my books and review them to help spread the word. Discoverability is hard, and your recommendations are a gift. And if anyone does any fan art, please tag me, @delilahsdawson, so I can gush over your work!

ABOUT THE AUTHOR

ISLA JEWELL is the author of the Arcadia Falls series. As Delilah S. Dawson, she is the *New York Times*-bestselling author of *Star Wars: Phasma*, *Star Wars Galaxy's Edge: Black Spire*, and *Star Wars Inquisitor: Rise of the Red Blade* as well as *It Will Only Hurt for a Moment*, *Bloom*, *Guillotine*, *The Violence*, *Ride or Die*, *Camp Scare*, *Mine*, the Hit series, the Blud series, the Shadow series, and the creator-owned comics *Ladycastle*, *Sparrowhawk*, and *Star Pig*. With Kevin Hearne, she co-writes the Tales of Pell. She lives in Georgia with her family and feels most at home in a bookstore.

delilahsdawson.com
Bluesky: @delilahsdawson.bsky.social
Threads: @delilahsdawson
Instagram: @delilahsdawson

For more fantastic fiction, author events,
exclusive excerpts, competitions, limited editions and more

VISIT OUR WEBSITE
titanbooks.com

LIKE US ON FACEBOOK
facebook.com/titanbooks

FOLLOW US ON TWITTER AND INSTAGRAM
@TitanBooks

EMAIL US
readerfeedback@titanemail.com